THE
PERIMETER

BOOKS BY SHALINI BOLAND

SHALINI BOLAND

THE
PERIMETER

SECOND SKY

Published by Second Sky in 2023

An imprint of Storyfire Ltd.
Carmelite House
50 Victoria Embankment
London EC4Y 0DZ

www.secondskybooks.com

Previously published as *The Perimeter* in 2014.

ISBN: 978-1-83790-016-9
eBook ISBN: 978-1-83790-015-2

This novel is dedicated to England, my home.
May you be fair, free and safe for everyone.
(And a little more sunshine would be nice)

CHAPTER ONE

RILEY

A sweeping wind blew in from the east, sharp with the tang of snow. The wind didn't care about the thickness of my wool coat, or the dense knit of my scarf. It sought out my skin and bones and chilled them despite the many layers wrapped around me. Shivering, I shoved my gloved hands deep into the pockets of my coat. I needed to get indoors where the air had been warmed by a crackling fire and a bubbling stove. But that would be hours away. I was here for a good while longer, queuing for provisions.

There was a queue for everything – mainly food and medicine. And these weren't normal-sized queues either. No, they were huge, great snaking lines which stretched so far back you couldn't see the end. I stamped my feet on the frosty ground and curled my toes inside my boots to get the circulation going again. Tried to ignore the icy burn which spread along my limbs.

I caught my warped reflection in a frozen puddle – pale face, dark eyes, chestnut curls. I might have looked the same as ever, but I barely recognised myself as the sixteen-year-old girl I was six months earlier, before my younger sister Skye was murdered and I'd tried and failed to find her killer. I still didn't even know who was responsible, let alone where they were now. My heart clenched as I thought of my sister, but I blinked and gritted my teeth against the pain, pushing it down for now.

The line inched forward a smidge. Not enough. What were they doing up there? Couldn't they move any faster? I watched my breath float in front of my face. It hung in the air for a few seconds, and then I swore it began to crystallize.

A woman with two children stood behind me and I toyed with the idea of letting them cut in front. But there were more women with more children behind her and I'd already let three families go ahead of me.

Pa's supplies were running low. Since self-appointed spiritual leader James Grey's aborted attempt to take over the south, people had been keeping more to themselves. They were hoarding, and this was making it increasingly difficult to get vital provisions. Fresh food and medicines were the most in demand. Especially since the weather had turned.

Sixteen years ago, the old world had collapsed in the wake of too much greed and poverty. Terror attacks, strikes, riots and the cost-of-living crisis led to a complete disintegration of society. I'd been born into a world of chaos, only I'd been lucky enough to live inside the walls of the Talbot Woods Perimeter – a gated, secure community where we had enough to allow us to live a decent life. Thanks mainly to my pa who'd had the foresight to build up a stash of supplies and create a safe haven for our family and neighbours. He was now respected as a leader. A man who could be relied upon to get things done and keep his community safe. But even for us, this winter was shaping up to be particularly bad.

Cutter's Quay, the place we normally traded, was a virtual graveyard these days and had become increasingly dangerous. Poverty and fear had made people more selfish. More violent. Pa had to take armed guards and refused point-blank to let me go with him. I hadn't complained. I'd learnt to pick my battles.

Today I was inside the Charminster Compound, and it was a whole different street scene compared to the last time I'd visited. Gone was the effervescent street market piled high with fresh produce and handmade crafts. The bantering stall holders had been replaced with the discontented mutterings of the sick and the scared.

Pa worried about the fragile balance of our part of the world. Yes, chaos always simmered beneath the surface, but at least we had the Compounds and Perimeters as some kind of protection. If society grew restless and fearful again... if there was no food, no perceived safety, then the people would destroy everything from the inside out. The walls and fences would come down and everything we had slowly built up would be for nothing. It would be the end of things. Again. Pa truly believed that this was a possibility. That our small patch of civilisation was in danger. He said frightened people were like spooked ponies, ready to bolt headlong over the edge of the cliff and into the abyss.

I realised that in front of me the queue was breaking up, the people drifting away. Some were crying, others shouting.

'There's none left!' a woman further down the queue cried. 'No bread, no eggs, nothing.'

'Mummy, I'm hungry.' Her son tugged on her arm.

My stomach lurched with fear. If the stalls were selling out already, what would these people do? How would they survive the winter? For me, it was an inconvenience – fresh provisions were a nice addition to our tinned and dried stores. But for most of these people, this stuff was a necessity. They relied upon it.

More raised voices joined the others. Pockets of arguments were breaking out around me. Silent discontent was fast becoming noisy anger. I turned to the mother behind me. She looked at me with wide eyes, gathering her children in close.

'Go home,' I hissed. 'It's not safe out here.'

'Can't go home yet, I got to trade for food. We've nothing left to eat. I need more firewood too or we're gonna freeze.'

I fished inside my rucksack and pressed a bag of dried peas into her hand, along with a precious jar of honey. 'It's not much, but take it,' I said. 'Hide it, before anyone sees.'

She stood there gaping. 'What? You're giving me this stuff? I've got some jewellery to trade you for it.' She shoved the items inside her clothes and began fishing around in a tatty cloth bag slung across her body.

'It's okay,' I said. 'There's no time. You better get out of here; it's turning nasty.' The queues had disintegrated and the street was now swollen with angry traders and frightened families.

'Thank you so much,' the woman said, her hand pressed over her heart where she held the food in place. 'I won't forget this.' She turned and left, her two boys shepherded in front of her.

It was time for me to leave too. There were no trades to be done today. But then I heard the unmistakable burst of rapid automatic-weapons fire. The sound was close and I dropped to the ground. A few people screamed. Some ran, others froze. And then things turned even uglier. Fights began to explode around me. A man yanked a bag of provisions away from a young woman and ran off. She yelled, outraged, pulled out a knife from her waistband and gave chase. I risked standing up again. I had to get out of there. Quickly.

Uniformed guards flooded the Compound firing shots into the air. Silence fell for a brief moment as though someone had pressed the pause button. But, as quickly as it stopped, the madness started up again.

Where the hell was Pa? He was supposed to meet up with me here after his meeting, but there was no way he'd find me in this chaos. I spun around as someone grabbed hold of my shoulder; my fist already pulled back ready to punch. But I relaxed when I saw it was the woman I'd given food to earlier.

'Woah,' she cried, leaning back, her hands up to protect her face.

I lowered my arm and realised my heart was thumping hard.

'It's not safe,' she said. 'Come with me.'

'It's okay, I'm armed.' I tapped the weapon at my waist.

'Against all this lot?' She waved her arm in a sweeping motion and I took in the pandemonium, the screaming and yelling, the running and shooting. 'Come on,' she urged.

I glanced wildly around one more time for Pa, but it was no good – I'd never find him here. The woman's kids were staring up at me and I gave them a quick smile before nodding and letting their mother lead the way.

To my surprise, we headed towards the exit wall and not the interior of the Compound where I'd presumed she lived. But this way looked infinitely more dangerous, with people shoving and stampeding to get through the main gates, creating a bottle-neck as they tried to escape the machine-gun fire and the violence of the crowd. A voice suddenly boomed through a megaphone.

'Clear the streets. Curfew now in place. Clear the streets. Curfew now in place. Clear the streets immediately.'

'Where are we going?' I yelled above the noise. But she either didn't hear me or chose to ignore me, keeping up her hurried pace. The children clutched at her coat, following on behind. She skirted the main body of the exiting crowd and made her way down a narrow side street to a cluster of large grey dumpsters at the entrance to an alley. Turning to check I was still following her, she and her children slipped into the alley.

I hesitated. It was deserted down here, the sounds of the riot already falling away. Footsteps behind me rang out on the cold concrete. I gave a start and turned. It was a man running towards me. My fingers inched down to my Saiga semi-automatic, but I needn't have worried; he kept on running down the road, away into the distance.

'Come on,' the woman said. 'Let's get out of here.'

'Do you live down here?' I asked.

'Yeah. Kind of. I'm Lou, by the way.'

'Oh, right. I'm Riley.'

The high brick walls of the alley looked like the backs of shops or houses, with small dark windows and the occasional door. It was creepy and deserted and smelt of rotting things. As I followed Lou and her kids, I worried about Pa and prayed he wasn't getting caught up in the violence.

'Maybe I should wait here,' I said. 'Till it blows over. I'm supposed to meet up with my father.'

'You can't wait in a deserted alley by yourself,' Lou replied. 'That's worse than being back there.'

'Okay,' I said, feeling foolish. 'Yeah, I suppose you're right.'

Lou headed over to one of the doors and knocked. I thought it funny she didn't have a key to her own house. Curtains twitched at the window. A few seconds later the door opened a fraction, and then all the way.

'Come in, come in, quickly.'

We filed into a dark narrow hallway. I couldn't see the person who had let us in, but the voice sounded as though it belonged to an old man.

'Thanks, Arthur,' Lou said. 'Don't go out tonight or tomorrow, okay? There's a bit of trouble on the main street.'

'Trouble? Pah, I can tell you about trouble. Who's your friend?'

'Her name's Riley.'

'Riney? What sort of a name is that?'

'It's Riley,' I said as we entered a tiny kitchen. 'With an 'L'. Riley.'

'Riney, Riley. Odd names you people have these days.'

The old man, Arthur, opened the back door and stood aside

while Lou and her children walked out of the house and into a miniscule back yard. Arthur was short and tiny and bald with a beak-like nose and huge bushy eyebrows. He looked more like a mythical creature than a man.

'Thanks, Arthur,' Lou said. 'Sorry I didn't bring you anything this time. The market's sold out.'

He waved his hand in a dismissive gesture and gave me a glare as I sidled past him into the yard.

'Thank you,' I said. But before I'd got the words out, he'd slammed the door behind us and I heard the sound of bolts sliding across.

I raised my eyebrows at Lou and she raised hers back. 'He's a charmer, isn't he,' she said. 'But he's lovely, really. Just not great on conversation.'

She raised her fist and banged on an old metal door set into the back wall of the yard, beating out a short, complicated rhythm.

'What are you doing?' I asked.

'Getting out of here,' she replied.

The door swung open and a dirty face appeared on the other side. My hand went to my gun, but I relaxed again as Lou briefly hugged the man. The children slipped through the exit and across a wide wooden board which spanned a metre-wide ditch. The smell rising up from it almost made me gag, it was way worse than inside the Compound, but I kept my reflexes in check and tried to breathe through my mouth. Lou turned and motioned to me to follow the boys across.

Taking a careful breath, I stepped through the doorway. The man with the dirty face gave me a harsh glare, but he let me past and closed the door behind us, sliding several large bolts across.

I found myself standing beneath a thick swathe of grubby beige material. Some kind of shelter I presumed. Lou tilted her head and I followed her out from behind the tent-like structure, across the makeshift bridge and back onto solid ground. My mouth dropped open.

We were now standing deep inside the encampment known as *the Walls* – an apt name as it lay immediately outside the Charminster Compound, in the shadow of its towering patchwork walls. Walls topped with glinting razor wire, sharp against the jewel-blue sky. With a thud of unease, I realised that Lou was a *shanty* – the name given to those outsiders who lived in shanty towns that had sprung up outside the walled settlements.

She smiled and I wasn't altogether sure it was a smile of friendliness. Her children had scampered off and I noticed everyone staring at me. Hostile glares from men, women and children.

I didn't look anything like these people, with my thick wool coat and shiny hair, my sturdy boots and unpatched jeans. I had the sudden lurching feeling that allowing myself to be brought here by a total stranger wasn't the smartest move I'd ever made.

CHAPTER TWO

JAMIE

Five Months Earlier

The quickening thud of his heartbeats throbbed in his ears as he squeezed carefully through the jagged hole in the fence. If he touched any part of the wire, he'd probably die. Probably get pumped with a zillion volts of electricity. Perspiration broke out on his brow. What would happen if a bead of sweat dripped onto the metal? He probably deserved to die anyway after what had just happened. But he finally inched his way through without getting zapped and now found himself safely back outside the fence. Straightening up, Jamie allowed himself to breathe once more.

Bending to retrieve his bundle from the ground, he darted a glance left and right, checking the vicinity. It was dark and he couldn't see much of anything. He held his breath and strained his ears. No human sounds. Only the swish of the leaves and the hum of the fence. What was he doing standing around? He needed to get out of here. Fast.

He gave himself a shake and began to run. Well, it was more of a limp than a run, because his leg was banged up good and proper. His feet pounded over the uneven heathland and his breaths came thick and fast.

The thing was, he hadn't even been looking for trouble. He'd been minding his own business when that snooty bitch in her posh AV had knocked him over and driven off without even checking to see if he was okay. That's how much of a nobody he was. No one cared if he lived or died. Then he'd noticed the hole in the fence and had stupidly decided to climb inside, ending up in some rich person's garden. When he'd spied the pool house with its comfy sofa and fully stocked fridge, he hadn't been able to resist. And who could blame him. He hadn't seen food like that for years – cold snacks and crisps and real beers, just like the old days. Pretty soon he'd fallen asleep and next thing he knew he'd been woken by a load of screaming.

All he had wanted was a decent night's kip, but a girl had come into the pool house, seen him, and assumed he was a dangerous madman. He'd tried to explain he wasn't a threat, but he'd been half-asleep and his words had come out rough and garbled. She'd panicked and he'd tried to calm her down, tried to stop her screaming and running off to get help. They'd struggled and tussled and that's when it had happened. She'd crashed through the glass door and a shard of glass had dropped from the doorframe, straight into her throat. It had been awful. And now she was dead. Because of him.

It was like a terrible dream. A nightmare. He wouldn't be safe until he got far away from here. Once they discovered her body, they'd be looking for the person who'd done it. He needed to run faster.

As he stumbled and staggered across the uneven wasteland that used to be Bournemouth, Jamie replayed the scene over and over in his mind. First convincing himself it had all been an unavoidable accident, and then berating himself for causing the death of an innocent girl. He'd seen some bad stuff throughout his life – worse than what had happened tonight, but he'd never been the cause of someone's death before. He knew he should've stayed and helped somehow, but the girl had been killed instantly and he'd been scared and hadn't known what to do. He'd panicked.

After a while, Jamie had to stop running. His leg now screamed in pain. Panting hard, he bent over with his hands on his thighs, trying to get his breath back. Finally able to breathe more normally, he stood straight, scratching at his beard. No wonder the girl had been so terrified of him. He must've looked like a wild crazy man and he probably smelt like an aging mountain goat. Pity he'd never got the chance to test out that shower in the pool house.

But there was nothing he could do about any of it. If he'd hung around inside to explain what had happened, the girl's parents would have killed him. They would never have believed it was an accident. They'd have assumed the worst. There would have been screaming and yelling and violence. No, better that he disappeared. Let them assume it had all been a terrible accident; that she'd tripped and fallen or something.

A girl like that probably had a lovely family who would cry for her. Who would never get over the shock of her death. How had his own life come to this? How had he become this outcast, this bringer of doom?

Was he really a bad person? Was he evil? He certainly didn't want to be. He wanted to be nice and good and always do the right thing. But somewhere in between this desire to be good, things got jumbled and messed up.

He strained his ears again, convinced he would soon hear the sound of vehicles coming after him, the glare of headlights seeking him out. But the night was silent and the air was still. He began limping again, moving away from the Perimeter in what he hoped was an easterly direction. But, to be honest, he had no idea where he was going. He was wandering blind. His panic had made him lose all sense of direction. He'd have to wait until morning to regain his bearings. Anyway, the sun would be up soon, it must be at least 2 or 3 a.m. by now.

Jamie was supposed to have been going to the Boscombe Compound that night to see a girl he'd met at the Poole Shanty. She'd told him there was work going at the 'pound. That he'd be able to get a job there no problem. He hoped his leg would heal quickly. He couldn't do any labouring in this beaten-up shape.

The girl from the shanty had been cute. Too good for him probably, but she'd definitely been interested – had said as much. She would help him forget tonight. She would chase the nightmares away. The problem was that every time he tried to picture her face, he saw the Perimeter girl's face instead. Her pretty features spattered with bright red blood. The shock in her eyes followed by the blank cold look of the dead. He'd seen that look many times over the years. The extinguishing of life. He'd just never been the cause of it before.

As he walked, he tried to put the image of the dead girl from his mind. What was one more dead person in this screwed up world? She was probably better off. Only Jamie knew this was merely a doomed attempt to make him feel better. A niggling voice insisted that it would never have happened if he hadn't broken through the fence and into the girl's pool house. But what was wrong with trying to find a bit of peaceful shelter for the night? Anyone would have done the same. Wouldn't they?

Jamie picked up his pace, staggering through the night, but his throbbing leg meant he soon had to slow down again. Come to think of it, it wasn't his fault at all. If that woman hadn't knocked him over in her AV and left him for dead, he would never have ended up inside the fence in the first place.

After fifteen more minutes of hobbling through the darkness, Jamie stopped and raised his face to the sky, suddenly overcome with exhaustion from everything. From the day's events, from the future ahead of him, from living on his wits for the past sixteen years. Here he was, surviving (just), but penniless, homeless and without a friend in the world. He'd killed a young innocent girl – unwittingly, but still his fault – and he came to the depressing conclusion that he had never ever done even one truly good thing in the whole of his pathetic life.

Jamie only had vague memories of his life before the bombs changed everything. His parents had loved him, he knew that much. But they had also smothered him with overprotectiveness. Spoilt him. And he recalled numerous times when he was mean to them. He was sarcastic and rude when they were only trying to be nice. He tried to remember – was he a good person back before the world collapsed? He didn't think so.

He'd been fourteen years old on the day when everything changed. He and his mum and dad had been returning home after spending a long summer holiday in France. The drive to the ferry had been boring and Jamie had felt an uncontrollable rage towards his parents. Their attempts to appease him had only made him angrier.

Now, years later, he couldn't for the life of him remember why he'd felt that way. There were times when he wished he could go back in time and slap the boy he'd once been. To go back and tell that boy to hug his parents; to tell them he loved them more than anything in the world. To thank them for loving him.

Too late for wishes.

After boarding the ferry, he'd given his parents the slip, and he remembered sitting on deck by himself during the journey home. Once they reached the chilly waters of Portsmouth, he had reluctantly obeyed the voice over the tannoy system and returned to their car in the transport hold of the huge ocean vessel. His parents were already down there, telling him how worried they'd been. How they'd looked everywhere but hadn't been able to find him. He remembered sliding into the car and ignoring them.

They sat there in tense silence waiting for the massive doors to open so they could drive out onto dry land and back home to their little house. And then the bombs had started going off.

First, a loud booming explosion. Seconds later, a crash above their heads and then a snowy white light had filled Jamie's vision. The explosion had been so loud that he almost couldn't hear it. Later, when he thought about this episode, the only thing he could liken it to, is when something is so cold, it feels hot. Then there was a silence that seemed to empty his whole being. He turned to look around at his parents and that's when the screaming started.

It had been a terrorist attack. Multiple car bombs on board the ferry which had killed over half the passengers. Jamie was one of the lucky ones (although he hadn't seen it that way). He recovered physically – amazingly he only received superficial cuts and bruising – but he still suffered vicious flashbacks of the horror of that day. The loss of his parents – killed in their car by the blast – was made doubly tragic by the fact that for the whole holiday, Jamie had been vile to both of them and felt massive guilt for the way he had acted towards them.

After he left the hospital, Jamie withdrew into himself. He spurned all help from the few relations he had and ran away from each care facility and foster home. Within ten months of his parents' deaths, he had spent his meagre inheritance and was living on the streets. Then came the post-terror attack shutdown and it was everybody for themselves.

Because he was out of the system, he had escaped being drafted, but maybe joining the army would've been better than living the lonely half-life of a drifter. Because, as the years dragged on, he was realising he just didn't have the energy for the harshness of the outside anymore.

Now, standing alone in the darkness, the true reality of his life hit him like a punch in the stomach. He was alone... a loser... a murderer. A sudden gust of wind snatched his breath away, making his eyes water. Or were they the tears of self-pity which trickled down his cheeks? There was no one to see him out here in the black wilderness, so why bother to even wipe them away? Who was he even crying for? For himself? For his parents? For this ruined place? For the dead girl?

He didn't usually dwell on his past; he preferred to blank it out. To forget. But tonight's events had totally unnerved him. Jamie closed his eyes and sank to his knees. And then he did something he had never done before. He began to pray. He asked God to forgive him and to help him. He needed guidance and he needed deliverance from the awful thoughts and fragmented images and memories which crowded his brain. He needed some peace.

CHAPTER THREE

RILEY

I shifted my gaze from the hostile shanties back to Lou. She glanced from my worried face to the others and then turned to grin at me. A sudden surprising smile which transformed her features from those of a downtrodden mother to a good-looking young woman.

'Don't worry about them,' she said. 'They're just being nosy.'

I finally let out a breath. 'Thanks.' Relief washed over me as I realised she didn't mean me harm.

'S'okay,' she said. 'I've never known it to kick off like that before. It's usually safe enough in the Compound.'

The man who'd let us out glared at Lou and then at me. I realised he was quite young really. Not that much older than me. His matted fringe hung over dark angry eyes. 'You can't be showing strangers our door, Lou.'

'It's crazy back there,' she replied defensively. 'A full-on riot. She woulda got hurt if I'd left her. Killed probably.'

'So?' He scowled.

'So...' Lou pulled out the dried peas and jar of honey I'd given her. 'Ta-da!'

'Are those...' He snatched the food from Lou and examined it carefully as though the peas were diamonds and the honey, liquid gold.

Lou smiled smugly.

'These yours?' he asked me.

'I gave them to Lou,' I said. 'For her and her children,' I said pointedly.

'We share everything here,' he replied, putting the food in his coat pockets.

I was about to protest, but Lou nodded. 'It's true,' she added. 'We share, and that way everyone gets something.'

'There's not gonna be enough of that for everyone,' I said, stating the obvious. 'How many of you are there?'

'Nine hundred and seventy-two,' Lou stated proudly.

'Seventy-three,' the man corrected. 'Marnie had her baby while you were inside.'

'She did?' Lou's eyes lit up. 'How's she doing?'

'Good, I think.' The man's eyes softened for a moment and then hardened again as he turned back to me. 'Where d'you get this stuff anyway?'

'I brought it to trade.'

'Where you from?'

'I should go back... I need to find my pa. He's still—'

'I asked you where you were from.' The man grabbed my wrists and looked at my hands.

I tried to pull away, but his grip was like iron.

'Soft hands, clean nails,' he sneered. 'Bet you're a Perimeter girl.' He spat on the frozen ground.

'Leave her alone, Reece. She was nice to me.'

'We don't need her pity or her charity.' He pulled the jars of peas and honey from his pockets, shoved them into my hands and stalked off. 'Get rid of her,' he called over his shoulder, 'and tell her not to come back.'

Charming, I thought. 'He's right,' I said. 'I'd better get back to the Compound.'

'Don't worry about Reece,' Lou replied. 'He's just mad at me for showing you our way in and out.'

'I won't say anything to anyone.'

'No, I know you won't. I've got a good feeling about you.'

'Me?'

'Come on,' she said, her eyes sparkling. 'I'll show you around before you go.'

'Hang on,' I said. 'You have to take these back.' I handed her the peas and honey.

She sighed and then smirked. 'Most people are fighting to get hold of food and you and I keep trying to get rid of it.'

'Well, take it and keep it this time. If Reece doesn't want it, that's his problem. You've got kids to feed.'

'They're not my children, you know,' she said. 'They're my younger brothers. My parents are dead, so I take care of them now.'

'I'm so sorry,' I replied. 'How old are you? If you don't mind me asking.'

'Twenty.'

I studied her more closely. I'd assumed she was older, but it was only because she'd had the children with her and was dressed in so many layers of old rags. She touched her face self-consciously and a strand of blonde hair fell out from beneath her brown headscarf.

'I know I probably look ancient.'

'What? No, don't be daft. You're really pretty. Are you and Reece? You know...'

'What? No. No, he's like this totally annoying pain-in-the-ass older brother.'

'Oh, okay.' I nodded, my thoughts straying to my neighbour Luc who had helped me hunt Skye's killer. I'd previously thought of him as an annoying pain-in-the-ass older brother too.

But now... I gave myself an internal shake. Now was not the time to be mooning over Luc Donovan.

'Hmm. Come on,' she said, shoving the food into her bag. 'I'll show you around our little village.'

I followed her into the encampment. Unfriendly stares accompanied us as we picked our way through tents, debris and smouldering fires. What must it be like to live virtually outdoors in weather like this, with only canvas or plywood for shelter? And hadn't Reece said that someone had recently had a baby? I shivered, thinking of our huge warm house with all its spare bedrooms and fully stocked cupboards. She would think I was a spoilt brat if she knew how I lived. No wonder these people looked at me with resentment.

'Have you always lived here?' I asked.

'Since I was eight. My parents didn't like living inside the Compound. Said it was too restrictive. Too many rules – like the old ways but worse. They liked the idea of being free. It's pretty good here, we're close enough to the Compound to trade and we have an okay relationship with the guards. As long as we pass them along a skinned rabbit every now and then, or some of our homebrew.' She winked. 'Winter's hard though. We always lose a lot in winter – friends, family, hope...'

She laughed at the expression on my face. 'Cheer up. I'm not dead yet. Being a shanty's not all bad, especially in spring and summer. We have pony races and go out on hunting expeditions. We grow our own food and the kids have a great life.'

'Sounds amazing,' I murmured.

'Don't get me wrong, it's not all sunshine and laughter. But I wouldn't want to live anywhere else. The Walls is as good a place as any.'

'Don't you get attacked by outsiders?'

'We *are* outsiders in case you hadn't noticed.'

'Oops. Yeah, course you are, I meant—'

'No, I know what you meant. Sometimes we do have to fight

off raiders or armed gangs. But you might have noticed there's a hell of a lot of us. And we can all fight. We decided years ago that protecting ourselves was top priority. We've had most of our weapons since the beginning. Getting ammo's always been a problem, but we hardly ever use it anyway. We hunt for food with bows and arrows and slingshots. The guns are only for self-defence.'

'I can see how that makes sense.'

'Yeah. I can take down any game bird with my slingshot. Only I haven't seen any game in weeks. We really need to go further afield. Here...' She gestured. 'This is my place.'

A long brick pier jutted out from the exterior wall of the Compound. Butted up against it sat a large wooden construction patched with rectangles of corrugated metal.

'It's not beautiful, but it keeps us dry.' She took a key from her bag and opened the wooden door's rusty padlock.

'I'd offer you tea, but I haven't got any. Hot water okay? We can put some honey in it.' She winked again.

'Great,' I replied, desperately needing to warm up. I couldn't wait to wrap my hands around a scalding cup. I ducked my head and followed her into a dark space that was barely warmer than outside. But she'd made it homely with mattresses and cushions on the floor. On one wall was a floor-to-ceiling open cabinet stuffed with books, crockery and other knick-knacks.

'Where'd you get all the books?' I asked.

'They were my dad's,' she said. 'I had to trade some of them when things got too bad. But I've managed to keep hold of most. Not sure they'll all make it through this winter though. It's a pretty cold one and books make great fuel.'

'How did your dad get so many?'

'He had them from before. Managed to keep hold of them throughout everything that happened.' Lou took a saucepan from the shelf and bashed it against a skin of ice on a bucket of water. The ice cracked and she dipped the pan into the water beneath, half filling it. 'It would feel wrong to get rid of his books though. They'd make a lovely fire, but every time I'm tempted, I take one down and start to read. They're irreplaceable.'

She opened another door in the side of the dwelling. It led through to a tiny courtyard, big enough to house a metal brazier and a couple of chairs. 'Sorry, I have to cook outside – no chimney. Come, sit. It'll be warmer once this gets going.'

She turned to a large wooden box and lifted the lid, pulling out a handful of dead plants. They had a strong smell; fishy, like down at Cutter's Quay.

'What's that?' I asked.

'Kelp.' She raised an eyebrow at my blank expression. 'You know... seaweed. Fuel.'

'You use seaweed for fuel?'

'Wow, you really do live in a different world.'

I swallowed and tried not to feel insulted because Lou was right. I hadn't realised people used seaweed as fuel, but at least I knew how to make a fire. Lou was using a flint and steel set to get hers going. It caught quickly and she covered the brazier with a metal grill and set the saucepan on the top.

'So was Reece right?' she asked.

'What do you mean?'

'Are you from the Perimeter?'

I nodded, embarrassed.

'What's it like in there? I've heard it looks the way towns used to look? Can you walk around unarmed?'

'We don't carry weapons inside, but that's because there are guards patrolling constantly.'

'I'd feel weird without my slingshot,' she said. 'It's like a part of me. So, inside the Perimeter, do you have wood to burn?' she asked.

'We mainly use gennies, erm... generators.'

'Ahh, yeah, you've got oil. We have to send out foraging parties for fuel. They go out to the west coast combing for kelp and driftwood. It has to be dried out, of course, and now we're running really low. Dunno what we're gonna do if we can't barter in the Compound anymore. There's nothing left to hunt out here and nothing growing this time of year. No trees left round here for firewood either. I reckon we're pretty much stuffed.' She didn't sound too upset, despite her words. 'You wouldn't happen to know where we could get hold of any fuel, would you?'

'I'll ask around,' I replied. 'And I'll let you know.' I thought of the great store of felled trees we had back home in the Perimeter. Mountains of timber stacked up so high we needed a mechanical grabber to lift it. But Pa said the store was precious because there were so few mature trees left growing now. We were planting more all the time, but not nearly enough.

'We can trade you for it,' Lou said, her eyes bright with hope. 'We make some great stuff. Sweaters and jewellery. Weapons. All kinds of things.'

'I can't promise,' I said, feeling guilty. 'Trees are scarce and Grey's men trashed everyone's stores when they were down here. They took a lot of local supplies and when I say "took", I mean "took". They didn't trade for it.'

'Tell me about it,' she retorted, her lips hardening. 'They barged through here, shoving their automatic weapons in our faces and taking anything they wanted. That's why we're so low on supplies this winter.'

'Creepy, aren't they. Did they do their chanting thing?'

'Chanting? No. None of them said anything. Just came in and took our stuff. Luckily we managed to hide some of it.'

'Did you fight them?' I asked.

'We couldn't. Not against those sorts of weapons. It would've been suicide. We're strong, but we couldn't compete with their fire power.'

'Do you think the riot's still going on?' I asked, worrying that Pa might think I'd been hurt.

'Hmm, dunno. The guards were clearing the streets, so I guess it's probably over by now.'

'I better get going then. My pa will be going mad, worrying.'

'I wouldn't go back. Not yet. Not with the curfew. They'll shoot you if you're out on the streets. Doesn't matter who you are.'

'But I have to.'

'Okay. Just wait a while longer. We'll warm up with our tea and then I'll come with you,' she offered, holding her hands out over the sparking fire. 'Help you find him. As long as we keep to the side streets I reckon we'll be safe enough. Maybe your dad'll know where I can get some more fuel.'

I scooched closer to the brazier, the smell of burning seaweed filling my nostrils, along with a pungent Christmassy smell. This little yard was almost cheerful, sheltered from the wind, with the fire crackling and popping.

'Where did your brothers go?' I asked, realising they'd disappeared the minute we reached the encampment.

'Probably off with their cousins.'

Steam began to swirl from beneath the pan lid and Lou poured the boiling water into two scratched and dented tin cups. She used a twig to drop a little honey into each, before passing me a cup. I cradled the warm metal container in my gloved hands and took a sip. It was scalding but good.

'Hello.'

I jumped at a man's voice behind me.

'Lou? You got that Perimeter girl here?'

'Haven't you ever heard of knocking, Tam?' Lou stood up, irritated. 'You can't just barge into my—'

'Riley? Riley, you in here?'

'Pa?' I stood and turned around to see one of the shanties – a young man with dirty blond hair and a matted beard. But right behind him stood my father, an expression of relief and anger on his face.

'What the hell, Riley. I've been going out of my mind.'

'There was a riot,' I replied.

'I know that,' Pa snapped.

'Lou helped me get out. I was going to come back and find you.'

'So what stopped you?'

'Just wanted to wait till the fighting blew over. How did you know I was—'

'This young man came and got me. Good job he did. There's me in the middle of World War Four doing my nut and you're out here, happy as you like gossiping over a cup of tea.'

Tam smirked.

Pa handed him some silver and Lou glared at Tam like she wanted to kill him.

'Let's go,' Pa said.

'Can I finish my tea?'

One look from Pa gave me my answer.

CHAPTER FOUR

JAMIE

At first it was the same dream he always had. It had never varied in theme or colour or feeling. Only it wasn't so much a dream as a memory. A nightmarish re-enactment of the day his life had disintegrated. When the whole world had crumbled into the mess it had now become.

But this time the dream was slightly different. This time, instead of the screams and explosions on the ferry, there was silence. And instead of his parents lying dead, it was the girl from the pool house and she was covered in blood and coloured glass. In the dream, Jamie closed his eyes to block out the image, but the picture stayed burned into his retinas.

He awoke with the sun on his face before it all came rushing back to him, making him sit bolt upright and open his eyes. But he instantly closed them against the glare of the morning. His heart still raced and his scalp prickled with terror at the memory of the dream. Only it wasn't a dream. It was real. It was all real.

He buried his head in his arms and groaned. Why couldn't he have those amazing fantasy-type dreams like everyone else? Why did his dreams have to be a technicolour montage of his worst memories? It was torture. A nightmarish reality he had to endure night after night. And now his recurring dream included this new reality – the murder of a young, innocent girl. Murder. He, Jamie, had unwittingly murdered someone. A girl who had begun to haunt his sleep.

He needed help. Either that, or he needed to never fall asleep again. An overwhelming rush of guilt threatened to crush him. He should pay for what he did, but how? There were no police, no prisons, no justice system. He'd been too much of a coward to stay and face up to the girl's family. He could go back and turn himself in. But he dismissed that thought as soon as he had it. He was too chicken.

Jamie stretched and then winced as a shooting pain travelled the length of his leg, from his hip to his toe. Cracking open an eyelid, he squinted up into the sun-soaked morning. Still too bright. He closed his eye, lay down again and willed himself back to sleep, but it was only a half-hearted attempt. It was dangerous to hang around here. He'd been so upset last night that he'd fallen asleep on rough ground, out in the open. Big mistake. Added to that, his head throbbed and his body felt like he'd had a fight with a grizzly bear and a gorilla and lost.

Last night's tears of despair had dried on his cheeks. Probably why his face throbbed so much. He also remembered praying. Things must have been bad if he'd resorted to talking to God. Strangely, despite his battered body and the guilt, things didn't feel quite as bleak this morning. He was alive at least. And the sun was shining, warming his stiff bones. Jamie felt different. Like he could tackle whatever was coming his way. If there was a punishment waiting for him out here, he would accept it. He took a breath, sat up and opened both eyes.

'Good morning.'

Jamie's heart gave a lurch and he leapt to his feet, clutching his bundle. Stupid and reckless of him to have fallen asleep in such an exposed place. He found himself facing a man: short, bald, clean shaven, quite a bit older than him. Not an outsider by the look of him. No, definitely not an outsider. Jamie glanced about to see if the man was alone. He couldn't see anyone else, but that didn't mean anything. There was a vehicle parked nearby; an old black AV. Maybe there were others inside it.

'Who are you?' Jamie asked, his voice still thick with sleep.

'You can call me Mr Carter. And you are?'

'Jamie.'

'Not a very wise place to fall asleep, Jamie. If I was so inclined, I could have stolen your possessions as you slept.'

Jamie tightened his grip on his bundle. 'Nothing worth stealing,' he retorted.

'Is that why you're clutching your bag as though it's full of diamonds?'

'It's just my clothes and stuff.'

'Don't look so defensive. I'm not a thief.'

'Good,' said Jamie. 'Well, I'll be on my way then.'

'Can I give you a ride?'

'No thanks. I like walking.' He turned away from the man and tried to get his bearings. The man spoke again:

'That way is west towards the Talbot Woods Perimeter and that way is southeast to—'

'I can tell my east from my west thanks. I know I look a bit rough, but I'm not stupid.'

'I'm sure you're not. You do seem disoriented though.'

'That's because I just woke up.'

'Well, the offer of a lift is there if you need it.'

Jamie waved him away with his hand and made off in an easterly direction, towards the rising sun. He would go to the Boscombe Compound as planned. Try to meet up with that girl.

'Hurt your leg, did you?' Mr Carter called after him. 'You're limping quite badly.'

'Some woman knocked me over in her AV. I'm okay,' he called over his shoulder.

'I'm headed that way and I've got fresh bread, fruit and water. You're welcome to share breakfast.'

Jamie kept walking, but his stomach whined at the thought of fresh bread. He could almost smell it. His leg was becoming more painful with each step. He was mad to even be considering this. How could he trust this man? This stranger. He stopped and turned.

'Who are you anyway?'

'Mr Carter, I already told you.'

'No. I mean, who are you? Where you from? What do you do? Do you always offer lifts to random strangers you find lying on the heath?'

Mr Carter chuckled. 'No, not everyone. In fact, hardly anyone. But I have a feeling about you. You look like you could use a break and I'm in the position to give you one.'

'That doesn't exactly answer my question.' Jamie took a step towards Mr Carter.

'Have you heard of James Grey?' the man asked. 'Grey's Church of the Epiphany?'

'Oh, right, you're part of the God squad.' Jamie's heart sank. 'I've heard about you.'

'We help people in need.'

'Thanks, but no thanks.'

'Have you done things you're ashamed of, Jamie?'

An image of the dead girl flashed into Jamie's mind. Shiny beads of blood and glass.

'I can help you come to terms with those things. I can give you peace. Absolution. Are you tired, Jamie? Are you sick of the road and the hostility of your fellow man? Do you crave a warm bed and a clear purpose?'

Jamie wanted to tune out Mr Carter's voice, but the soft seductive words crept into his brain like a virus. Part of Jamie knew that this man was skilled in the art of telling people what they longed to hear. That he wasn't doing anything out of the goodness of his heart. That he had an ulterior motive for approaching him. But the other part of Jamie was tired. Bone-weary in fact, and this Mr Carter bloke knew it. Knew how to press his buttons and get him to do what he wanted.

'Okay,' Jamie said, giving in. 'I'll have breakfast with you.'

'Good. I have fresh white bread from the Compound. Baked only half an hour ago. We'll split it.'

The drive across the heathland was more uncomfortable than walking had been. Jamie's bones rattled together and the pain in his leg intensified with every jolt.

'Not exactly a smooth ride,' Jamie grumbled. But the food more than made up for the rough journey. The bread tasted like heaven itself. Soft and warm with a thick crust. The water was good too – clean and clear. Not like most of the cloudy crap he usually had to choke down.

Thankfully, Mr Carter hadn't said a lot on the journey so far. Jamie would've laid money on the man trying to preach to him. Trying to convert him. But Mr Carter was quiet. Merely chewed his bread thoughtfully as he drove.

'So do you live with Grey then?' Jamie asked through a mouthful of bread. 'What's he like?'

'I live out here, in the open air. Just me and my vehicle. Sometimes I have the company of my brethren, but generally it's me alone.'

'So what's the deal with Grey?'

'I do his work out here.'

'Huh?'

'I find lost souls and I bring them to safety.'

'Was that what you were trying to do with me?'

'Maybe. I'm not sure yet. I'm not convinced our life is for you.'

'Oh.'

Suddenly, it seemed very important that Mr Carter should like him. That he should find him... worthy. Jamie's sleepiness vanished. The world outside was bright and clear. He had a full stomach and a safe ride. He remembered that he'd prayed for guidance last night. He'd actually got down onto his knees and spoken to God. Maybe this man right here was his answer.

CHAPTER FIVE

RILEY

As we drove back to the Perimeter, Pa was silent and I was lost in my thoughts. Life felt weird at the moment. Like we were all waiting for something to happen. For years, life in the Perimeter had been predictable and reliable. Safe. But since my sister Skye's death, everything had changed. Knowing that some stranger had broken into our Perimeter and killed Skye... it had been a horrific shock. The fence didn't feel as solid as it used to. As well as deeply mourning Skye's loss, we all felt vulnerable. Added to this, for the first time ever, supplies were running low. And then there was the FJ situation...

Putting it simply, FJ was unhinged. It wasn't all his fault. He'd been abducted by a religious cult when he was a kid and had been totally brainwashed by James Grey's church. Earlier this year, Luc and I had been captured by Grey, but we'd managed to escape when Luc had shoved a fork down Grey's throat. Gross, I know, but it had done the job and the injuries had resulted in Grey losing his voice. FJ had been selected to speak on Grey's behalf and had since become known as 'the Voice of the Father'.

Back in October, we'd managed to take Grey and FJ

hostage. We'd done it to try to prevent them from annexing our part of the country. But FJ had got away. Before he'd left, he'd given me some disturbing news, saying that he knew who had killed my sister, Skye. I didn't know whether to believe him or not. Luc was convinced he was lying, but I wasn't so sure.

Anyway, after thinking long and hard about it, I'd eventually told my father what FJ had said about Skye. Pa hadn't replied. He'd simply nodded his head and chewed the inside of his lip. Then he'd stood up and walked out of the room. Grabbed his coat from the hook and left the house.

I followed him. Worried about what he was going to do. I asked him where he was going, but he didn't reply. Just kept walking. But I knew where he was going. I knew what he would do. He marched straight into the Guards' House and demanded to speak with the prisoner – James Grey.

The guards let Pa into his cell. Maybe if Roger Brennan had been on duty that night he would have talked Pa out of it. But I doubt it. Grey was in a weakened state. His sudden capture had affected his health and we hadn't expected him to last the winter. He didn't even make it through the night. Pa saw to that.

Pa sent me home, so I don't know exactly what happened. And I don't think I wanted to know. It was a pretty insignificant ending for the legendary James Grey. He wouldn't be missed by many, except perhaps his brainwashed followers.

And it turned out we had lost our bargaining chip for nothing as Grey hadn't given my father any further information about Skye's killer.

Pa and I hadn't mentioned it since. It wasn't common knowledge that Grey was dead and we wanted to maintain the illusion that he was still our hostage. Otherwise, there would be nothing to stop FJ marching straight down here with his army.

FJ – otherwise known as 'the Voice of the Father'. But the Father was dead now. So what did that make FJ? He was out there somewhere and he was unpredictable, vindictive and dangerous. He also had a big problem with me. But I pushed that uncomfortable thought from my mind.

The AV blasted out deliciously warm air and my fingers burned as they thawed. Pa turned and gave me a smile.

'Manage to get any trades before the riot?'

'No. The queues were ridiculous and the traders sold out of everything before I got there.' I didn't tell him that I'd given away some of my trades to Lou. If he asked, I'd pretend I lost them in the confusion. 'Pa,' I began.

'What?'

'Do you know anyone with fuel to trade, for the shanties? They're desperate.'

'Fuel?' Pa said. 'What sort of fuel?'

'Wood and stuff. For their fires.'

'They'll be lucky. Apart from our stores, there's nothing around for miles. Everything was stripped and chopped up when Grey's army came through.'

'There must be something somewhere,' I pushed.

'Look around,' Pa said. 'There's nothing. Whatever we have at home, we need.'

I gazed through the glass at the bleak, grey December land-scape, the sky hanging low above the frost-tinged earth. All the summer bracken and bushes had gone. It was a barren waste-land. 'Can't we at least give Lou some of ours? She's got two younger brothers to look after and—'

The AV stopped with a jolt, cutting me off mid-sentence. Pa turned off the engine, plunging us into a sudden eerie silence.

'Riley,' he said after a few long seconds. 'Take another good look at the scenery. Because unless you want to end up living out here with nothing, you better put all thoughts of this misguided charity out of your head.'

'I'm not talking about a lot – maybe a few logs and some bundles of kindling.'

'A few logs can be the difference between life and death.'

His voice softened. 'I know I seem harsh, but if it's a choice between you and a bunch of strangers, I know who I'd pick.'

Pa's eyes bored into my own, willing me to see his point of view. But I didn't agree with him. How could I? We had mountains of timber at home. I'd seen it. Why should I have the protection of the fence and the warmth of the generators? What had I ever done to deserve so much? Nothing. I let my eyes drop to my lap. If Pa wouldn't help them, then I would.

As we approached the Perimeter, I gazed at the still unfamiliar red brick wall behind the fence. It had been Luc's idea to build it – a double layer of security. Since Grey had tried to take over the south, we'd had to think about upgrading our defences. They had bombs and weapons which now matched, if not outgunned, our own armoury. An inner wall would buy us time if they attacked again. It also shielded us from prying eyes. Pa had traded a lot for the extra bricks and we'd also had to dismantle several Perimeter buildings. But everyone agreed it was worth it.

Luc was on the gates today. He didn't usually go on gate duty, but half our guards were currently recovering from some kind of flu virus, so we were short-handed, meaning everyone had to pitch in. I had to admit, Luc filled out his guard's uniform really well. He was tall and broad shouldered with an easy confidence that had me catching my breath at the sight of him. Pa drove through the double set of gates, came to a stop and buzzed his window down, letting in the icy air.

'You okay?' Luc asked, leaning in with a worried frown. 'Heard there were riots at the Compound.' His sapphire eyes flicked to me and then back to Pa.

'We're fine,' Pa replied. 'But the Compound's in a bad way. They're gonna have to find supplies from somewhere soon or they'll tear the place apart. A lot of desperate people over there.'

'Not good,' Luc said, straightening up.

'No,' Pa replied grimly. 'Anyway, see you later.'

Luc nodded and then looked past Pa to me. 'Want to come round for dinner, Riley? After my shift?'

I felt a thud of something in my chest. Nerves? Excitement? Hope? Luc and I had barely spoken since we'd got back from Salisbury a couple of months ago. And, when we had talked, neither he nor I had mentioned *us*. If there even was an *us* anymore.

'Erm, yeah, okay. Sevenish?'

'Cool. See you later.' He straightened up and waved us on.

Pa closed the window. To my relief, he didn't comment on Luc's invitation.

We cruised up Glenferness, the Perimeter's leafy, wide main avenue, and over the bridge. There was no one else around. Probably all inside trying to keep warm. Turning into our road, Pa nosed the huge AV into the drive. Ma's face appeared briefly at the window, smiling before she vanished. Seconds later the front door opened.

As Pa and I crunched across the gravel to the house, Pa shook his head at my mother. Her face dropped.

'No flour?' she asked.

'Sorry, Ellie. No nothing. The whole place is empty. Or everyone's hoarding.'

'Oh, that's such a shame. I was going to bake a cake. Maybe Rita will have some, but I hate to ask. I'll pop over later. Come inside, quick. We're letting all the cold air in.'

She kissed Pa on the lips and me on the cheek, ushering us into the hallway.

'I'm going next door this evening,' I said. 'If Rita's there, I'll ask about some flour for you.'

'Thanks, darling. That would be great. I borrowed three eggs from Ellen's mum and if I get the flour from Rita, I should have everything I need. Tell Rita I'll bring her over a few slices once it's baked.'

'See you girls later,' Pa said, picking up some paperwork from the hall table. 'I need to call a meeting.'

'Okay, darling,' Ma replied, tucking a loose strand of dark hair behind her ear. 'Have fun.'

I shook my head. Ma just didn't get it. She didn't seem aware of the dangers or the precariousness of our life. She treated everything like a game and viewed Pa's business like some kind of hobby he indulged in. But deep down I knew it was her way of coping with stuff. She hadn't been the same since Skye died. She'd withdrawn into herself and didn't seem to want to know about the reality of things. Pa humoured her and I tried to do the same, even though her attitude irked me.

The front door slammed behind my father and Ma gave a dramatic sigh. 'He's always so busy. We never have time to do anything interesting anymore.'

'I know, Ma. There's just a lot going on at the moment. But, anyway, I met someone really nice today at the Compound.'

'Oh, yes? Tell me about it.' She took my arm and steered me into the sitting room. 'I think we should sit in here like civilised people and light a proper fire,' she said. 'What do you think? It's like the Arctic.'

'Ooh, a fire sounds nice,' I said. 'But we shouldn't really.'

The hearth was already laid with kindling. A big stack of split logs by the side. We weren't supposed to light it ever. It was strictly for emergencies only. We used the gennies for light and power, but our main source of heat was from the massive range in the kitchen which was hooked up to several radiators throughout the house. However, our place was so huge, that even with the range going, the rooms felt cold. An open fire sounded like heaven.

'No,' I said, not giving in to temptation. 'Let's sit in the kitchen. It's warm enough by the range.'

'You're right, I know,' she replied. 'I just fancied a change from being in the kitchen. It gets a bit dull after a while. What's the point of living in a grand house if only one room's comfortable?'

'I'll tell you about my new friend,' I said. 'That'll cheer you up.'

She smiled and we left the chilly sitting room for the warmth of the kitchen. Cradling cups of apple tea, we chatted until the light faded. I told her about the girl outside the Compound and how she'd helped me. I played down the violence though; Ma didn't need to hear about that. Then I realised it was nearly time to go next door to Luc's. I stood up and yawned, stretching my arms above my head. I wanted to shower and change before I left.

'Riley,' Ma said as I stood up to go. 'What's going on with you and that boy?'

Her question took me aback. She'd never openly asked me about Luc before. The subject had kind of become taboo. I thought she still blamed Luc somehow for Skye's death. Even though we'd all known Luc and his family forever. It was a question I wished I was able to answer better because, truthfully, I had no clue what was going on with Luc and me. We'd had something and then it had vanished.

'Nothing's going on,' I said, walking to the door.

'That's a shame,' she said.

'You think so?' I turned.

'Of course. It's obvious the boy worships the ground you walk on.'

'Not anymore,' I replied.

'Don't waste time overthinking things. I've made so many mistakes, Riley. If Luc's the one for you, then don't worry about making a fool of yourself. It's worth the risk. If you let him go without trying, you'll regret it for the rest of your life.'

I left the room and tramped up the stairs. Ma's advice was easier said than done. My non-relationship with Luc was a mess. He'd wanted us to be together a few months ago, but I'd felt guilty because my little sister Skye had a crush on Luc and then we did briefly get it together, but that had ended as soon as it had begun. Right now, I had no idea where we stood, except I was pretty sure he was sick of the whole 'us' scenario and just wanted to be friends.

Ma was right – I didn't want to talk about things with him because I knew I'd end up making a complete idiot of myself. But I also didn't want to ruin our friendship. But... but... Ugh! What I needed was to put Luc Donovan right out of my head.

Maybe cancelling dinner would've been the best option. But the truth was, I wanted to see him. In fact, the thought of spending a whole evening with him made me dizzy with anticipation. I was disgusted with myself for being such a slave to my emotions. Despite all that, I needed to talk with him about helping Lou and her family. That girl had done me a serious favour and I needed to repay her kindness. Plus, I liked her and I was sure Luc would too.

But I could sort all that out later, because right now I had the more important and impossible task of trying to decide what I was going to wear tonight.

CHAPTER SIX

JAMIE

Five Months Earlier

The Boscombe guards opened the heavy iron gates, nodding respectfully to Mr Carter as he drove in. He wound down the window and slipped something into one of the guard's hands.

It had been four years since Jamie had last been here. It had always been a bit rougher than the Charminster 'pound. A place you really had to watch your back. Last time he'd visited, it had ended disastrously. He'd been seeing someone, but her father had caught them and gone ballistic. Apparently, Jamie was too old for her. There was only a six-year difference – Jamie had been twenty-seven while she was twenty-one – but Jamie knew it wasn't his age. It was because Jamie wasn't good enough for his little princess. The man was some kind of big shot around here and he'd had Jamie thrown out of the 'pound, threatening to shoot him if he ever returned.

It was a shame, because the girl was cute and funny and had a swanky little apartment right above a bar. They'd had a good thing going. Later, Jamie came to the reluctant conclusion that the girl probably hadn't even liked him. She was just a spoilt brat who'd shacked up with him purely to annoy her dad. Well, her plan had worked. That was about five years ago, so he wasn't too worried that the father would remember him. Anyway, by now the girl was probably married to someone suitably boring and respectable with half a dozen sprogs.

Jamie sighed. These sorts of things seemed to happen to him wherever he went. But not anymore. No. He was going to be a lot more careful and a lot more... *thoughtful* about things. Maybe he should go against his natural urges for a change. Maybe he should forget about the cute girl who had told him to meet her here. Instead, he should see if this Carter bloke was legit. Maybe the man could set Jamie up with a proper place to live. A job even. Somewhere safe to lay his head at night. Pity; the girl he'd arranged to meet was prettier than a nugget of silver and Jamie was sure they'd have enjoyed each other's company; for a while at least.

Mr Carter parked the vehicle in the vast parking lot. Jamie eased himself out of his seat and gingerly tested his bad leg, putting weight on it. Yeah – still hurt really bad. Man, that sun was hot already, its rays glinting off hundreds of abandoned car roofs. Jamie scratched at his beard for the umpteenth time. He was pretty certain he had lice again.

'I have a good friend who lives here,' Mr Carter said, getting out of the vehicle. 'I'm sure she would very much like to see you. Would you like to meet her, Jamie?'

Jamie stared at the man. What was he talking about – *a friend*? How should *he* know if he'd like to meet her? He didn't even know who she was or what she did.

'Um.' Jamie stared blankly at Mr Carter. Then he remembered his new resolution to take a chance on the man. 'Er, yeah, okay.'

'Splendid.'

Maybe this friend was another member of Mr Carter's God squad. She was probably going to try to brainwash him or something. Well, bring it on. He could do with a bit of brainwashing. Heaven knows there wasn't much inside his head worth hanging on to.

They walked through the car park and up to the inner doors, which opened automatically before they even reached them. Carter had influence here; that much was obvious.

Jamie struggled to keep pace with the shorter man. His leg had almost seized up now and he could no longer bend it at the knee. He felt a wave of dizziness and nausea sweep over him, but gritted his teeth and kept going. He wasn't sure enough of Mr Carter's motives and he worried that if he saw how weak Jamie was, he wouldn't bother with him anymore. The last thing Jamie wanted was to pass out on the 'pound floor and be left for dead. He'd be picked clean in seconds, and the guards would sling him outside without any thought for his well-being.

Houses, people and various livestock flashed past Jamie's field of vision, but he couldn't focus properly. He could hardly see where he was going. The sun beat down on his damp forehead and beads of sweat slipped into his eyes. Mr Carter's back had become a hazy shape ahead of him, but Jamie was determined to hold on to the image. To not let it fade to black. The 'pound noises were nothing but a dull roar in his ears. A merging of voices, barking, the clatter of hooves and the banging and crashing of manual labour. Distant echoes.

'Here we are,' Mr Carter said, his voice clear and close, grounding Jamie, giving him something to anchor himself to.

'Where's here?' Jamie croaked.

'A place for you to rest while I go about my business.'

Sounded good. Jamie leant against the brick wall of the house he found himself in front of. He forced his eyes to focus on his surroundings. They were in an empty side street, the usual garbage smell hung in the air made worse by the heat. The buildings were run-down, crumbling and black with grime.

Dark, dirty windows stared down at him, greying curtains at their sides. Nothing new here. Nothing to make his heart sing.

The door opened and Jamie straightened up, shuffling closer to Mr Carter. A middle-aged woman stood in the doorway. Middle-aged? Jamie laughed to himself. She was probably about the same age as him. Did that make *him* middle-aged? How depressing.

'I've brought you a present, Miriam,' Mr Carter said. 'He's on temporary loan. See what you can do with him. I think his leg is damaged.'

'He's a sorry looking one,' she agreed. 'But I'll do what I can.'

'I know you will.'

'What's going on?' Jamie asked, his voice still thick and slow. 'Who's she?'

'*She* is Miriam. You will be polite to her at all times.'

'What do you mean, I'm "on loan"?' Jamie asked, panic rousing him from his dizzy spell.

'In you go,' Mr Carter said. 'I'll be back tomorrow or the day after, by which time, Miriam will have worked her magic.'

'Come straight through,' the woman said in a no-nonsense kind of voice. Jamie was bigger and stronger than her, but she didn't seem at all afraid of him. She had one of those teacher-ish voices – half-kind, half-condescending. Jamie followed her through into a blissfully cool hallway with a tiled floor. Glancing over his shoulder, he saw that Mr Carter had gone. Well, whatever this place was and whoever this Miriam woman turned out to be, it couldn't be any worse than outside. Could it?

She led him into a plain room with bare plaster walls. Jamie took it all in – the desk, the wooden chair, a metal cabinet and a high bed, the kind that doctors used to use in the old days.

'Can you remove your trousers and get up on the bench for me?' Miriam asked, handing him a small cotton sheet.

'What? Why?' Jamie held onto the top of his trousers, at the same time realising how ridiculous he must look.

'You have a bad leg and I'm a doctor,' she said. 'Use the sheet to cover yourself if you're embarrassed.'

'A doctor? Really?'

'Would you like to see my credentials? I qualified over twenty years ago and I've had plenty of practice since then.'

'Erm, nah, that's okay.' Jamie figured he could easily overpower her if she tried any funny stuff. As long as she didn't pull a gun on him. He wrapped the proffered sheet around his waist, lowered his trousers and levered himself up onto the table, wincing as he was forced to put pressure on his bad leg.

Miriam was of a medium build with a nondescript face and short mid-brown hair greying at the temples. But she had full lips and wasn't completely unattractive. As she prodded and poked at his flesh, Jamie wondered what he was even doing here in this strange house with this odd woman.

'What happened to you?' she asked.

'There was a woman in an AV. She knocked me over and drove off.'

'No breaks,' she said after a minute or so of checking. 'And luckily for you, no femur or tibia fractures.'

'It feels really bad,' Jamie said. 'Are you sure it's not broken?'

'You wouldn't be so calm if it was. You wouldn't have been able to walk here either.' She pressed the outside of his lower leg and Jamie yelled out in pain. 'Localised swelling,' she said. 'Looks like you may have fractured your fibula.'

'Fractured my what?'

'Fibula. But it's nothing to worry about. Get cleaned up first and then I'll strap an ice pack on your leg.'

'You have ice packs?'

'We're lucky here. God provides.'

Not normally he doesn't, Jamie thought.

'In the room next door, you'll find a shower, some soap, a toothbrush and a towel. When you're dry, use the powder on the shelf. It's good for getting rid of lice. I'll be back in a minute with a nightshirt and some clean clothes.'

A bathroom? Clean clothes? Was he dreaming? And a *toothbrush*? Jamie hadn't seen a toothbrush for years. He'd always used twigs whenever he could be bothered.

'Are you hungry?' Miriam asked.

Normally his standard reply to this was a big fat *yes*. But on the way here, Mr Carter had let him eat his fill of bread and fresh fruit – way more food than he normally ate in one sitting. 'I'm okay, thanks,' he replied. 'Maybe later.'

'Fine. Come back and see me when you're clean. I'll dress your cuts and put that ice pack on your leg.'

Jamie felt a flicker of some long-forgotten feeling. He couldn't quite put his finger on it, but his shoulders had begun to relax and that constant tight feeling around his head eased ever so slightly. Maybe it was because someone else was looking after him, worrying about his well-being. He hadn't figured out why they were doing it yet. He didn't buy into all that Christian charity crap. In his experience, no one did something for someone else without getting something in return. Not these days anyway. But for now, Jamie was going to get on board with it. He was going to pretend that everything was okay, that these people only had his best interests at heart. He would get cleaned up, rest, allow his leg to heal, eat his fill and then decide what to do later.

CHAPTER SEVEN

RILEY

Luc's mother, Rita, opened the front door, her hair pulled up into a messy bun, a pair of glasses perched on her nose. 'Hi, you. Come on in quick, it's freezing out there.'

'Hi, Rita. How are you?' I stepped inside and rubbed at my arms.

'Yeah, not bad. We're off out so you and Luc can eat in peace without Eddie hovering around you being nosy.'

'I heard that.' Eddie's voice wafted through from one of the back rooms.

'You were meant to,' Rita called back. 'Give me your coat, Riley. I'll hang it up.'

I shrugged off my parka and handed it to her. 'Thanks.'

'Luc'll be down in a minute. His shift finished later than planned. We're short staffed what with this flu bug thing that's going round. He's just having a shower. Poor boy's exhausted, bless him.'

'We can always make it another night,' I said.

'No, no. It's good for him to unwind. He's been looking forward to you coming over.'

'Okay,' I said. 'If you're sure.'

She smiled, wrapping a patterned scarf around her neck and loosening her hair from its bun.

'Oh,' I said. 'Before I forget, have you got any flour? Ma wants to bake a cake. She said she'd give you all a piece each.'

'Oh, yum. Your mother's cakes are spectacular. Ask Luc to give you a cupful. It's in the larder.' She took off her glasses and set them on the side.

'Oh, that's brilliant. Thanks. Ma'll be really pleased.'

Rita smoothed my hair absent-mindedly. 'Good. Well, we're going now, so will you be okay waiting for Luc? He shouldn't be long.'

'Hey, Riley.' Eddie popped his head around the door. 'Come on, Rita. We're going to be late.'

'I was waiting for *you*,' she said. 'See you, Riley.'

'Bye, Rita. Eddie.'

The front door slammed and I slid down onto the battered kitchen sofa to wait for Luc. Footsteps creaked on the floor-boards above and I chewed the corner of my thumb, trying to quell my butterflies. Before too long, I heard him coming down the stairs and my nerves intensified.

Luc walked into the kitchen wearing jeans and a navy sweatshirt, rubbing at his newly cropped hair with a towel. I stood up and he almost jumped a mile high, bashing his hip on the corner of the table.

'Ow!' he cried. 'I didn't see you.'

'Sorry,' I replied, laughing.

'Glad I amuse you. You almost gave me a heart attack. When did you get here?'

'Sorry, haven't been here long. Your mum and dad left a couple of minutes ago.'

'Yeah, I heard the front door slam. You okay? Hungry?'

'Starving,' I lied. Food was the furthest thing from my mind.

'It's only veggie soup and bread,' he said. 'Sorry it's not more fancy. We've got stuff, but Mum's rationing.'

'That's okay. Soup's great and I haven't had bread in a while.'

'Luc draped the towel over one of the kitchen stools, turned another stool to face me and sat down. I sank back into the sofa, slipped my trainers off and brought my feet up underneath me.

'So what happened today at the 'pound?' he asked, running a hand over his damp hair. 'Everyone's going on about it, but only you and Johnny were actually there. Spill, Culpepper.'

I grinned. 'What's it worth?'

'I'm making you dinner, aren't I?'

'Oh, yeah. Okay then. Well, it was pretty full on. Just kicked off without warning.'

While Luc heated up the soup, I sliced some bread and proceeded to tell him about the queues and how it had all turned ugly once people realised there were no provisions left to trade for. Luc tipped the contents of the pan into two bowls and we carried them across to the kitchen table.

'I've never known it this bad before,' Luc said, sitting down and blowing on a spoonful of soup. 'It's Grey's fault. His army ransacked the area. So now everyone's hoarding. At least you got out of there okay.'

'Only because of Lou.'

'Who?'

'Lou. She lives outside the Compound. She got me out of there when people started shooting the place up. Nice soup by the way. Did you make it yourself?'

'Yeah, I did actually. Made it this morning. Thanks. Did you say she lives *outside* the Compound? A shanty helped you out? It's usually the other way around. They usually help themselves, not others.'

'Well, Lou was really nice.'

'Hmm.'

I glanced up at his sceptical tone. 'What are you "hmming" about?'

'I've dealt with the shanties before and, not to be prejudiced or anything, but they don't usually help people from the goodness of their hearts. It's usually about what *you* can do for them.'

'Lou isn't like that,' I replied. 'After it all kicked off, she came back to see if I was okay and then when I couldn't find Pa, she told me she'd get me out. Once we got back to her camp, she got in trouble with this guy called Reece for helping me...'

'Who?' Luc's eyes narrowed.

'Reece – one of the shanties. He had a go at her for showing me their route out of the Compound. Anyway, I said I'd see if I could find Lou some fuel. She's got two younger brothers and—'

'There you go,' Luc interrupted.

'What?'

'You said you'd get her some fuel. She helped you out so she could get some fuel.'

'No. It wasn't like that. She didn't say she'd get me out of there for a price. She helped me and I offered afterwards.'

'Well, of course she wouldn't say that. She'd have to be a bit subtle about it.'

I tore off a piece of bread and started chewing. 'Not everyone's out for themselves, Luc. Some people can be kind without wanting something in return.'

Luc didn't reply, but I could tell he didn't agree with me. I also had the feeling he was being antagonistic on purpose. Like he was spoiling for a fight.

'Well,' I continued, 'whether or not you believe me, I want to help her. I'm going to try to get her some firewood or kelp or whatever. Anyway, even if she had helped me out for a price – which she didn't – that's not so bad, is it? Everyone deserves to have food and heating.'

'Do you think she'd give you *her* supplies if you needed them? Course she wouldn't.'

'She's not asking for charity. She's willing to trade.'

'What? Some jewellery made from old stones, I bet, or a palm reading where she tells you you'll meet a tall handsome stranger. That won't feed you or keep you warm in winter. It's junk and lies, Riley. Not worth anything. And she knows it.'

I knew if Luc met Lou, he'd see she wasn't like that at all, but talking about her only seemed to make him irritated. 'She helped me out, Luc. She probably saved my life.'

'You can look after yourself, Riley. You were armed, and Johnny was close by. Nothing would have happened.'

'You weren't there. You didn't see what it was like.'

'She knew there'd be something in it for her if she helped you. I bet you gave her something, didn't you. Tipped her off that you were wealthy.'

My cheeks reddened as I remembered the jar of honey and the dried peas. Both worth a fortune by anyone's standards.

'I knew it! What did you give her?' Luc grinned.

'Nothing much.'

He rolled his eyes. He wasn't normally so mean. I didn't know what had got into him.

'So basically you think I'm a gullible idiot. Is that it?'

He softened his grin. 'Course not. I just think you were played a bit.'

'Cheers.' I scowled and stood up. This evening hadn't gone at all how I'd expected. I thought we'd have a laugh and that there'd be the usual bit of banter tinged with expectation. I'd even stupidly thought that something might happen between us. But it was obvious to me now that we were way past that. He thought I was naïve and stupid.

'Calm down, Riley. I'm not having a go.'

'Well, it sounds like it.'

'I'm not.' A smile still played on his lips and it made me mad as hell.

'It's late. I should go home.'

'It's not late. We haven't had pudding yet.'

'I'm full up, but thanks.'

'You're sulking,' he said. 'Because I disagreed with you.'

He was right, but I wasn't going to tell him that. Anyway, it was more than sulking – it was disappointment. It was a sick feeling in the pit of my stomach. It was my heart breaking just a little, because I felt like I was losing him. Like he was pushing me away. He'd always been sweet to me and had faith in me. Trusted my judgement. Tonight he was being antagonistic on purpose.

'I'm fine, Luc. Not sulking, just tired.' I wanted to ask him why he'd even invited me over here tonight if he was going to act this way. But I didn't have the energy.

'Okay.' He stood and scraped his chair back. 'Well, I guess I'll see you...'

'Yeah. Night.' I turned and headed for the door feeling unsteady on my feet. My eyes brimmed with unshed tears and I prayed I could keep them at bay until I left the house.

'Riley,' Luc called after me. 'Riley... you okay?' His voice had lost that mocking edge and I heard the old Luc in there. But it was too late. I was too upset.

'Fine,' I called back without turning around. 'Night, Luc. Thanks for supper.'

I grabbed my coat off the hook and stumbled out through the front door. What just happened? We hadn't really argued and he hadn't said anything truly horrible to me. So why was I feeling like the world just ended? But it wasn't what he'd said, it was the way he'd said it, like I irritated him. He'd been condescending, treating me like a naïve little girl. Like I didn't know how the world worked. Like he didn't really even like me anymore.

I pulled up my hood and shoved my hands deep into my parka pockets as I walked slowly back down Luc's driveway, towards his front gate. I half hoped he'd come running after me, but by this time I was crying and I definitely did not want him to see my tears. All I wanted now was to throw myself on my bed and sob like a child. What had happened back there? Nothing really. So why did I feel so awful?

I turned into the deserted road and trod carefully so as not to fall flat on my backside on the ice. That would be the perfect ending to a crappy day. Half a minute later and I was walking in through my own front door.

'That you, Riley?' Ma's voice came at me from the kitchen.

'Yeah. I'm tired. Going to bed.'

'You okay?'

Her voice sounded closer. Oh no, she was obviously coming to see if I was all right. What if she saw my tears? The last thing I wanted was a heart-to-heart with my mother about why Luc Donovan was being a dick.

'I'm fine,' I called, quickening my pace and heading up the stairs two at a time. 'Just tired.'

'Want some tea?' she called up the stairs at my retreating back.

'No thanks. G'night.' I hoped she'd leave it at that.

'Okay, darling. Night. Oh, did you get my flour?'

I stopped at the top of the stairs and called down. 'Sorry, Ma. I forgot to pick it up. Rita said that's fine though.'

As soon as I closed the bedroom door behind me, I let it all out. I clenched my fists and gave a sob. Maybe it was post-traumatic shock from the riots or something. Maybe I was losing my marbles. I didn't even bother to take off my coat and shoes. Just lay face down on the bed. I wanted to hurl something at the wall. Break something. Punch a hole in the door. But I didn't. I felt so mad at Luc Donovan and mad at myself too. I should've stayed and told him he was being an idiot, but I hadn't wanted him to see my tears. Why had he been so mean? He'd been spoiling for a fight and I should've stayed and fought back.

I sat up and wiped my face with my sleeve. Should I march back over there and tell him what I thought? But tell him what exactly? No. I'd only end up making things worse between us. If that were possible.

CHAPTER EIGHT

JAMIE

She lay there, dead, unmoving on the ground; the coloured glass fragments decorating her body like precious jewels set into alabaster. Jamie reached down to touch them, but instead of hard glass, they were soft and smooth, like they were part of her skin. He moved his finger to another piece of the glass – a clear fragment embedded in her cheek. It felt gross and spongy like jelly. But suddenly the place he touched began to bleed, a trickle at first and then a spurt of dark red blood, staining her face and pooling around his thick dirty fingers. The dead girl opened her eyes and Jamie screamed.

Sweat coated his face and his heart pumped. It was a dream. A nightmare, that was all. The girl was dead and far away from here. But Jamie knew that the image of the girl would never leave him. She was part of his waking and dreaming life now. He sat up and tried to slow his breathing. The room was dark and quiet. He was in the Boscombe 'pound, he remembered. That woman doctor had fixed up his leg and let him get some sleep. Only sleep wasn't good. Sleep was scary. Such a waste of a good bed. He hadn't slept in a proper bed since forever. It even had a pillow stuffed with feathers.

Jamie's face felt odd. When he reached up to scratch his beard, his fingers found nothing but smooth skin, and then he remembered – he'd shaved off his beard earlier. It felt strange, like his head was lighter. It probably was.

After adjusting the pillow, Jamie eased himself into a sitting position. A tin cup sat on the bedside table. He picked it up and sniffed at it. A faint metallic scent. He took a sip – water. He gulped all the liquid down and set the cup back on the table. What now? He closed his eyes and the girl's face appeared. Jamie tried to banish it with thoughts of the doctor and of Mr Carter and of the other girl he was supposed to meet here, but the dead girl's face kept shimmering back into focus. This was bad. He was cracking up.

He needed to get away from his own company. Maybe the doctor, Miriam... maybe she was somewhere around here. Maybe she could give him something to stop him freaking out. He swung his legs off the bed, gasping as the pain from his damaged limb shot through his body. More carefully this time, he eased his legs onto the floor. But he wasn't sure if he dared put weight on his bad leg. The ice pack was still strapped to it, but the ice must've melted because it didn't feel cold anymore.

Then Jamie saw something propped up against the wall next to the bed. Two long sticks of metal with circular attachments – a pair of crutches. Miriam must have left them for him. Jamie reached out and took hold of the walking aids. He positioned the cuffs over his forearms and gripped the handles. Then he levered himself upright.

Jamie realised he was still wearing the cotton nightgown he'd put on after his shower. Should he get changed? A pile of homespun clothes lay on the floor. No, he would put them on later, but right now he had to get out of this room. Find some company to keep out the images of the girl. Once more he saw the shard of glass drop from the doorframe. Saw it slice into her white throat. Saw her look of surprise before the life drained away. He shook his head to dislodge the pictures. If he didn't get himself under control, he would start blubbing again, or screaming. They would think he was mad and throw him out.

The door to his room was closed and Jamie hoped they hadn't locked him in. If they had, he would definitely start pounding on it. He manoeuvred his way across the room, working the crutches, his bad leg slightly bent at the knee. But he needn't have worried; the door clicked open and Jamie poked his head out into a darkened landing. He wondered what the time was. Was it late evening? Or maybe the early hours of the morning.

'Hello,' he called out, his voice still croaky with sleep. 'Anyone there?'

Four other doors led off the landing, all closed. Should he knock on one of them? He didn't think he'd make it down the stairs on his crutches; the treads looked too narrow, the staircase too steep.

Footsteps from below. Jamie froze and then relaxed. It would be Miriam. He stepped back nonetheless and realised he could use the crutches as a weapon if he needed. A dim light filtered up and then the figure of a woman appeared on the stairs.

'You're awake.' It was Miriam. She reached the landing, a glass candle lamp in her hand, the flame casting strange shapes around them.

'What time is it?' Jamie asked.

'A little before midnight. You should get some more rest. How's the leg?'

'Sore,' he replied.

'That's normal. I see you found the crutches.'

'Yeah. Thanks.'

'You really should go back to bed. Sleep is the best medicine.'

'The thing is,' Jamie began, 'I... I can't sleep.' His voice cracked and he willed himself not to cry. He took a breath to get himself under control. 'I could really do with some company. Maybe a drink...'

'We don't drink alcohol here,' she replied.

'No... I meant tea or something.' He hadn't meant that at all, but he didn't want to offend her.

'Come on then,' she said. 'I was about to go to bed myself, but I'll make you a cup of tea first if you like.'

'Oh, sorry. Don't worry. You go to bed if you're—'

'No, no that's all right. I'll join you in a cuppa. You can tell me a little about yourself.' She turned and headed back down the staircase. Jamie hesitated at the top, not sure how to negotiate the stairs. Miriam stopped and turned. 'Lead with the crutches,' she said. 'Then follow with your good leg.'

Jamie did as she said and found that it wasn't as hard as he'd anticipated. All the same, he felt better once he'd reached the bottom. He followed her to the back of the house and into a small kitchen where she set the lamp upon the shelf of a wooden dresser.

'Is it just you here in this house?' Jamie asked.

'There are four of us,' she replied, pouring a jug of water into a metal pan.

'You all doctors?'

'I'm the only qualified physician, but my sisters are just as capable.'

'Isn't it dangerous?' Jamie asked, leaning against the doorframe. 'Four women on their own in a nice house. Aren't you scared someone will steal from you or hurt you or something? I mean, I'm a stranger. You don't know me.'

'No,' she replied. 'I've been here for more than ten years and nothing like that has ever happened.' She placed the pan on the stove.

'Doesn't mean it won't happen though.'

She smiled. 'Mint tea?'

'Yeah. Please.'

'Or chamomile to help you sleep?'

'That would be better.'

'What's troubling you, Jamie? Why can't you sleep?'

'Nothing. Just can't, that's all.'

She nodded. 'The tea will relax you.'

It'll take more than tea to do that, Jamie thought.

'There is only one way to truly achieve peace,' she continued. 'There is only one man who can help you.'

'Let me guess,' Jamie said. 'Grey.'

'Our Father is blessed by God. He alone can take away your troubles. Tea will calm you momentarily, alcohol will blot it out for a short while, but only when you have spoken your sins aloud and taken Our Father's blessing will the nightmares leave you.' Her words were soft and soothing and, although he didn't necessarily believe what she was saying, Jamie enjoyed the calming timbre of her voice.

To his relief, that was the last she mentioned of James Grey. They stayed in the kitchen, talking into the early hours of the morning, sitting at the tiny square table, sipping tea and eating homemade biscuits. Miriam wasn't like anyone else he had met before. She didn't judge. Didn't tell him what he should be doing or what he shouldn't be doing. She merely listened and nodded and made sympathetic noises. Not that he told her anything important. He certainly wasn't going to mention the dead girl or his proximity to the Perimeter yesterday. He skimmed over his life story, telling her how he'd lost his parents and how he'd been living on the outside ever since.

Finally, some hours later, she suggested that it would be a good idea to try to get some sleep. Jamie's heart rate increased at the thought of being alone with his nightmares again. His thoughts blurred into a panicked feeling of dread. But it was as though Miriam knew how he was feeling. She put a hand on his arm and he instantly felt calmer.

'It will be all right,' she said. 'Take a deep breath; slow your breathing right down.'

He took in a breath and held it.

'Now slowly let it out,' she said. 'Every time you feel your thoughts begin to stray to places you don't wish them to go, take a slow breath and let it out. I cannot vanquish the nightmares, but I can lighten your waking hours.'

Jamie felt tears welling behind his eyes.

'When you're in bed,' she continued, 'and the darkness threatens to overwhelm you, try praying to God and asking him for forgiveness.'

Jamie inhaled, listening to her words. To the softness of her voice.

'If and when you are lucky enough to be welcomed into our church, you will eventually find what you are searching for. Our Father will listen and you will be rewarded with a dreamless, healing sleep.'

Jamie exhaled. He desperately wanted to believe her.

'You go on up,' she said. 'I'll wash these cups.'

'I'll do it, if you want?'

'No, that's all right. You go up.' Jamie stood and Miriam held out his crutches. 'Lead with your good leg to go up the stairs.'

'My good leg? Okay, thanks. G'night then.'

'Goodnight. God bless you, Jamie.'

Jamie lay awake in the darkness mulling over Miriam's words. She had told him to breathe slowly and so he did. In through his nose and out through his mouth. All he thought about were the slow exhalations and inhalations. The pale face of the girl was banished into the darkness for now.

Sleep came quickly to him, but sleep was not his friend. His dreams were worse than ever – bloody montages of death and fear, screams and explosions. All his worst memories mixed together in a nightmarish concoction of guilt and terror.

When Jamie awoke the next day, he felt exhausted, as though he had fought in a battle. Sweat clung to his body and his heart rate was insane. The girl's face was still imprinted in his brain as clear as if he were looking at her right now. This couldn't go on. He couldn't endure another night like that. He would have to stay awake forever, until he lost his mind completely. Maybe the nightmares were his punishment for everything he'd done.

Miriam had said Grey would be able to take the terrors away. Was she right? Did he have that kind of power, or was it just a load of religious nonsense? Anything was worth a go. At this point he would have sold his soul to the devil to get a good night's sleep.

CHAPTER NINE

RILEY

In the morning I felt stiff and cold. Exhausted. I remembered last night and had the feeling I'd made a total idiot of myself. Made a drama out of nothing. But then I remembered how Luc had spoken to me and I felt a surge of anger. He was wrong about Lou. She was a good person and I was going to help her. Just how I was going to do that, I had no idea. But I'd figure it out.

I splashed my face with cold water, trying to take down the swelling in my cried-out eyes. Then I dried my face, got changed out of yesterday's clothes and pulled open the curtains. Daylight drowned me, making me scrunch up my eyes. I hadn't seen the sun in a long time and it felt good, even though frost still laced the window panes. I bounced down the stairs and into the kitchen.

I must have been the first one up. The kettle was cold and there were no dirty breakfast dishes. Breakfast these days was porridge, porridge or porridge. I missed my morning toast, but bread had been scarce for the past few weeks, so I had to make do. I shook some oats into a pan with a splash of milk and some water. Pa still had a ton of supplies, but it was the fresh goods we were lacking.

While I stirred the mixture, the image of Luc kept popping into my head. Thinking about him made me alternately cross, upset or nervous. I needed to focus on something else. Getting hold of fuel for Lou was the perfect distraction. First, I needed to lay my hands on the actual timber. And second, I needed a vehicle to transport it to the shanty camp. The outline of a plan was forming in my head. It was risky, and probably a little foolish, but I wasn't in the mood to worry about anything. I would just have to blag it. I made up my mind I would do it and I would do it today.

A burning smell wafted into my nostrils and I realised I'd forgotten to keep stirring the porridge. It had stuck to the bottom of the pan and, as I scraped at it with the spoon, I saw it had turned into a sticky black mess. I'd have to salvage what I could and bin the rest. Cooking had never been my strong point.

Footsteps creaked overhead and I realised I'd better move quickly before either of my parents came down. If I saw them, I might lose my nerve. I shovelled a couple of mouthfuls of partially burnt porridge into my mouth and scraped the rest into the trash, feeling guilty at the waste of food. I'd have loved a cup of tea before I left, but I didn't have time, so I sipped at some freezing water instead, feeling the icy burn as it travelled down to my stomach.

Leaving the kitchen, I peered up the staircase and listened hard. The drumming whoosh of the shower started up. I didn't have much time, so I slipped into Pa's office and quickly located what I was looking for – the requisition pad in the top drawer of his desk. I tore off the top sheet and scribbled: *1 pallet seasoned timber plus transport for collection by R Culpepper*. Then, with a trembling hand, I forged my father's signature and shoved the slip of paper into my back pocket, returning the pad to the drawer. Back in the hallway, I grabbed my coat, gloves and woollen hat and slipped through the front door as quietly as I could manage.

The air outside was still, the sun cold and bright as diamonds. Chill air cut through my jeans and sliced at my cheeks, but somehow I liked its fierce intensity. I'd soon warm up once I started walking. I held my hat and gloves between my teeth as I shrugged on my parka, zipping it right up to my chin. Then I put on my gloves and tugged my beanie down over my ears. Taking a couple of steps across the noisy gravel, I glanced back at the house, my heart still beating hard from what I'd just done. Ma looked down from the upstairs window and I waved. She mouthed something, but I turned away, pretending not to see.

Heading in the direction of the stores, I walked quickly. My cloudy breath puffed away from me as I tried to work out how I would play it with Denzil, who was on guard duty there this week. Denzil had saved my life and Luc's twice now, and Luc had seen to it that he got a job as a guard in our Perimeter. Denzil was ex-army, a good guy, but I wasn't convinced he'd help me out, despite the forged requisition order in my pocket. He might question it and want to speak to Pa.

I became aware of a figure up ahead. Someone running, getting closer. I stopped. He wore black tracksuit bottoms and a grey top, the hood pulled up. As he approached, he glanced up at me and slowed down to a halt.

'Luc,' I said.

'Hey, Riley. You're not usually around this time of the morning.' He hadn't shaved yet, and a haze of stubble shadowed his face.

'What are you doing out here?' I asked.

'Running. I run every morning.'

'Oh. I didn't know.'

'Gonna do some stretches and have some brekkie. Wanna join me?'

'Uh, no thanks. I'm going to meet someone.'

'Oh, okay.' He jogged past me and turned around so he was running backwards for a moment. 'Maybe see you later?'

'Yeah,' I said with a shrug.

'Okay... well... see ya.' He turned away and pounded on down the road towards his house. Well, that was awkward. He'd been overly cheerful and we'd talked to each other like strangers without even acknowledging last night's weirdness. I looked back at his receding figure and felt a pang of something. Then I shook myself out of it and carried on walking, attempting to distract myself by focusing on the tiny birds which darted in and out of the neighbours' hedgerows.

I crossed Glenferness and turned left, trudging down the curve of Leven Avenue, the slap of my footsteps sounding overly loud in the quiet morning air. Tall red-trunked evergreens lined the wide avenues, interspersed with cherry trees, oaks and sycamores. These were trees that we didn't want to fell, but we would if we needed to. Fast-growing saplings had been placed in amongst them to supplement our timber stores, and I marvelled at the relative excess of everything inside the fence compared to the barrenness outside. Sure, we occasionally ran out of things, but it was only ever an inconvenience, never a matter of life and death. Not yet anyway.

Up ahead, the high metal fence of the stores glinted in the sunshine and, as I rounded the bend, I caught a glimpse of the edge of the timber mountain jutting out behind the huge old manor house where the majority of our goods were stored.

Pa had his own underground supply of stuff, but it was secret and separate from these general Perimeter stores. All council members (including Pa) were able to requisition supplies, but they had to first agree how much, who to, and when. So what I was doing was very much against Perimeter rules. I stopped walking and took a deep breath. I could turn back now and no harm would be done. Lou wasn't expecting anything from me, so why was I risking so much to help her? I guess I just didn't like the inequality. I wanted to make her life more comfortable. I'd never had a friend on the outside before. Pa's and Luc's attitudes irked me. If you couldn't help out a friend, then what was the point of anything?

I crossed the road, stopped outside the gate and pressed the buzzer. Almost immediately, a guard stepped out of the brick-built hut at the entrance. His face broke into a smile and I grinned back at him.

'Hey, Denzil.'

'Hello, stranger,' he said. 'Haven't seen you for a while. You coming in?'

Back in October, Denzil had helped me and Luc take FJ and Grey hostage, but I hadn't seen much of him since.

'I've got a req order from Pa,' I said.

'Hang on then.' He went back into the hut and a moment later the right-hand gate swung slowly inwards. As soon as the gap was wide enough, I slipped through and followed Denzil into the chilly hut. He stamped his feet and crossed his arms, shoving his hands under his armpits for warmth.

'How can you stand it?' I asked. 'It's like an icebox in here.'

'It's not too bad. I do a lot of running on the spot and I stand outside in the sun when I can. Anyway, what can I do for you? You said you've got an order?'

'Yeah. For some timber and transport.'

Denzil ran his finger down the chalk board on the wall. 'I don't have a record.'

'No, you won't have. It's a last-minute thing. After yesterday's trouble at the Compound, we're delivering some supplies over there to calm things down. Pa's sent me here, while he gets some other stuff.' I knew I was starting to babble, and forced myself to stop.

Denzil looked at the forged order, appearing to think for a while.

'D'you need me to get Pa over here?' I asked. 'I don't mind. But he sent me to save time, and going to get him will take a while.' A light sweat broke out on my forehead. I'd be in so much trouble if I got caught. Taking supplies could get you locked up. Kicked out of the Perimeter even...

'Nah, that's okay, Riley. I've got his signature. That should be good enough. Go around back and see Pauly, he'll sort you out with what you need.'

'Cheers, Den. We'll have to catch up properly when I get back. Come over for a cuppa when you get some free time.'

'Sounds good. You and your dad go careful. I hear it's pretty volatile in the 'pound these days.'

'We'll be okay.'

'I know you will, girl. You're badass.' He laughed and I couldn't help joining in.

'What are you like, Denzil.' I gave him a last smile before heading round the back of the big house to get what I'd come for.

Half an hour later, I was driving out through the Perimeter gates into the wasteland of Bournemouth. I'd done the journey with Pa so many times in the last few weeks that I didn't feel nervous out here anymore. All I felt was an anxious fluttering that Pa would find out. But I knew he had a million and one meetings to occupy him today, so hopefully my little foray would go unnoticed. The flatbed had been loaded up, a huge green tarp stretched over the top, but my illicit truckload hadn't even made a tiny dent in the Perimeter's giant timber mountain.

The truck was a way harsher ride than the AV and much less secure. I hoped I wouldn't run into any bandits. My Saiga lay across the passenger seat just in case and I also had two revolvers and my knife, so I wasn't too worried. I hummed a tune to myself while I negotiated the bumps and dips of the heath, squinting against the sun's glare and wishing I'd thought to bring my sunglasses.

It dawned on me that I wouldn't be able to simply drive up to the Walls with a truckful of firewood. The shanties would take one look and strip it clean in minutes. Then Lou might be left with nothing. And I wanted her to benefit. To at least get the credit for such a big haul. This meant I would have to park up somewhere, walk into the camp alone and try to find Lou first. Not ideal.

If I carried my machine gun, they'd treat me as a hostile, but if I left it behind, I'd be vulnerable walking outside on my own. I didn't feel safe enough with only the revolvers. I really hadn't thought my plan through properly. Maybe this whole thing hadn't been such a good idea after all.

Once I was within half a mile of the Compound, I cruised up and down the area looking for somewhere to park the truck. But this was exposed ground. There were no buildings or trees to conceal a large vehicle, or even a small vehicle for that matter. The landscape was all frosted earth and rocks. It was no good – I would have to risk driving up close to the camp.

Before continuing, I stopped the truck for a moment and scanned the area. No one appeared to be around, so I hopped out and reached in for my Saiga, slinging it across my body. Despite the sunshine, the wind was vicious. I walked around the back and checked the tarp was still fixed on properly. I didn't want any of my precious load to be visible when I rolled up to the Walls. Either way, it wouldn't make too much difference – a truck loaded up with *anything* was fair game out here.

It was a rush to be alone out on the heath, its raw silence terrifying yet beautiful. Inside the Perimeter I was safe. I could walk around unarmed and relaxed. But outside, the safety catch was off. The silence deceptive. Anything could happen.

I wondered about before, when people had been able to walk around the country freely, unarmed with no fear of attack.

As relaxed as if they were inside a Perimeter. Apparently, there had been a proper army and a police force who would actually come to your aid if someone did something wrong, or even if they spoke to you in a threatening way. I wasn't sure I believed those tales. I suspected that memory made it all seem rosier than it really was. People couldn't have changed all that much, could they?

Well, whatever things had used to be like, they certainly weren't like it any longer. And I doubted they ever would be again.

Satisfied the tarp was adequately secure, I climbed back into the cab, restarted the engine and continued on my journey.

Within a few minutes, the patchwork walls of the Compound came into view, a huddle of dark shapes at its base. I decided to park up close to the settlement and wait for someone to approach me. Then I could ask them about Lou and hope they'd fetch her for me. I wish I'd thought to ask her last name. As I drew closer, I made out the shapes of makeshift dwellings – the tents and shacks and low barbed wire fences. Several shanties with rifles stood and stared as I came closer, their faces weathered and impassive.

I drew up as near as I dared, not wanting to be perceived as a threat and risk them firing on me. I stopped the truck but left the engine idling, and waited. One of the men leaned across to another and said something. The two of them sidled through a gap in the wire and headed towards me. My heart sped up, but strangely my mind felt quite calm. I had to keep telling myself that I was doing them a massive favour by coming here. I was doing something good. Even though it didn't feel like it.

The men were youngish with beards, wearing layers of filthy clothing. One of them had a face-full of piercings – lip rings, eyebrow studs and a hoop through his nose. They were both skinny and hollow-cheeked with deep-set eyes. As they drew closer, I saw pure hostility in their faces and it took all my strength of will not to throw the truck into reverse and gun it all the way home.

'What's your business here?' the man with the nose hoop called out.

I lowered the window a fraction. 'I'm a friend of Lou's.'

'Lou?' They took a few steps closer, their weapons still lowered.

'Yeah. Fair-haired girl with two younger brothers. Lives up close to the Compound wall.'

'I know who Lou is,' nose-hoop replied. 'What d'you want with her?'

'She helped me out yesterday. I've come to say thanks.'

'Get out of the truck and I'll fetch her over.'

'I'd rather stay inside till she gets here, if that's okay?'

They stopped a few yards away and talked to each other in low tones so I couldn't hear. By now, several other shanties had come close to the wire fence to see what was going on. I'd started to cause a bit of a stir – exactly what I hadn't wanted to do.

'Out of the truck,' nose-hoop repeated, aiming his rifle at the windscreen. 'Slowly. Hands in the air.'

I hadn't come here for a gunfight, so it didn't look as though I had much choice. I would have to do as he asked. This had seemed like such a good idea earlier, but I was starting to realise that maybe I should have stayed home after all.

CHAPTER TEN

JAMIE

Jamie spent the next couple of days recuperating. He took long cool showers and ate hearty home-cooked meals, but the problem was, he was still too scared to fall asleep. Despite his new safe environment, exhaustion crippled him. Shadows ringed his eyes and he had a constant hollow feeling of dread in his chest. Every small sound or movement made him jump. He was a bundle of nerves. Miriam and the other women were always busy so he didn't get much opportunity to speak to them, but when panic threatened to overwhelm him, he remembered how she had taught him to breathe.

It was another hot summer's afternoon and Jamie was trying to rest in the small yard at the back of the terraced house. At least these cotton clothes were clean and cool and comfortable. Better than his old falling-apart threads. He figured if he couldn't sleep upstairs in bed, he might have more luck outdoors. After all, he'd been sleeping outside for the best part of sixteen years. Unfortunately, it wasn't the sleeping arrangements that were preventing him from falling asleep.

The yard was a clean bare space apart from a warped plastic chair and a leafy Buddleia tree which provided some much-needed shade. Amid its dying purple blossoms, a few fat bees buzzed among the branches, extracting the last few sips of nectar. Jamie was in that suspended space between waking and sleeping where everything feels heavy and warm. It was a luxury to relax without fear of being robbed or attacked. If he could only manage a catnap, well that would be something. But even now, with his eyes closed, the girl's dead image was trying to show itself.

'Jamie.' A man's voice startled him and he opened his eyes, bringing his hand up to shade them.

'Mr Carter.' Jamie felt a moment of panic. So, his short stay was over. He had known he wouldn't be able stay here forever, but the thought of going back outside terrified him. He'd always been pretty resigned to his life as a vagrant but, having tasted a few days of comfort, it would be a wrench to return to living on his wits again. Especially now, with all these unwanted images crowding his brain and the knowledge that he might be losing his mind. Jamie reached for his crutches which were balanced against the wall and hauled himself to his feet.

'Miriam fixed you up then,' Mr Carter said. It was a statement more than a question.

'Yeah. She's been really kind.'

'So are you ready to join us, Jamie?'

'What? Stay here, you mean?' He felt hope quicken his pulse.

'No. No one stays here. This is a transitionary place.'

'Oh.' Jamie had thought as much, but it was still disappointing to hear confirmation.

'Are you still looking for redemption? For peace?'

Jamie nodded. No doubt in his mind.

'Good. Then you are needed.'

'Where?'

'Salisbury.'

His heart clutched with nerves. He'd heard all the rumours

like everyone else. But surely it couldn't be as bad as he thought – not if the people there were anything like Miriam. She'd said he would find peace in Salisbury. He should have quizzed her more about what went on there and about James Grey, but all he'd done that night was waffle on about his own life. He hadn't thought to ask her anything important. Since then, he'd been too busy taking things easy to think about Grey. He cursed himself for being so complacent.

'You'll find out soon enough,' Mr Carter said.

'Find out what?'

'All those questions running through your head. They'll be answered soon enough.'

'Oh. Right.'

'Ready then?'

'What? We're going now?'

'We are.'

'Okay. I'll get my stuff.'

'You don't need it.'

'I...'

'You'll be starting a new life, Jamie. A better life where your old things are no longer required.'

'Right.' Jamie didn't suppose it was the end of the world to let go of a few mouldy old clothes, but it made him a little light-headed to leave his bundle behind. He'd had it with him for years. Felt strange without it. 'I better say goodbye to Miriam. Thank her for—'

'No goodbyes or thanks are necessary. Miriam knows you're grateful.'

'Oh.'

Mr Carter turned and walked through the kitchen and out into the hallway. Jamie followed him. 'What about my crutches? I can't walk without them yet.'

'Bring them with you. I'll return them once your leg's healed.'

The doors off the hallway were closed and there were no sounds from above. Mr Carter had said Miriam didn't need any thanks, but it felt wrong to be leaving without a word. Seemed sneaky somehow. A week ago, Jamie wouldn't have given it a second thought, but now he felt different. Something had shifted within him. He already felt like a better person. Ironic, really, that the death of an innocent girl should turn him into Mother flipping Teresa. And he was sure this was only the start. Yeah, there was a shedload more craziness to come his way, he was pretty certain about that.

Mr Carter's beaten-up AV was parked outside. Jamie arranged himself on the passenger seat, sliding his crutches into the back. The engine started up and they headed off. A momentary pang of nostalgia caused Jamie to turn his head and stare back at the nondescript house. He wondered if he'd ever see it or Miriam again. Probably not.

He was giving up his freedom for something else. Something unknown. He hoped it was for something better, but it surely couldn't be much worse than the alternative. On the outside, the older you got, the worse chance you had at survival. Especially now with his dodgy leg and recent aversion to sleep.

They left the Boscombe Compound behind and traversed the familiar scrubland of Bournemouth. Jamie remembered the girl he was supposed to have met at the 'pound. He wondered if she was disappointed that he never showed up. He liked to think she would've at least wondered about him. He must need his head testing – instead of meeting up with a fit girl, he was heading off with a middle-aged bald bloke who was part of the God squad. Jamie grinned to himself. He must've injured more than his leg when that woman knocked him over.

'How long will it take to get there?' Jamie asked.

'As long as it takes,' Mr Carter replied.

Jamie sucked in a breath. 'Roughly.'

'Depends.'

'On?'

'Whether we go straight there, or whether we meet any other lost souls.'

'Lost souls like me you mean?'

'Everyone is different.'

'Do you only take people who want to go with you? I mean, do you ever take people against their will?'

'People don't always know what they want.' He turned to look at Jamie. 'Do you know what you want, Jamie?'

Jamie was taken aback by the question. 'A decent night's sleep would be nice.'

Mr Carter nodded and turned back to concentrate on the drive.

'How did you join Grey's church?' Jamie asked.

'I was one of the first.'

'So you're a big shot then?'

'None of us are important. We're only here to serve.'

Nah, Jamie thought. He wasn't going to be serving anyone. He just needed help getting his head straight.

'You'll see,' Mr Carter said with a smile.

Rough hands shook him and he lashed out with his fists, emitting a garbled cry. Sweat coated his forehead and his whole body trembled. Opening his eyes, he saw he was face-to-face with a man who had hold of his fists.

'You're having a bad dream, lad,' the man said.

Jamie tensed up again and tried to free his hands, but the man held them tight. He recognised him. It was Mr Carter. They were in the AV on their way to Salisbury. He must've fallen asleep. As the tension left his body, Mr Carter released Jamie's fists, relaxing back into the driver's seat. They were parked in the middle of a pitted track alongside a fallow field. Birds sang in the hedgerows, but the noise sounded eerie and alien. The air outside shimmered with midday heat.

'Not going to punch me again, are you?' the older man said.

'Did I... I'm sorry. I didn't mean—'

'I've endured worse.'

Jamie turned to look at Mr Carter and saw a bright red mark on his cheek. 'Oh, mate, I'm really sorry.'

Mr Carter held his hand up to silence Jamie. 'No need to apologise. You're troubled, anyone can see that.'

'I was trying not to fall asleep,' Jamie said, 'but the drive must've made me drift off.'

'We'll be there in a few minutes. You've been asleep a while. Had some nasty dreams too by the sounds you were making.'

Jamie wondered if he'd talked in his sleep, worried in case he'd babbled about the dead girl. What if Mr Carter worked out what he'd done? He realised he was shivering, his legs trembling and teeth chattering. He tried to get himself under control but his body refused to keep still. What the hell was wrong with him? He was definitely cracking up, no doubt about it.

If Mr Carter noticed, he didn't say anything; simply restarted the engine and carried on driving. Jamie rubbed his eyes and tried to shake the nightmare from his thoughts. The AV rattled and whined as they continued on down the rutted track. Jamie reckoned this old heap wouldn't last much longer. Sounded like it was falling to bits. Looked like it too.

At the end of the track, Jamie made out a tall, barbed wire fence, which ran in both directions as far as the eye could see. As they drew closer, a heavy duty metal gate came into view, set into the fence with three huge padlocks. Mr Carter brought the vehicle to a stop.

'Wait here,' he said, sliding out of the AV. He had a bunch of keys attached to his belt and used one of them to unlock the gate. He climbed back in and drove through the open gate.

'Want me to lock up for you?' Jamie asked.

'No thanks.' Mr Carter left the vehicle once more to re-secure the gate and they continued on their way.

'Is this Salisbury?' Jamie asked.

'It is.'

Jamie felt wide awake now and stared around looking for clues about their destination. But all he saw, other than the track, were fields and hedges, trees and fences. His shakes had subsided a little, but not a lot, and he clasped his hands together to steady them.

Eventually, in the distance, he made out a long solid shape – a brick wall. Jamie turned to look at Mr Carter to see if he was going to mention it, but the man had his eyes fixed firmly ahead. Beyond the wall, a tapering grey construction reached into the sky.

'What's that?' Jamie asked.

'What?'

'The pointy thing up there.'

Mr Carter took a breath. "That 'pointy thing" is the spire of Salisbury Cathedral.'

'It's high.'

As they drew closer, the wall reared up like a tidal wave. The thing was massive. Must've taken months to build. There was no way you could break in and probably no way you could break out. That thought made him more than a little nervous. Now he was here, he wasn't so sure he'd made the right deci-sion. Mr Carter must have sensed his hesitation.

'It'll be fine. You'll be glad you came. Your life will have purpose, your fears will be put to rest and your sins absolved. You will never go hungry and you will finally sleep in peace.'

The 'sleep in peace' part sounded very appealing, but he still had huge reservations. 'What if I get there and I don't like it?'

'What if, what if. Let's get you there first and you'll see: it will all be okay.'

The man had a talent for not answering questions, but Jamie let himself be soothed and tried to put his worries aside. A massive set of studded wooden doors opened inwards as they approached the wall. Freaky robed guards stood inside the doors either side of the entrance, guns and swords at their sides. The nerves started up again. Big time.

'Holy moly.'

'Every settlement needs its guards, wouldn't you say?' Mr Carter said.

'Yeah, but those guys look like something out of a horror movie.'

'Lucky they're on our side then.'

Your side maybe. As they drove through and the doors swung closed behind them, Jamie took a deep breath and hoped he hadn't just made the biggest mistake of his life.

CHAPTER ELEVEN

RILEY

Heart racing, I opened the door and stepped out of the truck, raising my hands in the air. I wore one of my revolvers beneath my coat and the other strapped to my ankle. I'd stashed the Saiga in the footwell under the passenger seat, reasoning that they might mistake my intentions if I approached with such a powerful weapon. I took a couple of steps towards the two shanties.

'Okay, that's far enough,' the one with no piercings said.

The one with the nose hoop gave a long whistle and a boy came running. Nose-hoop said something unintelligible and the boy nodded and ran off. I hoped he was going to get Lou. There was a long silence and I shifted from one foot to the other, feeling exposed and vulnerable with weapons trained at my head and so many pairs of eyes looking me up and down.

'What's in the truck?' one of the men asked.

'Just some stuff to trade.'

'Where you from?'

'I'd rather wait until Lou—'

'Oh, look, it's Perimeter Girl,' came a mocking voice.

I gazed across and saw the crowd had parted to let someone through. It was the man from yesterday – Reece.

'I thought I told you not to come back,' he called out. 'What? You enjoy slumming it over here?'

This incited a ripple of laughter from the other shanties.

'I've come to see Lou.'

'She's busy.'

'No she's not.' An out-of-breath Lou pushed past him, along with one of her younger brothers.

I exhaled and lowered my hands. I'd been on the verge of turning around, jumping back in the truck and racing home.

'Louisa, this is nothing to do with you,' Reece said. 'The girl's obviously up to something.'

Lou put her hands on her hips and glared at him. 'Reece, she's my friend. Do I have to get your permission to invite my friends over now?'

'Yes,' Reece replied. 'You do when they start showing up in armoured trucks with semi-automatic weapons.'

I turned to see that Nose-hoop had opened the passenger door of the truck, and had already discovered my Saiga under the passenger seat.

'Hey!' I cried.

He unclipped the magazine.

'Put that back.'

'It's fully loaded,' he called out to Reece.

'Put it back, Keon,' Lou said, walking up to him. 'Riley's cool.'

Keon didn't let go of my weapon, but I ignored him for the moment. Hopefully, once Lou explained why I was here, they would start to treat me with less suspicion.

'Can I talk to you for a minute, Lou?' I asked, desperate to dispel all the tension.

'Course,' she replied before turning to her brother. 'Joe,

thanks for fetching me. Go home now.' The boy pouted, but left, casting a few backward glances.

'Riley,' she said, walking up to me. 'Caused a bit of a scene, haven't you? Beginning to think you like trouble.'

'Sorry,' I replied. I really didn't want to speak to her with Keon, Reece and the others pointing their weapons at me, but it didn't look like I had much of a choice.

'What's in the truck anyway?' she asked.

'You said you needed fuel.'

She frowned and walked up to the tarp. Keon and Reece joined her while she loosened one corner and peeled it back. 'Holy mother of all that's sweet and good.'

Keon let out a long low whistle, but Reece glared at me again, his long fringe diluting the hatred a little.

'You serious?' Lou asked.

I nodded and turned to Keon. 'Can I have my gun back now?'

'I think I'll hang onto it,' he said, smiling at me. He fiddled with the magazine, trying to lock it back in. 'I could do with a nice shooter like this.'

'Give it back, Keon,' Lou said. She turned back to me. 'But, we haven't got enough to trade you for all this lot,' Lou said. 'Maybe a tenth of what it's worth? Or a hundredth.'

'That's okay,' I said. 'We've got more than we need.'

'You want to *give* us all this fuel?' Reece said. 'For nothing?' His voice was icy. 'D'you think we're charity cases? Is that it?'

'Of course not,' I replied. 'Lou more or less saved my life yesterday. This is my way of saying thank you.'

'We don't like being indebted to anyone,' he replied. 'Especially not rich little Perimeter girls.'

'There's no debt,' I said. 'I told you, it's to thank Lou for yesterday. She saved my life.'

Keon was still fiddling with my Saiga, swearing under his breath as he tried to force the magazine into place.

'For Christ's sake, Kee,' Reece said. 'What are you doing with that bloody gun?'

'There's a knack to it,' I said. 'Here...' I held out my hand for the weapon, but Keon shook his head.

'Not falling for that,' he said.

'Give it back to her, Keon,' Reece said. 'You're doing my head in.'

He glowered at Reece but handed the gun and magazine back to me. I locked the mag easily back in place.

'How d'you do that?' Keon asked.

'Keon, shut up or go away,' Reece snapped.

I caught Lou's eye and she smiled as Keon shoved his hands into his pocket and kicked at the ground.

'There's got to be a catch,' Reece said, turning back to face me.

'No catch,' I replied. 'You can thank Lou.'

'Why are you *really* doing this?' Reece asked. 'Are you setting us up, is that it? We gonna get a load of Perimeter guards come down and start kicking off that we nicked their fuel?' He stepped up close to me, his eyes blazing. I held his stare.

'Easy, Reece,' Lou said, putting a hand on his arm. 'I'm pretty sure she's on the level.'

'*Pretty sure* isn't good enough.'

'We've got no choice. We need this fuel,' Lou replied.

'So...' Reece said, still staring at me.

'So...' I replied, holding his gaze.

'How about we trade you something for it?' Lou said.

'You don't have to,' I replied.

'We want to.'

Reece walked off a little way, his head bowed and his fists clenched. Then he stopped, turned around and walked back.

'Fine,' he said. 'We need the fuel, so we'll do a trade. But if this comes back to bite us, it's on you, Louisa.'

She grinned. 'Let's get this baby unloaded.'

'Come and see me when you're done and we'll talk terms.' Reece turned his back on us and strode back into the camp. Keon let out a piercing whistle and soon we were joined by about fifty men, women and children; maybe more, I lost count after a while. They studied me curiously, some with distrust, others with a glimmer of friendliness. Within minutes they'd unloaded the flatbed and re-secured the tarpaulin. The timber had been squirreled away to some unknown destination, lifted over the heads of others and hidden within the vast encampment.

'Let's go to Reece's,' Lou said. 'We need to talk about what we owe you.'

'We'll guard your truck if you like,' Keon said with a wink.

I looked at Lou who smiled at my dubious expression. 'It's okay,' she said. 'Keon'll make sure it stays in one piece.'

'Really?' I replied. 'He tried to steal my gun a minute ago.'

'Trust me,' Lou said. 'Your truck'll be safe with Kee.'

I turned to him and his friend. 'Okay.'

'Chuck us the keys then.'

'I'll keep hold of them, if you don't mind.' I didn't trust him not to unlock the fuel cap and drain the tank.

'Whatever,' he replied.

'Cab's open though, so feel free to sit inside and warm up.'

'Nice one.' The two men turned and walked over to the truck, pulling a group of noisy children out from the cab and ruffling their hair as they sent them on their way. This elicited a bunch of friendly swearing and rude gestures.

'This way,' Lou said.

I walked beside her as she led me through the chilly maze-like camp. Once again, I noticed how raggedy and skinny everyone was and I felt self-conscious in my good-quality warm clothes. The makeshift paths were hard and frosted over, but I could imagine that with a little rain they would become mud baths.

'Here we are.' Lou pulled back the flap on a large marquee-like structure with a tall post running up through the middle of it. It looked as though it had been constructed from animal hide and smelt like it too. I followed her inside. Natural light filtered in from the entrance and other window-like flaps, but the air inside was thick with smoke. Thin plywood and mismatched squares of worn-out carpet dotted the muddy floor. However, the beauty of the place was that it was lovely and warm inside. A squat black wood-burning stove sat in the centre of the tent, its chimney running up alongside the central tent pole and out through the roof. An assortment of shabby chairs and cushions were strewn about the place and people sat talking in small clusters.

'This is our gathering place,' Lou said. 'It's usually the only warm spot. Sometimes, on really cold nights, we sleep in here too.'

Lou led me across the marquee to a screened-off area behind the stove, where a scrawny man with weaselly eyes stood in front of a patched-up wall of some kind. When he saw Lou, he grunted and told her to wait.

'We're here to see Reece,' she said.

'And I told you to wait.'

'Fine,' Lou replied.

As we stood in silence, I let my eyes wander further and realised that the screen was covered in charcoal and pencil drawings. They were pictures of people – faces. Mainly children.

'What are those pictures?' I asked Lou.

The weaselly man scowled at me.

'That's our Lost Wall,' Lou replied. 'Our artists draw portraits on here every time someone dies or goes missing. So we'll always remember them.'

'So many children,' I said, gazing at the young faces on the wall.

'Most of them disappeared,' Lou said, making my heart sink. 'Recently?'

'It's been going on for years. Makes me scared for my Joe and Mikey. But there's nothing any of us can do about it. We don't know where they've gone. They just disappear. Reece's younger sisters disappeared a few years ago. He doesn't like to talk about it.

My thoughts flitted to James Grey, but now was not the time to mention him.

'You can go in now,' the weaselly man said. I had the feeling he'd kept us waiting for no reason other than to please himself.

I followed Lou past the man and along to the end of the wall. We went around it into a large open space at the back of the marquee where Reece was sitting at a scrubbed wooden table. With him sat two men and two women, all considerably older. Reece, however, sat at the head of the table and it looked to me like he was in charge.

'Sit down,' he said.

Lou and I sat opposite each other on the only two free chairs. There was a long silence and I wasn't sure if I was expected to speak. I cleared my throat to say something, but then Reece spoke.

'Thank you for bringing the fuel,' he said, looking directly at me. He didn't smile and I guessed it cost him a lot to say thank you.

'You're welcome.'

'But I still don't understand why,' he said. 'And we want a decent explanation.'

'It's simple,' I said. 'Like I said before, Lou did me a good turn yesterday and I'm repaying the favour. We have enough fuel and I thought it would be good to have more links and co-operation between settlements.' I hadn't planned to say that, but it sounded good to my ears.

Reece interlinked his fingers and thought for a moment.

The others looked at me with curiosity. They were all shabbily dressed, but they had a certain dignity about them. A pride that shone through their rags.

'What would you like in return?' Reece asked. 'If we have it to spare, we'll give it.'

I'd already had a quick think about what I would ask for. They didn't want my charity and yet I didn't want to ask for too much and leave them worse off. Food was scarce and so were raw materials.

'I would like three pairs of your leather-worked boots,' I said. 'And a short-handled hunting knife.'

'Done,' Reece said. 'But that can't be all. You're holding something back, I can tell.'

'I'd also like it if Lou could come to the Perimeter to give us some slingshot lessons.'

Lou choked back a cough and stared at me.

'You want me to come to the Perimeter?' She asked the question as though I'd asked her to fly to the moon.

'If you don't mind. Yes. The slingshot would be good to learn. We're too reliant on guns and ammo. Stones will never run out.'

'Lou?' Reece turned to her.

She shrugged. 'I guess. Sure, why not.'

'Great,' I said.

'Are those your terms of trade?' Reece asked. 'Or is there more?'

'No,' I said. 'Those are my terms.'

'Then we're agreed.' He looked around the table and everyone appeared to be relieved. One of the women smiled at me and I smiled back.

'It's nearly noon,' she said. 'Would you like some broth?'

'Yes please,' I replied. 'That would be lovely.'

'Good,' she said. 'Stay sitting. I'll fetch it.' The woman stood and leaned down to kiss Reece's head. He reached up and squeezed her hand. 'Thanks, Mum,' he said.

I was surprised. I hadn't imagined Reece was the type of person to sit and negotiate terms with his mother present. I wondered if the other people at the table were also his family. I'd have to ask Lou later. Reece caught my eye and I realised I'd been staring at him. He smiled. The first smile I'd ever seen from him and it made him look like a different person. I returned the smile and saw Lou watching me curiously. A warm feeling flickered within me, but I quickly shook it off.

CHAPTER TWELVE

JAMIE

Mr Carter drove the AV across the vast courtyard and came to a halt by the far wall, beneath a sycamore tree. Jamie's nerves kicked in hard, but he tried to quell the swimming feeling in his head and struggled out of the vehicle, gripping his crutches for both physical and moral support.

The two of them walked a little way, their steps ringing out across the flagstones, until Mr Carter stopped right in the centre of the courtyard in front of a row of grand red-brick buildings. They were beautiful, nicer even than the houses in the Talbot Woods Perimeter, and that was saying something. They looked in good nick too, with clean windows and freshly painted doors.

So... he was inside Salisbury.

This place was for real.

Jamie absorbed his surroundings feeling somewhat exposed. He glanced over his shoulder, back at the gates, unable to discern if the guards were staring at him or not. It was impossible to tell with those hoods pulled menacingly low over their faces. Jamie was surprised to realise that Mr Carter seemed a little agitated. It was the first time he'd seen the man flustered.

'Wait here,' Mr Carter instructed.

Like, where else was he going to go? Jamie repressed the urge to say the words out loud as he watched Mr Carter stride off without a backward glance. After a few seconds, he disappeared through a gap between the houses and so Jamie turned his attention back to his surroundings. The courtyard was quiet and warm. Jamie stood awkwardly, balancing self-consciously on his crutches, still hyper-aware of the robed guards, wondering what kind of men hid beneath those ominous hoods. He counted six of them flanking the wooden doors, standing still as stone.

The sun hung high in the sky and it was hotter than hell. It must've been only a little after midday. Jamie let his eyes roam across the houses. He thought he caught a glimpse of someone's face at a first-storey window. But they vanished as soon as he saw them, so he wasn't sure if it really had been someone, or simply a trick of the light. Would he be staying in one of those rooms? Was this place really going to become his home? All his adult life, he'd never had a home. He let go of one of his crutches and reached up to scratch his beard before remembering he didn't have one anymore. He scratched at his bare chin instead. Maybe he should grow his facial hair back; he felt wrong without it.

Footsteps... Jamie turned to see Mr Carter returning with another man dressed in a plain brown homespun shirt and trousers. As they approached, Jamie noticed the man's face was badly disfigured with deep pink scars. They looked like burn marks and covered almost three quarters of his face. Only the lower quarter of his face was untouched and this made it hard to determine his age. If Jamie had to guess, he would've said he was quite young. No more than twenty.

'Welcome, Jamie,' the man said, his voice so soft that Jamie had to strain his ears to make out the words. 'My name is John. We're pleased you've decided to join us. Will you come this way.' He began to walk off without even acknowledging or mentioning Mr Carter who was already heading back to his vehicle.

'Uh, hi, John,' Jamie said. 'Thanks!' he called after Mr Carter. His voice sounded too loud in the hushed courtyard. He thought he saw Mr Carter nod his head, but he couldn't be sure as the man continued to walk away. *These people aren't very big on goodbyes*, Jamie thought.

Swinging his crutches out in front of him, he attempted to keep up with John, who was already several yards ahead. The man had a bald patch on the back of his head, pink and pitted with more wrinkled scars. Jamie wondered what had happened to him, but he wasn't about to ask – John didn't seem to be the chatty sort.

They passed in front of several of the houses before cutting through a pathway which ran alongside one of the buildings. This led them into a smaller courtyard with yet more buildings. These houses were less grand than the others. Not shabby by any means, just plainer. Above the buildings, the cathedral spire was visible once more. Now he was closer, Jamie could make out more detail – darker bands ran around the grey stone and a simple cross adorned its tip.

Several boys crossed the courtyard, crunching slowly over gravel, heads bowed. They were dressed similarly to John and didn't even glance up as they passed. Jamie, on the other hand, was gawking at everything. The whole place was spooky. It was too clean and too quiet and Jamie kept thinking he was going to put his foot in it big time. He wasn't the most subtle person in the world. It looked like he was going to have to be on his best behaviour every minute he spent here and Jamie wasn't sure he was up to that.

But then he remembered that he'd killed a girl. That she was haunting his sleep. That he needed this place. So he would try his best to give it a go. He would learn to be like John and these quiet boys who were happy to mind their own business. He could do that. Surely.

A door creaked open and several more young boys filed into the courtyard, led by an adolescent. Again, they didn't speak and they all seemed to move with a noiseless grace, apart from the crunch of gravel beneath their feet. John led Jamie through a gap in the buildings into another alleyway. At the end, a wrought-iron gate blocked their exit, but John unlocked it and they continued on. Now, they were in a narrow street, lined with the backs of tall buildings. It reminded him of the street where Miriam the doctor lived. Only this alley was cleaner and fresher smelling than back in the 'pound. This place was *cared for* – not a state he was used to seeing.

Jamie's arms began to ache. He wasn't adept at walking long distances on crutches. His throat felt scratchy and dry. 'Could I have some water?' he called to John.

'Not much further,' came the quiet response.

'Better not be,' Jamie muttered under his breath. 'I'm knackered, mate.'

They crossed a grassy expanse. It was so open and green and beautiful, it made Jamie forget his tiredness and want to run across it with his arms outstretched like an aeroplane. He smiled at the thought. The scent of cut grass wafted into his nostrils making him strangely hungry – not that he wanted to eat grass. Tall trees bordered the massive park-like space, reminding him of being a child, visiting places like this with his parents. Stately homes and National Trust properties. He hadn't even thought about those sorts of places in years. He remembered as a teenager being bored stiff, dragged around all kinds of historic buildings and gardens with his parents. Now, here he was in some thousand-year-old Cathedral Close. But this time he wasn't here for the sightseeing.

A square, grey-stone building came into view beyond a thin stand of trees. It looked like John was heading that way. Jamie hoped he'd have a chance to rest and eat and drink before they got on with whatever they were going to be doing here today. Come to think of it, he hadn't really given it too much thought, and Mr Carter hadn't exactly been clear on what the deal was. Maybe it would just be praying and stuff like that. That would be okay, he supposed.

Jamie found himself hobbling around the side of the grey-stone building and following John through a side door and into a small lobby. It was a relief to be out of the glaring sun. They slipped through another door until they reached a large hallway bisected by a wide staircase. Staying on the ground floor, they headed to the rear of the building and into a kitchen where two men were washing pots at a double sink.

A rough circular wooden table dominated the room with about a dozen mismatched chairs ranged around it. John gestured to Jamie to sit. Jamie didn't need asking twice.

John took a jug and two tin cups from a painted wooden dresser and joined Jamie at the table. 'Lunch was over an hour ago, but you may have some bread if you're hungry.' John spoke while pouring them a cup of water each. Jamie gulped his down in three mouthfuls and John refilled his cup.

'Bread sounds good,' Jamie said. 'Please.'

John stood and went to a wooden box on a shelf. He lifted out a bread roll and placed it on the table in front of Jamie. 'You may wash your hands in the sink over there.'

Jamie had thought his hands were clean enough – they were cleaner than they'd been for fifteen years, what with all the showers he'd been taking – but he did as he was asked, even though he was dying to stuff the bread roll into his mouth.

One of the washer-uppers moved aside while Jamie self-consciously scrubbed at his hands in the soapy water. He began drying them on his trousers, but one of the men passed him a cloth, so he made a pretence at using it despite the fact his hands were pretty much dry already. Then he returned to the table and tore off a piece of the bread. John sat in silence while Jamie ate. Once the last crumbs had been gathered up and eaten, John began to talk.

'This place is very different from outside,' he said.

'You're telling me,' Jamie replied. But John lifted his hand to silence him.

'We do not speak when there is nothing important to say. You do not have to say these empty words. We have our faith, we work hard and we live peacefully.'

Jamie wasn't sure he believed the 'peacefully' bit. He'd heard a few rumours to the contrary. But, so far, they'd done nothing aggressive that he could see. Maybe they really were peaceful, like he said.

'All we ask,' John continued, 'is that you abide by these tenets. You must embrace our ways or leave.'

'I only just got here. Can we see how it goes?'

'I think, perhaps, Mr Carter was wrong about you. I think this place is too serious for a man such as yourself. Maybe you would do better to return to the wilderness.' John stood.

'Hold on a minute, mate. I do want to be here, don't get me wrong, it's just a bit much to take in. It all feels a bit – *final*.'

'That is where you are wrong – it is not *final*, it is *ever-lasting*. There is a difference.'

Jamie realised that he'd better at least pretend to be fully committed to being here, or John would get the hump and chuck him out.

'Okay,' Jamie said. 'I'm in.'

'Very well. Follow me.'

Jamie swigged the last of his water, wiped his mouth with the back of his hand and followed John out of the room. 'Where we going?'

'It is better if you don't ask questions. If you are happy to be here, accept that everything we do is for the good of all. We will guide you and speak to you when you need to be spoken to.

Other than that, maintain your silence and use the quiet for contemplation.'

Jamie had to restrain himself from rolling his eyes. He wanted to be here, he really did. If only it didn't sound like a load of bullshit mumbo jumbo, he could get on board with it a bit more. But that was the old Jamie. The new Jamie had to be more open and less cynical. If he wanted to regain his sanity and lose the nightmares, he'd have to get with the program.

They were now back in the main entrance hall, heading for the wide staircase. Jamie tramped up the stairs after John, wondering what on earth was coming next. At the top of the stairs, John opened a wooden door and ushered Jamie inside. It was just an empty room with wooden floorboards and faded walls. There wasn't even a chair. What now? Jamie thought. Two curtainless windows looked out onto trees and sky. Jamie stared out at the motionless leaves, dark and heavy against the pure blue sky.

'Today you will confess your sins,' John said.

'Eh? What?'

'Before you can continue with us, you must purge your soul and confess your sins. You must be completely honest and speak your innermost thoughts.'

'What? You mean like tell you any bad stuff I've done?'

'Not me. But yes. Anything you are ashamed of, you must tell the Listeners.'

'The who?' Jamie was getting a bad feeling. The freaking Listeners! Who the hell were they? This was major cult territory and he was starting to get the heebie-jeebies.

John's voice suddenly lost its impersonal tone and softened for a moment: 'I know it sounds strange,' he said. 'But we've all done things we're ashamed of, and by getting them off your chest, you'll feel lighter and freer. You'll sleep like a baby and wish you'd done it sooner.' He looked directly into Jamie's eyes. 'I promise you, you'll be glad you did it.'

'Is that all I have to do?' Jamie replied. 'Just tell them what I've done? What if I've done really bad stuff? Won't they lock me up?'

'Believe me,' John said, 'there is nothing you can say about your past that will make them punish you for it. Just confess and you'll be fine.'

'They're not going to want my blood or anything weird like that are they?'

'Whatever you've heard about this place, forget it,' John said. 'Nothing untoward is going to happen. Just a simple confession is needed, that's all.'

'I can do that,' Jamie said. But he felt nervous, nonetheless. Would he really have the courage to tell these people what he'd done? That he'd killed someone. But wasn't this what he had prayed for? A way to lessen his guilt and a chance for a decent night's sleep, free from the terrors. 'Who are these Listeners anyway?'

'They are Our Father's disciples. They will listen and not judge.'

'Why can't I just tell God about my sins? Why do I have to tell people? If they won't do anything about it, what's the point?'

'It doesn't work like that. You have to speak your sins out loud. It's the only way for you to move forward here.'

'Right. Okay.'

'Are you ready? Or do you need time to think about what you want to say?'

'I'm ready.' Jamie felt his heartbeat quicken. He must be mad.

'Come,' John said. He held the door open so Jamie could walk through more easily with his crutches.

Jamie's mind raced. Should he lie or should he confess it all? He couldn't make up his mind. On the one hand, it could put him in danger to tell anyone what he'd done, but on the other hand, wasn't this why he had come here in the first place – to wash that girl's image from his mind. But what if they turned him over to the army and he had to face the girl's family? What if they executed him here and now? He could go ahead and confess and everything and they might shoot him on the spot. Clammy and slick with sweat, Jamie's hands slid on the crutch handles. He had to stop to wipe his palms on his trousers.

John didn't walk very far along the landing. He opened the next door but one and gestured to Jamie to enter. Jamie felt panicked. He still hadn't made up his mind what to do. He tried to catch John's eyes to glean any kind of clue or sign from his expression, but the man's gaze cast firmly down to the floor. This was all happening too quickly. Jamie took a steadying breath and walked into the room. The door closed behind him.

CHAPTER THIRTEEN

RILEY

The truck felt lighter on the drive home without its illicit load. Or maybe it was me who felt lighter. I had done it. I had made Lou's life a little easier and it felt good. The shanties were decent people. They had always seemed so fierce and terrifying to me, but I now came to the conclusion they were basically the same as us. The only difference was that they lived in a harsher environment. They had to be more on their guard, less trusting. They had no Perimeter fence to keep them safe.

The sun did a good job of cheering up the barren landscape, the sky now a clear cornflower blue. The truck had a stereo, so I pressed play in the hope someone had left a CD in the slot. A woman's voice filled the cab. I recognised the song: "Shake It Out" by Florence and the Machine. Ma had this album. I wondered where the singer was now. Did she survive the country's collapse sixteen years ago? Was she still singing somewhere? I decided to drive straight back to the stores, return the truck and head home. Hopefully no one would notice I'd been gone.

Far in the distance, the Perimeter fence glinted up ahead and I felt a sweep of apprehension. In fact, I felt more nervous returning home than I had when I approached the shanty camp. If the guards found out I'd taken the timber without permission, I would be in so much trouble. Pa would go ballistic. Nothing I could do about it now.

I shifted my attention back to the bumpy scrubland. A pack of wild dogs came into view and I had to adjust my course to avoid them. There must have been about thirty or forty, all skinny and mangy, different shapes and sizes, heads low, tongues lolling. A couple bared their fangs at the truck, but the majority seemed to be distracted by something else. Probably fighting over a rabbit or, if they were lucky, a deer. It looked like the appearance of my truck had interrupted them. I slowed and squinted into their midst, not really wanting to see in case it was some gruesome carcass. But then I caught a glimpse and slammed my foot hard on the brake.

I turned off the music and slowed the truck, cracking the window open a little. The dogs were growling and snarling and it was hard to see through the dense pack, but I was pretty sure I'd seen a person crouching on the ground. A sudden scream tore through the air. That was definitely a human sound.

I kept hearing Pa's voice in my head: 'Never stop on the road, not for anything', but I ignored it, wound down my window fully and fired my Magnum into the sky, feeling the sharp recoil in my arm. The deafening shot echoed around the landscape and spooked the dogs. They sprang away just far enough so I could get a clear view of what had got them so excited – two figures huddled together on the ground – girls. One of them held a backpack out in front of her, like a shield. The gun had startled them too, and they scrambled to their feet in a daze, stumbling backwards. They were headed away from me, but the dogs had recovered themselves and had begun to stalk the girls.

I drove hard at the pack, trying to scatter them. Up ahead the girls were losing ground. Bundled in thick coats, their movements were awkward and panicked. One of the smaller dogs – white-grey with prominent ribs – leapt and went for one of the girls' arms. She was knocked off balance and crashed face down onto the ground. The other girl stopped and tried to help by kicking at the dog, but then the pack descended. I rammed my hand down on the horn and drove into the pack, making them scatter.

I worried that the girls had been seriously hurt, but they lurched to their feet again, glancing from the truck to the dogs in panic. Most of the dogs backed away as I drew closer, snarling and yipping, but the white-grey was more persistent. Flanked by a couple of larger dogs, it growled and snapped at its prey. One of the girls thrust her backpack out in front of her again for protection, her dark blonde hair shining in the sunlight. Her eyes locked onto mine and my heart skipped a beat.

I recognised that face.

It was Liss, FJ's sister! But she looked terrible – pale and gaunt. I then realised that the other girl was Annabelle, her friend. We'd rescued the two of them from Salisbury a couple of months ago where they'd been held captive by Grey and FJ. What the hell were they doing out here alone, so far from their home?

I revved my engine once more, edging closer. I had to get the dogs to disperse, but they weren't as scared of my truck as I'd hoped. Hunger was making them brave. The grey mutt prepared to attack again, crouching, its ears flattened to the side of its head. I stopped the truck, leaned out, aimed and fired. I love dogs, but these were born wild and ready to kill. My aim was true and the bullet sank into the creature's head. Its companions yelped and then, with only a moment's pause, they fell upon the dead creature, tearing it to pieces.

The girls, making the most of this distraction, turned and

ran. But unfortunately they were running away from my truck. I leant out of the window and yelled.

'Liss! Annabelle! It's me, Riley!' They kept running so I drove after them as fast as I could, bumping around in the cab as the wheels jolted over ruts and dips. I quickly overtook the girls and swung the truck to a halt across their path. But they swerved out of my way and continued to head away from me in a blind panic.

'Liss!' I called.

She stopped, turned and narrowed her eyes at the truck windscreen. Perhaps she didn't recognise me. When she'd first met me I'd had dyed blonde hair, but now it was back to my usual brown. I glanced in the rearview – the pack was a few hundred yards away making short work of the dead dog and snarling over the scraps, so I stepped out of the truck, my revolver lowered at my side.

'Liss, Annabelle, it's me,' I said. 'Riley.' I glanced at the dogs again, paranoid they would strip the carcass and make me their next target.

'Riley?' Annabelle called back in a cautious half-shout half-whisper.

'You okay?' I asked. Annabelle's dark curls had been scraped back into a ponytail and her pale freckled face was smeared with dirt. Liss's ash-brown hair had been cut into a short bob, making her appear even younger than her friend. They both looked exhausted and terrified, their eyes sunk deep in their sockets, their breathing jagged and harsh.

'It *is* you,' Liss said, her eyes still wide with terror. 'Thank goodness. I thought we were going to be ripped to pieces back there. Then when we saw the truck we didn't know what to think.'

The girls walked carefully towards me, their eyes constantly flicking back and forth to the dogs on their right.

'Riley,' Annabelle repeated, relief on her face.

'Did they hurt you?' I asked. 'The dogs? Did you get bitten?'

'Only my wrist,' Annabelle said. 'But I don't think the skin's broken.' She pulled the ripped sleeve of her coat back, examining her pale forearm.

'I'm all right,' Liss said, still panting. 'Just got scared, that's all.'

'I'm not surprised,' I said. 'Quick, get in the truck.'

They followed me into the cab and I locked the doors and restarted the engine, relieved to be safely inside.

'Thank you,' Liss said. 'I can usually handle dogs okay. But that pack was starving, desperate.'

'And there were so many of them,' Annabelle added.

'Yeah,' I replied. 'They're always around, but I've never seen them so vicious before. What are you doing out here anyway? It's not safe, especially not on foot.'

'It's a long story,' Annabelle replied.

'Well, wherever you're headed, you're coming back with me first for some decent food and somewhere safe to stay the night.'

The Perimeter entrance loomed large up ahead.

'Let's get inside,' I said. 'Then you can tell me everything. There's water if you're thirsty.' I pointed to the floor where my bag lay. Annabelle reached down and pulled out my flask. 'Finish it,' I said. They took turns gulping down the liquid.

As I approached the gates, they began to swing slowly open. One of the guards, Liam, stood outside the hut and nodded as the truck rolled past. I briefly debated stopping to tell him about the girls, but then I figured it would be less complicated if I could get in without explanations. So I gave him a wave and kept going.

So far so good. Liam let me drive straight though, opening up the inner gate set into newly constructed brick wall. The fact that I got in so easily threw up some questions about internal security though. If it was that simple for me to take supplies out and bring people in, then we needed to upgrade the system. I hoped that it had been easy for me because of who I was; because no one would question Johnny Culpepper's daughter.

The girls were silent as we drove along empty roads and within minutes we were on Leven Avenue, the Perimeter stores directly in front of us. I hoped it was still Denzil on duty and not Roger Brennan or Charlie Duke, who might not be quite as easy going. I pulled up and slid out of the cab.

'Wait in the truck,' I said to the girls before walking up to the gates.

'Hello,' I called out.

'Hey,' Denzil said, stepping up to the gates. 'Jump back in, I'll get the gates.' He glanced up at the truck and did a double take. 'Is that...'

'Yeah,' I replied. 'Liss and Anna. I found them wandering around outside. A pack of dogs were eying them up for lunch.'

'Hang on,' Denzil said. He went into the hut and a moment later one of the gates began to creak open. Then he reappeared and walked out through the gate, stepping up to the cab. 'You girls okay?'

They nodded.

'Hello, Denzil,' Annabelle said.

'What you doing down this neck of the woods?' he replied. 'Where's your mum and dad, Liss?'

She didn't reply.

I pulled at Denzil's sleeve and ushered him over to the side. 'I think something bad must've happened,' I said. 'They haven't said anything yet, but I'm going to take them home and hopefully they'll tell me what's going on.'

'Where's your dad?' Denzil asked me. 'Does he know they're here?'

'Not yet. I'll tell him when I get home.'

'Thought he was out with you,' Denzil said, his brow creasing.

'Yeah, we had a change of plans.'

He gave me a sharp look. 'I'm not about to get a bollocking, am I, Riley? That load of firewood was legit, wasn't it?'

'What? Yeah, course it was. You've got Pa's req order, haven't you.'

Denzil nodded slowly, a doubtful expression clouding his features. 'Right, bring the truck back inside then.' He walked into the hut without saying goodbye. I could tell he wasn't happy with me and I couldn't really blame him. I only hoped he wouldn't rat me out to Pa.

I did as he asked and drove the truck through the gates and back round to the vehicle depot. No one there said anything untoward and so I signed the form and left, Liss and Annabelle walking in a daze by my side. When I waved at Denzil on my way out, he looked up through the window and waved back, but he didn't smile.

Fifteen minutes later, I was walking in through my front door with Liss and Annabelle. They'd been quiet on the walk back home and I hadn't pressed them for information. I figured they needed a while to recover from the dog attack and whatever else it was that had brought them all the way down to the south coast. Anyway, it would be best if Pa was here when they told their story.

Ma came out of the kitchen, a worried look on her face. 'Riley, where have you been, and who's this?'

'Just had some stuff to do. This is Liss and this is Annabelle.' The girls hung back and I ushered them forwards. 'This is my mother,' I said.

'Hello, I'm Eleanor. You girls look exhausted. Are you hungry? Would you like to get cleaned up and I'll make you some porridge?'

They didn't reply.

'I'll show you up to my room,' I said. 'You can have a warm shower and come back down for something to eat if you like.'

Once I'd shown them the shower and laid out some of my

clothes for them to change into, I came back down. Ma had already fetched Pa and they were sitting in the kitchen.

'Where've you been, Riley?' Pa asked.

'I left my bag at Lou's yesterday. So I nipped back to get it and ran into Liss and Annabelle on the way home.'

'The Walls isn't somewhere you "nip" to without telling anyone,' Pa replied. 'Especially not at the moment with all that's going on at the Compound.'

'I'm fine,' I said. 'Nothing happened.'

'Not to mention the waste of fuel,' he continued. 'I don't want you going out alone anymore. Not at the moment anyway.'

'Okay,' I said, eager to change the subject. 'So I wonder what's going on with Liss and Anna.'

'Didn't you ask them?' Pa said.

'Yeah, but they said it was a long story, so I figured I'd let them get cleaned up first.'

'What about Fred and Jessie?' he asked.

'I don't know,' I said. 'The girls were out there alone on foot, not far from the fence. A pack of dogs was attacking them.'

Pa exhaled and stood up, rubbing his chin. 'Dogs?'

'Yeah. We scared them off though.'

'Good. Those dogs are getting cheekier by the minute.'

'They were more than cheeky.'

'Might have to do something about them.'

'Liss and Anna can stay with us, can't they, Pa?' I asked.

'We'll see,' Pa replied.

'I'll make some porridge,' Ma said, walking over to the pan cupboard.

'Something's not right about all this,' Pa said, a grim expression on his face. 'I don't like it. We need to find out exactly what it is those girls are doing here.'

CHAPTER FOURTEEN

JAMIE

The room lay in semi-darkness. Black curtains had been drawn across two windows, but still a thin film of sunlight managed to creep inside. Before him, two figures sat unmoving, dressed in dark, hooded robes. Jamie's eyes flicked to an empty wooden chair in the centre of the room. He guessed that was meant for him. Jamie stood, indecisive for a moment, and then he came forward and sat in the chair, laying his crutches beside him. They clattered down onto the floor and his chair leg scraped as he sat. The silence soon settled back around him and he became aware of his own rasping breath.

Was he supposed to say something? Was he simply supposed to begin listing out his sins for these 'Listener' people? Sweat trickled down his forehead and a droplet landed on his top lip. He licked it away and blinked several times. Suddenly, a loud continuous hiss flooded the room, like a relentless wind or fast running water. Then, over the top of the hiss, came voices:

'Speak, we are listening.'

Woah! Jamie almost jumped out of his skin. *What the...* The words had seemed to come from the room itself, not from the men in front of him. The blend of voices had been deep and otherworldly, like God himself had spoken. Jamie quickly realised they must be using some kind of loudspeaker; that would explain the hissing sound he'd heard a second ago. He glanced around the room, but even if there were any to be found, there wasn't enough light for him to spot them.

'Speak, we are listening,' the voices came again.

The figures in front of him raised their heads so they appeared to be looking right at him, but the freaky thing was, Jamie still couldn't see their faces. It was as if the robes were worn by invisible men.

Jamie told himself this was all just trickery and technology, intended to spook and intimidate him. Well, they'd done a pretty good job, but he was here for a reason. He needed to do this.

'My...' He cleared his throat. 'My name is Jamie. I've come here because I'm sick of life on the outside.' He paused for a moment and swallowed. 'It's hard... It's harsh and you end up doing things you shouldn't...' He paused again. Was he really going to do this? Was he going to gamble with his own life by confessing? The loudspeaker hiss suddenly ceased.

'Go on.' This time it was one of the figures who spoke; not the loud crackling God-voice. It was a man's voice. Someone quite young by the sound of him.

'I did something. It was an accident. But it was terrible. I...' The girl's blank, unseeing face flashed into his mind again. The blood, the glass, the terror. A tear slid down Jamie's cheek. 'She was only a young girl and it was all my fault,' he said. 'I know that now. She died because of me. I had no business being in her garden, but I was only looking for somewhere safe to sleep. And now she's dead.' Jamie's voice had broken down into a gulping, gasping mess. He had done it. He had confessed to his crime.

Perhaps a bolt of lightning would pierce the room and strike him down. But nothing stirred, no one moved. The two figures stayed seated without a word.

'Is that it?' Jamie asked. 'Or should I explain some more?'

'Go on,' the young man's voice repeated.

Jamie tried to compose himself. He wiped away his tears and cast his mind back to the night when the woman in the AV had knocked him down. He would tell these listener-guys the whole sorry story. Might as well; he'd already confessed to murder, the rest was just for himself, to get it all out of his system.

As Jamie told his story, he felt a lightness of being creep over him, a sensation he hadn't felt in a long time. It was as if, with every word, his body and mind was coming slowly back into focus. Maybe Mr Carter and John had been right. Confession was good for the soul.

Jamie didn't let himself think about what would happen afterwards. He just spoke the words and let the Listeners listen. His voice threaded itself around the small room, twisting into the dark corners and wrapping itself around the chairs and over the Listeners. As the words left Jamie's mouth, they took on a separate entity, as though his past actions no longer belonged to him. They now belonged to the room and to the Listeners. Jamie talked and talked, leaving out no single detail.

Finally, his story was done and the room no longer seemed threatening. It was simply a normal room with summer sunlight filtering in through the gaps in the curtains. Jamie thought that whatever happened next he would be able to deal with it. Even if they chucked him in jail, or lined him up against the wall to be executed, he would accept it. But, somehow, he didn't get the impression that was to be his fate.

The faint sound of birdsong from outside made him feel almost euphoric. He wondered whether he was now supposed to leave the room, but before he could make up his mind whether to stay seated or to get up, the Listeners rose to their feet and began to remove their deep hoods.

Jamie was curious to see the faces of the two figures who had listened to his confession. He imagined them to be of another world, perhaps like beautiful angels or terrible demons. But as the Listeners removed their hoods, he saw that they were merely men. One was short and quite elderly with wrinkled skin and thin grey hair, the other was much younger – a boy really. Good-looking though, and almost like an angel, with his halo of fair curls. Jamie guessed it had been this younger one who had prompted him to keep speaking during his confession. Both their expressions were neutral, neither warm nor cold.

'Thank you for your words,' the younger one said.

Jamie nodded.

'My name is Matthew, and this is Michael.'

'What I told you,' Jamie said, 'are you going to do anything about it?'

'You need dwell on it no longer,' Matthew replied.

Jamie wasn't sure what he meant by that, but at least no one was pointing a weapon in his face or battering the door down to take him away. And these two seemed remarkably unfazed by his awful story.

'Come with me,' Matthew said, crossing the room to where Jamie sat. Matthew bent down to retrieve the crutches and pass them to Jamie who took them with a murmur of thanks. He stood and turned to follow Matthew out of the room. Before leaving, he glanced back at Michael, but the man had now replaced his hood and stood unmoving, his features concealed once more.

As Jamie followed Matthew out of the room and down the stairs, he felt like a completely different person to the one who had climbed the stairs only a short while earlier. He realised he was less afraid, and the constant worries and questions that had dogged him these past days now seemed entirely unimportant.

They were still there, under the surface, but he didn't let himself examine them. He was quite happy to accept whatever was about to happen. It was a liberating feeling.

They were now outside once again and the sun sat lower in the sky, making the heat a touch less fierce. Matthew's robes swept along the dusty ground and Jamie's eyes fixed on several brown holly leaves which had attached themselves to the robe's hem, making a rustling scraping noise as he walked, dragging and jumping in his wake. This time, as Jamie followed Matthew, he barely noticed his surroundings and paid no attention to the route they took; his mind was clear and blank and free with just the rustle of the holly leaves, the dull thud of his crutches and the warmth of the sun on his back.

After a time, they arrived at another building, traversed another wide cool hallway, climbed another winding flight of stairs and crossed another landing. Matthew had come to a stop outside yet another door.

'I am taking a personal interest in you, Jamie,' Matthew said. It was uncanny the way the boy spoke with such self-assurance. It made him seem much older than he first appeared. Before coming here, Jamie would have hated the boy's confidence; he would've thought him an arrogant and precocious idiot, and would've answered with smart remarks to put him in his place. But now he found he wanted to impress him, to earn his favour.

'I will leave now,' Matthew said, 'and trust you back into the care of John. But we shall meet again quite soon. There is something about you, Jamie...' He trailed off and looked thoughtful for a moment. 'You will be useful here, I am sure of it.'

Jamie wondered if this speech was used on all the newbies, or if he, Jamie, truly was being singled out as special. He couldn't help but feel flattered by Matthew's words. The boy was charismatic, that was for sure. Matthew held the door open and Jamie entered the room. It was a regular dorm-type space with some bunks and a few bedside tables. Nothing fancy, but not too bad either.

'Wait here,' Matthew said. 'John will be along shortly.' Then he turned and left.

Jamie assumed this room would be where he was staying. He plonked himself down on the end of one of the beds and looked around. His eyes felt quite heavy all of a sudden, like he could sleep for a hundred years. It must be all the adrenalin of the past few hours leaving his body. Would John be cross with him if he fell asleep on this bed? Quite frankly, he was too tired to worry about that. He eased himself down on top of the covers and closed his eyes.

It seemed only moments later that he was shaken awake. Jamie turned his head and blinked his eyes open. The room lay almost in darkness, the afternoon sun a distant memory. His neck felt stiff and sore. He must have slept at a funny angle.

'This is not your bed,' came a soft voice.

Jamie squinted in the half-light and made out the shape of a round, doughy face belonging to a man who was pointing at the next bed along.

'What?' Jamie croaked.

'This is my bed. You take that one.'

'Oh, okay. Sorry.'

'It's all right.'

Jamie shuffled off the bed and managed to hobble to the next bed along.

'What's the time?' Jamie asked.

'You've missed supper,' the man replied.

Jamie's stomach growled a reply.

'John said we should leave you to sleep,' the man continued. 'But you were on my bed.'

'Yeah, sorry about that,' Jamie apologised again.

'I'm Jeremiah.'

'Jamie.'

'Both our names begin with J.'

'Yeah.'

'They'll change your name soon.'

'I don't think so.'

'Yes. Your new name might not start with a J. it might start with a K or an L or even a Z.'

Jamie rubbed his eyes and shook his head, trying to dislodge the sleep from his brain. Then he realised something – while he'd slept, he hadn't dreamt of anything at all. He'd managed to have a perfectly dreamless sleep for the first time in... well, forever. He looked up as the door opened and several figures filed into the room. John was among them, carrying a storm lamp which cast a yellow glow about the room. He nodded at Jamie who nodded back.

'I see Jeremiah has shown you to your bed,' John said. 'The bathroom is down the hall on the right. In your bedside cupboard you will find a nightshirt, a towel, a washcloth, toothbrush and a beaker.'

The room was full of hushed mutterings, a rustling of clothes and the intermittent creak of the floorboards. The men were preparing to go to bed. As they stripped off their clothes and changed into their nightshirts, Jamie did a quick headcount – ten men including himself. But it appeared as though everyone had some kind of ailment or disability. Jeremiah had a few learning difficulties, John was badly disfigured, one man was badly hunched over and some men were missing limbs. Jamie wondered why he'd been put in with them when there was nothing wrong with him. Then his eyes fell on the crutches which now lay propped against the wall. Of course – he had a disability too.

Half an hour later, showered, changed and with clean teeth, Jamie lay beneath the grey coverlet of his narrow bed. He was worried that the nightmares would return. What if he cried out in his sleep and woke everyone up? What if he let something slip about the girl's murder? It was one thing to confess his sins to a couple of robed priest-type guys, but it was quite another to blurt out his secrets to a roomful of strangers.

He cast his mind back over the events of the day. He couldn't believe how much had happened and how much all this had begun to change him as a person. He almost didn't recognise the old Jamie. The fact he'd actually told two complete strangers his deepest darkest secret was crazy. They hadn't even batted an eyelid. They were all like, *stay with us, we'll give you food and shelter and everything will be great.*

Could this place really be all it seemed? Was he now safe from the outside? Could he finally stop worrying about where he would sleep and what he would find to eat and whether he would be attacked by raiders or soldiers or anyone else who fancied their chances? Jamie only hoped it wasn't all too good to be true.

CHAPTER FIFTEEN

LISS

She had known they wouldn't be able to stay at the farm for long – FJ would've come for them; that much was certain. It was heartbreaking to leave her beautiful family home for a second time, but after everything that had happened over the years, leaving the farm was a relatively small price to pay. At least she would still be with her parents, able to live a normal life. Whatever normal passed for these days.

Liss was sixteen – pretty much an adult. But at the age of seven she and her nine-year-old brother, FJ, had been abducted by James Grey's men and taken to the Cathedral Close in Salisbury, the headquarters of Grey's Church. That was where she'd first met Annabelle. She'd taken the younger girl under her wing and, over the lonely months, they had become as close as sisters. But Liss and her brother had been separated and she hadn't seen him again until nine years later.

For years she had lived under the austere rule of the church. Talking in hushed whispers and living half-lives with no purpose but to serve James Grey and his strict God. She and Annabelle had managed to resist being brainwashed like the others and had kept strong for each other in the hope they might one day escape.

Then their prayers had been answered and the girls were finally rescued from Salisbury. Liss's parents, Fred and Jessie, had enlisted the help of Luc, Riley, Denzil and Connor. They had arrived at the Close one night to save her and FJ. Only they hadn't realised that FJ had become part of the regime. He was now Grey's right-hand man, known as 'the Voice of the Father'.

FJ had tried to prevent Liss and Annabelle from leaving the Close, but he had failed. Instead, Luc and the others had got Liss and Annabelle out of there and reunited Liss with her parents, while at the same time managing to take Grey and FJ hostage. It was a miracle really. She still couldn't believe she was free. They later found out that, although Grey was still held captive at the Talbot Woods Perimeter, FJ had escaped.

After being rescued, she, Annabelle and her parents had returned to their farm, but they realised it would be too dangerous for them to remain as FJ and his men could come for them at any time. So her mum and dad had decided to move them to the neighbouring Compound. Part of her had wanted to stay at the farm in spite of the danger. It was crazy that her own brother should be the one to drive them from their home.

They had soon settled into the Compound. It was a relief to be in a protected environment with regular people. They had a sweet two-bedroom labourers' cottage on the edge of the settlement which provided them with a long garden, meaning they'd been able to bring some livestock from the farm. Most of their animals had been used as payment for the cottage, but they still had two cows, two sheep, the chickens and a goat.

Despite the possible threat from FJ, they had travelled back and forth to the farm each day to harvest the rest of their crops. Liss's mum wasn't keen on this plan at all. If she'd had her way, she would've let all the produce rot, but her dad said that the harvest would set them up for the winter – they could sell what they couldn't use and save the silver for when times grew tough. They had to be self-sufficient or they'd struggle to survive in the coming years.

Today was to be the last day of the harvest. They would gather in the rest of the crops and close up the place for good. It was a sad day and Liss was eager for it to be over. She felt like she couldn't move on with her life until they had said their final farewells to their family home. Although it was only a few miles from the Compound, it may as well have been a hundred because after today they had agreed to never go back.

The sun was sinking, throwing its golden light across the farm and Liss welcomed the cool of evening after their long day's exertions. The land looked more beautiful than it had ever looked before – perhaps because she knew she would never see it again. Once they left, the fences would fall into disrepair and nature would swallow the place up. Or perhaps outsiders would claim the property for themselves. Either way, Liss knew she wouldn't want to return to find out.

'Let's go back and check around the house one last time,' her dad said, climbing into the jeep which they'd parked up at the edge of the field. 'Make sure we haven't left anything important behind. It's later than I'd like. Gonna have to drive back in the dark. Everyone got their weapons?'

Fred had been training Liss and Annabelle to use a shotgun and they'd both gotten pretty good in the last few weeks, especially Annabelle, who seemed to have a knack for it. They joined her dad in the jeep, squeezing in beside him. He started it up and they trundled back across the fields to the house.

The building looked sad and Liss felt a welling of emotion. Back in Salisbury, she had dreamt of this place almost every day. It was the place of her heart. Dad pushed the scullery door open. They had never used the smart, wooden front door; only the faded and peeling back door, which stuck in the doorframe and always needed a firm push or two. They tramped through into the kitchen, wiping their feet from force of habit.

The place was bare now and already had the faint scent of desertion. They had taken most of their furniture with them to their new house. The rest had been sold at the Compound market, fetching good prices.

'Okay,' Jessie said, 'let's all have a last scout round the house. Make sure we haven't forgotten anything vital.' Liss heard the crack in her mum's voice.

Fifteen minutes later, Liss tramped back down the stairs and into the kitchen where she joined the others. After a final check of the rambling farmhouse, none of them had found anything of worth, but it had been good to revisit her room one last time, to memorise the view from her bedroom window – across the yard and over the fields beyond.

The light was fading, the sun dipping behind the western hills. Dusk was almost upon them, the kitchen rapidly turning chilly.

'What was that?' Annabelle asked, her eyes wide. 'Sounded like a man's voice.'

'It's the house, love,' Liss's mum replied. 'Makes all kinds of funny creaks and groans. Bit like my knees.'

'Hang on, Jess,' her dad hissed. 'That wasn't the house.'

Liss strained her ears, but all was quiet.

'Should've brought the dogs with us,' her mum said. 'They'd soon let us know if anyone was—'

Without warning, the door flew open with a bang and the room swiftly filled with men. Not just any men – for they wore the hooded robes of Grey's Church. They were soldiers. *His* soldiers.

Liss gave a short scream, her stomach lurching. Her dad yelled something and tried to reach for his shotgun which lay against the wall, but they were overpowered before any of them could make a break for it or try to defend themselves. The men seemed to fill up the whole room, bringing with them the familiar odour of old classrooms and musty clothes, transporting Liss right back to the Cathedral Close. That smell made her almost swoon with fear, reams of buried memories rising to the surface – the silence, the oppression, the fear and the complete absence of hope.

These intruders had somehow got onto their land, past the fence and through the back door. Liss's mum had been right – they should have left the harvest to wither and rot. They should never have come back. And now it was too late.

'What are you doing in our house?' Liss's dad demanded, his eyes flashing with fury. 'This is private property. You're trespassing.'

'This land belongs to the church now,' one of the soldiers replied.

Their faces were all concealed behind overhanging hoods, giving them the illusion of being ethereal beings. But Liss knew they were very real flesh-and-blood men. She wanted to struggle against her captor who had hold of her arms, but she was paralysed by fear, locking eyes with Annabelle, who looked more defeated than scared.

'We were sent by the Voice of the Father,' the soldier said. 'You are to surrender your house and lands and come willingly to serve him.'

'And if we refuse?' Liss's dad asked.

'If you refuse, you will be taken anyway, or put to the sword as heretics.'

'Where is he?' Liss's mum sobbed. 'Where's my son? Where's FJ? He's not the voice of anything, he's my boy. If I could talk to him, make him remember who he really—'

'Quiet,' the soldier said, giving her a violent shake.

'Leave her alone,' Liss's dad cried. 'Don't touch my wife.' He made a grab for the soldier.

Liss watched in horror as the soldier reached back and sideswiped her dad across the face, knocking him to the floor. His head cracked hard on the tiles. Liss gave a short scream, but the soldiers did nothing. They left her dad on the floor and tried to bundle the three of them out through the door.

Liss resisted. 'Dad!' she cried, turning back. 'Dad, are you all right?' But he lay unmoving. Liss gave a sob. What if he was dead? She, Annabelle and her mum were shoved out through the back door, which now hung grotesquely off one hinge, like a half-pulled tooth. Outside, dusk was already dissolving into night.

'Let them go.'

Liss turned. Standing in the doorway her dad was pointing his shotgun at them. Alive, if a little woozy looking.

'Put it down,' one of the soldiers said calmly. 'Or you'll all die.'

'Better that than to go with you,' her dad replied. 'Let go of them or I'll start shooting and I don't think FJ would want that.'

No one did or said anything for a moment, and then the guards finally released their grip.

'Run!' her dad yelled at them. 'Run! Now! I'll hold them off. You know where to go!'

Liss turned and fled towards the darkness of the fields. She felt Annabelle beside her; felt her hand slip into her own. Where was her mum? Should she stop to check? But Annabelle was pulling her onwards, the thump of their footfalls and their ragged breaths loud in her ears. Scuffles and shouts from behind. Then a gunshot filled up the night, ringing through the blackness and instilling a wild terror in her heart.

She glanced over her shoulder and saw her mum coming towards them out of the darkness. Thank goodness. But no – her mum's face registered shock. She stumbled and fell down onto her knees. Liss stopped dead, letting go of Annabelle's hand.

'Mum!' she screamed.

'Keep going, don't stop,' her mum cried. 'Annabelle, make Lissy go with you.'

'Come on, Liss,' Annabelle hissed. 'We have to keep moving.'

'No! *Mum!*'

'Please,' her mum said. 'I want you to go. Don't break my heart, Lissy.'

Her mum's eyes closed and she collapsed onto her side.

'No!' Liss moaned. And then another shot tore through the air. She felt Annabelle's hands on her arm and on her back. She tried to shake her off.

'Come on,' the younger girl said.

'I can't leave my parents.'

Annabelle tugged at Liss's arm. 'You have to.'

'No.' Liss's voice rose to a shrill screech.

'Please,' Annabelle said. 'I can't go back to the Close. I can't.'

'I can't leave Mum and Dad.'

'FJ will kill us if we go back now. Your parents want you to escape. They both told us to run. Do it for them.'

Liss shook her head, but she let Annabelle lead her away across the fields. She ran as if in a nightmare, tears streaming down her cheeks. They squeezed through a high hedge and then ran some more until their lungs felt fit to burst. They heard the soldiers' cries and footfalls in the distance, but it was night and the dim lights of the robed men's torches were ineffective in the vast darkness. No further shots were fired. Perhaps her brother didn't want her and Annabelle harmed, despite what the soldiers had said.

But what about her parents? Were they dead already? Had the guards found her mum's body lying in the grass? Had her father escaped? All these thoughts tore her up as they staggered through the black night. She should go back. But what good would it do? She had to protect Annabelle now. They would hide and then they would rescue her parents when they had a plan. She would kill FJ if she had to. He was no longer her brother. Grey had fashioned him into an unrecognisable monster.

Liss knew where they should go. She led Annabelle towards the tunnel they used for getting in and out of the farm. It was concealed behind a dense clump of bushes and was hard to find in the darkness. Her hands tore at grass and brambles before finally locating the wooden board which served as an entrance hatch. They crept down, under the ground, into the cold, dark passageway, hearts pounding.

CHAPTER SIXTEEN

RILEY

Pa and I stood as Liss and Annabelle entered the kitchen, awkward and uncomfortable, wearing the clothes I'd laid out for them, hair damp from their showers.

'Come and sit down,' Ma said, ladling out a couple of bowls of porridge. 'You girls need some nice warm food. You look half-starved.' Ma was right. They were nothing but skin and bones. The fact they were wearing my clothes highlighted this: baggy and rolled up at the cuffs and trouser bottoms, they hung off them like children wearing adults' clothes.

Annabelle and Liss sat hesitantly at the table. They seemed eager to eat, but the porridge was blisteringly hot and they could only manage tiny amounts off the tip of their spoons.

'Are you feeling any better?' Pa asked.

The girls nodded, but didn't look like they meant it.

'Where are your parents?' he asked Liss.

She stopped eating, but continued to stare at her porridge. After a heartbeat of silence she spoke. 'They're dead.'

'What?' I sat down heavily on one of the kitchen chairs. 'No. I don't believe it. What happened?'

Liss continued to stare down at her bowl, dry-eyed.

'I'm so sorry, Liss,' I said, thinking of Fred and Jessie and how happy they had been to get their daughter back after so many years. To think they were now dead and unable to live the kind of family life they'd been dreaming of was awful.

'I'm sorry,' Pa said.

'I'm sorry too,' Ma added. 'That's terrible. You poor things.'

'What happened?' I asked Liss. 'Are you okay to talk about it?'

'It was a while ago,' she said. 'Grey's men came to the farm.'

'You stayed on at the farm?' Pa said. 'But you were told how dangerous it was to carry on living there.'

'No,' Liss said. 'We were only there to finish off the harvest. We'd moved to the Compound. We've got a house there.' Liss stopped eating and went on to tell us exactly what had happened. How her mum had been shot and how she and Annabelle had hidden in a tunnel.

'I was sure they'd find us,' she said, 'but they never did. We waited down there for hours. We were too scared to come out.'

'I don't blame you,' Ma said.

'We waited till the next day. By then, the soldiers had gone, so we crept back to the farmhouse. Mum and dad were in the kitchen...' She swallowed. 'Dead.'

'Liss, I am so sorry.' I put my arms around her small frame, but she stayed unmoving, her arms wrapped around her body. I was pretty sure she was still in shock.

'After burying them, we didn't know what to do,' Liss continued. 'Or where to go. We didn't want to stay at the Compound, not with it being so close to Salisbury. Eventually we decided to come here. I hope that's okay.'

'Of course it is,' I said. 'Of course. You did absolutely the right thing to come here. Surely you didn't walk all the way?'

Annabelle nodded. 'It took us weeks using an old map. We got lost more than a few times.'

'You were lucky you didn't get attacked by raiders,' Pa said. 'It's dangerous out there.'

'We kept off the roads,' Annabelle said. 'And we hid if we saw anyone.'

Ma put the kettle on, shaking her head and muttering something to herself.

'You okay, Ellie?' Pa asked.

'I just... sometimes I forget what kind of world we're living in. It's so barbaric.'

'I'm so, so sorry about your parents,' I repeated, knowing how inadequate those words sounded. 'FJ has a lot to answer for. I know he's your brother, but—'

'FJ is coming here,' Liss said, cutting me off.

'What?' I wasn't sure I'd heard her right.

'Liss!' Annabelle cried.

'He's coming here,' Liss whispered it this time. 'I'm sorry.'

'FJ's coming here? When?' I asked. 'Now? To rescue Grey? Or is he after you?'

'No,' she said, looking up at me for the first time. 'Riley, he's coming after *you*.'

A chill entered my bones. I glanced from Liss to Annabelle and then back to Liss again. Ever since that evening when FJ had caught me in the clearing, I'd had nightmares about him. In my dreams I would be running away from him, but at the precise moment I thought I'd got away, I would realise that I was running *towards* him. And he'd be standing there in front of me, waiting, with a half-smile on his face.

'FJ's coming after *me*?' I don't know why I sounded so surprised. Back in the clearing when he'd had me in cuffs, the look he'd shot me was one of pure hatred. I guessed that sooner or later he would be coming for me, or that I would go to him – after what he'd said about knowing who Skye's killer was. It was inevitable – but it still sent chills down my body to know that he was possibly on his way here right now. That he was thinking about me with revenge on his mind.

'What are you talking about?' Pa said, getting to his feet and glaring at Liss. 'Why is FJ going after Riley? I can understand him wanting revenge, but it wasn't only my daughter responsible for Grey's capture. There was Luc and Denzil. Connor. Why Riley? Why has he singled her out?'

'I... I don't know,' Liss said, her face flushing. 'I don't even know why I said that. I must've got things mixed up. I'm not thinking straight. I was wrong. Sorry.'

'Don't lie,' Pa said, his eyes narrowing. 'You seemed very clear a minute ago. Just tell us what you know.' His face darkened. 'If that boy wants trouble, he's found it.'

'Pa, it's fine,' I said. 'I'm here, aren't I? And I'm perfectly safe.'

'I'm sorry,' Liss replied. 'His disciples mentioned something when they came to the farm but, like I said, I must've got it mixed up.'

'What exactly did they say?' I stood up shakily and took a step closer to Liss. She seemed vague. Exhausted. Perhaps, like she said, she wasn't thinking clearly.

'That can't be right,' Ma said. 'What would Liss's brother want with you, Riley?'

'I don't know,' I replied. I'd kept Ma in the dark about most of what had gone on since Skye's death. She couldn't take anymore trauma and I'd been scared that if she knew FJ was out to get me, she'd have another breakdown. Likewise, Pa would go crazy if he knew FJ had a personal vendetta against me.

'No, no. I'm sorry,' Liss said. 'I made a mistake.' She picked up her spoon again and scooped up some porridge, but her hand was shaking uncontrollably. Something wasn't right. She was hiding something.

'Annabelle...' I turned to the younger girl. 'Did the soldiers say anything to you about wanting to find me?'

She shook her head and carried on eating.

'There,' Ma said. 'I told you it was a mistake. Why would the boy be interested in you, Riley? If he wanted to come here for anyone, it would be to rescue that dreadful James Grey.'

'Pity he's dead then, isn't it,' I said.

'Riley,' Pa warned. It wasn't common knowledge that Grey was dead and I shouldn't have said anything in front of Liss and Annabelle. But the words had slipped out.

'He's dead?' Liss dropped her spoon and it clattered onto the tiles.

'Yeah,' I replied. 'Grey died in custody after he got here. I think the trip from Salisbury weakened him.'

'But he can't be dead! He can't. No!' Liss was crying now, almost hyperventilating. Annabelle tried to calm her, whispering soothing words, her arm around her shoulders.

'I'm sorry,' I said, 'I didn't realise Grey meant so much to you. I thought you hated him.'

Liss stood up and looked around wildly. Ma kept telling her to calm down while Annabelle held her arms and told her it would be all right, but by now she was completely hysterical, sobbing and shaking.

'Liss,' Pa said, trying to get her attention.

'What's wrong?' I asked her. 'This is Grey we're talking about, the man who had you kidnapped and brainwashed. You can't be upset he's dead, surely?'

'Liss!' Pa's deep voice cut through the hysteria in the room. 'Tell us what's going on. Is there something you're hiding from us? We're your friends. But we can't help you if you don't tell us what's really happening.' He splayed his hands on the table and stared at her.

Liss looked up at him, tears streaking down her face, her whole body trembling. But still she didn't speak.

'Annabelle?' I said. 'What's going on? Why is Liss so upset?'

'Liss,' Annabelle said. 'Liss, it's no good. We'll have to tell them.'

'No!' Liss cried. 'You can't. They'll kill them. What are we going to do?'

'They'll help us, I'm sure,' Annabelle said. 'I'm telling them.'

'Telling who? Kill who?' I said. Why was Liss so upset over the death of a man she hated? 'Annabelle?'

'We don't have any choice,' Annabelle pleaded with Liss.

'All right, all right,' Liss said, wiping the tears from her face. 'I'll tell them. I'll tell them.'

'Please,' I said. 'What's going on?'

'Just understand,' Liss said. 'I didn't have a choice.'

'Tell us,' I said, sitting back down, nervous about what she might say. Ma came and sat next to me and Pa, and we all three fixed our attention on the girls.

'Mum and Dad aren't dead,' Liss said.

'What?'

'They're alive. I lied to you before.'

'Why? Why would you lie about something like that?' I asked, confused.

Liss stared down at her porridge.

'Is this a joke?' I said. 'So that story you told us before – about Grey's men coming to your house – that was all a lie?'

'No,' Liss said. 'Not a lie. Just... just not the whole truth.'

CHAPTER SEVENTEEN

LISS

Cold terror and shock permeated the tunnel as Liss and Annabelle crouched in the slimy darkness waiting to be discovered, their frightened breaths amplified in the small space.

'Will they find us?' Annabelle whispered.

'No one knows about this place,' Liss said. 'We should be safe. This tunnel leads to the outside.'

'So why don't we just keep going then?' Annabelle asked. 'We could go outside and get as far away from them as we can? Run back to the Compound? Get help.'

'We can't leave Mum and Dad behind,' Liss said. 'They shot my mum, Annabelle. They shot her. Do you think she's dead? What if they're both dead?' Her last word came out as a shriek.

'Shh, shh,' Annabelle soothed, putting her arm around her friend. 'They'll be all right. You saw your dad, he was fine. And your mum will be too.'

'Do you think so?'

'Yes. Yes, definitely. We'll stay here till the soldiers have gone and then we'll help your parents, all right? Are you sure they won't find us in here?'

Liss stifled a fresh onslaught of tears. 'Maybe we should

help them now. Sneak back. Save them. We could get my dad's shotgun. Kill them all.'

'We'd never be able to kill them all,' Annabelle whispered. 'There's too many. They're too strong.'

'We have to try. We have to do something. We can't just save ourselves and leave them to—'

Annabelle shook Liss's shoulders. 'Keep your voice down. They'll hear.'

'We should never have come back. Mum was right. We should've left the harvest and stayed safe in the Compound. And now it's too late.' A chittering squeak came from the ground and Liss felt something small scuttle past her legs. Probably a rat, but she didn't care. What was she even hiding for? If her parents were dead, she had lost everything and there was no point in anything anymore.

'I'm going back,' she said, feeling behind her for the narrow steps which led back up. 'You stay here, Anna.'

'No. Please, Liss. Don't go. Don't leave me. You're all I've got in the world. If you let them take you, I'll be alone. I'll have no one.'

'Go back to the Compound. You'll be safe there. They won't take me. I'll kill them first. Or they can kill me. Either way—'

'Liss, please. You're not thinking straight.'

'If I stay here and my parents die, I'll never forgive myself.'

A sniff in the darkness. 'Well, then I'm coming with you.'

'No... you stay and—'

'I'm coming, Liss.'

But they were saved further debate about whether to stay or go, for at that moment the wooden board to the hatch was removed and a beam of light found their frightened faces. Liss's shoulders drooped.

Grey's soldiers had discovered them, and there would be no rescuing anybody.

'We can get out the other way!' Annabelle cried. 'Come on, Liss!' she tugged at her friend's arm.

'The other exit has been blocked.' A monotone voice filtered into the tunnel.

Annabelle let go of Liss's arm and sank to the ground.

'Come on, Anna,' Liss said, pulling her upright again. 'It's no good. We're caught.'

The two girls trudged up the steps and back out into the hostile night, a phalanx of robed soldiers awaiting them. The men formed a tight circle around the girls and herded them back across the field towards the farmhouse. Lights, once cosy and welcoming, now flickered threatening and harsh. Their home had been violated.

As they crossed the yard and approached the back door, Liss saw dark, robed shapes moving about the kitchen through the lamp-lighted window. But there was no sign of her parents within. Her footsteps faltered. What would she find inside? Would her mum and dad be there? Please let them be okay. Tied up, injured. Anything was better than dead. A prod in the back got her moving again. She lowered her eyes and clenched her fists, steeling herself against what she would discover inside.

'Good evening, sister.'

FJ.

'You,' she spat as she stumbled through the door and entered the kitchen.

'I'm glad to find you unharmed, Deborah.'

'That's not my name. My name is Melissa. What have you done to Mum and Dad? Where are they?'

'Your parents are fine. They've been taken to one of our vehicles for their own comfort.'

'They're *our* parents, not just mine. *Your* mother. *Your* father. Have you no memory of our childhood? Of their love and care for us? They adored you, FJ. But you throw it back in their faces like the spoilt brat you always were. And you talk about their *comfort*? What's your definition of comfort? A bullet in the back? Kidnap? Murder?'

'Careful, sister. If you want to keep your little playmate safe, you'd better watch your tone.'

'And now we see your true Godly self,' Liss said. 'Bullying threats.' Liss knew her pleas and accusations were falling on deaf ears. She had to try to reach him. To make him remember his younger self. 'They're our parents, FJ!' Liss cried. 'And I'm your sister! Your blood! Does that mean nothing?'

FJ nodded to his soldiers.

Liss struggled against the flowing black shapes that came to her with rope to bind her and cloth to silence her, but it was like trying to fight steel with paper. Within seconds, she and Annabelle were trussed like sheep, as they had been all those years ago. Would she never be free of Grey and his minions? The girls stared at one another, but there was no point in sorrowful looks, so Liss closed her eyes and turned away.

They were carried outside, back the way they had come. Liss in the arms of a huge, robed warrior. Annabelle next to her in the arms of another. Carried easily, as though they were no heavier than freshly shorn wool. Her captor's breath came even and steady as he made his way through the yard, across the field, down into the tunnel and finally up to the outside. This was the way FJ must have entered the farm. *Of course.* FJ knew about their secret entranceway. Stupid of them. They should have blocked it up ages ago. Too late now.

Bundled into the back seat of a waiting vehicle, Liss cast her eyes about wildly, but even in the darkness she could tell her parents were not here. Two figures slid into the front – not FJ though. Car doors slammed. The engine started up and they moved off into the night.

Liss and Annabelle were delivered back to Salisbury, to the Cathedral Close. The place they had hoped never to see again. Carried down to the stinking cells, they were untied and locked up. FJ hadn't shown his face again and the guards said nothing to tell them why they were here or what was to happen to them. But there was one consolation – a few hours later, two new prisoners were led into the cell: Liss's mum and dad.

Liss fell into her father's arms, sobbing. Grim-faced, he held her. She would've hugged her mum too, only she saw that she had a bandage taped across her shoulder and carried herself awkwardly like she was in great pain.

'What happened, Mum? I'm so glad you're okay. I thought they'd killed you.'

'I'm fine, Lissy,' she said with a trembling voice. 'It's just my shoulder. Thank goodness you two are okay. I wish to goodness you'd got away though. What happened?' Ashen, she looked like she was about to keel over. Annabelle helped her down to sit on the cold, wet floor.

'It's disgusting in here,' her dad said. 'Not fit for beasts. What sort of boy has our Freddie Junior become?'

'Are you okay, Dad? Are you hurt?'

'I'm all right. Bit of a headache, that's all. It's your mum I'm worried about.'

'At least they bandaged her up.'

'Yeah. Kind of 'em, wasn't it,' her dad growled. 'They obviously don't want us dead yet.'

'Why couldn't they have just left us alone?' Liss cried. 'We weren't doing them any harm.'

'Some people can't leave things alone. They pick and pick, until the world turns from a thing of beauty into a festering scab. I'm afraid our FJ has become one of those people.'

Liss shivered. 'They caught us in the tunnel. It was how they got into the farm. FJ showed them the way.'

'We've got to get you out of here,' her dad said. 'We'll work out a plan.'

'But no one knows where we are,' Liss said. 'And this place... we'll never get out.'

'Don't worry, girl,' her dad said. 'I'll get you out. Whatever it takes. You're not going to end up rotting in this hellhole. You're going to have a beautiful life, somewhere good.'

'We all will, Dad,' Liss said, resting her head on his shoulder.

But, several weeks later, still locked up in the rancid underground cell, their defiance had vanished, their hope dwindling to a pinprick of nothing. The guards gave them just enough food that they didn't starve and just enough blankets that they didn't freeze. And that was it.

Annabelle had used one of the blankets to mop up the slimy floor, to try to make it a little more comfortable, but after a few weeks they gave up on trying to improve their surroundings and reluctantly succumbed to the filth. Liss tried not to torture herself with thoughts of warm baths and clean sheets, but some days she would give in to the seductive images, letting herself wallow in the unobtainable fantasy.

She, Annabelle and her dad were holding up better than her mum, whose shoulder didn't seem to be healing. A doctor had visited on a couple of occasions, but he was silent and unapproachable, with no thought of the additional pain he might be causing as he poked and prodded. Liss's dad had to be restrained by a guard during these visits, threatening to break the doctor's neck if he didn't treat his wife with more care.

As the days rolled on, Liss was convinced they'd been forgotten. That they'd eventually die in their cell. A slow uncomfortable death. The lack of natural light meant they had no idea whether it was day or night and so found themselves dozing on and off, rather than enjoying a full night's sleep. It was disorienting and Liss felt as though trapped in a dream, unable to distinguish between waking and sleeping nightmares.

The day things changed was not a good day. Liss's mum had fallen into delirium, moaning and muttering in her sleep. Her wound had become infected and her skin burned with fever.

They had been calling and yelling for hours, for someone to come and help. Banging on the door to their cell. But no one came. So Liss cried into her father's chest and decided she'd better prepare for the worst. At least her mother was asleep, unable to witness their distress. Pretty soon, they all fell into their own versions of sleep. Light slumber and tortured dreams. Shallow breaths and fractured nightmares.

Liss awoke to brightness. A lantern flooding their cell with yellow light. She blinked and squinted, shielding her eyes against the glare. A hooded figure pointed at her and beckoned with a long pale finger. She stood shakily and turned back to see the frightened faces of Annabelle and her dad. Her mum still slept, head resting on her husband's lap. Liss knew she had no choice in the matter. She would have to go with this figure to wherever it was he wanted her to go. Back to her old life at the Close? She didn't think so. To her death, more like.

It was worse.

He took her to FJ.

'Sister, I hope you appreciate the weeks of silent reflection you've been given.'

Liss had never felt such burning anger as she did then, faced with this smug creature who shared the same blood as her. How could someone so radiantly perfect on the outside have such an ugly soul? And this room – so obscenely opulent, alien in its beauty. Its warmth and fresh clean scent. The rich furnishings, lush paintings and soft carpet. She hated this room more than her prison cell. It signified all that was wrong with this place.

Before bringing her to him, they had disposed of her filthy clothing, bathed her and dressed her in a simple skirt and blouse. Newly fragrant and presentable, she wanted to spit in his face and claw at his eyes. Instead, she stood and stared at him, trembling with rage, unable to speak for fear she would lose control altogether. Willing him to shrivel and die on the spot. But of course he did no such thing.

'Nothing to say?' he prompted.

She looked him in the eye, still unable to voice the torrent of hatred she felt towards him.

'Good,' he said. 'I need you to listen to what I'm about to say. Lives depend on it.'

She almost laughed at that. *Lives?* What did he care for lives? Unless they were vital to his precious plans.

'I am letting you go free, sister. You and your little friend.'

Liss heard the words, yet she didn't quite believe it.

'But I need you to do something for me.'

Of course he did. For when had he ever done anything out of the goodness of his heart? There *was* no goodness in his heart – he may have the face of an angel, but his heart was a pustule-ridden sack of evil.

'I need you to go south of here, to the Talbot Woods Perimeter. I need you to locate Riley Culpepper and her family, and win their trust.'

Liss was beginning to understand where this one-sided conversation was heading.

'You must find out where they are holding Our Father hostage,' said FJ.

'You want me to get James Grey for you?' she said.

'I want you to locate him. Find out where he's being held. My warriors will march on the Perimeter and we will crush them, but before we burn it to the ground, we must save Our Father and we must punish the girl who started this.'

'Who? You mean Riley?'

'Who else.'

'You want me to find Grey for you?' Liss said quietly. 'And you want me to betray my friend?'

'*Friend?* This shows me how lacking in judgment you are.

This girl is the essence of evil and she must be punished. You will hand her over to me and she will bleed for her sins.'

Liss shook her head. 'No.'

FJ smiled. 'Very well. Say goodbye to your mother and father.' He clicked his fingers and looked beyond her, to the doorway. Three guards entered the room, her parents between them – two to support her mother, and one to restrain her father. Her mum and dad were still dressed in the same clothes, hair wild and dishevelled, faces pale and gaunt, their mouths stuffed with rags. Their appearance was all the more shocking against the backdrop of this luxurious room.

'Shall we shoot them?' FJ asked her. 'Or should they hang?'

'All right!' Liss cried. 'All right, you've made your point. I'll do it.'

'What's that?' FJ cupped a hand around his ear.

'I said I'll do it. Whatever you want. I'll do it. But you have to treat them better. Mum's really ill. She needs a proper doctor and clean clothes, a good meal. I'll only do it if you—'

'You do not bargain with me,' he drawled. 'They will return to their cell and they will remain there until you do what you're supposed to do. Heretics and evil doers do not receive privileges. It is the will of God.'

'The will of FJ more like,' Liss muttered under her breath, despair clutching at her like a drowning man. 'How do I even know you'll keep your word?'

'I am a man of God. I always keep my word.'

Liss had no choice. She would have to do it.

CHAPTER EIGHTEEN

RILEY

Liss's porridge had gone cold. We stared at her, appalled by her terrible story. I couldn't believe what I was hearing. Her parents captured. FJ's army coming to destroy the Perimeter. And FJ had singled me out. He wanted me dead or worse. Liss had been put in an impossible position. No wonder she was so distraught.

'He said he'd kill Mum and Dad unless we did what he told us. And he will do it too. They're still down there in those horrible cells. I'm so sorry I lied. I really didn't know what else to do.'

'Okay,' Pa said. 'It's okay, Liss. I understand. You're in a terrible position. You did the right thing telling us the truth. Thank you. We'll sort this out.'

Liss raised her eyes to look at him and relaxed her shoulders when she realised he wasn't angry with her. 'I didn't want to lie, but he'll kill them. If only Our Father – I mean Grey – was still alive, it wouldn't have been so bad. I could have just rescued him somehow and taken him to appease FJ. I could've left Riley here. What am I going to do about Mum and Dad?'

'We'll do everything we can,' Pa replied. His eyes darkened.

'Why does he only want Riley? Surely he'd want Luc and Denzil too if this was all about revenge.'

'I... I don't exactly know,' Liss replied. 'But he seems to hate her.'

'We didn't exactly get along when we met,' I said. 'I think I pissed him off.'

'More likely he wants to use you as leverage,' Pa said. He turned back to Liss. 'When's he coming? And where are you supposed to meet him? I need you to tell me exactly what the plan is. How were you supposed to get Grey and Riley to FJ?'

Liss turned away from Pa and looked at Annabelle, shaking her head. 'I can't tell them... it's too awful.' She turned to me and met my eyes. 'I would never have betrayed you, Riley. You helped save my life. FJ is a terrible person.'

'It's okay, Liss,' I replied. 'You're not responsible for his actions. You can tell us and we won't judge you. I promise.'

Liss continued shaking her head, her hands twisting in her lap, and so Annabelle spoke up. 'We were supposed to find a way of getting Riley outside the fence. And then... bring her to FJ in exchange for Fred and Jessie. He was planning on using Riley as a bargaining chip to get Grey back. He was going to torture her until you did what he asked.'

Ma's eyes widened, brightening with tears, while Pa's face turned a deep shade of red, his whole body tensing. But I couldn't feel anything. It was a scary thing to hear, but for now I was numbed to scary things. Or perhaps I was too shocked to react.

'When's all this supposed to take place?' I asked, my voice calm.

'Wait a minute, Riley,' Pa said, his voice deathly quiet. 'I'm trying to take this in.' He got to his feet, his face dark, his eyes glittering with rage. He began muttering to himself. 'That boy planned to harm my daughter to get what he wanted. I'll kill him. I'm going to hunt him down and I'm going to kill him.'

'Pa, wait,' I said. 'There are better ways to do this. If you go out there, you'll be killed. You can't go up against an army on your own.'

'Watch me.'

'Pa, please!'

'Johnny!' Ma said, sternly. 'Sit down. What you're doing is not going to help anyone. Least of all Riley. She's here. She's safe. You need to work out a plan, not go storming off half-cocked.'

Pa tensed and then his shoulders sagged.

I had to hand it to her – Ma had talked him around. I took her hand across the table and squeezed it.

'When are you supposed to make the trade?' I asked. 'And where?'

'He said he'd meet us two miles due north of here at five a.m. on Christmas Eve,' Liss replied.

'Christmas Eve?' I said. 'But that's only a couple of days away.'

'Is he coming alone?' Pa asked. 'Or is he bringing his army?'

'Once he has Grey, he's planning on taking the Perimeter by force. He wants to destroy it,' Annabelle said. 'So, yes, he'll be with his army.'

'But what should we do now that Grey's dead?' Liss said. 'What about my mum and dad? When I don't show up, he'll kill them.'

'Not if I kill him first,' Pa said through gritted teeth.

'It'll be okay,' Ma said to the girls. 'Johnny will sort it out.'

'Right, we need to get organised,' Pa said. 'And, Riley, we'll need to get you away from the Perimeter.'

'I'm not going anywhere.'

'I don't want you here when FJ and his lot arrive. You can go to your grandparents in Uley.'

'No,' I replied. 'You need me here.'

'It won't be safe. Too much can go wrong. Go with your mother.'

'No,' I repeated, frustrated that Pa was still treating me like a helpless child.

'It's a good idea,' Ma said. 'A trip away will do us both good.'

'I'm not going,' I said. 'Anyway, you can use me as bait.'

'Like that's going to happen,' Pa replied. 'We'll talk about it later. Right now we need to lock this place down tight and I've got a few ideas.'

'Me too,' I said, standing up. 'Let's get started.' I figured if I could make myself useful, Pa might reconsider sending me away. It was either that, or go into hiding, and I wasn't one to run away.

Liss and Annabelle had moved into Luc's house for the time being. Pa didn't want them staying here in case they were tempted to try to turn me over to FJ. I didn't think they would betray me, but Pa reminded me that Liss's family's lives were at stake. That most people would do anything to save the lives of the ones they loved – betray a friend, kill even. He ordered them watched at all times.

Plus, Ma couldn't really cope with anyone staying at our house. Sometimes I didn't think she would ever return to her normal self again. Since Skye's death, I'd been treating her like a delicate child who might throw a tantrum at any moment. But there wasn't time to dwell on Ma's state of mind. We were all too busy, working round the clock, fortifying our home.

The Perimeter had always had its fence. That's what made it what it was – its towering, unscalable electrified fence, keeping us safe inside and everybody else out. But it was only ever built to keep out raiders and looters, vagrants and anarchists. It was never built to withstand an army. To withstand bombs. Since the threat of Grey, the Perimeter Council had built a secondary line of defence inside the boundary – a double-skinned wall, built of brick and stone, almost as high as the fence, totally obscuring the inside from view.

Towards the top of the wall, a series of wooden walkways jutted out, running almost halfway around the northern Perimeter. They were to be used as lookout posts and, in the case of an attack, as shooting platforms. Small gaps had been left in the wall for the guards to fire out of – an idea borrowed from the walls which enclosed Salisbury.

The day after Liss and Annabelle's arrival, hundreds of us lined the Perimeter, busily topping the new brick wall with razor wire and glass. I worked in a team with Liss, Annabelle, Luc and a guard called Jenny who'd been posted with us to keep an eye on Liss and Annabelle. We had one ladder between us, some clay-grass cement, and a bucket of broken glass.

The sun shone and the temperature had warmed up a little from previous days, but the mood was sombre and quiet. We spoke to one another in hushed whispers, everyone anxious about the approach of FJ and his army. What would he do once he discovered Grey was dead? Was he really only coming for me and Grey? Or did he have another agenda? Pa was convinced he was after our oil supply and most people agreed.

Luc and Liss stood on one of the high platforms, setting vicious shards of glass into wet cement, Annabelle was halfway up the ladder and Jenny stood at the bottom, passing up the glass. I, meanwhile, was mixing up the next lot of clay-and-grass concrete, adding water to achieve the right consistency.

We'd tried to tell Liss and Annabelle that they didn't need to work today. That they should rest. It was obvious they were half-starved and exhausted, but they said they wanted to be useful and we couldn't persuade them otherwise. Thankfully, Pa hadn't mentioned packing me off to my grandparents again. I think he was too busy. Either that, or he'd given up once he realised I wouldn't back down.

I hadn't even had time to think about Lou and the shanties. Yesterday's visit to the Walls felt like a lifetime ago. No one had mentioned the missing firewood, so I hoped I'd gotten away with it.

Liss gasped, interrupting my thoughts. 'Are you all right?' I heard her say.

I jerked my head up to see Luc holding his hand, crimson blood soaking into his gloves.

'Luc, come down,' I called. 'I'll run and get some bandages. Won't be a minute.' I turned to go.

'It's okay,' Liss called down from the platform. She reached under her coat and tore a strip of material from her shirt – well actually it was *my* shirt. She carefully peeled the glove off his injured hand and Luc held it out while she wrapped the cloth around his sliced fingers.

'You should get that cleaned,' I called up. 'You don't want it to get infected.'

'I'll be fine, Riley,' he said without looking down. 'Liss has sorted me out.' He smiled at her and she flushed, bowing her head.

Annabelle saw me staring at them and I gave her a quick smile and got back to mixing my cement. What had I just witnessed? Did Liss have feelings for Luc? Were her feelings reciprocated? I told myself not to be ridiculous. The girls had only arrived yesterday. They'd spent one night at the Donovans' house. Liss was simply being helpful, that was all.

Things were still awkward between me and Luc. He hadn't initiated any conversation with me today and I couldn't think of anything to say to him either. I folded more grass into the clay mixture. Liss was very pretty. Petite and fair, she reminded me of one of the flower fairies from a bedtime story book that Ma used to read us when we were little. I, on the other hand, was tall and ungainly. Liss was quiet and self-contained, while I was outspoken and emotional. Was it any wonder Luc preferred her calm, sweet company.

'Ready for the next lot of cement?' I called up.

'Be down in a sec,' Luc replied. 'We need to move along to the next platform.'

'Okay.'

Liss climbed down the ladder while Luc finished setting the last few shards of glass, ignoring his blood-soaked bandage.

'I don't think broken glass will be enough to stop my brother,' Liss said. 'He's always been very determined. You don't know what he's like.'

'I think I'm learning,' I replied. 'And the glass is only one line of defence. We've got other strategies.'

'Good,' she replied. 'You'll need them.'

As the minutes rolled away, we worked steadily along our section of the wall, hardly speaking, just concentrating on the job in hand. Tension hung in the air like a thick mist. Liss had been right – it didn't feel like we were doing nearly enough. What if Grey's army used explosives like before? All it would take was a single blast in the right location and our defences would be breached.

As soon as we broke for lunch, I decided to make an excuse and leave. We'd all brought food, but I didn't think I would be able to bear the awkward silences and overt politeness between me and Luc.

'I'll be back after lunch,' I said.

'We're only stopping for twenty minutes or so,' Luc said. 'There's loads left to do.'

'That's okay,' I replied. 'I won't be long.' But I had no intention of returning. I would go up to the Guards' House and see if they could find me another job. Luc and the girls could easily manage without my help.

I walked quickly, eating my lunch of fruit loaf as I went, giving myself indigestion. But when I got there, a double security detail was guarding the main gate and they wouldn't let me in.

'I need to see Roger Brennan,' I told Liam.

'I'll get him for you,' he said. 'Wait here.' He turned and disappeared into the red brick building. Two minutes later, he re-emerged with Brennan.

'Hello, Riley,' he said. 'What's the problem? I thought you were working on the wall today?'

'I am... I was. But I wondered if...' This wasn't going well. He was probably only giving me the time of day because I was Johnny's daughter.

'Can you make it quick, Riley,' Brennan said, not unkindly. 'I'm leaving for Charminster in a minute. Their radio's down so we haven't been able to warn them about FJ. I could do without the trip. There's too much to sort out here.'

'I'll go,' I offered. This was perfect. I'd wanted to warn Lou about FJ's approach anyway. Last time Grey's army had come down this way, they had terrorised the shanties and looted their camp for provisions. What if they did that again? Lou and the others wouldn't survive the winter after another raid; they were low enough on provisions as it was. There was no way Denzil would let me 'borrow' a truck again, so this could be the perfect opportunity to tell them.

'You want to go to the Compound after what happened last time?' Brennan said, lifting a bushy eyebrow. 'I heard you were caught up in the riots.'

'I'll be fine. I won't go inside. I'll just tell the guards on the gate and then I'll come straight back.'

He shook his head. 'It's too dangerous. No civilians are allowed outside the Perimeter alone.'

'I'll go with Denzil,' I said, knowing that was probably the only way he would let me out of here.

'Denzil's busy.'

'Liam then.' I smiled up at the guard, who looked at Brennan for confirmation.

'Liam's on duty.'

'Okay, well who can you spare?'

'I don't know if I can spare anyone, Riley.'

'There must be someone. It's not far. I can be there and back in a couple of hours. You're needed here. It's a simple errand. It makes sense to send me.'

'I suppose you could go with Luc.'

Great. Of all the people he could have suggested, why him? 'He's busy on the wall,' I said lamely.

'Well, so should you be, Riley,' he said, his patience running out. 'Look, either go with Luc or get back to work and I'll go myself. Either way—'

'Okay, I'll go.' Even as I said the words I was regretting them.

'Take one of the guards' vehicles,' he said, throwing me a set of keys. 'Do not enter the Compound, just tell them I sent you, inform the guards of the situation, turn around and drive straight home. I need you back inside the Perimeter before nightfall, or your father will have me hanged. No excuses.'

'Yep,' I said. 'I'll go straight away.'

My first thought was to drive out of here without Luc. I really didn't want to spend the afternoon in close confinement with someone who obviously couldn't stand to be in my company. Unfortunately, there was no way Liam would have let me out of the gates alone. I had no choice but to take him with me.

'Be careful,' Brennan said.

'I will.' I turned and jogged towards the parking lot around the back of the Guards' House. My stomach clenched with nerves at the thought of spending time alone with Luc. I didn't think he'd be too happy about it either.

CHAPTER NINETEEN

JAMIE

When Jamie awoke it was with a feeling of utter calm. Once again, there had been no nightmares. No dreams at all. This was some kind of miracle. Whatever Matthew and James Grey were selling, Jamie decided he was buying.

The other men were beginning to stir. Jamie felt a little intimidated at the thought of getting to know all these strangers. He was used to his own company. Sure, he'd spoken to other people on the outside, but it was generally safer to keep himself to himself. He'd hooked up with the odd girl from time to time – and they always wanted to talk – but that was different. Still, Jamie didn't think he'd have to worry about 'making friends' here, as people didn't speak much anyway. The guys in his dormitory certainly weren't the chatty type – there was no small talk, chit-chat, or one-liners. None of the usual banter you found among big groups of men. Just the quiet shuffling of people getting dressed and the odd cough. Well, that suited Jamie fine. He'd keep his eyes down and try to stay invisible.

After everyone had showered and dressed, they proceeded downstairs into a canteen-like room where there must have been a couple of hundred other men already seated at wooden tables. Jamie followed his roommates to an empty table with benches on either side. They all shifted up so there were five on each bench. Jamie found himself sandwiched between Jeremiah and a middle-aged man wearing an eye-patch.

Once all the tables in the room were filled, men came in carrying trays stacked with bowls of steaming porridge. A bowl and spoon was placed in front of Jamie and he grabbed his spoon and began to dig in. Suddenly, Jeremiah lunged for his wrist and forced his hand with the spoon back onto the table. He was surprisingly strong and Jamie had no choice but to let go of the implement.

'What are you doing?' Jamie asked. At first he'd thought the man was attacking him, but then he realised he was trying to stop him eating. Jamie was starving. The last time he'd eaten was yesterday lunchtime when John had given him that bread roll. And now this porridge smelt amazing.

Jeremiah waggled his finger at Jamie and tutted, shaking his head in disapproval. Realising that no one else was eating, Jamie reluctantly nodded and mouthed the word 'okay'. Jeremiah gave a smug smile and patted Jamie's shoulder.

A man at another table stood up. Everyone else bowed their heads and Jamie followed suit. The man recited a prayer out loud, thanking God and James Grey for the food they were about to eat. His voice was soft and clear. Once he was seated again, all the men began to eat.

Jamie burnt the roof of his mouth with his first spoonful, but he didn't care. The porridge was thick and sweet and lovely. Even Jeremiah slurping and burping next to him couldn't detract from how good it tasted. And he felt so awake and refreshed, energised for the first time in ages. All he needed was to get rid of these damn crutches and everything would be right with the world.

Once everyone had cleared their plates, all the tables began to empty except for Jamie's. The other men filed out in silent orderly lines. The lack of chatter was still strange and a little disconcerting, but Jamie figured it was better than a load of intimidating noise and the usual fights and scuffles you came across when you found large groups of men in any one place together.

Their table would probably be the next to leave the canteen. Jamie wondered what he would be doing today. Some kind of task maybe. He quite fancied gardening. That would be a pretty nice, easy job he reckoned – weeding and hedge cutting and whatnot. He remembered, as a child, seeing someone on one of those ride-on lawn mowers. Now that's a job he'd enjoy. Maybe you got a choice of what you could do here. He'd definitely opt for the ride-on mower job. He'd have a good chance of getting it, too, as it was a sitting down job, and what with his leg all banged up, he'd be a prime candidate for it.

Jamie's daydream was interrupted by the arrival of several serving staff with large metal vats, which they placed in the middle of their table. They then placed large hessian sacks on the floor behind them. Jamie turned to look and saw the sack immediately behind him was full to the brim with muddy potatoes. Jeremiah reached around and plucked a spud and a knife from the sack. He pointed at Jamie to do the same. Jamie sighed. Bang went his dream of the ride-on mower – he was to be a kitchen hand, a flipping skivvy.

Out of the window, Jamie spied the other men. But not just the men from their canteen, no, it looked like there were hundreds of men all lined up in a vast courtyard. Jamie craned his neck to see further, but he couldn't tell how far the lines stretched in either direction. Perhaps they were going to do some kind of morning exercise.

And then the men began to move away. They walked in an orderly, regular fashion – not quite marching, but almost. Each line peeled away one by one, leaving the courtyard to go who knew where. Maybe they were off to work in the fields.

Three hours later, Jamie's hands were encrusted with mud, blisters and tiny cuts. He'd peeled enough potatoes, carrots, swedes, parsnips and turnips to feed the five thousand. Apart from the sorry state of his hands, he'd actually quite enjoyed getting lost in the monotony of the work. The earthy smell of the vegetables had soothed him. He reckoned he could get on board with this type of work. It was all right.

Lunchtime was a short break where they ate bread and cheese and a few raw vegetables. None of the other men returned for lunch; it was just him and his roommates. Jamie reckoned the others were probably eating in the fields and would be back for their evening meal. He was proved right – the other men did indeed return for supper and the canteen was full once more. While eating his stew, Jamie realised he'd been inside all day. He yearned to poke his nose out into the fresh air, but it didn't look as though he was going to get the chance. He wasn't used to spending so much time indoors. Maybe he could ask John about it. Once supper was over, Jamie cleared his throat and spoke in a loud whisper.

'John...'

John looked up with a frown.

'Can we go outside to get some fresh air?'

John shook his head and put his fingers to his lips. Jamie felt like a child in kindergarten, but he didn't pursue his question. Some of the men on the other tables were throwing him disapproving looks and he didn't have the courage to continue speaking.

Later, once they were back in their dormitory, John approached him.

'You've done well today,' he said. 'You've worked hard. Contributed. I'm pleased.'

Jamie gave a nod.

'Some days we work outside. Not this week though.'

'Right,' Jamie replied. 'Thanks for letting me know. It's just I'm used to—'

John held his hand up to silence him. Jamie stopped mid-sentence. They looked at each other for a moment and then John turned away to continue getting ready for bed. Jamie felt foolish and annoyed, but he guessed he'd have to get used to this not-speaking malarkey if he wanted to stay here. All in all, it wasn't too hard a price to pay. Was it?

It was the kind of summer that Jamie normally loved – warm and dry with the odd thundery shower. Before, when he'd lived outside, he'd always welcomed warm summer evenings and the chance for a comfortable night's sleep, not the usual damp and chilly affair that Britain had to offer. But now, here, under James Grey's hospitality, he had an actual bed in a dry dormitory, clothing, food and safety so the weather was almost irrelevant.

It was amazing how quickly you could get used to something different. He'd been living at the Close for over a month and the days drifted into one another like clouds in an autumn sky. The routine was comforting, the quietness addictive and he'd even grown used to Jeremiah and his childish ways.

John had been true to his word and Jamie alternated his peeling and chopping duties with work outside in the kitchen garden; and this was what he enjoyed the most. There was still no sign of any ride-on mower, but Jamie was content to lose himself in the weeding, cultivating and harvesting of all the many fruits, vegetables and herbs which flourished in the well-stocked garden. Most of them he'd never heard of before, let alone tasted. Today, he was gathering herbs to dry, for use during the winter. The mingling scents of basil, mint and rosemary were making him hungry, so he stuffed a couple of mint leaves into his mouth to chew on. That should keep him going until it was time for lunch.

Jamie mused that he would probably be happy to remain here for the rest of his life. Sure, he missed certain things – alcohol, girls and privacy were his top three – but those were minor in comparison with the safe and secure life he now enjoyed. The rest of the people here were all a bit lifeless, but Jamie reasoned that it was because they had found peace. They were no longer troubled or anxious. They had found a safe place in this violent world.

His leg was healing quickly and he had already discarded his crutches. A slight limp remained, but the doctor he'd seen last week had told him he should be walking normally within a week or two. Jamie stood and heaved up his full basket to bring back to the kitchen. The sun burned the back of his neck, his throat was parched and he could do with a cup of water. As he walked, he sought out the shade of a line of sycamores, their leaves hushed in the still air.

Last week had been his naming ceremony – Jeremiah had been right about his name being changed – and now he was Jamie no longer. He didn't miss his old name. What had it ever brought him? Nothing but misery. He had needed a fresh new name to go with his fresh new life. Jamie had thought it might've been James, but apparently there was only one James around here. Made sense he supposed. No, Jamie's new name was now *Jacob*.

He and a handful of other men had been taken to the cathedral where James Grey had conducted the ceremony himself. It had been a humbling and emotional experience. Jamie touched the metal cross which hung around his neck. It had been presented to him when he'd received his new name, and Jamie treasured it. The only problem was that the chain from which it hung irritated his skin, and an angry red weal had appeared around his neck that itched and burned. They weren't allowed to remove the cross ever – not even when they went to bed – and so Jamie was forever trying to rearrange the chain so that it sat on top of his clothing, away from his bare skin. It was impossible though and the metal kept slipping back. Perhaps it was divine punishment for his sins. A small price to pay.

Jamie nudged open the narrow back door that led to the kitchen. Strangely, there were voices within. John was talking to two robed men. They turned to look as Jamie walked through the door, but he avoided eye contact and placed his full basket on the table, picking up an empty one and turning back around. He would forgo the cup of water for now. These men looked important and he didn't want to hang around as they might think he was eavesdropping.

'Jacob, wait.'

After a moment's hesitation, Jamie realised John was addressing him. It would take a while to get used to this new name of his. He stopped and turned.

'Come here.'

Jamie walked towards John. He felt the men's eyes on him and wondered what they were doing here and why John needed to speak with him.

'This is him?' one of the men asked John. 'This is Jacob?'

John nodded.

The man addressed Jamie. 'We have consulted the doctor and he says you are fit and well. He assures us your leg is healed. Does it trouble you at all?' the man asked.

Jamie shook his head.

'Good. You will come with us now.'

Jamie thought he'd misheard and remained standing when the men began to head to the door.

'Come.'

Jamie looked at John who nodded. John's expression was one of regret and acceptance. What did his expression mean? Why did Jamie have to leave? Perhaps it was temporary and he would be coming back. But the look on John's face told him otherwise.

Woodenly, Jamie put one foot in front of the other and followed the two strangers out of the back door and into the sunshine. He wished he'd been brave enough to take that cup of water now. The heat was punishing, his nerves magnifying his discomfort. The two men were silent, but Jamie wouldn't have expected anything else. He wanted to ask where they were leading him, but his mouth remained shut, his throat dry. Besides, they wouldn't have replied anyway.

They left the courtyard and the kitchen gardens, following a long wide pathway which ran alongside a row of buildings, across a bridge and along the river. At least there was a slight breeze here. Jamie's neck itched and he attempted to wipe the sweat away from the inflamed skin with his muddy fingers. His mind was numb and he couldn't even begin to think where they might be going.

They headed away from the river and into a lush, green water meadow bisected by a huge metal fence which stretched off in both directions. As they approached a sturdy-looking metal gate, one of the men took a set of keys off his belt. They waited as he deftly unlocked it. Once through, he relocked it and they continued walking. So, now he was locked out of the Close. Would he be returning?

There was no one else around and Jamie's nerves intensified further. Perhaps they were actually kicking him out of the Close. Maybe his confession wasn't a secret anymore and they had decided they couldn't shelter a murderer. But how could Jamie go back to a life on the outside after sleeping in a comfy bed and eating three meals a day? The thought filled him with panic. Better to die. Maybe that would be his lot anyway. Or maybe they were going to hand him over to the army for justice. That would be another fate worse than death. He had to stop speculating; he would soon find out. He simply had to be patient.

The grass swished around his ankles as they walked unhurriedly through the meadows. Jamie wasn't sure how long they travelled, but it must've been at least an hour when, up ahead, he spied something glinting in the sunlight. A wall. A high metal wall. Maybe it was a Compound. As they continued, the wall came into focus. Part brick, part metal, about twenty feet high. It reminded him of the Charminster Compound, only there was no shanty settlement outside and there wasn't the usual accompanying stench. The only thing Jamie could make out was a faint sighing hum, like the gathering breeze you might hear before a storm. But there was no wind on his face and the air was still. What was this place? Was it a Compound? A prison? Or was it someplace worse?

CHAPTER TWENTY

RILEY

The guards' AV was a mess. I cleared some papers and bits of machinery off the passenger seat and shoved them onto the back seat, which was covered in a whole heap of other crap. Drumming my fingertips on the steering wheel, I tried to quell my nerves. I really didn't want to spend time alone with Luc, but I had no choice.

He walked towards me with long, loose strides, taking his time. Once he got close, I restarted the engine and slid my sunglasses down over my eyes. He wasn't smiling when he got in.

'I told Liss and Anna they shouldn't be out here working,' he said. 'They look like they're ready to drop. Honestly, they're half-starved and totally exhausted.

'No, I think keeping busy is probably better,' I countered. 'There'd be more time to worry if they were home doing nothing.'

'Mm, Maybe.'

'How's your hand?' I asked.

He lifted it off his lap and looked at it. The blood on the cloth had darkened.

'S'all right.'

'D'you want to stop off at the surgery? Get it looked at?'

'No. It's fine.'

I threw the AV into reverse, swung it back and then slid it into gear before heading for the exit.

Soon we were outside the Perimeter. No sign of any dogs today. The silence between me and Luc was verging on awkward, but I didn't know what to say that would sound natural, so I stayed quiet and kept driving. I still needed to warn Lou about FJ's army and I knew Luc would try to stop me seeing her, so I decided I wouldn't ask him. I'd just do it.

'You okay, Riley?'

'Yeah, fine.'

'You're very quiet.'

'So are you.'

'Worried about FJ?'

'What? No.' I turned to give him a half-smile. Truth was I was bloody petrified of FJ, but I hadn't really let myself think about him. There was so much going on that I hadn't had time to focus on why he was coming here. The Perimeter would keep me safe and so would Pa and Luc and all the guards and our friends. If, against the odds, he did somehow make it past all of them, I would sort him out myself. He was only a boy, nothing more. A boy with too much power.

The circular shape of the Charminster Compound soon came into view. It seemed less daunting than usual and I wasn't sure why. Maybe because it was more familiar now I knew some of the people who lived in its shadow. As we passed the shanty encampment and drew closer to the Compound, it was apparent that the metal entrance gates were firmly shut. There were no people or vehicles hanging around outside on the ramps as usual. We drove past the Walls and I kept glancing across to see if I could spot anyone I knew, but the few faces I saw were unfamiliar.

Driving straight up the noisy metal ramps, I came to a stop outside the gates. Nothing happened. No one came out.

'Use the horn,' Luc said.

I pressed it once, a crease of noise in the smooth silence. We waited. I pressed it again. After a few seconds, one of the smaller side doors opened and two armed guard stepped through. One trained his weapon on the windscreen while the other examined the AV. I buzzed down the window.

'Step out of the vehicle,' the second guard said. 'Hands where I can see them.'

Luc and I did as he asked, raising our hands. The first guard trained his weapon on Luc and gestured for him to stand next to me. Luc walked around to my side of the AV. This wasn't usual protocol for the Compound, but I guessed they'd upped security since the riots.

'Afternoon,' the second guard said, stepping forward and eying me and Luc. 'This isn't your vehicle.'

'It's a Perimeter-guard vehicle,' I replied. 'We're here on guards' business.'

'Your name?'

'Riley Culpepper.'

He nodded. 'We're not allowing entry or exit today.'

'Why's that?' I asked.

'There's been some... unrest.'

'You mean the riots?' I said. Well, that explained the heightened security.

He nodded.

'We're not here to come inside,' I said. 'We've come from the Perimeter to warn you.'

'Warn us?' The guard raised an eyebrow.

'Yes,' I said. 'James Grey's men are on the march again. They're coming this way.'

'Okay,' he said, scratching his cheek. 'Thanks for the information.'

I looked at Luc and then back at the guard. The other one still had his weapon trained on us. 'So... aren't you going to do anything about it?' I asked.

'Like what?'

'Uh, like tell your superiors. Triple security. Warn people. Make some kind of plan.'

'A plan?'

'Your radio's down,' Luc said.

'How did you know that?' the guard snapped, taking a step closer to us. 'How did they know that?' he said to the other guard.

'Because our Perimeter has been trying to contact you to warn you about what's coming,' I said, starting to lose my patience.

'This is Riley Culpepper, Johnny's daughter, and I'm—'

'You're Luc Donovan!' the guard said, his attitude shifting. 'I know you.'

'So Grey's army's really coming here?' the other guard said, concern creeping into his voice.

'We don't know if they'll bother you,' I said, 'but yes, they're expected to reach here on Christmas Eve. What happened to your radio?'

'It's being fixed,' he replied. 'How do you know they're coming? What do they want?'

'It's a long story,' Luc said. 'But they're coming for the Perimeter. You might get lucky,' Luc said. 'They might not stop here.'

'Thanks again for the warning,' the guard said. 'We'll pass on the message. You need to turn around now and go straight back. Stay safe.'

'Thanks,' I replied. 'We okay to get back in our vehicle?'

'Sure.' He turned and walked back to the door. The other guard backed in after him, his gun trained on us the whole time.

The door clanged shut and the silence of the afternoon enveloped us once more.

'Looks like they believe us,' Luc said. 'Let's go.'

We got back into the AV and slammed the doors. I started up the engine and reversed us back down the ramp. 'Just gonna make a quick stop at the Walls to warn Lou.' I braced myself for an argument.

'Thought you might,' Luc replied.

Well, that was a turn-up – he didn't kick off. 'They're exposed out here,' I said. 'It's a shame they can't stay inside the Compound until FJ's gone.'

'They wouldn't want to do that,' Luc said.

'How do you know?'

'They chose to live out here. They could've got jobs inside anytime they wanted, but they prefer to live *their* way.'

'Yeah, but this is a slightly different situation. They're in real danger.'

'They're always in danger. It's how they live. But they'll appreciate the warning. At least they'll be able to stash any valuables away before Grey's army strips them clean.'

I nosed the AV towards the camp and pulled up at the entrance. Two men and a woman were chatting by the wire fence. As soon as they saw us, they stopped talking and tightened their grips on their weapons. The woman came forward. She had dark hair and large silver hooped earrings. Her eyes shone a startling blue in her brown weather-worn face.

'Wait here,' I said to Luc.

'Yeah, right,' he replied.

I got out of the AV and Luc did the same.

'It's okay, it's only the firewood girl,' the shanty said to the men. She turned back to me. 'Who's your friend?'

'This is Luc.'

'Firewood girl?' Luc muttered, turning to me with raised eyebrows. 'You didn't!'

'Talk about it later,' I hissed.

'Unbelievable.'

'Is Lou around?' I asked the woman.

'Sure. Come in,' she replied. 'No weapons.'

We'd already stashed our weapons under the seats. One of my pistols was strapped to my ankle, but they didn't need to know about that. I locked the AV and we strode into the camp. The men nodded at us.

'You know where you're going?' the woman asked.

'Kind of.'

'She'll either be at home or at the gathering place. Head to the 'pound wall, taking every left turn.'

'Thanks.'

'My pleasure, lovey.'

Luc and I headed into the encampment. We'd attracted the attention of a group of children who stared and pointed before coming alongside us. I recognised one of Lou's brothers.

'Hello... Joe, isn't it?'

'Hello,' he said. 'My sister said she's coming to the Perimeter to teach slingshot. Can't you use one?'

'No, I'm afraid I can't.'

'But you're a grown-up,' he said, staring at me in disbelief at my lack of skills. 'I'm really good on slingshot,' he said. 'Everyone knows you'll starve if you can't use one. You better get some lessons quick. Who's he?' Joe pointed at Luc. 'He your boyfriend?' At this, the children tittered.

'This is Luc.'

'Hello,' Luc said. 'Nice to meet you.'

'You her boyfriend?' he repeated.

I was interested to hear how Luc would answer that question, but he was saved by the timely appearance of Lou.

'Now I know you're stalking me,' she said. 'Either that or this place is swankier than the Perimeter and you can't get enough of it. Maybe all the rumours are a lie and it's actually a total dive in there.' She came over and we hugged.

'This is Luc,' I said.

'Hey,' she said. 'Welcome to the Walls. Got time for a chat and a brew?'

I looked at Luc, who shrugged.

'A quick one,' I said to Lou.

'We'll go to the gathering place. Reece'll wanna see you too.'

We walked with her through the narrow paths, chatting while fielding questions from the children, who were growing more outspoken with every step.

'That's enough!' Lou snapped at them. 'Go pester someone else.'

The children grumbled, but did as she asked, melting away into the camp until it was only the three of us left. The tall metal post of the gathering place soon came into view and we followed Lou into the massive tent.

Walking inside, we attracted all the usual stares, but this time they didn't feel quite as menacing. I even got a couple of polite nods. It felt chillier than last time and I noticed the wood-burner wasn't lit. Lou saw me shiver.

'We only light the stove when it's really freezing,' she explained, scanning the room until her eyes landed on a group of men sitting cross-legged on battered cushions at the far end of the tent.

'There's Reece,' she said.

We crossed the space, picking our way through clusters of people, some sitting, some standing, their cloudy breaths hanging in the frigid air. Luc stayed by my side and I felt the tension pulsating off him. I found myself wanting to take his hand, but then I remembered I was still pissed off at him. As we approached the group of men, Reece looked up and caught my eye, his face registering surprise, and then his expression softened into a smile. His gaze shifted to Luc and his smile hardened.

'Lou,' he said, rising to his feet. 'Riley.' He nodded at me. The other men also began to stand, their hands automatically travelling to their weapons once they caught sight of Luc. But Reece made a calming motion with his hands and they stayed seated.

'This is Riley's friend, Luc,' Lou said.

'Come and sit,' Reece said. Some of the men shifted around to make space for us and Luc and I stepped in to join their loose circle. We sat next to each other, sharing a damp floor cushion.

'I'll get you some tea,' Lou said. I watched her disappear into the crowded space, feeling more ill at ease without her.

Reece introduced the five men who sat with him, but their names trickled over me and away like running water.

'We can't stay long,' Luc said.

'Sorry to be blunt, but why are you here?' Reece asked, turning to me. 'Was there a problem with our deal?'

'Not at all,' I replied. 'We came to warn the Compound that Grey's army is on the march again. They'll be passing this way any day. Just thought you'd like to know too.'

Reece swore under his breath and the other men began muttering among themselves.

'How come they're marching?' Reece asked. 'I thought you were holding Grey prisoner at the Perimeter?'

'We are,' Luc replied quickly, not revealing that Grey was in fact dead. 'But his army has a second in command. A boy named FJ. They call him the Voice of the Father. He's calling the shots now.'

'Thanks for the heads-up,' Reece said. 'Appreciate it.'

'They might not even stop here,' Luc said. 'They're coming for us at the Perimeter.'

'All the same,' Reece replied. 'It's good to be forewarned.' He held out his hand to Luc and they shook.

'Here you go,' Lou said, arriving with a tray of tin cups. 'Nettle tea.' She set the tray on the rug and plonked down next to me. Everyone reached forward and took a cup of the steaming liquid. 'What did I miss?' she asked.

CHAPTER TWENTY-ONE

JAMIE

The walls were high, their metallic glint making Jamie's head swim. He needed a drink or he would surely pass out. There were no other guards or people in sight. As Jamie and his two robed escorts drew closer to the wall, a door swung inwards and they walked through. No matter what lay on the other side, Jamie didn't hesitate to enter; he desperately needed to escape the sun's glare.

Thankfully, they came to a covered corridor. It was dark and cool and when one of the men offered Jamie a canteen of water, Jamie almost snatched it out of his hand. *Why couldn't he have offered me some of that an hour ago?* Jamie thought, gulping down the warm liquid. He could easily have polished off the lot, but thought he'd better not. Dribbles ran down the side of his mouth and he wiped them away with the back of his hand, then handed back the half-full canteen.

As his eyes grew accustomed to the low light, he noticed four more robed men. Three stood to attention, their hoods covering their faces, while a fourth talked in a whisper to his companions, or guards, or whoever the hell they were. They were now leaning over a small wooden table filling in a form.

The corridor seemed to curve outwards, following the line of the brick walls – perhaps wrapping itself around the whole Compound. Jamie wondered just how big this place actually was.

An inner door opened, letting in a faint glimmer of sunlight. Jamie silently groaned. He really didn't want to face that heat again, but he had no choice as the two men bade him follow. They walked along another corridor lined with doors. It soon ended and Jamie found himself stepping out into a wide, open amphitheatre.

In his head, Jamie swore several times, his jaw slack with amazement. For spread out before him, the gigantic arena was filled with thousands of dark-robed men. At least Jamie assumed they were men; they might well have been women too, for all he knew, as their faces were concealed by deep hoods.

On either side, and indeed all around them, was some kind of grass-covered seating arrangement that stretched up and around the whole place. Maybe it used to be an old sports stadium or something.

With a jolt, Jamie realised what this place truly was. It seemed the rumours about James Grey were right. Salisbury was not the Godly place of quiet reflection and service it first appeared. For this place was in fact a massive army training camp.

The sight was surreal, for the soldiers were performing some kind of complex fighting manoeuvres in perfect synchronization, the movements both beautiful and terrifying. All the while, they chanted in a low whisper, weird foreign-sounding words. It gave Jamie chills, and he began to wonder – was he being brought here to be punished by this army? Or to join them?

Amid this tumultuous swirl of emotions, he was thankful that the day's heat had finally dissipated. Glancing up, he saw why – an arrangement of cloth sails had been drawn across part of the open roof, presumably to shelter the soldiers from the sun. Casting his eyes back down, he saw swirls of red dust spiralling up from the ground as the men moved upon the dirt floor. The whole area must once have been grassed over, but now most of it had been burnt away by the sun to nothing but patches of earth and straw. Surely it would become a mud bath in here when it rained.

As he and his companions skirted the arena, Jamie's eyes were drawn to a high wooden platform, like a diving board, on which stood a figure who moved with such grace and force that Jamie's jaw dropped still further. Barefoot and with a shaved head, the man wore loose trousers and a vest. He was too far away for Jamie to make out his features, but his graceful movements were being imitated by the soldiers on the ground.

It gave Jamie vertigo to watch the man. The platform was narrow – about six feet by six – and it must have stood at least twenty five feet off the ground. There was no safety fence around him and no soft landing if the man should fall. Jamie couldn't even work out how the man would have got up on the platform, as there were no steps or ladder to be seen.

The two men continued to lead Jamie around the arena in their regular unhurried manner, before turning off down another corridor, under the stands, away from the rows of chanting soldiers. Jamie reluctantly turned away from the sight of the man on the platform and followed his companions through an innocuous wooden door set beneath the raised seating.

He found himself in a room, and it took a moment for his eyes to adjust to the dim light which filtered in through a number of open metal grilles in the wall. A large group of men sat cross-legged on the wooden floor, while a robed soldier spoke to them in a quiet voice. The soldier glanced across at their approach, caught Jamie's eye and pointed to a place on the ground. Jamie's companions nodded and pointed at the same spot on the ground. Self-consciously, Jamie crossed the room and sat with the others. They were dressed the same as him, in loose-fitting, brown, homespun trousers and shirt. They were all clean-shaven with closely cropped hair. None of them acknowledged his arrival but instead kept their eyes focused on their teacher.

Jamie realised his two companions had disappeared. Strangely, he experienced a pang of loneliness. So was this place to be his new home? Was he to train as a soldier? To become one of the robed warriors like those in the arena practicing complicated fighting manoeuvres? The thought thrilled and terrified him. Part of him would love to be able to move like that and maintain such a level of dedication and control, but the more realistic part of him knew that he was no soldier. That they would soon realise he was a coward and a weakling.

'I know some of you are wondering why you are here,' the robed teacher said, mirroring Jamie's thoughts. 'But you do not need to wonder. You are here because Our Father has willed it and He believes you are strong enough to endure it. Because "right" is on our side. So you will gather your courage and draw up your strength and you will become the strongest army this land has ever seen.' He spoke in a calm, measured tone without the yelling or fist-pumping that Jamie might've expected from a soldier.

Jamie trembled inside at the man's words. So he really was to become a soldier. It was all very well this hardened warrior giving a pep talk and trying to inspire them, but there was no way on earth he was cut out for this. He just wasn't. Glancing left and right, he was disappointed to see every other pair of eyes locked onto the teacher, lapping up his words. Was he the only one with doubts and fears?

'Repeat after me,' the man continued. *'We are of God, and the whole world lies in wickedness.'*

'We are of God, and the whole world lies in wickedness,' they chanted, copying his low whispered tone.

Jamie joined in hesitantly.

'*The wicked shall be overthrown and the house of the righteous shall stand,*' the man said.

'The wicked shall be overthrown and the house of the righteous shall stand,' they repeated.

'*God is my Light.*'

'God is my light.'

'*While we live, we serve.*'

'While we live, we serve.'

'Good,' the soldier said. 'These words will sustain you in battle. You will think of them as you fight. You will think of them as you sleep and as you eat. These are the words spoken by Our Father and which will carry you through this world and into the next. We will say these words in our own language and then we will say them in the ancient tongue. You will learn them as they were meant to be spoken. Repeat after me:

'We are of God, and the whole world lies in wickedness – *Scimus quoniam ex Deo sumus et mundus totus in maligno positus es.*

'The wicked shall be overthrown and the house of the righteous shall stand – *Verte impios et non erunt domus autem iustorum permanebi.*

'God is my Light – *Deus lux mea est.*

'While we live, we serve – *Dum vivimus servimus.*

'*Scimus quoniam ex Deo sumus et mundus totus in maligno positus es. Verte impios et non erunt domus autem iustorum permanebi. Deus lux mea est. Dum vivimus servimus.*'

Jamie's voice joined the others as they sat and chanted, their voices merging and whirling, like the whispering of trees or the sighing of the wind. At first the words felt odd on his tongue, like an unknown food or a first kiss. He stumbled over their strangeness. But after a while, he grew used to the sound of them and it seemed as though he might never stop. At moments, the chanting sounded so quiet he could barely make out the words, and other times it would fill his head so it was all he could do not to clap his hands over his ears. But soon, he relaxed into the chanting; his worries dissipating as he lost himself in the sounds, his mind floating upwards and away from himself.

'*Scimus quoniam ex Deo sumus et mundus totus in maligno positus es. Verte impios et non erunt domus autem iustorum permanebi. Deus lux mea est. Dum vivimus servimus.*'

Push-ups, sit-ups, squats, leg thrusts, weights. Gone were the lazy contemplative days of life as an injured kitchen hand. No more weeding and peeling vegetables, or losing himself in idle thoughts. For now Jamie spent all his days training. He really was to become one of James Grey's warriors.

His head had been shaved to a peachy fuzz and every millimetre of his body ached from the punishing exercises he undertook each day. Those beautiful, synchronized fighting moves that Jamie had witnessed on his first day at the camp were not for the likes of him and the other new recruits. Perhaps they would eventually progress to that. But, for now, he and the others rose at dawn, prayed, ate and then followed their trainers as they ran, sprinted, stretched, lifted weights, walked with heavy packs and swam back and forth across the river until they were fit to drown.

Occasionally they might have a rest day where they prayed and chanted, but these were few and far between. There was no quarter given, no slacking off, no sick days. You woke, you trained. In the beginning, some of them would throw up or pass out from the sheer physical effort – Jamie included. But there was no sympathy or relief. You pushed on through without complaint.

After several weeks of intense physical discomfort and

sheer panic that he wasn't cut out for this life, Jamie eventually adjusted to the new routine. His leg was as good as new and his whole body had grown sleek. His previous life on the outside had kept him pretty tough, but now he'd acquired a seemingly unlimited energy that he'd never before possessed. Muscles defined his body and gave strength and grace to his movements. But there was no time to contemplate any of this. No time to worry or analyse what he was doing, or what he was becoming. His thoughts were all about keeping up with the others and making it through each new set of pain barriers. At night, he fell into a deep slumber the moment his head hit the pillow and in the morning he was up and dressed within minutes of his eyes snapping open.

He and his brothers, as he now thought of his fellow trainees, ate and slept on the floor inside the walls of the training camp and they trained outside in the water meadows, whatever the weather. Aside from their trainers, no one else spoke. No conversation lit up the hallways by day, no whispered discussion echoed around their chamber at night. The only words Jamie uttered were prayers or the warriors' chant, which looped around his brain like a mantra. Jamie couldn't imagine life without it. The words grounded him and focused his energy:

Scimus quoniam ex Deo sumus et mundus totus in maligno positus es. Verte impios et non erunt domus autem iustorum permanebi. Deus lux mea est. Dum vivimus servimus.

He fell asleep with the words swirling about his brain and he awoke the following morning with the chant fully formed on his lips. He could not remember their meaning word-for-word, but he knew that there was something in there about 'the light of God', and he liked to imagine this holy light was fuelling him on. Infusing his body with purpose and energy.

One warm September morning, Jamie awoke as usual and dressed in his loose trousers and tunic. He and the others knelt on the dusty wooden floor to pray, but instead of their trainer leading them in prayer, the man issued a curt command:

'All stand and follow me. Stay in line.'

Jamie and the others did as they were bid and filed out of their quarters. As they exited the room, others joined them in the corridors, everyone moving slowly and surely towards the outdoor central arena.

Once Jamie and his brothers reached the arena, it quickly began to fill up. More trainees joined them, along with the robed warriors and their trainers. Row upon row of them. Hundreds became thousands. Only inches separated each person and it soon became warm. Uncomfortably so. The smell of earth and sweat hung thick in the air, and dust fogged Jamie's vision where so many feet had disturbed the dry earth. A relay of barking coughs started up and then gradually grew silent. There was no murmuring or whispering speculation as you might expect. The soldiers remained still, eyes facing forward. Then, through the heavy silence, the loudspeaker squealed to life.

CHAPTER TWENTY-TWO

RILEY

Despite the apparent civility between us and the shanties, Luc's left heel jigged up and down – a sure sign that he wasn't relaxed. This small show of insecurity endeared him to me again and I remembered the Luc who was my friend, the Luc I trusted, before all the weirdness had started up between us. And now I'd brought him into this place. A place he didn't want to be. But he'd come anyway. Because of me.

I tried to catch his eye, but he was on alert, scoping out the immediate vicinity while keeping one eye on Reece and his buddies. His jawbone flexed and his eyes narrowed. I could see him working out escape routes and contingency plans in his head.

'Riley, got a minute to talk?' It was Reece.

'Yeah, sure,' I said. I felt Luc tense up some more.

'Alone,' Reece said.

I raised my eyebrows, not sure how to answer.

'Why alone?' Luc asked Reece, his eyes narrowing further. 'Why can't you say what you need to say here? In front of me.'

He ignored Luc, his eyes resting on me, waiting for my reply.

'It's okay, Luc,' I said. 'I'll only be a sec, okay?'

Luc scowled as Reece and I rose and left the circle. Reece led me a little way off, out of earshot of the rest of them before speaking. He leant in close, his breath warm on my ear.

'What's the deal with your friend?' he asked.

'Who? Luc?'

'He doesn't like me,' Reece said. 'And he doesn't like you being here. Is he going to cause us any trouble? Should we be worried about him?'

'Luc? No, definitely not. He's just looking out for me, that's all.'

'You and him together then?'

I considered his question – were Luc and I together? No. I didn't think we were. The thought made me die a little inside. I wondered why Reece was even asking me such a question.

'No,' I said. 'No, we're not together.'

'Good,' Reece replied. And then he smiled, his shoulders relaxing. 'Send him home and stay a while. I'll drop you back later.'

Why was he being so nice? And then I realised... oh no, did he *like* me? No. He couldn't. This was Reece, who'd made it abundantly clear he didn't want me around.

His invitation to stay here without Luc made my stomach flip, but not in a good way.

'Thanks,' I said, 'but I can't. I have to get back. My pa... there's too much to do at home.'

'Just one drink then. One for the road. Lou can entertain your friend while we talk.'

'I don't think Luc will want to—'

'Lou!' Reece called out, cutting me off. 'Give Riley's friend a tour of the Walls. Show him the sights.' And then he casually placed his arm around my shoulders. I froze.

'Another time, Reece,' I stammered. 'I really have to get back.'

'You really don't,' he whispered in my ear.

Whatever I'd thought of Reece before – his charm and his looks – I definitely wasn't feeling it now. His arm around me felt proprietorial and threatening and I was pretty sure it was only done to piss Luc off.

It worked.

Luc stood and strode towards us, a snarl distorting his face. Lou followed, putting a restraining hand on his arm. 'What's going on, Reece?' she asked.

'Yeah, Reece,' Luc said. 'What's going on?' His voice sounded quiet and measured, but his expression was murderous.

'Nothing's going on,' Reece replied, a smile curling on his lips. 'Just thought you might like a tour of the place. Riley's already had the honour, so it'd be a bit boring for her. But I can keep her company while you and Lou have a wander round.'

'Riley,' Luc said. 'Why's that *shanty* got his arm around you?'

'Not sure I like the tone of your voice, mate,' Reece said, tightening his hold on me and tilting his head. 'You're a guest here. Wouldn't hurt to show a little respect.'

A couple of Reece's friends rose to their feet, all pretence at friendliness forgotten. The whole place had suddenly grown quieter.

'Guys,' Lou said. 'Let's take it easy, yeah? We're not enemies. There's a bigger threat out there. We need to get things sorted before Grey's hoodies show up.'

'Riley,' Luc said. 'We should get going.'

He and Reece glared at each other and I prayed nothing would come of it. Luc would get battered, or worse, if things kicked off. Luc's fingers flexed and I held my breath. Reece's grip on my shoulders meant that it wouldn't be easy to extricate myself without him losing face. And if Reece felt humiliated, that would only make the situation worse. This thing would escalate out of all proportion if I didn't do something to stop it.

'Thanks, Reece,' I said, with what I hoped was a flirty smile. 'I'll come and have a drink with you another time, but I can't right now. Not with everything that's going on. I have to get back. They're expecting us.'

Lou caught my eye and raised an eyebrow. 'Reece,' she said. 'Should I start warning people about Grey's men? Do you want us to post more lookouts?'

I could have kissed her for attempting to help me out.

Reece's hold on me loosened as he stared at the faces around him looking for some kind of leadership. He cleared his throat. 'Yeah,' he said to Lou. 'We need to call up the council. We'll meet in fifteen minutes round the back.' He finally dropped his hand from around my shoulder. 'Riley,' he murmured. 'Sorry, but that drink will have to wait. There's too much to sort out here at the moment.'

'That's a shame,' I said. 'But we'll do it another time.' *Like hell we will*, I thought.

'I'll hold you to it,' he replied, tipping my chin up with his finger. 'You're not a girl to break your word, are you?'

I shook my head. 'Course not.'

Luc took another step closer, murder in his eyes, but I stepped between him and Reece, took Luc's hand and pulled him away towards the exit.

'I'll show you the way out,' Lou said quickly.

Reece's friends sank back into their cushions as he sauntered back to join them. I couldn't believe I'd actually been attracted to him. What had I been thinking? Yes, he was good-looking, but he was also intimidating and, as I'd just discovered, a bit of a bully. He scared me.

As we made our way out of the marquee, Luc's hand dug painfully into mine. He pulled me along, anger radiating off him and I wasn't looking forward to the conversation we were about to have.

'You okay?' Lou said. 'Awkward, or what.' She gave a nervous laugh.

'Yeah,' I replied. 'Just a bit.'

'What are you boys like?' Lou smirked.

Luc's scowl deepened.

'No offence,' she said to him, 'but I think it's probably best if you don't come back to the Walls.'

'You think?' Luc replied.

'Thanks for coming though,' she said. 'It was good of you to warn us about Grey. We're grateful, even if things did get tense back there.'

Once Lou had walked us safely back to the AV and waved us goodbye, I realised what an idiot I'd been. I'd been so keen to prove Luc wrong about Lou and the shanties, to show him I knew better, that I hadn't once considered his safety. I was glad I'd warned Lou, but that was it.

'What the hell, Riley,' he spat once we were in the AV. 'What *was* that? Are you and that moron together or something?'

'Of course not. I just didn't want to make him angry, that's all. You two looked like you were about to beat the crap out of each other. I'm sorry,' I said. 'I shouldn't have asked you to go there.'

Luc didn't speak. I was pretty sure I'd pissed him off for good. But part of me dared to hope he might've been just a tiny bit jealous. I started up the engine and we headed back towards the Perimeter in silence.

If I'd had any hope that our afternoon trip together might have mended mine and Luc's relationship, I was wrong. It had pushed us still further apart and shown Luc that I wasn't worth his effort. I didn't blame him for being mad at me. After every-thing that had happened, I'd only succeeded in making things even worse between us. And now we had to go home to try to save our settlement from a crazy boy with a God complex. I bit back an irrational wave of laughter. Maybe I was losing it.

I drove slowly, not wanting to reach our destination, not wanting to think anything or feel anything because it was all too bloody depressing.

'Stop the car,' Luc said.

'Huh? What?' I replied.

'The car. Stop the car.'

I did as he asked and brought the AV to a reluctant halt.

We were in the middle of nowhere, the Charminster Compound a dim shape behind us and our home not yet in sight. The December afternoon was ending early with a darkening sky and a bleeding sun. A couple of birds streaked through snow clouds in the direction of the Perimeter.

I was sick of everything. Sick of trying to do the right thing. Sick of trying to help people. Sick of trying to patch things up with Luc. Sick of the whole situation. But I had to keep it together for a short while longer. I'd let Luc have his say and then I'd go home and stick broken glass on the walls and do whatever other tasks were required of me. I was torturing myself with a mental image of Luc and Lissy as a loved-up couple when I realised Luc was saying something.

'Can you turn off the engine?'

I did as he asked, a feeling of doom enveloping me, the silence loaded and painful.

'What's wrong with you?' he asked.

'Everything. Apparently.'

'What? Stop wallowing and tell me what's wrong. Why are you so determined to help everyone except yourself? And why do you keep putting yourself in unnecessary danger all the time? I'm worried about you, Riley.'

I stared ahead at the bruised sky.

'Riley.' His voice was heartbreakingly soft. 'Did you hear what I said? I'm worried about you.'

I felt his eyes on me, but I didn't turn to face him. Instead, I concentrated my gaze on the outside, seeing nothing.

Suddenly, I decided that things couldn't go on as they were. I had to tell him the truth. About how I really felt. What did I have to lose? Except my pride, and that wasn't worth a damn. Any day, FJ would be arriving with his army. There was no time left for worrying about what Luc might think of me, when we might not even make it through this thing alive. The whole Perimeter might not make it. I didn't want to die regretting my stubborn, fearful silence. But first I had to check something. I cleared my throat.

'Are you and Liss...?'

'Me and Liss, what?'

'You know?'

'No, I don't know. Riley, why do you always do this?'

'Do what?' I finally turned to look at him, but now it was him looking straight ahead out of the windscreen.

He shook his head. 'Why do you always imagine things that aren't there? Put words in my mouth? Cut me off before I've finished talking?'

'What? I don't do those things.'

'You do. You think you know what I want, but you have no idea and you don't ever stick around long enough to listen. You drive me totally crazy.' He threw open the passenger door and got out, standing next to the AV, the chill wind ruffling his clothes and hair.

I sat where I was for a moment before opening my door and walking around to join him. It was freezing outside.

'Why do you want to push me away, Riley?' he asked, his voice small in the vast wilderness.

'Me push you away?' I said. 'It's not me. It's you doing that.

You've been really weird lately. Criticising me and questioning my judgement all the time.'

'When have I ever done that?' he said.

'That night I came to yours for dinner. You were really mean.'

'What? I was worried about you, that's all.'

'Well, thanks, but I don't need your concern.'

'Really? You'd rather I didn't care? Do you want me to agree with you all the time? Even if I think you're making a mistake that could put you in danger.'

'No.' I scowled. 'But—'

'I was worried about you,' he repeated. 'I still am. I can never win with you, Riley. Why do you always take things the wrong way?'

'Because I'm scared,' I replied without thinking, and realised it was true.

He faced me, unsmiling, and I didn't know what to think or say next. His normally blue eyes had turned dark grey against the wintry sky. I hugged my body to keep warm.

'Riley—'

'Luc, you're—'

'Shh, let me finish for once.'

'Sorry. Go on.'

'Thank you.' He relaxed his glare and gave me a smile and an eye-roll. 'Liss is a lovely girl, but we're friends. That's all. She's only been here a day and we've barely even spoken. She's worried about her parents and that's it. I'm just trying to make the poor girl feel welcome. The rest is in your imagination.'

Embarrassment washed over me. Luc and I weren't even together and I'd accused him of having feelings for someone else.

'Riley,' he said. 'Ever since I've known you, it's always been *you*.'

I wanted to say something, but more than that, I wanted to

hear what he would say next. So I kept my mouth shut, biting my bottom lip to stop myself interrupting again.

'It's always been you, Riley.' He said the words again and put his hand out to briefly touch my cheek. 'It was never Liss and it was never Skye. There was never any chance of that. I loved Skye like a sister and she knew it. She would've dropped her crush eventually and been happy for us. That's who she was. She was a sweet, generous person with a big heart who hero-worshipped you and had a little crush on me. But because she died, we never got past that stage. We're stuck in this... this guilt-ridden limbo.' He sighed. 'Riley, it's only ever been you and you're crazy if you think anything else.'

I revelled in his words, not quite believing he was actually saying them.

'And I know all sorts of strange crap's been getting in the way of everything,' he continued, 'and we've still got more to get through before any kind of "normal" can happen, but...' He broke off.

My heart was pounding and my mouth had gone dry. I licked my lips and tried to form a word, but I couldn't speak.

He ran a hand over his head and stared at me. 'I love you.' There was no smirk, no joking. Nothing but his deep blue eyes staring into mine.

I still couldn't speak, so I did the only thing I could possibly do. I stepped forward and put a hand on his cheek, guided his face to mine and kissed him. A long slow kiss that made my insides disappear and my mind spin into nothingness. He felt warm and strong and alive and beautiful. His arms came around my body and his grip tightened, gathering me in closer to him.

How had I got it so wrong before? How had I managed to convince myself he had just wanted to be friends? Or maybe I'd done it on purpose. Too afraid to let myself have this kind of happiness, so I'd pushed him away. But this, right now, right here, felt so good that I must have been crazy to deny what had been there all along.

Luc's kiss was deep and warm. Demanding. Urgent. He broke off and unwound my scarf, moved his mouth to my neck, to my ear where he whispered, 'I love you,' before bringing his mouth back to my lips. His hands moved from my back to my waist. He sought out the skin beneath my sweater and moved his hands across my hips, lighting up nerve endings. Electricity in his touch as he trailed cool fingers across my stomach, letting them drop below the line of my jeans.

I gasped and he pulled me closer, our kisses deepening further. Even as we became so immersed in each another, I knew we'd have to stop. There was no time for us. Not yet. It was too dangerous out here. But I wasn't going to be the one to pull away first. It wasn't physically possible. My body was too desperate for his. My hands pushing their way beneath his T-shirt, feeling the smooth muscles of his back and wanting to feel more.

As he lifted me up, I wrapped my legs around his waist, my arms moving from around his body, up to his hair and the nape of his neck. His kisses touched the core of my body as though we were connected from the inside out.

'Luc,' I whispered.

'I know,' he replied.

'Can we go somewhere?' I asked, picturing a warm quiet place for just the two of us.

Easing me back down, he kissed me again, his hands in my hair. 'We have to get home,' he murmured. 'If we're out any longer, Johnny will kill me for putting you in danger. He'll send out a search party.'

I knew he was right about Pa, but I didn't want to go back. I wanted to run away, just Luc and me, and forget about our responsibilities. Forget about the dangers. Forget about FJ.

Luc and I had found each other again and I didn't want our

twisted situation to get in the way of us anymore. As I breathed in the warm scent of him, I was overwhelmed, consumed, terrified and euphoric.

'Promise you'll never doubt me again,' he said. 'I love you, Riley. Nothing and no one will change that.'

'I promise,' I replied. 'I love you too.'

CHAPTER TWENTY-THREE

JAMIE

Standing in the arena with his brothers, trainees and warriors alike, Jamie flicked his eyes to the raised platform where a man stood, dressed in dark robes with the crimson trim, denoting he was one of Grey's favoured disciples. His voice pierced through the loudspeaker, stabbing at Jamie's ears after weeks of hearing nothing but whispers.

'There has been a vile and vicious attack,' the man said, pausing to let his eyes skim across the thousands of bowed heads. 'Our Father's life hangs in the balance...'

At this, a collective gasp from the arena. Even a couple of shouts from behind. Jamie resisted the urge to turn his head to see who had cried out.

'We must all now speak to God and beg for Our Father's recovery,' the disciple continued. 'Every one of you must kneel, bow your head and pray for Our Father. For without him, we are lost. We are nothing. We are cast back out into the wilderness to become dust.'

There was a moment's silence before he spoke again.

'Kneel!' he commanded.

As one, Jamie and his brothers sank to their knees and

bowed their heads. While they began to mouth the prayers, Jamie wondered what on earth could have happened to James Grey. Attacked? How? Was it soldiers? Army? Raiders? Had the whole Close been attacked or was it one person acting alone? An inside job perhaps?

As the hours passed there was no let-up. One speaker was replaced by another to lead their prayers. And then another. The hours spent on the ground meant his neck now ached from supporting his bowed head. His legs had grown numb, his stomach growled and his bladder complained, but Jamie told himself that everyone else must be in the same predicament.

They stayed kneeling like that on the hard ground from dawn until dusk, when they were at last invited to stand and return to their quarters. The men creaked to their feet and shuffled from the arena. They were given bread and water and told to pray in their beds as they fell asleep. The next morning, after being led back outside into the blazing heat, Jamie prayed more fervently than the day before. He begged God to return Grey to health and to punish the people who had carried out the attack. But this wish for his leader's recovery was not entirely altruistic. It was mainly so that he, Jamie, would be allowed to continue with his new warrior life and not be forced to leave Salisbury. He also threw in a few sly prayers to request an end to his discomfort, to relieve the heat and to ease his bent back and sore knees.

Jamie adjusted his position, putting more weight onto his left leg to try to stop the cramp developing in his right calf. He preferred the tough days of training to this uncomfortable inactivity. The disciples' prayers had now merged into an incomprehensible drone and Jamie had to keep pinching his fingers to stop himself falling asleep. What would happen if he accidentally nodded off? He'd be punished for sure.

The following day, prayers in the arena continued, but summer's heat had been replaced by cool winds and spattering raindrops. Jamie didn't know which was worse – to be thirsty and dripping in sweat, or to be cold, shivering and damp. He was dismayed that he still had these old self-pitying thoughts. Over the past few weeks, Jamie believed he had left his old persona behind; that he was now *Jacob* – a better, more Godly human being. That he was a warrior who truly belonged to Grey's Church of the Epiphany. So why did he still have these doubts and feelings of resentment when all these other men were so obedient and true?

While he was trying to come to terms with his failings as a human being, a commanding voice on the tannoy system punctured Jamie's thoughts:

'All stand.'

Jamie blinked his eyes open and chanced a look up at the speaker's platform. A robed man stood unmoving. Nothing new about that; but this particular disciple had a presence about him which the others had not possessed.

Jamie found himself rising to his feet along with his brothers. His muscles enjoyed this chance to stretch out, and Jamie had to stop himself from rolling his shoulders and pulling at his limbs. He chewed the inside of his cheek as he stared up at the disciple and, when the man began to speak, Jamie realised he knew that voice. He had heard it once before, back when he first arrived at the Close. It was one of the Listeners, one of the men who had heard his confession. The younger one – Matthew.

'I am here to introduce myself to you,' Matthew said, his voice reedy but confident through the loudspeaker. 'Our Father is gravely ill and we do not yet know if he will recover.' He paused to allow the impact of his words to permeate the arena. 'But he is still Our Father and we will pray for him with every ounce of strength in our bodies and souls.

'It pains me to tell you that his voice was damaged during the attack and He is unable to speak at present. Therefore, he has decreed that I should become *His Voice*.

'I am now *the Voice of the Father* and all his words will go through me. When I speak to you, it is His words I speak. I am *the Voice of the Father*. All kneel.'

Jamie sank to his knees once more, Matthew's words spinning through his brain. If James Grey died, would this young boy take his place? Jamie didn't know if he liked the idea of that.

The soldiers' days of prayers lasted a full two weeks, until finally, miraculously, James Grey was considered healed and out of danger. It transpired that Grey's vocal cords had been damaged beyond repair and so Matthew's position as the Voice of the Father was made permanent.

Jamie's days continued as before, only they were now so busy that he barely had a moment to think of anything other than the increasingly gruelling exercises they were expected to complete. Their fitness regime was also interspersed with weapons training: rifle, handgun, short-handled knife and sword practice.

Some days, they were taken to a separate nearby Compound containing hundreds of horses. There, they were taught to ride and fight on horseback. To Jamie's surprise, he excelled at everything, with sharp reflexes, a steady hand and a keen eye. He and several others were quickly moved up to a different, more challenging group.

They had also begun to train inside the actual arena where Jamie had first seen the robed warriors. In fact, Jamie hadn't seen the warriors inside the Compound for quite a while now. Had they gone? Did this mean the warriors were training somewhere else? Or were they actually fighting a real enemy on the outside? Maybe it was something to do with the attack on Grey.

Jamie wouldn't want to be in their enemy's shoes. Grey's robed warriors were terrifying. He wondered if he would ever be expected to go out and fight. Although he was competent in training, he wasn't so sure he'd be brave enough in a battle situation. Would a day come where he would be made to fight for real? He guessed so, but he hoped not.

Another month passed. The weather grew stormy and the arena, as Jamie had predicted, now churned with thick oozing mud. This did not mean they could slack off in their training. The men continued on in all weathers, learning to put up with the conditions, their clothes constantly damp, their quarters dripping and chilly, their muscles always aching. To Jamie, these squalid living arrangements were a step up from what he was used to – hardened to the elements as he was – but many of his brothers suffered discomfort and illness, although they never dared complain.

Jamie's question about the warriors was soon answered as several wounded soldiers began to return. A makeshift hospital was set up on the east side of the Compound in a couple of training rooms, and medical staff were brought in from elsewhere. Jamie idly wondered if he would see Miriam, the doctor who had fixed up his leg all those weeks ago. He probably owed her his life; there was no way he would've survived on the outside with that kind of injury. But any medics he happened to glimpse were male.

There was obviously some kind of conflict out there, but as usual he was kept in the dark. Jamie attempted to stifle his curiosity, but the fact of the matter was he was burning to know what was going on beyond the walls. He tried to ask a few subtle questions, but everyone else seemed content to remain ignorant.

Unfortunately, it wasn't long before Jamie and his brothers were back in the arena on their knees praying for their leader once more and this time it was worse – James Grey had been captured by their enemies, held hostage for reasons unknown. This could only mean one thing – a full-scale war was coming.

On his knees in the mud once more, listening to the

monotonous words of the disciples, Jamie tried to keep his mind on the prayers he was supposed to be sending to God. But the truth was, he was freezing cold and miserable. He believed they would be much more use to Grey continuing with their training, rather than kneeling in the dirt all day. At least the sun was shining now, but it was merely the shadow of a sun, with no real warmth.

He mouthed the prayers while practicing fighting manoeuvres in his head. He was anticipating his opponents' moves and blocking imaginary blows, when suddenly two sets of real hands grabbed Jamie's arms and hauled him to his feet. Without thinking, Jamie twisted out of their grip and assumed a fighting stance. Then he opened his eyes wide and blinked in the bright sunshine, remembering where he was. As his eyes adjusted, they focused on two robed guards, their faces concealed. Jamie immediately lost his aggression, bowing his head in submission.

After a couple of moments' hesitation, one of the guards gave him a sharp nudge sideways on the shoulder with the tips of his fingers and so Jamie turned and began to walk ahead of them, picking his way through a sea of bowed heads, his heart hammering in his chest. Had they read his mind? Could they have known that he wasn't really praying? Not one person glanced his way. Every head remained bent, eyes presumably shut tight. The disciple on the platform did not miss a beat as Jamie was led from the arena.

In order to calm himself, Jamie began to recite the warriors' chant. Though he did not speak it out loud, the words instantly soothed him and slowed his heart rate to a steady thud. Once out of the arena, the robed men headed along a corridor and into one of the dimly lit exit chambers. Keys were procured, locks undone, doors opened and closed once more. They passed through a final door which clanged shut behind them with solemn finality.

Unshaded sunshine now assaulted Jamie's eyes as he found

himself outside the arena walls with just his two enigmatic guards for company. The world beyond the walls appeared vast and empty without the familiar security of his warrior brothers around him.

Was he being evicted or were they returning him to the Close? Why now? Why at such a critical time, when James Grey's life was in jeopardy? Was it a coincidence or did they somehow think that Jamie had something to do with the attack? He tried to push out these thoughts by clinging to the mantra in his head, but he was so familiar with the words that he was now able to chant while thinking other things at the same time.

Here, beyond the metal walls of the arena, snatches of the disciple's prayer came to him on the chill autumn breeze, the loudspeaker sending the man's words out into the wide sky, sometimes dipping low and other times swooping high and out of earshot. As they walked, the words of the prayer gradually faded. Jamie and his companions were moving inexorably further from the Compound, back across the water meadows where stubborn beads of morning dew still clung to the long grass.

Would nothing remain stable in his life? When Jamie had first arrived at the Close he thought he was fated to become a kitchen hand and had grown strangely content to chop vegetables and weed the garden. But just as he was accepting his lot, he had been wrenched from it and thrust into the world of the warrior. This too, he had gradually come to accept. So now what? Jamie was in their hands. He had no free will in this place. He had to follow where they led and ask no questions. He had to live a life of acceptance.

If his life was no longer his own, he should stop questioning and give himself over to these people. He should recite their words and block out all other thoughts. Suddenly, up ahead, a flapping of wings as dozens of goldfinches took to the air like overgrown bumblebees, their black-and-yellow markings catching sunbeams. Jamie watched their playful flight, envying such uncomplicated freedom. No one told the birds what to do; they just did their thing, followed their natural instincts. They had no choices to make; nature chose for them.

The meaning of the mantra suddenly came to him:

Deus lux mea est – God is my Light.

Dum vivimus servimus – While we live, we serve.

Up until now he'd been going along with things because of the benefits of this place, the safety and security it offered. But now he realised he needed to truly commit. The birds served nature. Nature was their god. Jamie would be like these joyful goldfinches. He would follow his God. He would let James Grey dictate his life, because it would be easier that way. He would stop worrying and wondering and just accept what came to him. The mantra filled his thoughts and a smile lit his face as he continued walking across the dew-sodden grass, the hopeful sound of birdsong in his ears.

CHAPTER TWENTY-FOUR

RILEY

'You nearly finished?' Luc asked.

'Not yet,' I replied, running a cloth through the barrel of my Magnum. 'Still got another one to do after this.'

It was late evening and we were sitting cross-legged on the floor of one of Pa's underground storerooms cleaning our weapons and sorting out ammunition supplies. Although faced with an impending dire situation, I had never felt happier. Since this afternoon, everything had taken on a brighter hue, a less sinister aspect. The rations were low, but we would manage. The weather was harsh, but spring would return. An army was coming, but Luc loved me.

Luc loved me. And I loved him. And nothing else mattered.

With Luc I could face a hundred FJs.

Throughout the Perimeter, work continued at a fevered, panicked pace. Everyone pitched in no matter what their age – children, adults, the elderly. No rest, no sleep. With only the briefest breaks to eat.

We had sent two copters out that evening to see if they could spot FJ's army. We knew they marched by night and so it would be almost impossible to spot them, but we had to try. We needed to know how far away they were. How much time we had left.

Would FJ really have the nerve to attack if he didn't get what he wanted, i.e. me and Grey? We would soon find out, as Grey was dead and Liss wasn't about to betray me to her psycho brother. FJ would be a fool to attempt an outright attack on the Perimeter. We could last out for weeks in here. Months. But then I remembered the sight of Grey's men surrounding the Ringwood Perimeter – the dead guards and the rigged explosives – and a drop of doubt tainted my conviction. My moment of worry was blotted out with a long deep kiss from Luc. His hands cupping my face. His touch tangling my thoughts. This thing with FJ had become an inconvenience rather than a fear, taking me away from where I wanted to be. Here. Now. In this kiss.

Luc and I broke off at the approach of footsteps.

'This way.' Pa's voice. He ducked his head to enter the subterranean room, followed by some of our guys from the Perimeter, along with Luc's Uncle Rufus, all lugging wooden crates.

Luc gave me a rueful smile and jumped to his feet. He took some of the crates from Pa, stacking them with the others against the wall.

'Luc,' Rufus said, putting the crates on the floor and holding out his arms. 'Not too old to give your uncle a hug, are you?'

Luc grinned and complied.

'Is that you, Riley?' he said. 'I hear you've become quite an asset to the Perimeter.'

I blushed at the compliment. Luc's uncle had always been larger than life. But in a good way. I laid down my weapon and got a hug too. It had been ages since we'd last seen him. The room grew crowded as several more men and women appeared, laden with crates upon crates.

Rufus was rumoured to be a weapons manufacturer – either

that or an extremely competent arms dealer – but it was something he would never confirm or deny. Knowledge like that was dangerous to his health. He didn't even tell us where he lived – as much for our own safety as his.

'Are you staying?' Luc asked his uncle.

'Sadly, no. I'm needed elsewhere. But I'll come back if things get too hairy, okay?'

Luc nodded. 'What goodies did you bring us?'

'Ammo mainly. But there are a few hand guns and I also managed to get hold of some grenades.'

There was a moment of stunned awe at this revelation.

'I know, I know,' he said, hands up in false modesty. 'I'm a superstar genius, right?'

'I'd have to agree with you, Uncle,' Luc said. 'Those could come in very handy.'

'Good. Well, sorry to drop in and run, but I have to go. Great to see you guys. Take care of each other and let's hope you won't have to actually use any of this stuff.'

We hugged again and he turned and made his way out of the room.

'Riley,' Pa said, before leaving. 'Can you get this ammo distributed to all the guard posts on the wall.'

'Sure. Anything else?'

'That's it for now. It'll take a while. Come and see me or Eddie when you're done.' He singled out four of the men who had entered the room with him. 'Wait here. Riley'll tell you where these boxes are needed.'

And so the rest of the night was spent distributing ammunition and counting and allocating weapons. It was a mammoth job. One of too many. I hoped that if FJ did show up, it wouldn't be any time before his expected date of Christmas Eve.

We worked until we were done. I managed to get about three hours sleep from 4 a.m. to 7 a.m., and then when I opened my eyes at the sound of the alarm clock, my first thought was of

Luc. I smiled and curled into myself for a moment, allowing myself the brief luxury of remembering yesterday's journey back from the Walls, before flinging back the covers and preparing for the day ahead.

I opened my blackout blinds and had to shield my eyes. Another bright, crisp morning. A day for walking in the woods, for talking in the sunshine. A day for lovers, not a day for war. But we had no choice in the matter. Trouble was coming to our door and we had to deal with it head on. No point hoping for the best. Not in this world. My room was freezing as usual, so I showered briefly, enjoying the heat of the jets, and threw on some warm clothes.

As I came down the stairs, Pa was coming in through the front door. The skin beneath his eyes bruised from lack of sleep.

'Morning, sweetheart. Did you manage to get any shut-eye?'

'Yeah, a few hours. You look like you could use some too.'

'Later,' he said. 'I'll just have a coffee and rest my eyes for a minute or two.'

I followed him into the kitchen where a note from Ma rested on the table:

Morning darlings, Gone to the crèche with Liss and Annabelle, see you later xxx.

Rather than build defences or distribute supplies, Ma had volunteered to help look after the babies and toddlers while their parents worked at securing the Perimeter. She had wanted me to help out too, but there was no way I was sitting inside with a roomful of babies. Not with everything else that was going on. It looked like she'd roped Liss and Annabelle into volunteering with her today.

Pa sat at the table and sipped his watery coffee, while I put some porridge on the stove.

'Want some?'

'No thanks.'

'Well, I'm making you some anyway,' I replied. 'You have to eat.'

He nodded vaguely.

'Did the copters get back?' I asked.

'They did.'

'And? Did they spot them?'

Pa shook his head. 'I didn't expect them to. FJ's not stupid. He'll have his army marching through the woods, under cover where we can't see them.'

'They'll have to come out sometime,' I replied.

'Yeah, but it's catching them when they do. They're sneaky buggers.'

'What do you need me to do today?' I asked. 'Are we on track? D'you think we'll be safe enough?'

'Truthfully?' he replied. 'I don't know. All we can do is keep up with the prepping. We should have done a lot more a lot earlier. The type of warfare we're facing takes years of planning, not days.' He closed his eyes for a moment and pinched the bridge of his nose.

'So what can I do? Shall I help Luc out with—'

'Eddie and Luc left early on a supply run.'

'What? They've left the Perimeter?' My head swam at the news. It had been okay when Luc and I were outside together. But now he was out there without me. If anything happened...

'Eddie heard some chatter on the radio.' Pa interrupted my worries. 'Something about a trading convoy travelling east of Christchurch. He thought it was worth a shot to try to track them down. Seems to think he can get to them before lunchtime. If they're trading decent food supplies, it'll be worth paying over the odds to get the lot. We might need it if we get... stuck in here for a while.'

'What time did they leave?' I asked.

'About five-ish this morning.'

I did a quick calculation in my head. That meant they'd

been on the road for two and a half hours already. They should have caught up to the convoy by now and then it could take two or three more hours to negotiate a deal and load up the trucks. Then another two hours to drive home. Hopefully they should be back by 2 p.m. at the latest. I would have to swallow my fear and get busy to take my mind off it.

I had an idea of my own I wanted to try and I couldn't work out whether it was completely stupid or whether it was genius. I was originally going to run it past Luc first, but now I'd have to tell Pa instead.

'Can I borrow the horse-box trailer and your AV?' I asked.

'Why? What for?'

'I've got a plan.'

CHAPTER TWENTY-FIVE

JAMIE

'You are sure this is the one?' the Voice of the Father asked the guards.

'Yes, sir,' one of them replied with a subservient nod.

In the hallway of a very grand and impressive house, Matthew scrutinized Jamie through narrowed eyes. Jamie recognised the disciple, but apparently Matthew did not recognise *him*.

'If it is you, you look well,' Matthew said. 'Very well indeed. Stronger. Unrecognisable from the wretch you once were. Are you the one who came here as "Jamie"?'

Jamie nodded.

'And now you are known as Jacob?' Matthew continued quizzing him. 'You confessed your sin to me? A particular sin involving a young girl?'

Jamie felt his cheeks colour with shame and nodded.

'Very well,' Matthew said, apparently satisfied that he had the right person. He turned to the guards. 'You may leave him with me.'

They hesitated.

'Did you not hear me? Leave.'

They turned and walked out of the front door. Jamie didn't blame them for not wanting to leave Matthew alone with him. How did they know Jamie wasn't dangerous? They hadn't even searched him for a weapon.

'Follow me, Jacob. I have need of you.'

Jamie followed Matthew up the wide wooden staircase, curious, but reminding himself he was here to serve and not to question. The rich scent of wood and polish made him suddenly nostalgic for a forgotten time and he briefly ran his hand along the smooth dark banister, before letting it drop back down to his side.

They reached a wide landing and Matthew walked up a couple more steps and into a room. Jamie followed him inside. The room was beautiful. Gorgeous. The most lovely space Jamie had ever seen in his life, steeped in luxuries from a long-ago era. Irrationally, its beauty made him want to weep, but of course he did not.

A huge picture window dominated the room, framed with bronze velvet curtains; a tranquil view of jewel-green grass, trees and sky beyond. The warm elegance of the place was even more startling to Jamie after the basic quarters he'd become used to at the arena. Paintings of landscapes sat inside gilt frames and a long gold mirror gleamed above a mahogany chest. Carved chairs and upholstered sofas sat upon intricate rugs, which in turn sat upon a thick cream carpet. Jamie realised his grass and mud-stained feet were now soiling this impossibly pale floor covering and he wondered if Matthew would notice.

The disciple bade him sit in one of the carved chairs. Jamie did as he was told and watched Matthew walk across to the window and gaze out. He seemed even more imposing than the last time they'd met. More sure of himself, if that were even possible.

'Tell me your confession again.'

Jamie's throat went dry and his heart sped up. Again? He thought all that was behind him. That once he'd got everything off his chest the first time he would never have to think of it again. That was how it was supposed to work. Right? But then he remembered this morning's goldfinches trusting to nature, and the promise he'd made himself to trust to God and His disciples, so he choked back his fear and began to talk.

'I accidentally killed a girl. I broke into her garden. Into her pool house.' Jamie's voice sounded strange to his own ears. He wasn't used to talking. 'She saw me and I was scared she'd run off to fetch her parents so I tried to stop her, but she fell backwards through the door. It was glass – the door, I mean – and a piece of it fell out of the frame and into her throat.' Jamie said the words, but he tried not to think of their meaning. He tried to keep the warriors' chant in his head to stop the image of the girl seeping into his mind. 'She died. Instantly. And I ran off.' Jamie bowed his head, shame revisiting him once more.

'Remind me, where did this happen?' Matthew asked, still turned to the window.

'At the Talbot Woods Perimeter.'

'When?'

'A while back. Two or three months ago I guess. It was the day before I met Mr Carter.'

'Do you know the name of this girl?'

Jamie swallowed. 'No,' he said. Did Matthew know the girl? Was that why he was here? Jamie didn't want to know her name. In fact, if Matthew told him her name, Jamie was quite sure he would break down. But the disciple changed the subject and Jamie was able to breathe once more.

'You know Our Father has been taken.' Matthew turned away from the window to face him.

Jamie nodded, twisting his hands in his lap. 'I've been praying for him.'

'He was attacked. Viciously attacked. His vocal cords are permanently damaged. And now he has been abducted. The people who did this will be punished.'

'Do you know who they are?'

'Do not question me.'

Jamie bowed his head, conscious that he had overstepped the mark. But Matthew didn't seem angry. Strangely, he seemed almost elated.

'I am the Voice of the Father now,' he said softly.

Jamie looked up at Matthew, who was unable to fully conceal his pride. No wonder the boy appeared so confident and commanding. He was in charge of the whole sodding place. Jamie didn't know whether to be flattered to have been brought to his attention, or terrified that he was here under scrutiny.

'Will... will Our Father be okay?' Jamie asked, unable to stop himself. 'Will we be able to rescue him?'

'Yes, when the time is right,' Matthew replied. 'But now you may resume your training. It suits you. You will do well as a soldier. I may have further use for you. Expect to return.' Matthew turned back to the window and signalled to someone outside, beyond Jamie's view. 'My brothers wait in the court-yard. They will return you to your duties.'

Jamie stood uncertainly, but Matthew remained with his back to him and so he left the room and made his way down the stairs, out into the courtyard where the two men were waiting. They accompanied him back to the arena where he re-joined his brothers to continue praying for James Grey's safe return.

Jamie still had no idea what this morning's visit had really meant. Why he'd been summoned to a private meeting with Grey's top disciple and why he had been asked to repeat his confession.

. . .

Jamie awoke to the sound of bells. He opened his eyes. It was still dark. In their damp quarters, his brothers stirred around him. What were those bells? They grew louder. A fire? Some kind of alarm? He sat upright and rubbed the sleep from his eyes. And then the bells stopped for a moment and a voice called out:

'Awaken, Warriors of Our Father, and prepare for Battle. Awaken, Warriors. To arms!'

The bells started up again, louder still, and a hooded figure appeared in the doorway, holding a lantern and swinging a hand bell. Calling them to battle. The disciple's body merged with the shadows, making him appear a giant, filling the door-frame, as the bells filled the room with their insistence.

Jamie rose from his place on the ground with a thumping heartbeat and a swooping sensation in his stomach. This was it. After weeks of training, they were finally to go into battle. He and his brothers stood, all eyes on their brother in the doorway. The figure moved away, calling along the corridors, ringing the bells and rousing Grey's Warriors from their slumber.

So today would be the day they would mount a rescue oper-ation. They would take back their Father and stamp out the hostile forces who threatened their way of life. Warriors and trainees alike were to fight and this evening they would leave the training ground. To travel by night and rest by day.

In their chilly quarters, Jamie and his brothers spent the morning kneeling on the ground to clean and sharpen their weapons. He found these familiar tasks soothing and he tried not to think too hard about using these deadly arms for real against a flesh-and-blood enemy instead of the usual cloth dummies and distant targets. But he would do what had to be done. He would make Grey's abductors pay for their wrongdoings.

They ate lunch in their quarters and then began packing

their kit. They were issued with ammunition, new warmer underclothing and water bottles. Extra ammo and supplies would also be brought along in supply vehicles. The day was almost done and Jamie felt the tension and anticipation in the air around him. No one spoke, but the atmosphere was fevered – part anticipation, part fear.

They were ready.

He and his brothers donned their warriors' cloaks and packs, left their quarters and made their way to gather in the vast, cold arena. Jamie's breath flowed before him like soft warm pillows. But that was something he couldn't think about, for he had a full night's march ahead of him before he could rest his head again. Torches blazed around the outside of the arena, though remnants of light still hung in the sky. Once the day fully gave way to the stars, they would abandon their training ground and head south.

Rising up into the night, the faint sound of the chant began to wend through the ranks. Inspiring and calming. A call to arms. A prayer for the righteous. Along the rows of soldiers, this grid of sound rose, swelling from a barely audible hum into a menacing battle cry. Jamie's voice merged with his brothers and his mind cleared as they prepared to leave the arena. He would put one foot in front of the other, like his brother before him and his brother behind. A movement in the ranks broke his meditation.

Two robed men. Matthew's guards.

This could only mean one thing – that Jamie was to be summoned once more for an audience with the Voice of the Father. Was it his imagination or did these guards seem more deferential this time? They did not grab his arms or prod him in the direction they wanted him to move. Instead, they had bowed and gestured that he follow them.

His warrior brothers did not so much as glance his way as

he was led from the arena. Jamie was used to their apparent lack of curiosity by now. If it had been someone else being taken away, he too would have been careful not to stare. The Voice of the Father had warned him that he would be summoned again, so this shouldn't have come as too much of a shock. But why now? At this crucial time.

The two guards flanked him as they left the training ground, but it felt like they were accompanying him, rather than guarding. Jamie was dressed for war, with a full complement of weapons, but Matthew's guards did not asked him to disarm. He was surprised when one of them spoke:

'The Voice of the Father requests your presence in the North Canonry.'

It was bewildering to him. What could he, Jamie, have to offer at a time like this? What could Matthew possibly want with him?

Out of the arena, without his brothers around him, Jamie felt the full force of the cold night air. It sharpened his senses and set his mind racing. Yet again, something was about to change in his life. He could feel it. But he didn't yet know if would be a great thing or a terrible thing.

Their footfalls crunched across the frosty ground and the night wind sliced through his cloak. He picked up a familiar scent and, sure enough, three horses had been tethered outside the main entrance. The guards mounted and bid Jamie do the same. He stroked his horse's nose, put his foot in the stirrup and swung his other leg over the saddle.

'We ride to the Close,' one of the guards said, before disappearing across the water meadow.

They galloped through the crisp darkness, stopping only to let themselves through the many gates. Jamie wished they could have kept going all night, enjoying the warm solidity of the horse and the chill wind on his cheeks. But all too soon they were within the Close, trotting along the narrow pathways and cantering over the wider grassy areas. Before long, the horses' hooves clopped to a halt outside the house Jamie had previously visited. He assumed it was where Matthew lived. The guards dismounted and Jamie did the same, patting the neck of his steed, reluctant to give her up and discover his fate.

CHAPTER TWENTY-SIX

RILEY

'I bloody hate those wild dogs,' Denzil grumbled. 'Give me a bunch of armed raiders any day over a pack of vicious mutts.'

'It'll be fine, Den,' I said. 'They won't be interested in you.'

'That's what you say now. But we'll be out in the open and they'll sniff out my weakness.'

I laughed. 'Denzil, what weakness? You're the toughest bloke I know.'

'Frickin' dogs though,' he muttered under his breath.

I heard a rattle and a crash behind us and whipped my head around to glance out the back window. 'D'you think the trailer'll be okay? It's not liking the potholes.'

'Yeah, be fine,' he replied, changing gear with a judder, almost tipping the horse-box trailer right over.

I was amazed that Pa hadn't totally ridiculed my idea. Sure, he'd raised an eyebrow a couple of times and wasn't overly enthusiastic. But, after I'd explained the plan, all he'd done was sigh and say it couldn't hurt and was worth a shot.

Good enough.

So now here I was with Denzil, outside on the heathland, scouring the frosted landscape for packs of wild dogs. We'd been out for almost an hour and there was no sign of anything. Not even a bird, let alone a dog. Pa wouldn't be happy if we emptied his AV of fuel with nothing to show for it. Maybe we should've turned back and given up before we wasted the morning completely. Truth was, I felt a bit embarrassed about the whole idea. It could turn out to be a total non-event and make me look like an idiot.

'Over there,' Denzil said, reluctantly. 'Lassie and co.'

'What?'

'Never mind. Before your time.'

I looked out of his window to where he was pointing and smiled. For off in the distance, a large smudge of canines loped towards us.

'Turn the AV around,' I said. 'Quick.'

'Thought we were gonna round 'em up?'

'We might not have to,' I said. 'Look, they're headed this way anyway. They're hungry. Coming to see if there's any lunch.'

Denzil put the AV on a hard lock and turned it around so the horse box faced the approaching pack. I opened my door and hopped out, revolver aimed in front of me. Then I jogged around to the rear of the trailer and began fumbling with the ramp. Denzil joined me, his weapon trained on the dogs, who had now broken into an all-out run, yipping in excitement.

'Come on,' Denzil cried. 'Hurry up, girl. Them dogs is hungry. They're liking the look of my tasty black ass.'

I spluttered out a hysterical giggle. 'Shut up,' I hissed. 'Stop making me laugh. I can't concentrate.' Finally, sweating and shaking, I managed to undo the latch, and the ramp dropped down to the ground with a crash. We'd already placed a couple of dead rats in the trailer to lure the pack in, and now I tossed a couple of mutton bones from my bag onto the base of the ramp.

We backed out of the way around the side of the trailer and waited. Yelps and growls preceded the hysterical pack. They looked even meaner than the last time I'd seen them. As they approached, they slowed, warier now that they were up close to us. I aimed my gun. The scary part was waiting to see if they would go straight for the bait or try to attack us instead.

But our plan appeared to be working. Inanimate food seemed to be preferable to live prey. Thankfully, the dogs began growling at each other rather than at us, as they stalked the mutton bones, ears flat, eyes narrowed. Each one working out if it could get to the food before their pack mates. A brindled mutt made a dive for the largest bone and suddenly they were all on the ramp in an all-out dog fight. Tearing at the bones and tearing into each other.

And then they scented the dead rats. A moment's hesitation before most of the pack tore up the ramp and into the trailer. A couple of them had remained outside with the mutton bones and now sloped away from us to enjoy their meaty prizes.

Denzil and I cautiously made our way around behind the horse box, weapons drawn. It was carnage inside the dark trailer and the dogs paid us no attention whatsoever. There must've been at least thirty of them, climbing over each other to get at the meat. Between us, Denzil and I heaved up the ramp and closed the trailer with a satisfying clang.

'Perfect,' I said.

'Not bad,' he replied.

A loud bang from inside the horse box made me jump.

'They're gonna kill themselves in there,' Denzil said, shaking his head.

'I hope not,' I replied. If they did, it would all have been for nothing.

'Better get back quickly before they do.'

We returned to the AV and Denzil started her up.

'What do you think, Denzil? About all this stuff with FJ?'

'It is what it is,' he said. 'We're doing what we can. If he turns up, we'll take him down. I think it's better this way.'

'What do you mean, "better"?'

'You don't want the likes of FJ out there doing Christ knows what. Getting more powerful. This way, he comes to us and we eliminate the threat straight away. It's better.'

I hadn't thought of it like that. What Denzil said made sense. We had to treat this as an opportunity, not a threat. 'I just wish we had extra time to prepare.'

'No,' he replied. 'Extra time to get scared, more like. We need to get this done as soon as possible. Anyway, we've already got a massive advantage.'

'How d'you figure that?'

'Well, FJ doesn't realise we know he's coming. He thinks he's gonna turn up here and surprise us, unprepared. But we've had a few days to get sorted. Get provisions. Build our defences. Liss did us a massive favour by warning us. FJ's gonna be pissed.'

'True,' I said.

'Too right it's true. And believe me, that stacks the odds in our favour. Way, way in our favour.' He nodded and started to hum a tune under his breath. I sank back into my seat feeling slightly more reassured than I'd felt on the way out.

During the brief journey home, I scanned the curve of the land, keeping a lookout for Luc and Eddie's trucks returning, but there was nothing to see. Not even a speck on the horizon.

To look at them now, you wouldn't have thought these were the same wild creatures out on the heath that morning. They were lying in an open barn in one of the farmer's livestock pens, docile as anything. Only a couple of dogs showing any sign of agitation, skirting the Perimeter of their spacious quarters in a frenzied attempt to find a way out. But I bet if we'd thrown any food in there, they'd have gone crazy.

After our first successful trip out, Denzil and I had brought back the dogs and then returned to the wilderness, heading in a different direction this time. We managed to track down another large pack. Then another. And another. Each time, capturing them had been as straightforward as the first, and we now had well in excess of two hundred.

The only problem was, they looked too placid, lying in the barn resting, tongues lolling. Some were badly injured, whimpering and licking their wounds. I felt a pang of sympathy before I remembered how they'd surrounded Liss and Annabelle. How they'd gone in for the kill. No matter how cute and harmless they looked now, they weren't pets. They were wild, dangerous creatures that wouldn't hesitate to attack and kill. And this was what I was banking on.

After our day's work, Denzil had gone straight back on duty. I was just about to head home to see my parents and check whether Luc was back yet, when Pa showed up at the livestock pens.

'You did it then,' he said, startling me.

I turned to greet him. 'Is Luc back?'

He shook his head. 'Sorry. No word yet.'

My stomach lurched. 'But they've been out the whole day. It shouldn't have taken that long. It's almost dark.'

'They'll be back any time,' he said. 'Might even be coming through the gates right now.'

'Well, if they're not, you need to send out a search party.'

'Eddie doesn't need me chasing after him. These things always take longer than planned.'

'But—'

'If they're not back by morning, we'll do something. Rita isn't worried, so you shouldn't be either.'

I highly doubted that. Rita was probably always worried about her husband and her son, just as they must worry about her. She just did a better job of appearing calmer than my mother, who was liable to make a fuss if I wasn't wearing a warm-enough sweater.

'So, are things serious between you and Luc?' Pa asked, shoving his hands into his pockets, eyes cast down to the ground.

'Huh?' I replied, not wanting to talk about it with Pa. It was... weird.

'Never mind,' he said, clearing his throat. Obviously not comfortable with it either. 'Luc's a good lad.' He coughed and changed the subject, to my intense relief. 'Nice work with the wild dogs today. But they look a bit tame for what we've got in mind.'

'I know. I'm worried about that too. They were vicious out on the heath though.'

'We'll give it a go,' he said. 'It can't hurt to try and it's a good idea in principal.'

'Thanks. What's the plan for this evening?'

'More prep. Come on. We can't hang around. Stuff to do. FJ's supposed to be making his trade tomorrow. When Liss doesn't show up with you, he won't be happy.'

We walked back in the direction of the house, the setting sun a yellow scorch behind us. Pa put his arm around me and kissed the top of my head. I hoped I'd find Luc back at the house.

CHAPTER TWENTY-SEVEN

JAMIE

Jamie was ushered into a room on the ground floor. A dining room by the look of it. Candles flickered in bronze candelabras, casting wavering shadows on the walls. At the head of a dark wood table, in a sparsely furnished room, sat the Voice of the Father. He wore a utilitarian warrior's cloak, and a hard look burned in his eyes. Jamie had heard a rumour that he too had been captured along with Grey but had somehow managed to escape. He wondered if that was true.

Once again, Jamie couldn't help the treasonous thought that this boy was way too young for the power that had been thrust upon him. What was he? Sixteen? Seventeen? Eighteen at the most. He was still confused as to why the Voice should be talking to a nobody like him, especially at a time like this. As Jamie stood in the warm room, his cheeks and hands afire from the contrast in temperature, he waited to hear if he was to receive a punishment, an accolade, or something entirely different.

'Jacob, you are to be awarded a great honour.'

All right then. But he couldn't for the life of him think what he'd done to deserve it.

'You are to become a favoured disciple of the Church.'

Jamie clamped his jaws together to stop his mouth from hanging open in shock.

'You will carry out Our Father's sacred duties. You will live here in the Close with us and be privy to our most revered secrets.'

Instead of revelling in this honour, Jamie felt suspicion. Why should he become a disciple? What was the real agenda here? It was just him and Matthew in the room. If he was really to be made a disciple, why wasn't there some kind of public ceremony? There was always a ceremony for these kinds of things. Every time someone moved up a rank, it was done before an audience, with prayers and thanks given to God. Jamie knew he didn't deserve such a privileged position. What was the catch? Or was he being too cynical? Had years on the outside left him incapable of trust? He realised Matthew was asking him a question.

'Do you have anything to say?'

'I... I'm honoured, of course. But I don't understand. Why me?'

'You do not need to understand, or ask why. You only need to accept. To become a true disciple of Our Father, you must prove you are worthy. Sometimes through faith or good deeds, other times through some kind of challenge or hardship.'

Okay, here we go. Jamie's senses became hyper-alert. He was about to discover what was in store for him. What this boy-priest really wanted from him. He had a feeling it wouldn't be anything easy.

'Does this mean I'll miss the battle?' Jamie asked. 'My brothers are leaving already.'

'You don't need to worry about that,' Matthew said. 'We will be joining our brothers-in-arms in a few days.'

Jamie didn't know whether to feel disappointed or relieved.

Matthew sat up straighter in his chair. His voice turned

more serious. 'From the thousands of trainees, teachers and warriors, you alone have been chosen to carry out this defining task that will bring you great honour. Know that you will be doing God's work.'

The boy was selling it to Jamie. If he needed to sell it, it definitely wasn't going to be good.

'What do you want me to do?' Jamie asked.

'You have been training for this holy war. Your teachers tell me you're a good student. You have learned well. You are... exceptional. And so, you will therefore have the honour of killing the one who has taken Our Father.'

Jamie let the words settle for a moment. Matthew wanted him to kill someone. This didn't sound like a battle situation. This sounded like an execution.

'I want to serve,' Jamie said carefully, 'and I'm honoured that you're happy with my training. But... just because I killed once before, doesn't make me a murderer. It was just... a really terrible accident.'

'Of course the girl's death was an accident,' Matthew soothed. 'I know you are not a cold-blooded killer. You have become a warrior and that is why you are suited to this. This is not murder, this is survival. We are fighting a holy war and you will kill this evil doer as a soldier kills his enemies. It is what you've been trained for and it is a great privilege to be selected.

'Our country lies in darkness, Jacob. There are those out there who seek to keep it that way. They have stolen the light from us. You will end the darkness and the bloodshed with the death of the one who has done harm to our beloved Father.'

'Why was I chosen?'

As Jamie realised what was being asked of him, he wondered for the hundredth time how he'd ended up here, in this religious settlement. He was Jamie the loser-vagrant, not Jacob the warrior.

'It will become clear,' Matthew replied. 'There is a purpose to this as there is a purpose to everything. Sometimes that purpose is hidden, and we must try to discover it for ourselves, but other times we are lucky enough to be shown the way. By coming here, you have allowed yourself to be guided along the right path and earn God's forgiveness. Forgiveness is a journey, Jacob.'

'Who was it?' Jamie asked. 'Who attacked Our Father? Why did they do it?'

'These are people who, if left unchecked, will never leave us alone. They will continue to attack, to try to destroy our peaceful way of life.'

'Yes, but, forgive me, who are they? Are they raiders? Or just random outsiders?'

Matthew leant back in his chair and steepled his hands together. 'They are a much greater threat than that. These are people who live a decadent life in a world of poverty. They do not deserve to have so much, when the rest have so little. They hoard their wealth and their resources with no thought for the rest of us. Not content with their lot, they also feel the need to come here and attack us in our home.'

Jamie marvelled again at how such a young person could speak with so much confidence and certainty.

'Jacob, you seek peace and an end to the haunting images in your mind,' Matthew continued. 'You doubt everything around you. You question your reason for being here.'

'Yes,' Jamie replied. 'How can you know so much about how I feel?'

'Because I too had doubts when I first came here. But God has a plan for us all, and your plan, Jacob, is very clear to me. It is part of the greater purpose. You were sent here for a reason.'

'Can you tell me the reason? The purpose?'

'You will discover it in time. You must trust me. Can you do that?'

Jamie nodded. He had to trust Matthew, or what else was

there for him? He had come here to give his life to this place, to be absolved from sin. To heal and move forward. He had never expected that murder would be asked of him. But perhaps Matthew was right. Perhaps this was a holy war and they were fighting for good. Casualties were part of war. These people, whoever they were, had attempted to harm their way of life. They had tried to kill James Grey, and that wasn't right.

Jamie was still no wiser as to why he specifically had been singled out, other than his prior confession. He didn't buy the reason that he was an 'exceptional' fighter. Sure, he was pretty good, but there were far better warriors than him.

Nevertheless, he would try to accept this responsibility and carry it out without hesitation. He had to. He was a favoured disciple now. After this, he would live in the main house and truly *belong* here. He had never belonged anywhere in the whole of his adult life.

'As one of Our Father's warriors, you are bound to kill our enemies,' Matthew said. 'It is what you have been training for. We say these words to remind us of who we are: We are of God, and the whole world lies in wickedness. The wicked shall be overthrown and the house of the righteous shall stand. Jacob, *we* are the house of the righteous. *Scimus quoniam ex Deo sumus et mundus totus in maligno positus es. Verte impios et non erunt domus autem iustorum permanebi.*'

Jamie recited the chant along with Matthew and as he spoke the familiar words, he felt a renewed confidence and the knowledge that they were right in what they were doing. They were blessed by God, and to carry out His work truly was the highest honour.

'*Deus lux mea est. Dum vivimus servimus.*'

'You will march south,' Matthew said as Jamie continued to mouth the chant. 'You will kill the one who holds Our Father. You are destined to kill this unholy murderer.'

'I will march south,' Jamie repeated. 'I will kill the one who holds Our Father. I am destined to kill this unholy murderer.'

Jamie stood infused with purpose and power as the Voice of the Father rose from his chair and walked towards him.

He kissed Jacob on his left cheek and then embraced him. 'We leave in three days.'

After a night spent in the Close, Jamie was woken by the peal of bells. Yesterday's events came rushing back to him and he briefly wondered if it had all been a dream. Opening his eyes, his surroundings told him otherwise. Gone were his quarters at the training ground, to be replaced by a comfortable bedroom, a dim lamp burning on the dresser. Brown drapes hung open at the window, the sky still dark outside. Jamie was in a proper bed, in a small cottage next to the big house. But there was no time to enjoy the unexpected comfort. His two roommates were already out of their beds and Jamie's mind was bright and alert. He rolled out of bed, stretched and reached for his clothes, which were folded on his bedside table.

Selected as one of Grey's favoured disciples, he'd been brought a robe to signify his rank: black with a crimson trim. Out of thousands, he was now one of the chosen few. It was hard to believe. Jamie felt self-importance swell within him, even though he knew it was a sin. The other two men were also of the same rank and he wondered if they were newly promoted too. If they had been charged with similarly important tasks.

Right at this moment, Jamie was unsure what he was supposed to do and where he was supposed to go. He had learnt enough during his time here not to ask questions. Had grown used to following orders. So he followed the other disciples' lead, dressing and then leaving the room. They walked down the narrow stairs in silence and entered a small dining room with eight places set. Jamie and his roommates were the last through the door. None of the others had raised their hoods, and so their faces were clearly visible, heads shorn like his own. The men appeared to be in their twenties and thirties, apart from one who appeared much older.

Now that all eight men were seated, including Jamie, breakfast was brought in by serving men. Jamie hadn't eaten a breakfast like this for years: toasted bread, mushrooms, tomatoes, bacon, sausages and fried eggs. The only thing missing was the baked beans. The smell, this delicious smell, was a dream of long ago. The memories hit him hard. What was it called, this breakfast? *A Full English.* His dad's favourite.

He remembered, as a kid, strolling down the road to the local caff for breakfast with his dad on Saturday mornings, while his mum stayed home to have a lie-in. How could he have forgotten such a wonderful memory? The mugs of tea. The men with their newspapers. The sizzle of the frying pans and the tinny radio playing the hits of the day. His dad pretending to steal a crispy rasher of bacon off his plate. Their chatter about what he'd done in school that week. His friends. Sports. The latest video game.

Jamie didn't want this memory. Not now. Not when he was about to do something so far removed from that time. The image of him and his father in that café produced such a physical ache beneath his rib cage that he couldn't enjoy a single mouthful of food. It stuck in his throat and he had to force it down. He seriously worried he might be about to cry. Everyone ate until their plates were empty. Jamie just about managed to do the same, squashing down the distressing memory.

The men left the table before their plates were taken away. No time for ceremony. They would be marching to battle in a few days. Jamie's first battle. Would he be at the front with the Voice of the Father? He hoped so. It would be a good feeling to be at the head of things. Respected. Playing an important role. He wasn't a loser anymore. He was going to make a difference.

Rescue their leader. Eliminate a threat so their people – *his* people – could live without fear of attack.

The eight disciples left the cottage without their weapons. The morning air was dark and damp, the tramp of boots the only sound as they walked the few hundred yards to the huge house which was the North Canonry. Entering through a rear door, they crossed the hallway and made their way into what appeared to be a small chapel. The room was almost full, with rows of warrior disciples seated on polished wooden pews. Jamie and the others took their places at the front. The Voice of the Father walked in and everyone rose to their feet.

The morning was spent in prayer and then, after a simple lunch, the men were sent back to their rooms to sleep. In a couple of days they would be leaving the Close, travelling by night, and so they needed to reverse their body clocks to become fully alert. For the next two days, they prayed and slept during the day and trained at night. Sword practice and hand-to-hand combat. It wasn't anywhere near as rigorous as the arena training, and Jamie breezed through it all without breaking a sweat. His fitness and reflexes far surpassed his fellow disciples.

On the third day, waking after his final afternoon nap, Jamie felt ready. He was up before his roommates this time. Dressed before they'd even opened their eyes. He opened the window and gazed up into the black sky, the cold air heightening his senses and catching at the back of his throat. He felt strong and brave. Purposeful and worthy. He smiled.

As he descended the stairs and gathered his weapons from the armoury, Jamie thought of his brothers from the training ground. They would have left the arena several nights earlier, as he was originally supposed to have done, before Matthew had summoned him. They would already have completed three nights' march. He wished they could see him now in his black robes with the crimson trim. Pity his hood was raised so no one would get to see his face.

To Jamie's surprise, he and his new brothers weren't to travel on foot or on horseback. The Voice of the Father and his elite disciples were to *drive* down to the south. Rows of jeeps, AVs, trucks and 4x4s cluttered the grassy area at the front of the North Canonry, as well as two massive fuel tankers.

An uncloaked man approached Jamie as he stood on the grass with his brethren.

'Sir,' he said, head lowered. 'I'm to escort you to your vehicle.'

Jamie gave the man a nod and followed the man to a sleek black AV. The man opened the front passenger door and waited while Jamie removed his sword and AK47. The man took them from Jamie and slotted them into a rack that had been fitted along the side of his seat. Once his weapons were secured, Jamie got into the vehicle. He didn't recognise the driver, another warrior. The back doors opened and closed as more soldiers got in.

This was it. They were going to war.

CHAPTER TWENTY-EIGHT

RILEY

It was half three in the morning before I got to bed, but I couldn't sleep. Two hours later I was still staring at the ceiling, my brain spooling back over everything that had happened and projecting forward to everything about to happen.

That evening, I'd worked flat out without stopping. Shifting supplies and checking weapons, trying to keep busy and not think about what was happening to Luc and Eddie, who were still out there somewhere. Once more, I had begged Pa to send out a search party, but he wouldn't do it. Said there was nothing to be achieved by sending guards outside at night. That it was better to wait. That Eddie had years of experience. That he and Luc would be fine.

It was all very well for Pa to say these things, but he didn't understand that I was in love with Luc. His whole world wouldn't come crashing down if Luc disappeared. He wouldn't spend the night feeling physically sick with worry. I wanted to yell. To defy him. But I stayed calm on the outside and told myself to wait until morning. Then, if Pa still did nothing, I would do something myself.

I lay in the darkness, wide awake. Ma was in bed and Pa

was still working, although he'd managed a catnap earlier, down in the stores. It hit me that today was Christmas Eve. The day when Liss was supposed to trade me for her parents. The day FJ was planning to attack our home. What if his army breached the fence? What if this was the last night I would spend in my house?

I glanced at the clock – 5.45 a.m. The deadline had already passed for Liss's trade. Did that mean FJ would be on his way here now? There was no way I was going to fall asleep. My whole body felt edgy, antsy, unable to stay still, let alone sleep. I closed my eyes again, but my brain was so hyper that I immediately snapped them back open. It was no good. I unclenched my fists and tried to take calming breaths, but my heart beat too fast, like war drums.

I sat up and swung my legs out of bed, deciding to go next door and see if Rita had heard anything. She was always up early. Maybe Luc and Eddie were back already and I was lying here worrying over nothing. I quickly pulled on some jeans and an oversized sweatshirt, tucked my Magnum into my waistband and padded down the stairs. I slipped my feet into my boots and grabbed my coat and keys, remembering to scrawl a note for Ma on the chalkboard. When I opened the door my heart sank.

Snow.

White whorls already settling thick on the ground. *Please let Luc be home already*, I said in my head, over and over again. If he wasn't, this weather wasn't going to help them at all. I pulled the door shut behind me and was consumed by the muffled hush of early morning.

My boots squeaked as I walked down the path and the cold seeped through to my skin, my toes tensing in complaint. The road outside was pristine white, the night sky lighter than it should've been at this hour, filled with spinning flakes. As I trudged next door, I didn't dare let myself hope they were home.

But turning into the Donovans' driveway, I saw a couple of lights burning and my heart lifted. Maybe...

Rita answered the door, a look of heartbreaking expectancy on her face, quickly replaced by a sad smile. So they weren't back then. I instantly felt guilty for getting her hopes up.

'Can't sleep either?' she asked.

I shook my head.

'Come on in.'

Following her into the hallway, I eyed the travel bags stacked against one wall. She saw me looking.

'Just in case,' she said. 'It's always better to be prepared. I'm going to load up the AVs. You should do the same. Plus a large rucksack with emergency provisions, in case we have to leave on foot.'

'You really think it'll come to that?' I asked, an unsteady feeling creeping over me.

'No. I don't. But for the one per cent chance that it might happen, you'll be glad you prepared for it.'

My mind was buzzing. The thought of actually leaving the Perimeter for good was about as terrifying as it could get. But... being made homeless by an arrogant seventeen-year-old boy?

'I could kill Eddie for going out,' Rita said, ushering me into the kitchen. 'He really didn't have to; we could've managed on our existing supplies. But he's always got to be the big man and go for the prize, the grand gesture. And to take Luc with him was just plain irresponsible. They should've been back by now.'

Her outburst surprised me. I'd always thought Eddie and Rita were equally tough, supporting each other in everything.

'Sorry,' she said. 'Ignore me. I'm worried, that's all. They'll be fine, like they always are. And when they get home, I'll murder the bloody pair of them.'

'Why do you think they're not back?' I asked, sitting at the table and resting my chin in my hands.

'I think maybe something's happened to one of the vehicles

and it's taking a while to sort out. The weather isn't going to help.'

'You don't think... FJ?' I said.

'No. Eddie went east and stayed off the main routes. If FJ's coming, he'll be coming from the north.'

'Waiting's painful,' I said. 'Can't we send out a search party? I'll go.'

'Eddie won't want that, but if they're not back by the time it's light, I'll go myself. The thing is, everyone else is needed here. With FJ so close...' Rita came and sat opposite me. 'Luc told me you and he finally got it together.'

Annoyingly, I blushed; surprised Luc had mentioned it to his mother. 'What did he say?' I asked.

She smiled. 'Just that I had to keep an eye on you while he was gone. He wouldn't have said anything else, but I pried it out of him. We mothers have a way of doing that you know. I'm happy for you both.'

I didn't know what else to say, so I just gave her an uncomfortable smile. I guess she realised I felt awkward because she stood up and changed the subject.

'I don't know about you,' she said, 'but I'm sick of this. Let's go down to the Guards' House and see if we can't get a bird's eye view of our men coming home. If there's no sign of them, we'll take a four-wheel-drive and get them ourselves.'

I scraped my chair back, relieved we were finally doing something. 'What about Liss and Annabelle?' I asked. 'Are they upstairs?'

Rita nodded. 'We've put a guard up there, just in case.'

'They wouldn't betray me.'

'I don't think so either,' she said. 'But it doesn't hurt to be overcautious. Come on, let's go.' She pulled on a sweater and scarf before donning her thick navy parka. Pa had done a deal a few years ago for a job-lot of these cosy coats and we had enough of them to last several lifetimes.

Rita and I left the house and walked briskly down the road, our feet sinking into the thickening snow. Slipping on a hidden kerb, I lunged for Rita's arm. She steadied me and we walked arm-in-arm the rest of the way. Everything looked so surreal and pretty. We rarely got snow this far south, so it was an oddity. Pity we couldn't enjoy messing about in it. The timing sucked.

CHAPTER TWENTY-NINE

JAMIE

The drive was uneventful. The night too dark to see beyond the glass of the AV's tinted windows. Nothing but his own faceless reflection – a hooded creature. Jamie recited the warriors' chant in his head, trying to remain calm and focused. Not thinking about what he was tasked to do; simply trying to conserve his energy. To keep his mind and body fresh and ready for whatever lay ahead. The trick would be to stay awake inside the warm thrumming cocoon of the AV.

How far would they have already marched? His brothers from the arena. Would they have reached their destination yet? Jamie realised he didn't even know exactly where they were supposed to be heading.

South.

That's all he'd been told. South could mean anywhere. It was a long coastline.

An hour passed. Two. The road was so rough and pitted they had to crawl along, but it was comfortable enough. Too comfortable – Jamie would have preferred to march or ride. It would've kept him sharp, rather than lulling him to sleep.

Another hour gone. The darkness outside was dissipating,

the sky pale. But it couldn't be morning. Not yet. Jamie suddenly realised the reason for the lightening sky. It wasn't dawn. It was snow clouds. He hoped they'd reach their destination before it fell to earth. Driving in a snowstorm would be tricky. And it would make finding their foot soldiers almost impossible.

Just as he was having these thoughts, their driver slammed on the brakes. Jamie looked up to see the brake lights of the truck in front as it slowed to a halt. Luckily Jamie's AV hadn't been travelling very fast, but even so, he braced himself as they skidded out to the side, finally stopping on a grassy verge a couple of inches from a spindly tree, leafless and shivering. The lead truck had stopped up ahead. Someone got out of the vehicle and started walking towards them. A disciple.

They remained in the AV and waited. A rap on the window and the driver buzzed down his window a little way. The bitter scent of snow flew into the vehicle.

The disciple stood at the window. 'We have caught up with our brothers,' he said, pointing to his left. 'Follow us. We'll take the next turning.'

The driver nodded and buzzed up the glass. They waited, their engine idling, while the messenger made his way along their convoy, passing on the news. Jamie flexed his fingers and went through his katas in his head, wielding his sword high and then low. Breathing through the movements. The driver put the AV in first and moved off once more, pulling back onto the road, headlights illuminating the rear of the truck in front. The lights from behind shone in through their rearview. They were all sticking close together now. No one wanted to get separated. Not here, so far from home. On enemy soil.

Jamie wondered where exactly 'here' was. Were they anywhere near his old stomping ground of Bournemouth and Poole, he wondered. The truck in front had its indicator on, flashing left. Jamie's driver followed suit, a clicking noise signalling their imminent turn.

The exit twisted down and around a narrow overgrown path. Branches scraped at the windows and the ground grew pitted and bumpy. Nothing more than a rough dirt track. Not meant for vehicles. Jamie's teeth rattled together and he reached out to steady himself against the dash. After five minutes of this, the path finally led onto a wider track. They stopped and their driver switched off the engine.

Jamie and the other disciples exited their vehicles and gathered by the lead AV. The Voice of the Father stood at the head of his men, hood draped about his shoulders, eyes glittering, illuminated by his vehicle's headlights. He looked young and powerful. Beautiful. Their cavalry and foot soldiers stretched out back along the forest track, black cloaks merging into the darkness.

'We are here at last with you, our brothers,' Matthew cried, his voice cutting through the chill night air. 'Four thousand of us ready to fight. To claim back Our Father, James Grey, who has been abducted.'

Four thousand. Jamie considered those numbers. It was an incredible amount of men. And when you thought about the level of training they'd undertaken, that made them ten times as deadly. The enemy didn't stand a chance. They would be obliterated. And so they should be. How dare they kidnap James Grey. He'd done nothing wrong to deserve being taken. Jamie was suddenly infused with a righteous power. God would make sure justice was done and he, Jamie – or rather, *Jacob* – would play his part in serving justice. He would destroy the people who had attacked their Holy Father. They would all pay.

'We are only a few miles from our destination,' Matthew continued, 'but first I have somewhere I must be. When I return, we will meet our enemy and do what needs to be done.'

Jamie wondered what errand could call Matthew away so

soon before they were due to attack. It must be important. How long would it take?

'Stay vigilant while I am gone,' the Voice said. He turned and climbed into an armoured truck. Four disciples followed him and with them they had... yes, they had prisoners. Two of them. A man and a woman by the look of them. Middle-aged, weak, bound and gagged. Who could they be? Jamie felt a moment's pity for them, before he remembered why he was here. To avenge a wrong doing. Those two people must belong to the enemy. If that was the case, they deserved everything they got.

The disciples lifted the prisoners into the back of the truck. Two climbed in with them, the other two got into the cab. The engine started up and they drove away.

Jamie watched the tail lights vanish into the pale night, feeling strangely vulnerable without his leader. And then he and the rest of them returned to their vehicles to wait.

CHAPTER THIRTY

RILEY

The Guards' House had been transformed from an ugly red block to a picturesque dolls' house covered in frosting. A cluster of guards huddled in front of the door, turning at our approach, thick flakes of snow landing on their heads and faces.

'Riley!' It was Pa. 'What are you doing out here? I thought you were back at the house.'

'Couldn't sleep.'

'Me neither,' Rita added. 'Any sign of—'

'Sorry,' Pa interrupted, his eyes softening. 'Eddie's not back yet.'

I felt Rita's body sag. Mine did the same.

'Did you go?' Rita hissed the words to Pa, but he cut her off with a look.

'Where?' I asked. 'Did you go where?'

'Didn't you tell her?' Rita said.

'No point her worrying,' Pa replied.

'Well, I think it's a bit late for that,' she snorted. 'Things have gone past the point of *worrying*, Johnny, in case you hadn't noticed. I think we're now somewhere in the region of *grave concern*, heading towards all out *panic*.'

Her attempt at black humour didn't fly with Pa, and he scowled before a look of resignation settled on his face. I raised my eyebrows for an answer.

'Nothing happened anyway,' Pa said to Rita. He turned to me to explain. 'I went to the rendezvous.'

His words slowly sank in. He had been to the place where Liss was supposed to have traded me for her parents.

'I took some men,' Pa continued. 'Set up an ambush. Thought we could rescue Fred and Jessie and take out FJ at the same time.'

'And?' I asked.

'There was nobody there.'

'Maybe you scared them off,' I said.

'We hid ourselves well,' Pa said. 'We waited for over an hour, but there was no sign of anyone.'

'That's bad luck,' Rita said. 'It would've solved a lot of problems if you'd got rid of FJ before—'

'They must've spotted you,' I said.

'Maybe,' Pa replied. 'But then why didn't they attack? If I was more ruthless, I'd have taken Liss along as bait. I should have done it. But it's too late now.'

'I'm glad you didn't,' I replied.

'Let's hope you still think that after today,' Pa said. 'When FJ's army arrives and starts killing people.'

'Do you think Liss was lying about FJ's plan?' Rita asked.

'I don't think so,' Pa replied. 'She'd have to be a pretty good actor. And what would be the point?'

'Maybe something happened to FJ and he couldn't make the rendezvous,' I said.

'Let's hope so,' Pa replied. He looked done in.

I leant forward and kissed his stubbled cheek. 'At least you tried,' I added uselessly.

'Come on,' Rita pulled at my arm. 'Let's go up on the wall.'

'What? Why are you going up there?' Pa asked.

'Riley and I are going on lookout duty,' Rita said.

Pa nodded. 'Go on then. But if you see anything moving outside, I want you straight back down here, Riley. Okay?'

Rita and I headed to the wall. The gun turrets were already manned, so we climbed the first ladder and made our way onto a wooden platform. Twenty feet up from the ground, the platform measured about three and a half feet wide with a double guardrail at our backs. Snow covered the wooden boards, already about a couple of inches thick, light and fluffy under our feet. But if many more people came up here, it could quickly compact into treacherous ice. We needed salt or grit.

Rita and I were of a similar height, and our heads just about poked above the snow-covered razor wire. The storm was slowing to just a few light flakes, but visibility was still poor. Rita took my hand and gave it a squeeze.

'Come on, boys,' she said, looking out across the land. 'Where are you?'

We gazed over to the east where the sky was lightening. That was where Eddie and Luc had gone, so it made sense that that would be where we'd spot them. But all I could see was white land, merging with white sky.

'Where are they?' I asked, trying not to let myself think the worst. Images of raiders, upturned vehicles and gun battles flew unbidden into my head.

'This is hopeless,' Rita said. 'I'm going out to find them.'

'I'll come.'

'Your father won't allow it,' Rita said. 'And he's right. FJ wants you, so you'd be playing into his hands if you left the Perimeter. You'd be putting everyone else in danger too.'

She was right. I already knew that if I went out there, it would be an opportunity for FJ to get what he wanted without any effort. But it still didn't make me feel any better about hiding away behind the fence.

I turned my eyes northward and saw a low black cloud

spreading across the horizon. A rain cloud? But it was snowing. 'Rita,' I said. 'Do you see that rain cloud?' I turned to her and saw her eyes narrow, her mouth clamp down in a hard line.

'That's not a rain cloud,' she said slowly, enunciating each word. 'That's an army.'

CHAPTER THIRTY-ONE

JAMIE

Less than an hour later, Jamie heard the sound of an engine bumping down the track towards them. He exited the AV and held his finger on the trigger of his gun. Several other disciples left their vehicles too. It was probably Matthew returning from his detour, but you couldn't be too careful.

Seconds later, Jamie relaxed once more as their leader's AV came into sight. The driver turned off the ignition, plunging them into silence once more. But the silence didn't last long. The Voice swept out of the vehicle, anger etched across his face. He stood and waited while his disciples gathered around him.

'I have been betrayed,' he spat, his breath clouding the air. 'By my own sister.'

Nobody spoke.

'But she will discover what it means to betray our church. To betray Our Father. To betray me.'

'What happened?' Jamie asked, before he could stop himself. As he spoke, he felt the disapproval of the other disciples.

The Voice turned to him, his eyes slits. Jamie immediately

wished he hadn't spoken. But then the boy's face lost its hard edge and he spoke. 'My sister had agreed to deliver the enemy to me today. But she never came. In her place, my scouts spotted a poorly concealed vehicle meant to ambush us.'

'Do you think maybe your sister's been captured?' Jamie said. 'Maybe there was nothing she could do about it.'

Matthew's face turned to fury. 'Are you questioning me?'

'No, no, sir. Of course I would never—'

'It makes no difference now,' Matthew replied. 'We will have to proceed to our final destination.'

'Tell us what you need us to do and we'll do it,' Jamie said.

'You will travel with me now, Jacob,' the Voice said to Jamie. 'We will lead our army to the Perimeter and we will crush them.'

Jamie was taken aback. He was to travel with the Voice of the Father. To lead the army. But something else was troubling him. 'Which Perimeter are we going to?' he asked.

'Talbot Woods. No more talk. We leave now.'

Jamie went cold. He was to return to the Talbot Woods Perimeter. The place of his nightmares. A place he'd hoped never to see again. But would it really be so terrible? His life had moved on. His nightmares had receded and he had been granted forgiveness and a chance at a new beginning. Maybe he needed to return to that place to finish this once and for all. If the people of the Perimeter were evil, maybe killing the girl hadn't been such a tragic accident after all. Maybe it had been God's will.

Gathering up the hem of his robes, Jamie followed Matthew to the truck. As he passed by, he saw the huddled shapes of the prisoners still in the back of the vehicle, their scared hollow eyes staring back at him. Jamie waited by the passenger door while one of his brothers brought his weapons from the AV.

Jamie had instantly acquired a new status among his brothers. He was now openly favoured by the Voice of the Father. His new life was taking shape. All he had to do was prove himself on the battlefield and he would be assured a life of power and fulfilment. His past was gone. He had to look to his future now.

Up in the cab, it was just Jamie, Matthew and the driver. The engine purred to life and they rumbled down the dark track in convoy once more, followed by their massive army on horseback and on foot. If only the old Jamie could see him now, he would be laughing his ass off at the magnitude of the situation. Scrub that. The old cynical Jamie wouldn't even believe it. Jamie didn't like to think of the fool he once was. He was ashamed of his years scrabbling around in the wilderness, doing nothing but surviving. Serving no earthly purpose.

Jamie didn't know how long they'd been driving for, when a noise in the distance made him strain his ears. 'Stop the truck,' he cried.

Matthew looked at him, first annoyed, then concerned. He turned to the driver. 'Stop,' he said. The driver slowed to a halt.

'Turn off the engine,' Jamie hissed. This time the driver complied without waiting for the Voice of the Father to repeat it. The other vehicles also whined to a halt behind.

'What is it?' the Voice asked Jamie.

Jamie held up his hand for quiet. There it was again – the distinct rataratarat of machine gun fire.

'Let me see,' Jamie said. Without waiting for a reply, he slid out of the cab, reached for his AK47 and pulled up his hood. Moving quickly, he melted into the trees, running back the way they had driven. Running towards the sound of bullets. But he felt no fear. Only power and adrenalin. The knowledge that he was trained to do this. He was good at this. He ran along the path, past their convoy of vehicles until he reached the foot soldiers.

As soon as they noted the trim of his robe, the warriors snapped to attention.

'What's going on?' Jamie asked.

'Our warriors are under attack at the rear,' the man replied, his voice deep and calm.

'And?'

'There's a convoy of trucks up on the main route. They opened fire on us two minutes ago. They've got the high ground. I've told most of our soldiers to fall back into the woods. We'll leave some snipers behind to eliminate them.'

'Who are they? The attackers?' Jamie snapped.

'I don't know.'

'Take a guess.'

'The enemy. A scouting party. A supply convoy. Raiders. Could be anyone.'

'How many trucks?'

'Four or five, but it's hard to tell.'

'Continue falling back,' Jamie ordered. 'And leave the snipers returning fire. I'll take some AVs up on the main route and cut them off. Inform our snipers we'll be coming. Tell them not to fire on us.'

The warrior nodded and Jamie powered back to the convoy as fast as he could. When he got there, the disciples were out of their vehicles, gathered around FJ once more. Jamie had no qualms about speaking up this time.

'Our foot soldiers are under attack,' he said. 'I need six heavily armoured vehicles up on the main route to outflank them.'

'Whatever you need,' Matthew said.

'Please,' Jamie said. 'You stay here. We'll take care of this.'

Matthew paused and then nodded.

Jamie ran down the line of vehicles and picked out six: three trucks loaded with soldiers and weapons, a couple of fast AVs and a heavy duty 4x4. He got into the driving seat of one of the

AVs, accompanied by three other disciples and pulled around the other static vehicles. The six vehicles travelled down the track until Jamie spotted a path leading back up to the main road. Turning sharp right, he angled the AV up the bank and onto the track. The disciples already had hold of their weapons.

Revving the engine in first gear, Jamie climbed the track and finally bumped up onto the dual carriageway. He recognised this route. It was the Wessex Way which led down into Bournemouth. His blood pumped and he felt a little light-headed, but he also felt exhilarated and in control. He drove on a few yards and waited for the others, then they all headed back along the main road towards the enemy. The road was relatively smooth here and they flew along.

After only a minute's driving, Jamie saw the dull silhouettes of the enemy vehicles up ahead. Heard the sound of bullets pinging off metal. He indicated, braked and turned, so his AV was parked across the route. The rest of his convoy followed suit, so they had now effectively blocked the road. Jamie cracked the window, aimed his machine gun into the night and fired. His brothers did the same.

After thirty seconds or so, Jamie stopped shooting and signalled to others to ceasefire. The sound of gunfire stopped altogether, and now the enemy's engines roared to life. Jamie waited, straining his eyes to see, wondering if the hostile vehicles were headed straight for them. Should they move? He fired his weapon once more. But the engine noise receded until it was just a faint growl in the distance. They must have turned tail or pulled off the main route. Either way, it looked like they had gone.

Jamie pointed the AV back up the Wessex Way towards the enemy's last seen position. He drove more slowly this time, his brothers aiming their weapons into the darkness, sweeping their surroundings for any movement.

Nothing. No one.

He felt the eyes of his warrior brothers upon them. Thousands hidden down on the forest road under cover of darkness.

And then, up ahead, he saw a lone truck in the middle of the road. Stationary with no lights. Jamie braked. The other vehicles drove on to form a semi-circle around the vehicle, blocking off any escape route. Jamie realised the others were waiting for his orders, but he wasn't sure what to do. He might have the ear of the Voice of the Father, but he wasn't experienced in these situations. He'd have to make a judgement call. The truck's cab appeared empty, but looks could be deceiving.

With more confidence than he felt, Jamie opened the AV door and slid out, dropping into a crouch and pointing his Kalashnikov at the truck. He braced himself to be fired upon. Several of the other disciples had followed his lead and exited their vehicles, approaching the truck with caution. Jamie's adrenalin was surging and strangely, he found himself almost enjoying the situation, revelling in the fear.

He had almost reached the truck now and sidled up to the passenger side of the cab. He pulled at the cold metal handle and the door clicked open. Then he flattened himself against the side of the vehicle and kicked hard at the door. It flew open and he stepped forward, firing into the interior without checking to see if anyone was inside or not. His heart battered his ribcage and he stopped firing to see what he'd just done. Nothing. There was no one inside. Jamie was half-disappointed, half-relieved.

While he'd been checking out the cab, two of his brothers had been around to the back. Jamie joined them.

'Empty,' one of them said.

Jamie peered in. Nothing inside. 'Maybe it ran out of fuel. Looks like they've fled,' he said.

'Here!' a voice called out.

Jamie turned and followed the sound to the front of the

abandoned truck. One of the disciples had noticed a piece of rope tied to the front of the vehicle. It had been cut.

'They were towing it?' Jamie asked.

'Yes,' the disciple replied. 'Should we give chase? The other vehicles—'

'No point,' Jamie said. 'We're only a few miles from the Perimeter now. Come on, let's get back to the others.'

Twenty minutes later, Jamie and the Voice of the Father led the army down along the main route into Bournemouth. The vehicles drove in rows, four abreast, spread out across all four lanes. The cavalry came behind and lastly came the foot soldiers, their robes merging with the cold darkness. Unshed snow hung heavy in the air and the breath of four thousand soldiers made its own clouds above them.

The vehicles moved at a slow cruising speed, a little way ahead of the main army. Jamie had returned to Matthew's vehicle, leaving the driving to one of the others. No one spoke. They would soon reach their destination and all thoughts turned to what might lie ahead. As they reached the end of the road, flakes of snow began to fall. At first, light and whirling, but too soon they grew heavy and thick. This was no flurry, it was a blizzard. The raw landscape transforming from a black wilderness to a whiteout.

The going was slow, but they inched along. At least they would be able to sneak up unseen, the snow shielding their approach. Jamie wondered how the main army behind was doing. He prayed the snow wouldn't settle too deep or they'd be done for.

His prayers were answered. The snowfall eased after about half an hour, just before dawn. The land was white, but the snow wasn't deep enough to hamper their progress.

'Nearly there,' Jamie murmured.

'Do you remember your task?' Matthew asked.

Jamie nodded. How could he forget. He was to kill the one who had taken their Holy Father.

'When the time comes, you must not hesitate. I will ask and you will act.'

'Yes.'

'There were many I could have asked to receive this honour, but I chose you. So you must not hesitate. You must not doubt what is asked of you. You must have faith and you will be rewarded.'

'You can rely on me,' Jamie said. 'I won't let you down.'

'Good.'

A loud squeal of brakes jolted Jamie and Matthew from their conversation. Their AV slowed and spun out. Up ahead, something glowed red, a soft light permeating the snowy morning haze. Two of them. Jamie quickly realised they were tail lights and, as his eyes focused, he saw more. Their own driver quickly straightened the AV up and they began to give chase.

'Faster,' Matthew said.

Jamie squinted into the snow-glare of morning to see the bulk of a hulking great snow-topped truck up ahead. And another. And yet another. They were the same model as the abandoned one they'd seen back on the main road.

'It's them,' Jamie said to Matthew. 'The ones who attacked us earlier.'

Their brothers in the other vehicles were matching their pace now, leaving the foot soldiers and cavalry behind.

'Run them down,' Matthew cried. 'I don't want them reaching the Perimeter.'

Jamie opened his window, letting in a hiss of frosty air. He aimed his machine gun and began firing.

The trucks sped off ahead towards the Perimeter. Jamie and his brothers gave chase, leaving the rest of their army to catch them up.

Within five minutes, the Perimeter fence had materialised in the distance, silver and white. It seemed bigger than Jamie remembered it. Taller, wider, more imposing. It wasn't at all how he remembered it. They fired at the trucks, but none of their shots seemed to find a target or slow them down. Jamie wondered what would happen once they all reached the fence. He wondered if he would survive this. Or if this was the day that his luck would finally run out.

CHAPTER THIRTY-TWO

RILEY

Spread across the northern horizon, a massive army marched towards us. It had come too close, too fast. The snowstorm had hidden its progress and now they would soon be upon us. Like gathering clouds, this swarm of men, shrinking the sky and smothering the land.

Death was coming to visit.

But Luc was still out there. Somewhere. Was he captured? Dead? If Luc was gone, there was no point in anything. FJ would pay. I would kill him myself. Army or no army.

I heard shouts from below. Pa's voice. The guards. Everybody scrambling to prepare for the inevitable. For several seconds, Rita and I were frozen in place on the platform, staring in horror at the distant army. Bright lights preceded them – pinpricks of yellow.

Headlights.

So FJ had vehicles too.

Of course he did.

The beams grew stronger as the vehicles drew closer. Spread out in front of their army, but still out of our firing range. I'd left my semi-automatic at home, so now I drew out my

Magnum. Rita had the same idea and aimed her pistol down through the razor wire, waiting.

Despite the cold, a thin film of sweat coated my breastbone and forehead, my blood pumping furiously through my body. Today was a day that was always going to come, but now it was here, it didn't feel real. I saw everything removed from myself, like I was watching a movie. But this was no movie. The snow, the enemy, my sweat and heartbeats – they were all real.

The racing vehicles drew ever closer, headlights flashing. The pitter-patter of automatic gunfire, muffled by snow.

'That's Eddie!' Rita cried. 'Those are our trucks.'

Luc! My heart jumped.

'I have to tell the others,' she said. 'Stay here.' Rita almost slid down the ladder, calling to the guards, telling them to cease firing.

The whine of engines deepened to a throaty roar as the trucks came closer still. But, through the milky morning, behind our trucks came another bank of vehicles accompanied by the lightning crackle of gunfire. Our people were being pursued. Still too far away to make out their faces through the windscreen. Right then I'd have given anything for my binoculars. Rita climbed back up the ladder, a battered-looking Kalashnikov now slung across her body.

'They're being chased,' she panted. 'Those Salisbury bastards are firing on them, but Eddie's lot are giving as good as they get.'

Come on, Luc, I chanted in my head. *You can do it. You can make it home. Not far now.* The lead vehicle was about five hundred yards away and I was sure I could make out Eddie in the driving seat. He had his hand on the horn, his headlights still flashing. Signalling us to open up the gates and let them in. On the passenger side of his truck, one of our guards was leaning out of the window, returning fire.

As they approached, it was as though everything slowed to a

single beat of time. The trucks in a line flashing their lights at the Perimeter, FJ's vehicles behind them and the bright sparks of gunfire. But then something happened, and that single beat of time splintered into a thousand fragments of horror.

A light zipped across the sky with a sound like a firework. There was a pause. And then our lead truck exploded into an orange ball of flames, the sound ripping across the sky with a sickening boom, sending metal and smoke out across the snowy wasteland. I turned from the sight of the burning wreckage to look at Rita, her face a mask of shock.

'No!' she yelled, her voice lost in the roar of flames and multiple explosions.

Our other three trucks were nearly home, but one skidded out in the blast and now it tilted at an impossible angle before crashing down onto its side in the snow, sliding away from the Perimeter gates. It came to a screeching stop, wheels spinning in the smoke-filled air. Behind our remaining two trucks came an assortment of black jeeps, AVs, trucks and 4x4s – FJ's vehicles.

From our vantage point up on the platform, I saw the outer gates had now been flung open, guards stationed either side, ready to swing them shut again once our trucks had made it safely through. Only they wouldn't all be coming through now. One was gone and the other was immobilised, fallen.

'Come on!' I yelled, tugging at Rita's arm. 'We have to go down and help.'

Her face was white and rigid, but she followed my shaky progress down the ladder, her machine gun crashing into each rung as she descended.

Was Luc okay? Had that really been Eddie in the lead truck, or had it been someone else? Back on the ground, we raced around to the Guards' House, skidding and sliding on the snow. Although she moved fast, Rita's face remained frozen, her mouth open, eyes glazed. In my heart, I knew Eddie had been in that doomed truck, but until it was confirmed there was always a tiny ember of hope.

The guards flung open the gates to the inner wall as the first truck reached the outer gates. The driver's eyes were wide as he hit the brakes and turned into a skid. Rita and I backed up instinctively, away from the entrance as the truck screeched through, scraping the edge of the wall on his way in. The second truck came in at a steadier pace and the guard had to scramble to get the outer gates shut before the enemy reached us.

FJ's vehicles were almost at the fence and they pulled up just as our heavily reinforced gates clanked shut, their armoured-steel sections ringing out, setting my teeth on edge.

As this was happening, a figure came hurtling towards the fence from behind FJ's vehicles. He wore a guards' uniform, and I realised it must be one of our guys from the toppled vehicle. But he was on the outside and the gates were shut.

It was one of Pa and Eddie's friends, a guard called Ethan who had been with us since before I was born. A nice guy. Quiet and hard-working. As he flung himself against the locked gate, he wore an expression of fear and defeat. The guards inside were trying to get the gates open once more, but if they did that, there was no way they'd get them shut again in time to stop FJ's vehicles getting in.

Ethan must have realised what would happen and he shook his head at them, yelling at them to leave it, but they continued to fumble with the lock. There was no escape for him now. Nowhere to hide – he was blocked in by the fence and cut off by the approaching vehicles. With a grim smile, he turned his back to us and faced the enemy, charging at them, spraying bullets uselessly into the armoured vehicles. Two seconds later he was dead. I covered my mouth to stop myself screaming. They'd shot him down.

I turned away, unable to believe what I'd seen. He had run

towards his death to stop us opening the gates for him and putting the rest of the Perimeter in danger. But there was no time to mourn Ethan and his sacrifice yet. I had to find out what had happened to Luc and Eddie.

Two guards climbed down from the first cab and two from the second, neither Luc nor Eddie among them. My hands began to shake and I thought I might throw up. What if Luc was in the overturned vehicle? Trapped out there among the hostiles. Rita ran to the two trucks, calling out for her family.

And then I saw him.

I saw him.

He clambered down from the back of one of the trucks, blood cascading down the side of his face. Had he been shot? Rita got to him first.

'Thank goodness,' she cried. And then, 'Eddie?'

But Luc shook his head, and I had to stand by and watch, as he wept in his mother's arms for his dead father.

CHAPTER THIRTY-THREE

JAMIE

It took some skilful driving to avoid crashing into the fence. The gates swung shut only seconds before Jamie and his army reached the Perimeter. But at least they'd managed to take out two of the enemy's trucks.

Jamie tried to slow his breathing, using the chant to calm him and channel his thoughts. Their main army was still a way behind. They would have to pull their vehicles back. Wait for the rest of them to catch up. Perimeter guards had already begun firing on them and, although they were in armoured vehicles, there was no point waiting here like sitting ducks.

'We should pull back,' he said. 'Wait for the rest of our—'

'No,' Matthew cut him off. His eyes glittered with excitement. 'We are here now and we will get what we came for.'

As he spoke, a hail of bullets began to rain down on the vehicles, deafening and relentless.

'Please, sir,' Jamie urged. 'Let's just pull back out of firing range, or we're not going to survive this.'

CHAPTER THIRTY-FOUR

RILEY

No time to dwell on the horror of what had just happened. We were under attack. As our guards scrambled to withdraw behind the inner wall, about thirty to forty enemy vehicles parked up outside the fence and began firing with assorted weaponry. Several of our men were hit and had to stagger to safety. But then our guards began returning fire from the parapet, driving the enemy back. In all the confusion, I couldn't see Pa. Where the hell was he?

I turned as Rita drew back from Luc to examine the wound on his head. He put his hand to his face and stared at the blood on his fingers – he hadn't even realised he was bleeding.

'I think I banged my head in the truck,' he said. 'I'm fine.'

I took a step towards them, unsure what to say. I went with the obvious choice: 'I'm so sorry,' I said, cringing at the inadequacy of the words.

Luc shook his head. 'We were almost home,' he said. 'Another thirty seconds...'

Rita suddenly turned from distraught to livid, her face darkening to a thunderous scowl. I'd never seen her so angry. She wiped away her tears, turned and headed for the platform once more.

'Rita!' I called out.

She turned. 'I'll kill them for what they've done,' she said. 'They murdered him. They murdered Eddie.' And then she carried on walking.

Luc looked dazed. I went to him, put my arms around his body. 'I'm so sorry, Luc,' I said. 'What can I do?'

'Nothing,' he said, staring ahead in a daze.

I felt sick for him, but he was right – there was nothing I could do to stop how he was feeling. Eddie was his father. A larger-than-life character who everyone loved and respected. A family man, a grafter, a figure of respect. You always felt safe around Eddie Donovan. And now he was gone.

I realised the gunfire had calmed down a bit. Now that all our guards were behind the wall, the shots were more sporadic. The panicked yelling had lessened as well, turning into barked orders and muffled conversations.

Through the gates, in the middle distance, the cloud of dark-robed warriors drew closer. They would be here soon. And then what? We would be trapped. Surrounded. Although we'd known this day was going to come, it was a different thing altogether to be faced with it. To see a vast enemy coming across the land to kill you. I tried to clear my mind of the creeping terror and turn it to more practical matters. Like, what I could do to help.

'There you are, Riley!' Pa strode towards us. 'I was on the platforms looking for you,' he cried. 'I thought you were still up there.' He looked at Luc. 'Eddie...?'

Luc tried to answer, but he couldn't speak.

I dropped my arms from around Luc's body. 'Eddie didn't make it,' I said to Pa. 'He was in the lead truck.'

'Son of a bitch!' Pa cried, his face contorting. 'I'm sorry, Luc,' he said, placing a hand on his shoulder. He took a moment and then turned to me. 'Where's Rita?' His voice was gruff, brimming with emotion.

I jerked my head up at the platforms.

'And your ma?'

'Still at home,' I replied. 'Liss and Anna are at Luc's. They're under guard.'

'Good. They all need to stay there. You need to join them too, Riley.'

'I'm more useful here. Put me up on the platforms. I can take out some of those vehicles.'

'Listen to me, Riley,' Pa said. 'And listen hard.'

I bit my knuckles and listened.

'FJ wants to kill you,' Pa said through gritted teeth. 'He wants to take you from here and he wants to *kill* you. So get your ass back home now before I order the guards to tie you up and take you there by force.'

'Fine,' I said. I was shaking, but whether it was from shock at Pa's tone, from the loss of Eddie or from fear of FJ, I wasn't sure.

He turned to Luc, speaking more softly now. 'Go with her. Make sure she does what I say. And get that head wound looked at.' Pa glanced over his shoulder at the scene through the gates and I followed his line of sight. The swarm of warriors was almost here, blotting out the landscape, dark cloaks billowing into a white sky. A low drone accompanied them. I recognised that sound – it was their warrior chant and it sent shivers through my already ice-cold body.

Then came a single voice, cutting a swathe through all the other sounds. A voice which demanded to be heard. Everyone in the Perimeter fell silent and listened to the calm, measured words being spoken. Amplified into the air through a loud speaker.

'Return Our Father, James Grey, to us.' A pause and then,

'Send out the girl, Riley, to account for her sins. Then we will leave.'

The sound was distorted, but even so, I recognised that voice. It was FJ. He really was here in person and he wanted his revenge. To hear my name spoken like that was the most chilling feeling in the world. Liss had said her brother hated me, but it hadn't sunk in how much, until now.

Pa's face turned white. Luc gathered me into his body as though he could protect me from those words.

FJ wanted two people.

Grey was dead. So that left me.

If I gave myself up, I could stop the attack.

I could save the Perimeter.

'Go!' Pa cried. 'Back to the house as quick as you can.'

'But, Pa, what about FJ's demands?'

'That was FJ's voice on the loudspeaker?' Pa said.

Luc and I nodded.

'So he's here in person,' Pa muttered. 'Good. That means we can sort this once and for all.' He looked at me once more. 'Now go.'

'If I give myself up, FJ said he'll leave the Perimeter,' I said. 'You should send me out there.' My insides trembled. I spoke with a lot more courage than I felt.

'If you believe that,' Pa said, 'then you've a lot more to learn than I thought.'

'So he's lying then?'

'I wouldn't trust him as far as I could throw him,' Pa snapped. 'Go back to the house, Riley. Or so help me I'll get the guards to carry you there. If FJ gets hold of you, we're doomed.'

'Okay.' I raised my hands in submission. 'What will you do?'

'Refuse his demands,' Pa replied. 'He thinks we still have Grey in here alive, so I don't think he'll launch an all-out attack. Thank God Liss didn't do what FJ asked. Go, Riley.' He kissed my forehead and waited for me to leave.

Luc remained silent. His father had just been killed. He was in shock. I took his hand and we turned away from the Perimeter entrance. Before we left, I glanced back at the guards, at the men and women gripping their weapons as they waited to see what would happen next. At least the shooting had stopped for the moment. FJ was probably waiting for his demands to be met. I worried about what he'd do when he realised he wouldn't be getting either of us.

As Luc and I hurried back home, we passed more of our people heading for the fence and I nodded my head in greeting, feeling guilty that I was going in the other direction. All the while, Luc said nothing, his head bowed.

CHAPTER THIRTY-FIVE

JAMIE

The air was quiet in the wake of Matthew's demands, the rest of the warriors fast approaching, a wave of black against the snow-covered plain. Jamie and his brothers waited in their vehicles, keeping a safe distance from the Perimeter gates, spread out in two rows.

Inside the AV, anger radiated off the Voice of the Father. 'Why don't those people listen to me?' he hissed. 'They've seen my army. They must know they don't stand a chance. All we are asking is for our leader to be returned to us. And for the girl to pay for her transgressions. These are fair and reasonable demands. Too reasonable.'

Jamie wondered about the girl. Who was she? Matthew was losing his composure. He was probably exhausted. Their leader hadn't undergone the same level of training as the rest of them. He wasn't used to these conditions. Jamie realised *he* was the strong one now. He was the one who was needed. Matthew actually looked to him for advice. And Jamie felt strangely protective towards his powerful leader.

'Did they hear me, do you think?' Matthew asked Jamie. 'Was the speaker turned up loudly enough?'

'I'm sure they heard.'

'So why don't they respond?' His temper rose.

'Give them a few more minutes,' Jamie said. 'They need time to understand what's going on.'

'I'd think it was clear what's going on – they must meet our ultimatum or face the consequences. I'll give them ten minutes before we start to tear this place down.'

'What about Our Father?' one of the disciples interrupted from the back seat.

Matthew turned to look at the one who had spoken. 'Who are you to question me?' he said, his voice deathly quiet. 'Take down your hood.'

The disciple lifted his hand and pulled down the thick material. The man's face was lined with age but had a strength about it. 'I'm sorry,' the man said. 'I would never think to question you, but—'

'But?' Matthew pronounced the word carefully, savouring the consonants.

The disciple shook his head. 'Nothing. I apologise.'

'But?' Matthew repeated.

Jamie's heart hammered. The Voice of the Father was far more terrifying than the enemy behind the fence. He realised how lucky he'd been that their leader hadn't taken offence at Jamie's own questions. He wondered why that was. The unfortunate disciple quivered. His head bent in deference.

His posture must have appeased Matthew, as he turned his face back to the front. 'Why are these people not replying?'

'I don't know,' Jamie said.

'Five more minutes,' Matthew said. 'Five more minutes and then we attack.'

CHAPTER THIRTY-SIX

RILEY

The snow was already turning to mush, brown smeary footprints staining the white pavements. Nearly home. What would I do once we got there? Could I really just sit around while people put their lives at risk to protect us? Maybe I could do as Rita had suggested and pack some bags. At least it would keep me occupied. As we turned into our road, I heard a shout.

'Riley!'

It was Ma.

She stumbled down the middle of the road, trying not to slide on the half-frozen slush, holding her fake fur coat in place over her nightie. 'Thank goodness you're all right,' she cried, taking hold of my arm. 'Is it true? Is Grey's army here?'

I nodded. 'How did you know?'

'Denzil came by earlier. What should we do?' she cried. 'Where's your pa? Is he okay?'

I nodded again. 'He's fine.' I hoped she wouldn't ask any more questions. I couldn't tell her about Eddie. Not in front of Luc.

'Your face!' Ma cried, putting a hand out to touch the dried blood on Luc's cheek. 'What happened?'

'He banged his head in the truck,' I said. 'I'll clean it up when we get inside.'

'It looks awful,' Ma said. 'You should see the doctor.'

'Don't worry, Ma,' I said. 'I think it looks worse than it is.' Luc rubbed at his chin. Ma's hysteria was going to send him over the edge. I could feel it. 'Go back in the house,' I said to her. We'll be there in a sec.'

'Come with me,' she said. 'Both of you. It's not safe out here.'

'It's fine, Ma. FJ's outside the fence. He can't get in.' But I'm not sure I believed the last part. I was pretty sure he *could* get in. *Would* get in. It was just a case of how long we could hold them off for. 'Just give us two secs, okay?'

'Okay.' She hesitated before turning back towards the house. 'I'm going to have a shower and get dressed.'

Once she'd gone, I faced Luc, his face devoid of expression.

'Luc, I don't know what to say to make things better,' I said, taking both his hands in mine. 'Your dad was amazing. He died trying to make things safer for everyone. He was an incredible person. What happened was terrible.'

He gave a small nod and then shook his head. 'I can't believe it's true,' he said. 'How can he be gone? He's my dad.'

'I know. I'm so sorry. What happened out there? Why were you gone so long?'

He took a breath. 'We found the supply convoy, no problem. Traded them for everything they had. They wanted silver, cigarettes and alcohol, we wanted food and medicines. It was the perfect deal. Dad was so happy. We all were. We got so much stuff, Riley, you wouldn't believe it. Enough to load up all five trucks and last us right through the winter.'

'Five trucks?' I said. 'I only saw four coming back.'

'Yeah, mine broke down. We tried to fix it, but we didn't have the part. So we had to unload it. Pack all the supplies into the other trucks. It took ages. By the time we'd done that it was dark. Anyway, we decided to tow the broken truck, which was really slow going. It took hours. It would've taken days to get home at that pace, so we made the decision to get off the heathland and chance taking the main route. As soon as we hit Ringwood, that's when we saw them.'

'Who? FJ's lot?'

Luc nodded.

'What did you do? Did they see you?'

'No. Not straight away. We were driving without headlights. They weren't on the main route, they were marching parallel to the Wessex Way, down along the forest path. Dad being Dad wanted to start shooting. We were up on the main road in trucks, they were down below us on foot. It was a no-brainer.'

'But—'

'But we didn't realise they also had a fleet of vehicles. We were too cocky and didn't do a proper recon. We did manage to wipe out some of their soldiers, but there was like a gazillion of them. Too many for just the ten of us to take on.'

'So what did you do when you saw their vehicles?' I asked.

'That's when we cut our broken truck loose and tried to speed home. But FJ's AVs were blocking the road, so we had to pull off the main route and make our way back the long way.' Luc shook his head and rubbed at his forehead with his fingertips.

I took his hand. 'You don't have to talk about it now if you don't want to,' I said.

'No,' he said. 'It's okay, I want to. Then it started snowing and we couldn't see a bloody thing. Once we reached the heathland outside the Perimeter, they were all there, coming at us. Their vehicles chased us all the way back. Fired some kind of RPG at Dad's truck.'

'Oh, Luc—'

'FJ is not going to get away with this,' he growled, his face tightening, darkening.

'No,' I said. 'He's not.'

'We should've ended him when we had the chance.' His voice cracked.

'Come on,' I said, pulling at his hand. 'Come into the house. Let me clean that gash on your head and then we can work out what to do.'

He let himself be led inside. The house was still. Just the usual hum from the genny and the faint sound of running water from upstairs. Normal morning sounds.

Only nothing was normal.

We shed our coats and went into the kitchen where I cleaned the cut on his head with a damp cloth, carefully wiping the dried blood from his face. Once the wound was clean and dressed, I made us some coffee, putting a large spoon of honey into Luc's cup and stirring it until it dissolved. He took a sip and made a face.

'Drink it,' I said.

'Too sweet.'

'You need it. You're in shock. It'll help.'

He nodded and took another sip, came over to the table and sat next to me, dazed. I put my drink down and turned my chair to face him. He was lost in his grief, his eyes unseeing, his hands still clasping his cup. I took it from him and set it next to mine. Took his hands and brought them to my lips. A tear slid down his cheek and I leant forward to kiss it away. Moved my mouth to cover his. Luc turned his chair to face me and suddenly his hands were on my neck, my hair, my arms, and we were kissing. Salt tears and desperation on our lips. The cold of winter on our faces, melting to warmth and heat.

I shifted from my chair onto his lap, closed the gap between our bodies until we almost inhabited the same space, breathing the same air. I took his grief and made it my own. His hands on my back. Skin-on-skin, sending jolts of electricity through my body.

In my peripheral vision, I saw Ma come into the kitchen. Heard her apologise, and then leave again. I felt a moment's discomfort, but not enough to make me want to stop.

Luc slowed his kiss and ran his thumb down along my jaw. I leaned my head into his touch.

'Was that your mother?' he murmured, a wry smile in his voice.

'Mmm.'

Luc sighed. 'I don't want to think about anything,' he said. 'I want to stay like this.'

'Yeah. Me too.'

'But we can't.'

'No.'

'Our home's being attacked,' he said. 'We should...' He made to stand up so I moved off his lap. His demeanour had changed from dazed and grief-stricken, back to the driven, focused Luc I knew. 'We should go next door,' he continued. 'Tell Liss and Annabelle what's going on. And we need to prepare ourselves to leave here. Just in case.' He leant down and kissed me again, grazing my lower lip with his teeth. A slow kiss with a meaningful gaze fit to knock my feet from under me. But it didn't linger nearly long enough.

'You go next door,' I said reluctantly. 'I need to speak to Ma and pack some stuff up. I'll come over when I'm done.'

CHAPTER THIRTY-SEVEN

JAMIE

A clank and jingle of metal and the snorts and whinnies of the horses permeated the frozen air as the first wave of cavalry finally caught up with Jamie and his convoy. The horsemen stayed back behind the vehicles awaiting orders. It would only be minutes until the foot soldiers caught up.

The electrified fence of the Perimeter towered in front of them. The brick wall behind it even taller, studded with razor wire. Curls of snow adorned the formidable fortress. Jamie wondered how they would breach it and how many guards were inside. He saw movement at the top of the wall and realised there were people up there, the tops of their heads just visible. This attack might not be as straightforward as the Voice of the Father had anticipated.

Jamie was suddenly assaulted by a sharp memory of the last time he was here and he shook his head to try to dislodge the image. Now was not the time to think of that night. Especially with the task that lay ahead of him.

Matthew took up the mouthpiece for the public address system and spoke:

'This is your last warning,' he said. 'Send out James Grey and the girl. You have two minutes to comply.'

Jamie stared at the gates. Nothing stirred behind them. No people could be seen. No activity. Nothing to suggest they were about to do what they'd been asked.

Suddenly, a small missile flew down towards them. Over the top of the wall and across the fence, to land at the foot of one of their 4x4s. Jamie's first thought was that it was a grenade, but then the passenger door to the 4x4 opened and a disciple got out, bent down and picked up the thing, whatever it was.

The disciple walked towards their AV. A slow unconcerned walk considering the enemy probably had him in their sights. Jamie wondered what the item could be. He held his breath, waiting to see if the enemy would begin shooting at the man. But there was no activity from behind the wall. And now the disciple stood at Jamie's window. Jamie withdrew the nose of his AK47 and rested it against his seat. He buzzed the window down further and took the proffered item from the man's hand.

It was a large rock. Cold and jagged with a note tied around it. Jamie slid the note from under the string and smoothed it out. He read the scrawled message in his head and then passed it along to Matthew. Matthew did not read it aloud either, but his face darkened, his fists clenched and the cold atmosphere deepened further.

'Read it aloud,' Matthew said to Jamie, passing the note back to him.

Jamie cleared his throat, unwilling to say the words which would further anger Matthew. 'We will execute your leader unless you withdraw immediately.'

A gasp from the back. 'We must do as they say,' came a stern voice.

Matthew ignored the advice. 'No,' he said.

'But we cannot risk Our Father's life,' the disciple said. 'He is the whole reason we are here.'

'Do you question me?' Matthew said. 'I am the Voice of the Father. I speak for Him. I know what Our Father would wish. Do you question his judgement in choosing me?'

'Of course not,' the disciple said. 'But I—'

'Prepare to attack,' Matthew said to the one who had delivered the message. 'Disable the fence and blow up the gates. Kill them all, but bring me the girl alive.'

'And what about Our Father?' the disciple said.

'What?' Matthew snapped.

'We must bring him out alive too.'

'Yes. Of course.'

The man gave a short bow and turned away, returning to his vehicle to deliver his orders.

Matthew waved a hand at their driver who started up the engine and drove around the other vehicles so that they were now towards the back at the western edge of their army, leaving the rest of their convoy at the head of their troops. Jamie still had a good view of the gates, but they were now much further from the front line.

Up at the front, the bank of vehicles cranked into life and began to crawl forward. Behind them, the first wave of foot soldiers swept past the cavalry. Moving silently across the snow, they took up the chant. Jamie mouthed along, willing victory to be with them. The whole mass of men and machines moved forward until they were in firing range, and then halted. It was as though they were waiting for something. Jamie was eager to know the battle plan. Glancing at the Voice of the Father and noting the grim smile on his face, Jamie dared not ask. He would have to watch and see.

Then a volley of shots came down from the enemy guards along the top of the wall. Some ricocheted off the metal roofs of the vehicles, others found their mark and sank into flesh. Grey's men returned fire with accuracy. Several bodies slumped down across the wall, some caught up in razor wire, others tumbling to their deaths. Cries of pain were heard from behind the battle-ments. But weapons fire still continued to rain onto the front line. And the warriors still held their positions, even as many of them fell.

Next, Matthew's snipers scuttled forward and crouched behind the front row of vehicles, rifles aimed at the gate. A tightly packed group of warriors settled behind them, and Jamie made out a large shape in their midst. A gun. A huge rifle so heavy it took two men to carry it. Soldiers fanned out around them, protecting the precious weapon. Taking fire. Dying. To keep the gun safe. To keep the marksman safe.

Once the weapon had been set up on the ground, the remaining warriors drew back and Jamie saw that it was some kind of anti-material rifle. It looked like it would have a wicked recoil. The gunner was already in place on the ground. He wore ear defenders and had his eye locked on the telescopic sight at the front. A second man lay beside him with his own scope – his spotter – picking out the targets for him so the shooter could concentrate on his aim.

Jamie held his breath, waiting.

After what seemed like an age, but must have been only moments, the gunner fired. The sound was incredible. Like a canon going off.

He had blasted a great hole in the fence and the wall beyond. Then he fired again and again until the hole was large enough for a man to get through. The gunner shifted position and focused on another area of the fence, doing exactly the same thing. Once he'd blasted half a dozen of these holes, the fence sparked, crackled and died as the electrical current shorted out.

The gunner now turned his attention to the outer gates.

Jamie flicked his eyes to the Perimeter and guessed the man was aiming at the spot where the gates met the posts – going for the hinges. He watched in awe as the heavy metal of the posts tore and buckled. The shooter fired again and again at each hinge until eventually the gates wobbled, groaned and crashed forward with an almighty bang, sending snow and mud spraying into the air, the gate posts now reduced to a mess of twisted metal.

The Perimeter fence was breached.

CHAPTER THIRTY-EIGHT

RILEY

We spent the next twenty minutes packing. I told Ma it was just a precaution. Like a fire drill. To my surprise, she didn't freak out. Said it reminded her of going on holiday as a child. She told me stories of fraught car journeys and early mornings at airports, where you could find people of every nationality. Of speeding down long runways and taking off above the clouds. A bit like copter travel, only much, much more exciting. Lazy days spent on warm beaches where everyone was relaxed and happy. Her brothers throwing her into the waves. Laughing.

It sounded like a fairy tale.

As she reminisced, we stuffed cases and bags with warm clothes, medicines and food supplies. I lugged crates of weapons and ammo from Pa's stores and we loaded up the two AVs and trailers. I also took Rita's advice and packed us each a rucksack of essentials. Ma tried to ask me about Luc, but I wasn't in the mood to share my feelings. I could tell she was hurt by this, so I gave her a hug and said it was still early days.

Once we were done, I sat halfway up the stairs, feeling the enormity of our situation. Would I get to stay here, in my house? Or would this army batter down our defences and kick us all out? I'd had these worries before, but now they felt like they could actually become a reality. It was crazy. We were the Talbot Wood Perimeter. We were the ones other people contacted for help, not the other way around. And now we might be brought to our knees. We might have to evacuate our homes. We might never come back. This place, my home, could very well be trashed and picked apart. The land claimed back by nature. I pictured it all in my head. Our beautiful safe home destroyed.

How would we be able to live out there? Permanently. Plus, it was the depths of winter. And with Eddie gone, we had lost so much of what made this place familiar and safe. What about Ma? How would she cope without her beloved house and Perimeter fence to protect her? I had to keep busy. Couldn't sit here and worry about what ifs. There was no point.

Ma came down the stairs and I stood to let her pass. Instead, she sat down and patted the stair for me to sit back down. I did as she wanted and she leant her head on my shoulder.

'I love you, Riley,' she said.

'Love you too, Ma.'

'I'm sorry.'

'What for?'

'For not being a great mother anymore. I know I'm not as strong as I should be. I know I pretend things are better than they are. I—'

'Ma,' I said. 'It's okay. You're doing the best you can. We all are. That's all we can do.'

'You're a good girl, Riley.' She kissed my cheek. 'I'm glad you and Luc have each other. Everybody needs to have a somebody.'

'You and Pa seem good now,' I said.

'Your father is an amazing man,' Ma said. 'I worry about him every second he's away from me.'

'Pa can take care of himself,' I said with a confidence I

didn't feel. I thought of Eddie's truck exploding across the snow, bile rising to the back of my throat. But I still couldn't bring myself to tell Ma what had happened.

A deep boom made me catch my breath. Louder than a gunshot, but not as loud as the devastating explosion earlier this morning. Ma and I looked at each other as another boom rattled the windows. We stood and slowly walked down the rest of the staircase.

'What was that?' Ma asked, her voice barely audible.

I shook my head. 'It sounded bad. I hope they haven't got through the fence.'

More blasts shook our bones.

'Johnny,' Ma whispered. 'What if your pa—'

'Stop,' I said. 'Wait here and I'll find out.'

'No, it's not safe.'

'Well, I can't just stay here, not knowing,' I replied. 'I'm going to get Luc.'

'Okay,' she said, as another explosion made us cringe.

'Wait here,' I said.

She gripped my hand and I had to pry it loose.

'Try not to worry,' I said uselessly as I reached for my coat on the banister post.

I opened the door just as a car pulled into the drive with a screech. My uncle Tom got out, his breaths coming hard, his face grimy with smoke and dirt.

'What's happening?' I asked. 'Is Pa okay?'

'He's fine, but—'

'What?' Ma said. 'What is it, Tom?'

'The fence is breached and the wall won't hold much longer.'

I sucked in a breath. I knew the explosions must have been something bad, but to hear that the Perimeter was breached...

'They've got through the fence?' Ma brought her hands to her mouth.

'We should've threatened them with killing Grey,' I said. 'FJ still thinks he's alive. Surely he wouldn't risk us harming his beloved leader.'

'We did that already,' Uncle Tom said. 'We sent a note threatening him with Grey's execution. But it didn't make any difference. He doesn't seem to care about their leader anymore. Either that or he doesn't believe us. You have to hide in the underground stores. Tell Luc. Tell everyone. But be quick. Get the children and the elderly. Make sure they all go down there where it's safe. Where FJ can't find you.'

'But we'll be trapped,' I cried.

'Your pa said it was vital everyone goes down there. Lock yourselves in, okay?'

I nodded, even though I was far from certain this was the best thing to do. 'What about Liss and Annabelle?' I asked.

'Take them with you. I've got to get back.'

'Will you and Johnny be coming down with us?' Ma asked, clutching her brother's sleeve.

'Johnny and the rest of us will come later. We're still needed at the wall to hold them off. Pray for a miracle.'

I stepped forward and gave him a hug. 'Be careful, Uncle Tom.'

'Please stay safe,' Ma said, squeezing his hand briefly.

He gave us a grim smile, turned and slid back into the vehicle.

I raced back into the house, took the stairs two at a time and grabbed my rucksack from the bedroom.

'Hurry, Riley,' Ma called from downstairs.

Part of me wanted to lie on my bed and savour the last few moments I might have left in my home. But I couldn't afford to be sentimental now. Every second counted.

CHAPTER THIRTY-NINE

RILEY

Luc and I divided up the Perimeter between us, visiting the crèche and then going to each road, delegating people to go door-to-door to let their neighbours know what was happening. I was met with panicked faces, tears and reluctance, but I told them there was no option. Anyone found at home was told to pack an emergency bag and come to my house, as access to Pa's underground stores was via our basement.

In less than an hour, the stores were rammed with children, the elderly and the sick. Basically, anyone who wasn't fighting or stationed around the fence. It was grim down there, with its stone walls and floors, lack of heating and the harsh buzz of the strip-lights on the ceiling. Crying babies and sickly moans added to the fear permeating the cramped space. The rooms weren't small but they were already packed with provisions, leaving little room for this many people. I believed Pa had made a massive mistake sending us down here. No way could we remain in such awful conditions for more than a day or two. The air was already tinged with the faint aroma of decay, fear and sickness.

Ma was doing her bit in the largest of the rooms. She had

most of the kids ranged around her and was reading them stories. Trying to keep their minds off what was happening.

The stores were laid out as a snaking corridor with various rooms branching off it. The whole area was much larger than our house and extended a long way out, beneath our back garden. I was at the back of one of the first rooms, stacking some boxes to make more floor space, when Luc arrived with Liss and Annabelle. I saw him scanning the crowded space and I waved to catch his attention. The girls didn't look much better than they had when I'd last seen them. If anything, they looked worse. Scrawny, pale and afraid. But Liss managed a thin smiled when she saw me. I waved again and beckoned them over.

'Are you okay?' I asked.

'Luc said my brother's here,' Liss replied, her eyes narrowed in a mixture of fear and anger.

I nodded. 'Liss, can you think of anything that would make him stand down?' I asked. 'Anything at all.'

'Only Grey,' she said. 'And he's dead.'

'What are we going to do, Luc?' I asked. 'We can't stay down here and hide.'

Luc smiled at Liss and Annabelle. 'Can you wait here?' he asked them. 'There's something I have to do.'

They nodded.

'Riley.' Luc tilted his head in the direction of the door.

I picked up my coat, gun and rucksack and followed him back through the crowd of bodies until we reached the corridor where the air was a little less thick.

'What's happening up top?' I asked. 'Do you know if Pa's okay? Your mum? Denzil?'

'I saw them. They're fine. We're managing to keep FJ's men back for now. But I don't know for how much longer. There's too many of them. I don't know what'll happen when we run out of ammo.'

'We have to hope they run out first,' I said. 'How are *you*?'

'Me?' Luc said. 'I'm taking one minute at a time and not thinking about anything else.'

I nodded. He'd just lost his father, but he was still worrying about everyone else. I wished we had some time so I could take care of him.

'Your pa told me to get you out of here,' he said.

'Good,' I said. 'Does he need me at the fence?'

Luc took my hands and made me look at him.

'What?' His strange expression was beginning to worry me.

'He wants us to leave the Perimeter and go to your grandparents' place in Uley. I've got a motorcycle ready. We need to leave now.'

His words didn't make any sense. 'Leave?' I said. 'No, Pa told me we had to wait down here.'

'No, Riley. He needed us to get everyone down here to safety, but now we've done that, he wants us to leave. He made me promise.'

'But we can't leave everyone. What about Ma? What about your mum? Denzil? The people down here?'

'Your dad thinks they'll all be okay. They're safe down here and anyway, FJ's argument is with us and with the guards.'

'If I'm going, then we should all leave,' I said. 'Pile everyone into trucks and get out.'

'No, Riley. They'll see us escaping.'

'Copters then.'

'Too dangerous. They'll shoot us down. And there are too many of us.'

'So how are *we* supposed to get out then?'

'There's a way,' Luc replied.

'What way?'

'Your dad told me. Come on.'

Luc led me along the corridor, past a group of elderly men who were leaning against the wall, chatting in earnest, the strip light buzzing and flickering above their heads. One of them, Joe Farley, tipped his hat at us.

'Are you all right?' Luc asked them. 'Do you need me to find you a place to sit in one of the rooms?'

'We're fine, lad,' Joe replied. 'Just needed some space away from the hordes.'

'We can't leave these people down here,' I said as we carried on walking. 'There's not enough room for everyone.'

'Trust me,' Luc replied. They won't have to stay here for long.'

'Where are we going?' I asked. 'There's nothing down this way.' As we left the main part of the corridor, we also left the light behind. There was hardly any illumination now. We rounded a bend and Luc flicked on a torch.

'Your pa told me something interesting,' he said.

I waited for him to continue.

'You know the steel door at the far end of the corridor?' he said.

I nodded. I knew it well. Behind that door was the place where Pa stored his most valuable things – gold, whisky and other stuff I knew nothing about. No one was allowed in there. Not me. Not Ma. Not anyone, as far as I knew.

'Well, I've got the key,' Luc said.

I stopped walking and stared at Luc. 'How did you—'

'Your dad gave it to me.'

'Pa gave you the key? What for? Do we need to get some stuff out of there?'

'There is no stuff,' Luc said.

'But—'

'Behind that door is an escape route,' he said.

The thought of another way out of the Perimeter just blew my mind. 'Where does it lead? Who else knows about it?'

'No one else knows. Your pa said he never told anyone

about it. Not even your mum. But you won't believe where it goes.'

'Where?'

We had finally reached the end of the corridor. A circle of torchlight flickered on the dull steel door.

'Apparently,' Luc said, 'it leads to an abandoned underground pumping station outside the Charminster Compound.'

'All the way over there? That's miles away.' I stared at the steel door with a new respect. I'd spent my life wondering what lay behind it. But now that I finally knew, I couldn't even enjoy the drama of Luc's revelation. Too much was happening too fast.

'I know what you're thinking, Riley.'

'What?' I said. 'What am I thinking?'

'You're thinking that it's wrong to leave.'

'Yeah. Well, it is.' How could I even think about leaving everyone here, while I snuck off like a coward.

'But I promised your pa we'd go. So please do this for him and for me. My dad was killed today. Do you think I want to run off and hide? Don't you think I want to go out there and kill FJ with my bare hands?'

I bit my lip.

'I'm taking you to safety, Riley. And then I'm coming back to help.' He turned and glanced behind us, making sure no one could see. Then he slid the bolts back on the door, took a bunch of keys from his coat pocket and fitted a thick brass one into the lock. He turned it and then put a Yale key into the lock above. Once the door was unlocked, he pushed down the handle and pulled hard.

The door swung open and Luc held out the torch, pointing into the gloom. In front of us lay a wide, dank, concrete tunnel and at its entrance sat a motorbike. All shiny chrome and dark, metallic green, looking like it had just rolled off the factory floor. Luc gave a low whistle.

'That's a nice machine,' he said. 'Looks like your dad kept it in mint condition. You got everything you need with you?' he asked.

I nodded. 'Are we riding this thing all the way to Uley?'

'No, just to the 'pound. Your pa told us to go to a lockup at 38 Lowther Road. Inside is a van with weapons and supplies. We'll travel in that. We can stick the bike in the back if there's room.'

'Have you got the keys?' I asked.

Luc took the bunch of keys from the door and jangled them.

'Okay,' I said.

'Good. Let's go.'

'Luc,' I said, 'does Ma know the plan? Does she know where we're going?'

'I don't know.'

'Could you... would you mind telling her for me. I don't want her to worry and I don't think I can tell her myself. She'll get upset and—'

'Sure,' he said.

I held out my hand for the keys. 'I'll wait here for you.'

'Okay, I won't be long.' Luc dropped the keys into my palm and shrugged off his backpack, dropping it onto the stone floor. He leant in to give me a quick kiss, but I pulled him towards me and kissed him hard. He responded, pushing me back against the wall. The torch clattered to the floor as Luc ran his hands down my body. Shocked by the force of his passion, it sent me into freefall. Chills running through every cell. The rest of the world was obliterated for those few seconds.

'Riley,' he murmured. 'What are you doing to me?'

I smiled as he drew back. He bent and retrieved the torch from the floor, putting it into my hand.

'Back in a minute,' he said, kissing me once more. Then he turned and jogged away.

Once Luc was out of sight, I opened my rucksack and

rummaged for a paper and pencil, scrawling a hurried note and leaving it on the floor in the hope he'd find it. Then I found the bike key and slotted it into the ignition. My heart thumped as I pulled on my gloves and woollen hat, and swung my Saiga and my rucksack onto my back. I closed the door behind me and swung my leg over the machine.

'Sorry, Luc.' I whispered the words into the darkness as I turned the key, put the bike in neutral and flipped down the kill switch. As I pulled the clutch and pressed the starter button, the engine roar immediately filled the narrow space. I had to get out of here. Luc would have heard the noise, I was sure of it. I located the headlight and stuffed the torch into my backpack. I kicked up the bike stand, my blood pumping through my veins like rapids over rocks. It had been a while since I'd ridden a motorcycle, but I was so fired up on adrenalin, I reckoned I'd be able to fly a spaceship right now.

Slowly at first and then faster as I built up confidence, I cruised along the tunnel. I felt terrible, misleading Luc, but he would never have let me do this and there was no way I was running away to my grandparents when everyone else was in danger. A plan had been formulating in my head and I knew I had to give it a go.

CHAPTER FORTY

JAMIE

The gunner fired once more, puncturing the second set of gates. He continued shooting at the metal, but as he reloaded, he was hit by an enemy bullet and collapsed over the gunstock. The warriors around him dragged the body away and he was swiftly replaced by another.

The next shooter took over, and soon the inner gates were shot from their hinges, the left hand side of the wall crumbling as the sniper continued blasting chunks out of it.

Turning his head, Jamie saw the Voice of the Father all but laughing out loud. And Jamie had to admit he was impressed. They had lost a few brothers today, but they had achieved so much. And soon they would have what they came for.

'Let me fight now,' Jamie cried.

'No,' Matthew replied. 'You are my disciple. You're needed here with me. Let my warriors finish this. Your turn will come later.'

Now that the gates were taken care of, rows of soldiers began to advance on the Perimeter in earnest. Enough of the wall had crumbled that sections of warriors had begun trying to force their way inside. However, it wasn't yet possible. They were taking too much fire from beyond the gates and from shooters up on the wall to get close enough. It was apparent they still needed to demolish more area to enable their army to get through. Jamie realised that too many brothers had moved in on the wall for the gunner to be able to get any more decent shots. He would be unable to fire without killing their own warriors.

Relentless gunfire came at them from within the Perimeter, raining down on their men at the base of the fence. Their warriors were being hit too hard and if they didn't do something soon, there would be nothing but a pile of robed bodies at the foot of the fence.

Something whistled across the sky, dropping into the settlement. A huge explosion rumbled beyond the wall. Screams. Flames. Smoke. Jamie exhaled in relief. That should give them something to think about. Another whistle. Another explosion. Grenade launchers firing death into the sky. This was going to be too easy.

Just then, Jamie winced at an ear-splitting blast in front of them. He witnessed a scene of utter devastation – burning vehicles and warriors zigzagging out of harm's way, while many more lay lifeless and bleeding on the ground. More than one of their vehicles had been hit. But it was hard to see how many due to the density of flames and smoke streaming upward. The enemy obviously had their own explosives.

Another blast shook the earth in front of the Perimeter and more of their brothers fell. But as the life left their bodies, still more swept forward to replace them. Smoke snaked and curled into the frigid air.

The noise of detonations and the acrid stench of smoke gave Jamie a painful spike of memory back to the day his parents had been killed on the ferry. His mind projected long-ago images of twisted metal and gushing water. Of flames and of the unseeing bloody faces of his mother and father. He squeezed his eyes shut, trying to reset his mind and flip it back to today. When he finally snapped them open again, he saw the smoke and snow and warriors once more.

'We need to pull back,' Jamie yelled to Matthew. 'It's not safe for you to be so close to the explosions.'

'No,' FJ said. 'I want to watch.'

More grenades were being lobbed from the wall, taking out tens of warriors.

'What are they doing? Matthew cried. 'They need to force their way in there.' He turned to one of the men in the back. 'Go,' he snapped. 'Tell them to send in more of my warriors. Overwhelm the wall. Get in there and find Our Father. Find the girl.'

The disciple bowed his head and left the AV. He skirted around the back and Jamie saw him disappear into the surging mass of warriors behind them. He waited, impotent and impatient, to see what would happen next.

CHAPTER FORTY-ONE

RILEY

Within minutes, I had reached the end of the tunnel and brought the bike to a stop. Another steel door loomed ahead and I cursed. I hoped it wasn't locked. Dismounting, I turned off the engine but left the headlight on. Then I slid the metal door bolts across with some difficulty. Pulling down the handle, I tugged at the door, but it wouldn't shift. Perhaps the key was on the bunch. I prayed it wasn't one of the ones I'd left behind for Luc, or my plan would be ruined. He would have returned to the tunnel by now. He'd have read my note. Would probably be running after me. But by the time he got here, I hoped I'd be long gone.

Taking the bunch of keys from the ignition, I tried one of the others – a lever mortice brass key. It went into the lock and turned with a beautiful clunk. The door still wouldn't budge, so I tried a couple of the Yales in the other keyhole.

Bingo.

The heavy door finally eased open and a stream of icy air rushed into the tunnel. I gave a shiver and used my rucksack to prop the door open. Then I wheeled the bike through before hastily locking the door behind me.

I now found myself in the pumping station Luc had told me about. It looked like it had been abandoned for years. I'd been okay while I'd ridden through the tunnel – the noise and speed had distracted me from its dark confines. But this place with its rusted pipes and scuttling, dripping sounds freaked me out. Despite having a serious case of the creeps, I angled the bike to get a better look at my surroundings. In the corner, a ladder rose up to a circular hatch. I kept searching. There must be an easier, wider exit here, otherwise what was the point of the motorcycle?

I wheeled the bike alongside the pipework and turned a sharp corner. There, before me, a steep narrow ramp led up to a door in the wall. I exhaled in relief and left the bike for a minute while I went up to have a closer look at the door.

What would I find on the other side? Pa wouldn't have sent Luc and me into any kind of danger so I was fairly confident the exit wouldn't lead anywhere too bad. As expected, the door was locked and bolted, but I quickly found the correct keys on the bunch. I pushed at the door and it opened; slowly at first before being suddenly tugged from my hand by a sharp gust of wind.

I blinked at the daylight brightness outside. As my eyes readjusted from the gloom, I saw an empty snow-covered landscape. I had no idea where I was or which way I would need to go. I'd figure it out. I pushed the door as far as it would go, wedging it into the ground so it stayed open. Then I ran back inside and hopped back on the bike.

Revving it hard, I rode up the ramp to the exit and through to the outside, into the cold still air, the sky an iron grey sheet. Dismounting, I glanced around. Then I pushed the door, easing it closed, pulling at it to check it was locked.

The exit had been set into the side of a low hillock, its exterior blanketed in grass and snow. If I hadn't disturbed it, the door would have been completely camouflaged. I was impressed. Pa had done a great job. And to have kept its existence secret for all these years was a feat in itself. I grabbed a few handfuls of snow from nearby and tried to cover it back over, but I couldn't quite recreate the look of undisturbed snow. I would have to leave it. At least the exit was locked.

Guilty thoughts of Luc assaulted me, but I pushed them aside. My worst fear was that he wouldn't forgive me. But I was doing this for him. For us. For all of us.

No time to linger here. I had to find my way to the Charminster Compound. If I kept heading in the same direction, I guessed I would reach it eventually. My hands were stiff with cold and I blew through my gloves to try to warm them. It was no good. I would have to resign myself to being freezing for a good while longer. A few flakes began to fall again. With any luck, they'd cover my tracks from the exit.

I sat on the motorcycle and steeled myself for a ride across the snow.

The wind cut into my cheeks and stung my eyes, making them water. My fingers almost froze in place on the handlebars and my legs were chilled to the bone marrow. Beneath the snow, rocks and potholes tried to fling me from my seat. But I clung on hard, and after only five or ten minutes of discomfort, the Compound finally came into view.

I cruised alongside the wire fence of the Walls. There was no one around. No one even guarding the fence. Just snow-covered tents sitting amid brown slush. I hoped everyone was okay.

'Hey!'

'I looked up to see a man striding towards me from inside the encampment. I slowed and drew out my magnum, fingering the trigger. As he drew closer, I realised I'd met him before. It was the guy with all the facial piercings and the nose-hoop. He aimed a rifle at my head.

'Keon,' I said. 'It's me, Riley.'

'Riley?' He peered through the wire and relaxed. 'Oh, yeah,

I remember you. Nice bike,' he said, lowering his weapon. 'You here to see Lou again?'

'I need to see Reece,' I said, holstering my gun.

Keon raised an eyebrow and pointed at the gate further along the fence. I rode up to it and waited while he fiddled with the lock.

'Didn't expect to see you back here so soon,' he said.

'Is Reece around?' I asked. 'It's urgent.'

Keon opened the gate and I wheeled the motorcycle through.

'If it's urgent,' he said with a grin, 'it'll be quicker to ride.' He took hold of the bike and hopped on, nudging me out of the way.

'Hey!'

'Get on then.' He patted the space behind him. 'Better hold on tight.'

I scowled, but did as he said, instantly regretting it as he pulled a ridiculous wheelie. I gripped his waist just in time to save myself from sliding backwards into the slush. He laughed and took off through the camp, spraying snow and mud in his wake. Curious faces peered out from huts and shacks, but I couldn't worry about what people thought, I was more concerned with working out exactly what I was going to say to Reece when I saw him.

I didn't have long to wait. We reached the gathering place at the main marquee within a few minutes.

'He's in there,' Keon said, skidding to a halt. 'I'll look after this baby for you.'

I got off, reached forward, turned off the ignition and pocketed the keys.

'You're no fun,' he said.

'Fuel's precious,' I replied. 'It better be here when I get back, or Reece will have something to say.'

'It'll be here. I looked after your truck before, didn't I? Kept it in one piece.'

I nodded and left him, pushing back the tent flap and stepping inside.

There was no way I could've come back here with Luc. Reece would never have agreed to see us, not after what happened last time. But I wished he was by my side right now. It would've made me feel so much braver.

The marquee was packed with people. The air smoky and dense, slightly warmer than outside, thank goodness.

Hundreds of pairs of eyes followed me as I picked my way past families and groups huddled together for what little warmth could be found. Reece was sitting in his usual spot, surrounded by his cronies. To pull this off, I would have to be brave. I would have to lie and I would have to act my ass off.

One of Reece's friends nudged him and pointed in my direction. Reece looked up and gave a triumphant smirk as I smiled across at him. He leant down and said something to his friend who laughed. I took a breath and walked up to him.

'Riley,' he said, taking my gloved hand. 'You're freezing. Come sit by the burner with me.' He twined my hand in his and led me over to the centre of the marquee. People made way for us as we walked and two men vacated a couple of floor cushions about ten feet from the huge stove with its blissful warmth.

Reece let go of my hand and sank down onto one of the cushions. He patted the other and I sat facing him. He leant forward and peeled off each of my sodden gloves, placing them closer to the burner. Then he took my frozen hands in his and started rubbing the skin, blowing on my fingers to warm them up. I didn't like the feel of his calloused hands over mine, but I let him continue.

'I'm glad you came back to see me,' he said. 'I've been looking forward to spending time with you.'

'Me too,' I said, forcing myself to look up at him. He was certainly good looking, with his dark eyes and stubbled jaw, but there was something too wild and unpredictable about him, despite the warm and genuine smile he showed me now.

'Reece, I need your help,' I said.

He carried on squeezing my fingers, rubbing each one individually till they tingled and burned.

'The Perimeter,' I said. 'It's under attack. We're under attack.'

'So you didn't come to see me,' he said, letting go of my hands. His smile melted away.

'We're in trouble, Reece. And you were the first person I thought of.'

'What about that lad you were with before? Can't he help you?'

'Who, Luc?' I said. 'He's just a boy. He can't do anything.' Those traitorous words made me burn with shame, but I had to tell Reece what he wanted to hear or he'd never help us.

'Grey's men,' Reece said without emotion. 'They came?'

I nodded, willing myself not to cry. 'They're going to destroy our home. I really need your help.'

'Why me?'

'You've got skills. Numbers. You can make the difference, Reece.' I took hold of his hands again. 'You could save my home.'

'What can we do with a few knives and rifles?' he said. 'We can't go up against an army like that. We're tough, but we're not idiots.'

'I can arm you,' I said.

'Go on...'

'I've got proper weapons you can use. State-of-the-art. But I need you to come now, before it's too late.'

'Wait a minute, Riley. I appreciate the firewood, I really do. But you're asking me to risk my people's lives for yours. Why should I do that?'

'You can keep the weapons afterwards. And I'll give you

ammo and supplies to last you through the rest of the winter.'

He looked thoughtful at this. 'I don't know,' he said. 'I'm not convinced. I'll need some time to think about it.'

'Reece, there is no time. If we don't get going now, it's game over.' I thought back to the Lost Wall – the one Lou had shown me with the sketches of missing children. I stood up and reached down for Reece's hand. 'Can I show you something?' I asked.

He nodded and let me haul him to his feet. I led him around to the back of the marquee where the Lost Wall was situated.

'What's going on?' he asked gruffly. 'Why are we here?'

'Which ones are your sisters?' I asked, pointing at the wall.

'What? How do you... that's nothing to do with you.' His face turned ugly and I knew I'd have to speak fast.

'I'm sorry to talk about them, but Lou told me they went missing.'

'Blabbermouth bitch,' he said. 'She should never have—'

'Thing is,' I continued, 'I'm pretty sure I know where they are.'

Reece stepped forward and took me by the throat. 'What the hell are you talking about? What are you really doing here? Start talking before I squeeze so hard you'll never talk again.'

'Grey!' I croaked. 'Grey's been stealing children! Help us defeat him and we can get them back. I swear! I swear it's true.'

He let go and I sank to the ground, clutching at my neck and swallowing hard. My hands shook and I tried to get my breath back, gasping and choking.

He crouched down and leant in close, his breath on my face. 'No one talks about my sisters,' he said. 'No one. Especially not a stuck-up Perimeter girl like you.' He straightened up. 'Follow me.'

I scrambled to my feet and followed. Reece gave a sharp whistle and a boy came running over.

'Gather the council,' he said. 'Now.'

CHAPTER FORTY-TWO

JAMIE

The mass of warriors surged forward through the newly blasted gates in the fence, trying to get beyond the wall, but it was impossible as bullets rained down on their heads and they were picked off like fish in a barrel. Not one of them retreated. Those who survived kept on pushing forward, trying to get through. Jamie could hardly bear to watch. And the bodies were piling up, impeding the warriors behind. If the Voice of the Father hadn't have selected him for his special task, then he too would have been one of those men out there in the thick of the violence.

And then Jamie saw something weird.

Once the warriors reached the wall, they were being driven back by more than just bullets. There was something else there. Creatures! Their men were being set upon by creatures. Tens of them, pouring out from gaps in the exploded brickwork. Jamie leant forward and squinted.

'Are those... dogs?' Matthew asked.

'I think so. Yes.'

'If that's the best they've got, we'll be inside the walls within the hour.'

But Jamie watched in fascinated horror as the creatures leapt onto their warriors, tearing into them and bringing them down onto the blood-stained snow. These wild dogs were an effective weapon. Distracting and vicious. The soldiers at the front were forced to drop their machine guns and use blades instead. It was terrible to watch. Jamie looked down at his lap. His looming task seemed simple by comparison: to carry out an execution. That is, if they made it that far.

CHAPTER FORTY-THREE

RILEY

The mood was tense as we sat around the table at the back of the marquee – Reece, his four councillors and me. My voice was croaky, but I managed to speak. Reece was in a foul mood and, although he had listened to my tale of Grey's children, I could tell he hadn't enjoyed hearing it. I thought he might stride around the table any minute and snap my neck. I guess I was the messenger and he wanted to shoot me.

I put forward my request for help. I told them that it was Grey who'd been abducting children over the years. I explained about Liss and FJ and how she had escaped and he had become one of them. About Grey being dead and how FJ had taken over. I said that now would be the perfect time to strike. That if we could get rid of FJ, the whole regime would be vulnerable.

'If we kill FJ, Grey's soldiers will be miles from home with no leader,' I said. 'We could go to Salisbury and find the missing children.'

'How do we know you're not spinning us a yarn?' one of the older men asked.

'Look at me,' I replied. 'I'm here, alone. At your mercy. Why would I offer you a vanload of weapons and ammunition if I was trying to trick you?'

'How many of those warriors are down there?' another man asked.

I swallowed. I couldn't lie, but if I told them about the thousands of men blotting out the horizon, they would never agree to help. 'A lot,' I said. 'More than a thousand.'

Silence settled around the table for a while.

The man leant across and whispered something in Reece's ear. Reece nodded and turned to me. 'Wait outside,' he said.

I nodded and stood up shakily, but before I left the room I gave a last plea. 'If you agree to this,' I said, 'you'll get your lost children, you'll get supplies for the winter and you'll never have to worry about Grey's army again.' Then I left the makeshift room and waited outside by the Lost Wall.

One of Reece's men stood guard at the entrance to the council room, but I ignored him and concentrated my gaze on the sketches of the missing people. Examining the faces of all the children. Yes, I wanted Reece to help save my family and my home, but I also wanted those children to be reunited with their parents. Grey's ethos was wrong. It needed to be exposed and stopped.

Heated voices filtered through the thin partition wall in the marquee. I caught odd snatches of words, but I couldn't make out which way the conversation was going. All I knew was that time was ticking and the longer I waited here, the less chance there was of saving the Perimeter.

'You.'

I looked up to see the scowling face of the shanty on guard.

'Back inside,' he said.

I walked past him to hear my fate, standing at the foot of the table with five pairs of eyes on me.

'Where are the weapons?' Reece asked.

'In a lock-up in the Compound,' I replied.

'And you'll give us supplies, enough for everyone here, to last through the winter?'

'You have my word,' I replied.

'What if you get killed out there?' he asked. 'Who else knows about this 'deal'?'

'Luc,' I said.

'He knows you're here?' Reece said. 'I don't believe that.'

'I... left him a note.' My cheeks reddened at the memory.

At this, Reece laughed. 'I'd love to have been there when he read it.'

I had the grace to look down at my boots.

'Come on then,' he said. 'Show us this secret weapons stash.'

'Do I have your word that you'll help me?' I said. 'I mean, I could give you the weapons and you could just say—'

'We may not have much here, in the way of comfort and supplies,' he interrupted. 'But we do have our honour. My men are hungry and not as strong as they should be, but our word is our bond. Cross us and you'll regret it, but you can always rely on our word.'

I would have to accept what he said. What other choice did I have?

Collecting the motorcycle from Keon on the way out of the Gathering Place, I ignored Reece's scowl, wishing the bike looked a little less shiny and a little more beaten-up. No wonder these people resented the Perimeter. We appeared to have it all.

Not any more.

While Reece and two of his men came with me to the Compound, the councillors headed off to round up the rest of the shanties to prepare for the battle ahead. I pulled in the clutch handle and wheeled the bike behind the three men, stumbling in their wake. Although the bike was relatively small, it was still unwieldy, and the pathways weren't exactly smooth.

Reece and his companions made no attempt to talk to me, not once turning around to check I was following. I didn't blame Reece for his cold attitude. He thought I'd come here to see him, but I hadn't. I'd come to give him some unwelcome news and a difficult decision.

We reached an area screened by dirty swathes of material and I followed Reece and his companions through. He held back the sheet for me as I pushed the bike; his first acknowledgment of me since we'd left the marquee. And now we were standing at the Compound wall, by the wide ditch which ran around its base. A bored-looking shanty sat in front of the ditch on an upturned metal drum. He stood as we approached.

Lying across the ditch, a wide wooden board ran up to a metal door set into the wall. It was the door through which Lou had first brought me to the Walls back when the riots had sent us fleeing from the Compound. That day seemed like months ago. So much had happened since then. The guard crossed the ditch and unbolted and unlocked the metal door in the wall. Reece took the bike from me and wheeled it across the ditch. Then he lifted it through the doorway and into the small yard.

Once we were all through, the guard shut the gate and I heard the bolts slide home. Reece pushed my motorcycle up to the back door and rapped hard on the wood. A few long seconds later, a shuffle of feet and a rattle of keys, and the door opened.

The old man, Arthur, stood there in his dressing gown and slippers. His face lit up at the sight of Reece.

'Reece, my boy, come in, come in.'

'Good to see you, Artie. We're in a bit of a rush today. But I'll come over next week and let you thrash me at cards. How's that sound?'

'Sounds about right. You young 'uns are always in a rush.' He chortled. His cantankerous manner had totally disappeared. Nothing like when Lou and I had been here.

'Can I bring the bike through?' Reece asked. 'One of my guys will clean the floor later.'

'Bring it through, my boy. Nice machine. Used to have a Triumph Tiger when I was younger.'

'You're a diamond, Artie,' Reece said, manoeuvring the bike over the threshold and into the house. 'How about I take you for a burn on this thing when the weather's better.'

Arthur's eyes widened to the size of horse chestnuts, making him look like an owl. 'You're on,' he said.

Reluctantly, Arthur opened his front door, allowing us out into the quiet alleyway beyond. Reece shook his hand and the old man gave him a nod before closing the door on us.

Reece turned to me. 'Where's this lock-up?' he asked, his pleasant manner evaporating.

'38 Lowther Road,' I said, hoping I'd remembered the address correctly.

'I know it. It's not far.' He mounted the bike and I got on behind. His friends stood to the side. 'Catch us up,' he said to them, before pulling away down the alley.

Reece and I turned into Charminster's main road, which was quieter than I'd ever seen it. People were staying home where it was safer and warmer. We turned down a relatively nice street with large, detached houses. Maybe the snow made it prettier than usual.

'Number 38?' he called over his shoulder.

'Yeah,' I replied. I counted along the even numbers. 32, 34 and then the house numbers jumped straight to 42. 'Go back,' I called out. 'It's got to be somewhere here.'

Reece turned the bike around. Between houses 34 and 42 was an alleyway. We rode down it. At the end were three garages with corrugated metal doors. The middle one was number 38. We got off the bike and I took the bunch of keys from the ignition, examining them for one which looked like it would fit the small keyhole in front of me. I got it right first time.

The key turned and I heaved up the door. It rolled upward with a clatter. Immediately behind it was a sturdier set of doors. Again, I found the key and opened them up. Behind them lay a surprise.

The doors opened up to a massive space which spanned the width of all three garages and stretched back three times as far as I had expected. Inside, I saw not one, but three black vans in a row.

'Let's get in and close the doors,' Reece said. 'Don't want anyone walking past and seeing this lot. I reached behind into my rucksack and fumbled for my torch while Reece shut the doors behind us. Clicking on the beam, I realised there were two more vans parked behind the first two, making five vehicles in total. All fully armoured with bullet-proof windscreens. I walked around to the rear of one, located the key and opened up the back.

Luc had been right.

Shining the torch inside the vehicle, I saw it was kitted out, floor to ceiling, with shelves containing military grade weapons. Reece and I stared wide-eyed at each other. If there had been any doubt in his mind about the truth of my story, these vans wiped it away. I turned and shone the beam around the rest of the lock-up. The walls were lined with metal crates. Stamped on the outside of one of them were the words:

```
200 cartridges
7.62 MM NATO M80
Cartons M13
```

A crate of ammunition. And there were a lot of crates in here – all containing different types of ammo.

Reece tapped the wall with his knuckles. 'This place is lead-lined,' he said.

I opened up the other vans. Two more were kitted out

inside, exactly the same as the first. The two at the back were stocked with ammunition, emergency medical supplies and dried food. Reece ripped open one of the boxes and took out some kind of shrink-wrapped food bar. He tore off the wrapper with his teeth and spat the plastic out onto the floor before sniffing the bar and taking a bite. He chewed, swallowed and took another bite.

'Rank,' he said. 'Like eating boot leather dipped in earwax.'

'Pass me one,' I said. 'I'm starving.' He tossed a bar in my direction and I peeled off the wrapping and nibbled at the corner. It wasn't half as bad as he'd made out.

A loud rapping on the door made me jump. Reece opened the lock-up and let his guys in. I doled out the keys and took one of the vans with the hardware. Reece helped me load the motor-cycle into the back of my vehicle and I found some rope to secure it to one of the shelving units.

'Give me the keys,' Reece said, 'and I'll send one of my men back for the last van and the rest of the ammo.'

I hesitated. Should I hand over Pa's keys and give him access to all this precious gear?

Reece shook his head. 'I should've known. You don't trust me, do you? What do you think happens out there in the field when we run out of bullets?'

I slid the keys off the chain with shaking fingers and passed them to him. He was right of course. We would need every last box in this place.

'Will the guards let us out of the 'pound okay?' I asked.

'Getting out of here's okay,' Reece answered. 'It's getting in that's the problem.'

I nodded and stepped up into the driver's seat. Reece drove out first, then me, then the other two. We pulled up in the alley, locked the doors behind us and moved out.

CHAPTER FORTY-FOUR

JAMIE

Grey's warriors clambered over the bodies of their fallen comrades as they tried to reach the Perimeter gates, all the while taking heavy fire from the battlements. The sheer number of soldiers meant that eventually they made progress. The dogs had been dispatched quickly enough, but not before they had killed or maimed many soldiers. The way Jamie saw it, until their brothers got inside and disabled the enemy shooters, there would be hundreds more deaths.

From his vantage point back here in the AV, it looked unreal. Like watching a movie from the old days, back when he was a kid. He glanced at the Voice of the Father, who was transfixed by the action at the gates. Matthew had probably never seen a movie in his life.

Little by little, their men made slow and steady progress. Warriors gradually disappeared into the Perimeter through the crumbling wall. More and more of them getting in with less and less resistance from above. And now Grey's warriors appeared on the top of the wall, near the entrance. Jamie made out their dark hoods as they fought, taking out the Perimeter guards. A full-scale fire fight erupted near the top of the gates. It was crucial they disable the snipers up there or FJ's warriors would never make it inside.

The skirmish on the battlements lasted only a short while and then everything fell quiet. Through the newly made silence, the sound of galloping hooves drew closer, and a rider appeared at Jamie's window.

'Sir,' he said, breathless, aiming his words at Matthew. 'We are victorious. We have secured the gates and are moving through the Perimeter, taking hostages. Posting guards at the entrance.'

'What about the girl?' Matthew asked. 'Riley Culpepper. It's vital you locate her.'

The rider shook his head. 'No sign yet, I'm afraid, but we're still searching. We're questioning her father, but he's not very talkative.'

'You can make him talkative,' Matthew replied. 'Or do I need to show you how?'

'We'll find her,' the rider said. 'And we're still searching for Our Father.'

'Good.'

'We've cleared out the guards' building,' the rider continued, 'and put the prisoners in cells. It's safe for you to enter now, if you wish. We've cleared a path through the entrance.'

Matthew nodded.

'There's one more thing, sir,' the rider said.

'Go on.'

'It's like a ghost town inside. There were only a few guards left up on the wall, but we've eliminated them. There's no sign of inhabitants. We're searching the buildings, but so far... nothing.'

'Have you surrounded the Perimeter?' Jamie asked. 'No one inside can escape, can they?'

'No. We've placed guards at intervals around the entire settlement.'

'Well then, the inhabitants must be in there somewhere,' Matthew said. 'And we'll ferret them out. Use the prisoners. We can get answers from them.'

'Very good, sir.' The rider turned his horse back to the Perimeter and urged him into a canter.

Matthew turned to Jamie. 'Jacob,' he said. 'We are getting closer to our goal. Before today is done we will have avenged a great wrongdoing.'

Jamie nodded.

'Come,' Matthew continued. 'Let us go inside and find Our Father.'

The driver started up the engine and led the motorised cavalcade up to the torn entrance where hundreds of warriors stood facing outwards to attention, both horsemen and foot soldiers. As the Voice of the Father and his disciples approached, the warriors parted in a wave to let them by, closing back over them as they drove through the double set of decimated gates and into the Perimeter.

CHAPTER FORTY-FIVE

RILEY

We moved across the snowy plain. Black vans leading the way, almost camouflaged against the darkening winter sky. I was in one of the vans with Reece and Lou. She'd volunteered to fight and I'd asked Reece if she could travel with us. He hadn't objected, and I felt more confident with her beside me. Behind us a tribe of around seven hundred able-bodied shanties followed on foot and horseback. Not nearly enough to match FJ's army, but we were still a fair number. And at least we were heavily armed. Reece had sent a scout ahead on horseback to check the battleground.

Our convoy slowed as the scout returned on his dun-coloured pony. Reece slid out of the driver's seat and walked over to meet him.

'Back in a sec,' I said to Lou and followed Reece out of the van.

The scout wore a woollen hat pulled down over his ears and a grubby cotton scarf across his mouth and nose. He pulled the scarf down and I was struck by how young he looked. He couldn't have been more than fourteen or fifteen. I felt guilty that I'd put him in danger, but then I realised I was only a year or two older.

'How many soldiers?' Reece asked.

'A few hundred more than what we got,' he said in a thick Dorset accent. 'Maybe a thousand. They're stationed outside the main gate like a load of statues.'

That was good news to my ears. There had been a hell of a lot more than that earlier in the morning.

'They got horses too,' he added.

'Is the battle still going on?' I asked.

The boy scowled at me but answered my question. 'No fighting outside. Dunno about inside though. Loads of bodies piled up out there.'

I shook my head, trying to keep my anxiety at bay. Trying not to think about who else might not have made it.

'Warriors' bodies,' the boy clarified. 'They was wearing cloaks.'

I exhaled. 'Any movement behind the fence at all?'

'Couldn't really tell – too many soldiers in the way. Gates is blown to pieces though. Wall's smashed up a bit. There's one of their men posted about every two hundred yards along the fence. They might be right the way around, but I only did a quick reccy.'

I considered the boy's information. If only a thousand of FJ's men were standing guard outside, that meant FJ had probably taken over the Perimeter, and the rest of his soldiers were either dead or had gone inside. I prayed all our people had made it safely into the underground stores.

'You did good, Pauly.' Reece patted his pony's neck.

'Yeah,' I said. 'Thanks.'

Pauly nodded, clicked his tongue at his pony and moved off to join the other shanties.

I looked up at Reece with some trepidation. What if he changed his mind and decided to order his people back to the

Walls? He turned away and walked back to the van. I followed, not wanting to speak in case I jinxed things. But I needn't have worried. He started up the engine and we continued heading in the same direction – south, towards the Perimeter.

Our plan was to split into three sections and approach the thousand-or-so soldiers that were stationed outside the fence. We would attack head-on, as well as from the western and eastern edges of the fence, where we would initially be concealed from the main entrance. Reece and I were to lead the western flank. I gave Reece and Lou a rough description of the Perimeter layout inside. Telling them about the shooting platforms along the top of the wall and the position of the Guards' House. I also described how to get to the main Perimeter stores. But I omitted to tell them about Pa's underground stores. I couldn't give away that secret.

Halfway across the heathland, before the Perimeter came into view, we split into our separate battalions. It was vital the eastern and western units weren't spotted by the main bulk of the army until we were almost upon them, otherwise our plan would fail. We had to get them surrounded.

The knot in my stomach tightened as we drew closer to the Perimeter. What would I find there? Would my family be safe? Would Luc?

Reece and I headed west, leading our section of about two hundred battle-ready men and women. Half were armed with semi-automatic guns, the rest carried rifles, crossbows, slingshots and knives. In the van we had grenades. Our first task was to take out the sentries around the western side of the fence. Reece sent his stealthiest people ahead to do this job. They would use silent weapons so as not to draw any attention. To my surprise, Lou was among them.

Inside the van, Reece looked at me for the first time since we'd been on the road. I noticed his stare and immediately stopped chewing at my fingernails. I must've looked pitiful because he dropped his scowl and tried to reassure me.

'My people are good at this,' he said. 'They're expert hunters. Can virtually kiss a deer on its nose before killing it.'

'Thank you,' I said. 'I don't know what I would've done if—'

'Okay,' he interrupted. 'Let's just get this done, yeah.'

I nodded. Reece was unpredictable to be around. But I felt confident in his abilities to lead his people. If anyone could make this work, he could.

Up ahead, the western edge of the Perimeter came into view. Dark shapes moving in the foreground.

People.

But who?

I looked through my binoculars and turned the focus wheel until it showed the mesh of the fence, sharp against the inner wall. I moved the lenses slowly along until I had the figures in my sights.

It was Lou and the other shanties.

I exhaled in relief. A couple of figures lay on the ground wearing the robes of Grey's church.

'Well, that's two down,' I said, passing Reece the binoculars.

'Don't worry,' Reece replied. 'We'll soon have the rest of them.'

I liked his certainty. But now it was our turn. We were about to face FJ's warriors.

CHAPTER FORTY-SIX

JAMIE

Inside the walls, Perimeter buildings smouldered and burned. The main road was a mess of slush and mud, ashes and blood. Jamie cast his eyes over scattered fallen men and women in civilian clothing. Their bodies bent at unnatural angles, their faces blank or shocked in death. He wondered where all the bodies of his fallen brothers had been taken. Units of warriors moved about the place with a proprietary air.

'Stop the vehicle,' Matthew said. 'I want to get out.'

'It may not be safe,' warned one of the disciples from the back.

'Nonsense. Look around.' Matthew said. 'Let us walk and enjoy our victory, instead of hiding away behind all this armour and glass.'

The driver pulled over to the side of the road and they exited the AV. Jamie pulled his cloak tight around his shoulders, the icy chill of winter cutting through his skin after the warm protection of the vehicle. As they began to walk, Matthew aligned himself with Jamie, and the other disciples fell behind. Matthew beckoned one of the high-ranking warriors.

'Where are we holding the girl's father?' he asked. 'Take me there.'

'This way, sir.'

They followed the man to a plain red-brick building at the side of the road. Inside, the place was crammed with their own men, inspecting weapons and rifling through cupboards, drawers and filing cabinets. They bowed as the Voice of the Father walked past. Matthew, Jamie and the other disciples were shown to a cell. The warrior peered through the grille and then opened the door. Matthew and the others swept inside.

In the centre of the room was a seated figure, a guard standing before him. Jamie's eyes were immediately drawn to the bloody knife in the guard's hand. As the entourage entered the room the guard looked up, bowed and stood back to fully reveal the prisoner: A shirtless man, seated on a faded plastic chair, hands tied behind his back. His torso was a mess of cuts and bruises, blood dripping from his mouth onto torn combat trousers.

'Has he told you where Our Father is being held?' Matthew asked the guard.

'No. He refuses to say anything.'

'Maybe you haven't asked nicely enough,' Matthew said.

The guard remained silent.

'Well?' Matthew prompted. 'Did you ask nicely?'

'I...'

'Here.' Matthew took the knife from the guard and walked up to the prisoner. 'This is how you ask.' He held the knife to the man's throat and pressed the flat part of the blade down firmly.

'Where is our leader? Tell me or I'll cut your throat.'

But the man only laughed. 'Do it, FJ. I don't care.'

Jamie wondered why the man had called him FJ.

Matthew's face clouded and he pressed the knife down harder, until the blade nicked the man's skin, drawing blood from his throat. 'Where is your daughter? Where is James Grey? Hand them to me and we'll withdraw. We will leave your precious Perimeter. It is a simple equation. Two lives for everyone else. Surely you wouldn't put your own selfish desires before those of your people.'

'If you think I would ever tell you where to find my daughter, you're more deluded than I thought.' The man spat blood onto the floor at Matthew's feet. 'And you may as well know that your beloved leader is dead. James Grey died weeks ago.'

'You're lying,' Matthew hissed.

'Am I?'

An explosion outside made everyone glance up.

'What was that?' Matthew asked, turning first to the guard and then to Jamie.

The faint sound of battle could be heard from outside and the prisoner smiled.

'Find out what's going on,' Matthew barked.

CHAPTER FORTY-SEVEN

RILEY

We came at them hard, with a roar of engines, a thud of horses' hooves and a battle cry which echoed across the wasteland. We were fighting for survival. For food, for warmth, for home and family, for love and for life. Everyone had grown weary of the relentless winter and the constant threats from hostile forces. And all our energy went into that charge. From the relative safety of the van, I fired my Saiga at the robed invaders, my bullets joining the others, zipping into the masses and finding their target every time – because it was an enormous target. More soldiers than I'd anticipated. Even Reece gave me a look that said more than words.

I hoped our eastern flank was doing as well as us. The majority of our shanty force was now coming to our aid across the heath. Charging like demons towards the enemy. After our initial attack from either side, FJ's soldiers were finally gathering themselves together and returning fire in earnest. But we were a moving, spread-out target, whereas they were closer together in a compact group. Plus, it didn't look like they were all armed. And, of the ones who were, many of them were out of ammo, reduced to using their guns as sticks or shields.

The shanties were ferocious. They didn't simply hang back to fire their guns. Instead, they careened into the ranks of soldiers, slicing them down with hunting knives and other more primitive weapons. Smashing at heads with the butts of their rifles and kicking their way through to the next soldier and the next. The warriors rode huge horses that towered above the shanty ponies, but the smaller steeds were nimble and brave, taking their riders where they needed to go, and delivering vicious kicks to the enemy.

Reece left the van and took some of his men closer, where they began to lob grenades into the middle of the warrior clusters. This forced the enemy away from the fence, sending them running straight into our gunfire. They were trapped and losing tens of men by the minute. But, despite the success of our attack so far, I couldn't feel triumphant, for we were losing people too. Reece's comrades were falling around us, bleeding and dying on the cold ground. I ran to help some of the wounded, taking them back to the van with the med supplies and leaving them to be patched up by people more capable than I.

Squinting up at the wall, I wondered why FJ's men weren't making full use of all the shooting platforms. As far as I could tell, we were only taking fire from the section nearest the gates. I was amazed how quickly we were able to cut through this army. At this rate we might actually make it through into the Perimeter soon.

I guessed it was now around mid-to-late afternoon. The sun would set soon and the temperature would plummet even further. We needed to get in there and finish this off. I worried about the people down in the stores. I was desperate to get down there to see if Luc and Ma were still safe. What if FJ had found them? What would he do?

CHAPTER FORTY-EIGHT

JAMIE

The cell door flew open and one of the warriors stood in the doorway panting hard.

'Yes?' Matthew snapped.

'I need to speak to you, sir,' the warrior said, glancing from Matthew to the prisoner and back again.

Matthew strode out of the room, into the hallway, followed by Jamie and the others. The guard remained with the prisoner.

'What's going on out there?' Matthew said. 'I heard an explosion.'

The warrior spoke quickly. 'Our soldiers outside... they're taking heavy fire, sir.'

'What are you talking about?' Matthew snapped.

'We've been attacked, and more than half the guards we posted at the gates are dead.'

'Attacked? By who? I thought the enemy had fled.'

'They appear to be shanties, sir.'

'Shanties? What are they doing here? How many of our men are outside?'

'Only about four hundred still standing.'

'But that means they're killing hundreds of our men. How is that possible?'

'Our men are good soldiers. Taught never to flee from an enemy, but they're caught in a crossfire.' The man lowered his eyes.

'Where are the shanties now?'

'Still out there, trying to get to the gates. At this rate, they'll have wiped out all the guards we stationed outside within the hour. We've got a few of our men firing from the parapets, but the enemy destroyed most of the platforms up there before they fled. We can't access the rest of the wall to fire down at our attackers.'

'Are there any platforms left at all?' Matthew asked.

'One.'

'I need you to get me up there.'

'Sir,' the warrior said. 'It's too dangerous. You'd be a target.'

'Don't argue. Get me up there.'

'Let me go up with you,' Jamie said. 'Take four of us. We can shield you.'

Matthew nodded. 'Let's go. Now.'

They swept along the corridor and back outside.

'Who are these shanties?' Matthew asked. 'What do they want? Are they mercenaries? Do they want money? Are they trying to take this Perimeter for themselves? How many are there?'

He kept up a steady stream of questions, but as yet nobody knew the answers. And they were all still reeling from the news about Grey's death. Jamie wondered if it was true. He thought it was very likely. That meant Matthew was their new leader.

Through the torn gates, Jamie saw the surging bodies of their warriors trying to keep this new enemy at bay. He heard raucous cheers beyond. Whoops and whistles, battle cries and rapid trill of machine-gun fire. More of Matthew's warriors were attempting to exit the gates to help engage the shanties, but each time a group tried to leave, they were driven back inside.

At the base of the wall, one of their men passed Jamie a megaphone. He carried it with him as he climbed the ladder, a tricky feat in his disciple's robes. The Voice of the Father climbed up after, followed by three other disciples. It was quite a climb and Jamie fought off a wave of dizziness, unused to being this high off the ground. At the top, they arranged themselves on the narrow platform, next to the marksmen who were already up there. It didn't feel too stable.

Ensuring that the Voice of the Father was not exposed, Jamie peered through the razor wire to witness a scene of total devastation below. Rows and rows of fallen warriors, as well as those still alive, pinned back against the fence and fending off the shanties with little or no ammunition. It was a bad joke. How could this be? Their warriors were trained for battle. They were the best of the best. But they'd been trapped, exhausted from the first battle, without enough weapons or bullets to fight back.

Jamie passed the megaphone to the Voice of the Father.

'Ceasefire!' Matthew called out through the loud speaker. 'Ceasefire!' Even over the noise of the battlefield, his voice carried authority.

Shouts rose up from the shanties below, along with more shots and catcalls. Matthew waited, his face rigid and tense, his eyes steely, focused on the scene below.

Gradually the noises died away and Jamie watched as more and more faces looked up at them, weapons trained on their position. But, mercifully, they didn't shoot. It was a risky move, coming up here, and Jamie was ready to step in front of Matthew should he need to protect him.

Up so high, the wind groaned and sighed, rattling the precarious wooden boards underfoot. Then a shout from below: 'What do you want?'

'I wish to speak to your leader,' Matthew said, his voice clear and otherworldly, floating across the wall and down to the enemy.

'You're speaking to him,' came the same voice.

Matthew scanned the chaotic scene below, trying to spot the speaker. 'What are you people doing here?' he asked. 'This is not your fight. If you do not leave within ten minutes, we will have no choice but to kill everyone inside.'

'Not my problem,' yelled the voice from below. 'Do what you want!'

'Gotcha,' Jamie murmured, as he spied a dark-haired shanty flanked by a dozen or so others. The man had an automatic rifle in one hand and a bloody machete in the other. Jamie tapped the closest marksmen on the shoulder and pointed out the man. The sniper nodded and aimed his rifle at the shanty's head. 'I have him in my sights, sir,' the marksman said. 'Shall I take the shot?'

'Do it,' Matthew ordered.

'Wait,' Jamie cried. 'I'm sorry, sir, but maybe we shouldn't make a martyr of him. They'll want to avenge his blood and then we'll have no chance of appeasing them.'

'Appease them?' Matthew said. 'Why would I want to do that?'

'If we shoot him, we won't get the opportunity to negotiate.'

'What are your orders, sir?' the sniper asked Matthew.

'Hold your fire,' Matthew replied.

'Know this,' the shanty yelled. 'If you kill those people inside, then as soon as we reach you, we'll make sure you die slowly and painfully.'

Cocky little runt, thought Jamie.

'What I don't like,' the man continued yelling up at them, 'is people who steal what doesn't belong to them. Like other people's children. There's no bargaining here, sunshine. What I want is your head on a spike. You won't be getting out of there alive.'

'I have thousands more men back at Salisbury,' Matthew replied. 'If you harm any more of my people, my warriors will march down here and they will seek retribution.'

'You still don't get it, do you, sonny,' the shanty yelled. 'You're not leaving here alive. None of you are. Put down your weapons and we'll promise to kill you quick.'

A chorus of cheers started up. And then a shot skimmed by Jamie's head. All four disciples and Matthew ducked behind the wall while the marksmen returned fire. But Jamie didn't see if they hit anything.

'Time to go back down,' Jamie said. 'We can't risk your life up here, sir. Especially if what they said about Our Father is true.'

Matthew's face was white with icy anger. 'We cannot let them get away with this. We are God's army with thousands of trained warriors. This cannot be happening. Who are these people? And how did we come to be trapped in here?'

'Sir,' Jamie said, 'we must rally our brothers inside and send them out to fight. We still outnumber them easily.'

'No,' Matthew replied. 'Our warriors must find the girl first.'

'But, sir, she's just one girl. We need to—'

'Silence!' Matthew hissed.

Jamie bowed his head and hoped Matthew's decision wouldn't cost them dearly.

CHAPTER FORTY-NINE

RILEY

Standing at the base of the Perimeter, listening to FJ's demand for us to stand down, only seemed to reinvigorate the shanties. They got their second wind and threw themselves at the warriors like rabid dogs. Those pale sullen faces I'd seen back at the Walls had now been transformed into an angry fighting machine.

The thought of FJ inside my home made me angry as hell. He had been standing on the very same platform that Rita and I had stood on this morning as we'd witnessed the approaching army and the destruction of Eddie's truck. I couldn't bear the thought of FJ's men trampling across our roads and lawns, defiling our houses and mistreating our people. How dare he! I reloaded my Saiga and stuffed my pockets full of ammo, before taking a breath and leaving the cover of the van to draw closer to the main battle. I was way out of my depth, but I couldn't hang back while the shanties fought with every ounce of strength in their malnourished bodies. I needed to get inside the Perimeter and find out what was happening.

We fired our guns and hacked with our knives. It was brutal and bloody and terrifying. Despite the battle noise, which raged around me, all I could truly hear was the harsh rhythm of my own breaths coming fast and loud. Animalistic cries issued from my own mouth as I flew at the enemy, convinced in that moment that this would be my last day on earth. That I would die here in this hellish bloodbath, defending my home.

Somehow, we were managing to force our way through the enemy, getting closer to the gates, but they were still hopelessly out of reach. My aim was to slip through one of the holes in the wall and try to get to my house and down into the stores. To find Luc and tell him what was happening. I couldn't let myself think about another scenario where Luc wasn't there.

Evening was almost upon us. The light turning its back on the violence of the day. I hoped darkness would make my plan easier. Suddenly, a warm burn spread across my face. I put my hand to my cheek and saw crimson blood. A stray cut from a wild sword to my right. I ducked and slithered through icy slush and dead bodies on my stomach. Then I pushed myself onto my hands and knees and tried to crawl towards the fence. If I stayed low and moved slowly, I might just go unnoticed. I needed to get inside and find Pa.

Crawling through the horror, I clamped my jaw shut and tried to stop shaking. My rucksack hampered my progress so I discarded it. But I made sure I kept hold of my semi-automatic. At least I wasn't a target down here and, as I crawled along, I managed to take out several warriors by shooting up into their faces and chests. No one even noticed me, they were so caught up in the violence at head height.

Finally, I lay on my belly and slithered through the gates, using my elbows to propel myself over the massacred bodies. While I was hidden in the murk, I tugged a robe off one of the dead warriors and slipped it on, cringing as I pulled the blood-stained hood over my head. To my left I spied a clear spot leading to a crumbled section of wall. It was dark enough to chance making a dash for it. So I scrambled to my feet and ran at a crouch towards the opening.

I was through.

I flattened myself against the brickwork, breathing hard. The scene before me was little better than outside. The whole place was a brutal bloody war zone. And something else was wrong. Nowhere in the fighting did I see the uniforms of the Perimeter guards. Nor did I recognise a single face. The only people here were FJ's men and the shanties. I had to move.

Following the line of the wall, I headed away from the fighting, towards the back of the guards' building. Maybe some of our people were being held prisoner inside. Peering through a lighted window, I saw four or five robed men inside. Ducking down, I swore. They were already making themselves at home. I had to find my people and let them know I'd brought help. They needed to come back and join the fight. What if they'd used the secret passageway and were already headed away?

I left the cover of the Guards' House and ran as hard as I could down the tree-lined pavements and away from the fighting, not looking back, just praying I wouldn't hear pounding feet behind me or feel bullets in my back. But luckily everyone was caught up near the entrance. The cries and screams and sounds of gunfire receded as my feet took me further into the heart of the Perimeter. I needed to cross the main road, but it was wide and exposed and I hesitated to leave the cover of the fir trees.

Just as I was preparing to cross, a squad of warriors came jogging out of the road opposite. They were headed back towards the entrance. Back to the battle no doubt. I shrank back behind a tree trunk, my heart pounding. I may have worn their robes, but there was no way I would be mistaken for one of them close up. Finally, their figures receded and I dashed across the road, glancing wildly about as I ran. Not far now. I was almost home.

I turned the familiar corner, but it all looked different now. Alien and scary. It was like looking at my road through a distorted mirror. The houses lay in darkness and I stumbled into my driveway, excited to have made it this far, but terrified at what I might find. The crunch of gravel under my boots made me wince. The sound seemed ten times magnified in the silent street.

I slipped off the dead man's robe with a shudder and let it drop to the floor. My frozen fingers went to my jeans pocket to pull out my house key. Such a familiar action, but everything was changed now. My home no longer safe. The key turned with a click and I opened the door, stepping into the pitch black hallway.

As soon I set foot inside, the door closed behind me and a hand came over my mouth. I tried to scream and reach for my gun, but someone else's hands pinned mine behind my back. Why hadn't I had my finger on the trigger of my gun? I was a fool. I tried to scream again, but the hand was firm against my lips.

'Shhh, Riley, it's me, Uncle Tom.' The hands let me go.

'Tom?' I hissed, almost weak with relief. 'Oh, Uncle Tom.' I flung my arms around him, as someone flicked on a torch, illuminating the faces of Liam and Denzil. 'I'm so pleased to see you guys,' I breathed.

'What happened to your face?' Denzil asked.

I remembered the sword cutting into my cheek. Had that only been a few minutes ago? It felt like weeks since I'd been in the thick of the battle. 'It's fine,' I replied. 'Where is everyone?'

'Once the wall was breached we had to withdraw,' Denzil said. 'Too many of them. Thousands. We couldn't have won with those odds, so we made the decision to get out. Everyone's down in the stores.'

'Everyone?' I said. 'But there isn't enough room.'

'They're crammed in,' Denzil said. 'Spread out along the

secret corridor. Your pa told Tom about the escape route, gave him a spare set of keys.'

'Where is Pa?' I asked. 'Downstairs with everyone?'

Silence.

I looked up at the men's faces and my head began to swim, a cold sweat broke out on my forehead.

'We don't know where he is,' Tom replied softly.

'What!' My voice rose to a screech and they all shushed me.

'Your pa, Rita, Luc and half a dozen others stayed on the wall to hold them off, so everyone else could get away.'

I shook my head, trying to focus on the present and not think about worst case scenarios. Pa and Luc would be fine, I told myself, swallowing bile at the back of my throat. They were probably hiding out somewhere, hatching a plan.

'Where've you been, Riley?' Uncle Tom said. 'Everyone's been so worried about—'

'We have to get everyone back out there,' I interrupted. 'All our guards. All our men and women need to come out of the basement and fight.'

'Riley, it would be suicide,' Liam said. 'There are thousands of warriors.'

'Not any more,' I replied. 'I brought help. I went to the Walls and got the shanties.'

'What!' Uncle Tom looked at me like I was from another planet.

I carried on explaining. 'The shanties have wiped out hundreds of FJ's men. Caught them in a crossfire and just obliterated them. You should've seen it. If you all come now, we can finish this thing easily.'

'But how did you—'

'Not now,' I said. 'Come on, we need to get back out there. Are the weapons still down in the stores?'

Tom nodded.

'Right,' I said. 'We arm everybody and we take back our Perimeter.'

Everyone able to fight filed out of the storerooms like a stream of avenging angels, hope and fire in their eyes. Up the hidden stair-case, into the hallway and out of the house into the cold night. They had thought they'd lost their home for good, but now they had a second chance to reclaim the Perimeter. As I saw all the familiar faces I was overcome by a wave of love and wanted to wrap it around everyone to keep them safe. I realised it was Christmas Eve. A time for family and peace.

I hadn't seen Ma or Liss and Annabelle yet, but Denzil said they were fine down below. Looking after the children and keeping everyone's spirits up. Hundreds of us gathered along the street, quiet anticipation threading its way through each of us. We would fight and we would drive these intruders from our home. Make sure they never returned.

CHAPTER FIFTY

JAMIE

Things weren't going as planned. Who were these shanties and what did they want? They had forced their way inside the walls of the Perimeter and didn't seem to be giving an inch. Jamie had watched the carnage from within the guards' building at the entrance. He, Matthew and the other disciples had locked themselves in. The building was secure for now, but they were pretty much trapped. The shanties' energy was astounding, and Jamie wished their own warriors would put as much fervour into battle. But Grey's people were controlled and competent. Skilled and focused. Tactics which usually worked well, but didn't seem to have much effect against such a chaotic, driven enemy.

In a cramped room at the back, Matthew's patience was running out and Jamie felt the boy's anger like a palpable thing around them. He hadn't mentioned James Grey yet and Jamie was inclined to believe the prisoner's statement that something terrible had befallen their leader. But he couldn't voice his fears to Matthew. Not given the cold fury which already emanated from every pore.

One of the disciples in the room cleared his throat. 'Sir,' he

said, approaching Matthew. 'Do you think we should...
withdraw?'

'No. Do you?'

The disciple didn't answer.

'I asked you a question. Answer me.' Matthew got to his feet
and faced the man.

'I think...' the man stammered, 'that if we stay here, there's a
chance those people out there will kill all our brothers.'

'And you, Jacob?' Matthew said, turning to Jamie. 'What do
you think?'

Jamie thought for a moment. He didn't want to say the
wrong thing, but the disciple was right. They couldn't wait it
out in this building, hoping that things would go their way. At
the moment, he guessed their chance of success was about fifty-
fifty. Just then, a warrior burst into the room, saving him from
answering.

'The Perimeter guards have appeared from nowhere with
hundreds of people. They're all armed. I'm sorry. It looks like
we're outnumbered.'

'Get out!' Matthew shouted.

The warrior backed out of the room, shocked.

Jamie had never seen the Voice of the Father lose his cool
before. He tried to think of a way to salvage the situation, but
his mind kept coming up blank. It seemed hopeless. He needed
to get Matthew focused once more.

'Sir,' Jamie said, daring to put a hand on Matthew's
shoulder in what he hoped was a gesture of comfort and solidar-
ity. 'What do you want to happen now?'

Matthew's attention snapped back to Jamie. 'What are you
talking about?'

'What would be the best outcome for you? Here. Now.'

'The best outcome here, now, is the same as it's always been
– to find Our Father,' Matthew said. 'And then I want to bring
this Perimeter to its knees. But most of all, I wish to get hold of

the girl who's responsible for all of this and I want you, Jacob, to slice off her head with your sword.'

'Right,' Jamie said, getting to his feet and leaning forward on the table with the tips of his fingers. 'I think we may have to face the fact that Our Father is gone from us. You are our leader now, Sir. You are Our Father.'

Matthew didn't speak and nor did any of the other disciples in the room, so Jamie continued.

'I don't know if we will win this battle here today. Not now that we're outnumbered. But... there is one thing we can definitely do.'

'And what is that?' Matthew said.

'I know a way to get the girl,' Jamie replied. 'As long as she's still alive.'

'Tell me,' Matthew said, his eyes glittering.

CHAPTER FIFTY-ONE

RILEY

'Reece!' I called, over the boom of an explosion. '*Reece!*' I'd spotted him and some of the others crouched behind one of the guards' vans. The vehicle was riddled with bullet holes and they were trapped, taking heavy fire. Denzil, Tom and I were only about a hundred yards away, concealed behind a couple of thick pine trees.

Eventually Reece turned and saw us. Tom fired at the enemy to cover him. Reece glanced left and right before darting over and skidding to a halt in front of me, panting hard, his face smeared with grime and blood. He pushed his fringe out of his eyes.

'Reece,' I said. 'Thank you. You and your people have been incredible.'

He nodded in acknowledgement.

'This is Denzil,' I continued, 'one of our Perimeter guards. Can you brief him? Tell him what's going on? What you need from us? More weapons? Ammo? Manpower?'

'More ammo for starters,' Reece replied. 'But we're doing all right considering the numbers we were up against.'

A bank of lights glared on, throwing the dark chaos into

relief. I squinted and shielded my eyes. We all looked over to see what was happening. It took a couple of seconds for my eyes to adjust. From the trees, we had a clear line of sight straight through to the entrance of the Guards' House. Someone had switched on the floodlights outside, illuminating the paved area at the front of the building and beyond. More exterior lights clicked on in turn. The fighting paused, everyone momentarily frozen by the illumination. The bloodshed around us now even plainer to see.

Seconds after the lights came on, the front door to the Guards' House was thrown wide, a figure in the doorway. Gagged. His hands bound behind his back. It was the Head of Perimeter Security – Roger Brennan.

A robed warrior stood behind, pointing a gun at his head and prodding him out of the doorway. Behind them, another guard, bound with a gun to his head. And another. They all stumbled out to stand beneath the lights, blinking and dazed. In a terrible state. Blood-soaked clothes and smoke blackened faces, barely able to walk. I clutched Tom's arm.

And then I saw Rita, also gagged and bound. A look of shock and pain on her face. It looked as though her shoulder was dislocated. I'd never seen her so scared before. She was always fearless. I wanted to run over and fling my arms around her, but she too had a weapon pointed at her head.

My heart was in my throat as I recognised the next face. It was Pa. But his expression was not one of defeat, it was one of pure anger. I crouched on the ground and hugged my knees, my legs unable to support my body. Tom crouched next to me and put an arm around my trembling shoulders. What was going to happen? We had to do something. Stop whatever was to come next. I didn't want to know what this wicked boy had planned.

And then the next figure came through the doorway...

Luc.

I shoved my fist in my mouth to stop myself screaming his

name. What could I do? What could I do? He shared my father's angry expression and I felt so bad that I'd left him here to be captured. All for nothing.

Lastly, FJ and an entourage of robed figures exited the house. If only I could shoot that boy dead. But I couldn't risk it. Not with guns at the heads of all the people I loved. What was this world, where the only thing that mattered was a gun and who it was pointed at? I'd had enough of this. Enough. I wanted to do something, but there was nothing to be done.

The hostages were lined up in front of the building and forced down onto their knees. Behind each, stood a robed warrior with a gun aimed at each head. FJ stood to the side, his robes pristine, his face untouched by smoke, his body unharmed, his fair hair shining beneath the blinding lights. Like an angel from hell.

A hooded warrior stood by his side holding a gleaming sword. The scene was something from a nightmare.

The silence had become oppressive. No shots, no yells or screams.

'We have to do something,' I whispered to Tom. He squeezed my shoulders tighter, but he didn't reply. I turned to see pity on his face and so I looked away and glanced up at Denzil. More pity. I didn't want to see pity, I wanted to see determination. A plan. Anything but pity.

'You have a choice!' FJ's voice cut through the silence. 'These people on the ground here can die. We can kill them one by one. And then we can continue fighting until the Perimeter is destroyed along with everyone in it.' He paused and cast his eyes around. 'Or...'

I knew what his alternative would be. I knew what he was about to say and I was ready for it. I attempted to brush the dried blood and dirt off my knees and tried to rise to my feet, but Tom's arm was still around my shoulders and he tightened his grip. I shook his arm off and got up anyway. He stood too while Denzil stepped closer to my other side.

'There is one person here who must atone for her sins,' FJ cried. 'If she gives herself up, we will leave.'

Pa's eyes widened and if he hadn't been gagged I knew he would've yelled for me to run away as fast as I could. But he *was* gagged and so he said nothing. No one said a word.

'Riley Culpepper, show yourself,' FJ called out.

Tom took my hand and held it tight. Denzil stood in front of me, his weapon pointed in FJ's direction. Even though we were standing behind the trees, I felt exposed. My name ringing in my ears like a death knell.

'Show yourself or I will execute every prisoner.'

I knew I had to do it and I tried to step forward, but Tom and Denzil wouldn't let me pass, gripping my arms and pulling me back. I briefly caught Reece's eye as he watched me, impassive.

'No!' Tom hissed. 'You're not going.'

'Here!' I yelled. 'I'm over here.'

Tom shoved his hand over my mouth to silence me, but he was too late, FJ had to have heard me. 'What are you doing?' Tom hissed. 'That boy will kill you. You can't give yourself up.' He took his hand from my mouth, and he and Denzil tried to drag me back.

'I should've given myself up in the first place,' I said. 'Stopped all of this from happening. Let me go, or I'll never forgive you. You know I have to do this.'

I stopped struggling and Tom and Denzil briefly loosened their grip. But before they could say another word, I elbowed them hard in the ribs, slipped out of their grasp and made a break for it.

'Riley, come back!' Tom cried.

Once I was clear of the trees, I slowed my pace and walked

towards FJ, keeping my eyes locked on his triumphant face, unable to bear looking at the people on the ground. Pa would be heartbroken to see me. And Luc... I couldn't think about him now.

The silence inside the Perimeter was heavy with dread and anticipation, broken by the soft tread of my final footfalls.

'As soon as you have me, you must let these people go,' I said, my voice echoing across the space between us. 'If you really are a man of God, you'll keep your word.'

I prayed he would do the honourable thing and act on his promise. But experience had shown me that FJ was not an honourable man.

CHAPTER FIFTY-TWO

RILEY

As the warriors continued to point their weapons at the prisoners on the ground, a robed man stepped forward to claim me. He chained my wrists and ankles while FJ looked on, a smile on his face, like a small boy on Christmas Day who just got his favourite toy. The robed man hoisted me over his shoulder and bundled me into the back seat of a black AV. FJ and three of his cronies got into the car and slammed the doors, two of them sitting either side of me on the back seat.

'Wait half an hour and then move out!' FJ called out the window to his remaining warriors. I prayed that meant that Grey's men would leave and release the prisoners unharmed. But then the AV engine started up and we headed towards the exit in convoy with another two vehicles, leaving me to only guess at what would happen to my home once we'd gone.

With some relief I looked over my shoulder through the back window. The prisoners still had guns pointed at their heads, but at least FJ had given no order to execute them. For now, the hostages would be the only means of Grey's men getting out alive. No one from the Perimeter would risk attacking the warriors while Pa, Luc and the others were in danger, but I wasn't so sure about the shanties.

I winced as the AV bumped and crunched its way out through the entrance. Rolling over the mounds of dead bodies. We drove for a short while, my mind blank and unfocused. I couldn't let myself think about what was about to happen to me. All I knew was that it would be extremely unpleasant and then it would end. Images of Luc forced their way into my mind; of the life we would never have together. But I pushed them away. Snowflakes began to fall once more, melting against the dark glass of the windscreen. No one spoke.

After a while, I didn't know how long, we stopped. And now I started to feel scared. My heartbeats skittering and jumping, my skin cold and shivery. Doors opened, letting the icy wind blow through the vehicle and I was dragged outside, made to stand on the snowy ground before these hooded creatures. The only face exposed was that of the boy. His pale skin illuminated by the headlights. Slivers of snow swirling in the beams.

I tried to get rid of my fear. To be defiant and uncaring, but I couldn't quite manage it. My chin wobbled and I pressed my lips together to stop from crying. Please, I told myself, don't give him the satisfaction. I thought about the lives I was saving by doing this. That by giving myself up, I had brought about the end of this pointless fight.

Ever since that time in the clearing, when I'd had FJ in handcuffs, he had wanted his revenge. I'd humiliated him and I doubt he'd ever been in that situation before. He needed to restore his ego. Humiliating and killing me would help him achieve that. Perhaps this was all this had ever been about. I wouldn't have been surprised. It was pathetic.

The robed men began to whisper their weird chant and one of them stepped forward, drawing a sword from beneath his robes. The sight of that gleaming metal threatened to send me over the edge. I had assumed they would shoot me, and that was bad enough. But seeing the sharp edge of the blade sent chills down my body, making my knees soft. I couldn't let myself collapse. I forced my body to remain upright, clamping my teeth together and squaring my shoulders back. I made myself stare FJ in the eye. I would not flinch and I would not beg for my life.

CHAPTER FIFTY-THREE

JAMIE

Jamie's hand trembled slightly as he held the sword. The girl was young and beautiful. Her eyes fierce, like a cornered cat. He would swing his blade and watch the flame in her eyes die. She would crumple to the ground and he would see her face in his nightmares. Was this really the way to salvation? Or was this the way to hell?

But what else was there for him? This was his life now. And the girl had threatened their existence. She had kidnapped their Father who was now likely dead. She had dragged them across the country on a mission of death and destruction. If it wasn't for her, he might still be in the kitchen garden, his hands deep in the good black earth. Growing things instead of killing things. He was resolved. This girl needed to die, so that all things could return to their natural order.

His brothers' chant swelled to fill the night sky. Rising above it, Matthew's voice came clear and strong. Jamie latched on to the words, waiting for the order to kill.

'Jacob,' he said. 'We will do to this girl what she has done to Our Father. And we will feel no remorse. Only joy that we are free from her hatred.' As he spoke, Matthew came forward to stand at Jamie's side. 'And once this is done we will return and finish off the rest of them. We will burn that place of evil to the ground.'

'You can't!' she cried out. 'You gave your word.'

'Hush,' Matthew said. 'It's no longer your concern. You will not be here to worry or cry.'

Jamie tensed his arm, preparing to do what had to be done.

'But first,' Matthew continued, 'she must know the person who ends her life.'

Jamie glanced across at his new leader, confused.

'Girl!' Matthew cried. 'This good disciple has undergone a transformation. Like you, he used to be nothing.'

At this, the girl narrowed her eyes and shot Matthew a venomous glance.

'He was a common thief. A murderer.'

Jamie bristled a little at the use of the words 'thief' and 'murderer'. He had stolen through necessity and killed by accident. But he supposed that wasn't important now.

'Before this man discovered the light, he killed a girl. A young innocent girl.' Matthew stared at Riley, a slow smile spreading across his face. Jamie was disturbed to realise Matthew was enjoying himself. That he wanted to draw this out and make her suffer before she died. Jamie wasn't so keen on having his sins made public either. But there wasn't much he could do about it.

Just then, Matthew pulled Jamie's hood back so that his face was exposed to the girl. Jamie tried to remain expressionless and mask his surprise, but it was difficult. He took a steadying breath and focused on the Latin words which streamed from the mouths of his brothers.

'Riley,' Matthew continued, 'I would like you to meet your executioner, Jacob. He was once a vagrant called Jamie and he has visited your Perimeter before, haven't you, Jamie? Last summer, I believe.'

Jamie was confused. What did all this have to do with the girl standing before him? Why was Matthew talking about this now?

'Jamie killed Skye,' Matthew said to Riley. 'Jamie killed your little sister. And now he's going to kill you. Perfect symmetry, wouldn't you say?'

The blood rushed to Jamie's head and his heart boomed in his ears like dynamite in a cave. This was the sister of the girl he'd killed! That's what all this had been about. That's why Matthew had chosen *him* to end her life. It was all done so Matthew could witness the total shock and devastation on the girl's face when she met her sister's killer. So he could break her before she died. Wipe the defiance from her eyes.

And sure enough, her eyes clouded and dimmed. She stared at Jamie in horror, her mouth open.

'My sister,' she hissed. '*You!* You killed my sister?'

Jamie felt as though he'd been punched in the stomach. He needed to end this now, unwilling to witness the raw pain and hatred on her face a second longer. But at the same time, unable to tear his eyes away.

'Do it now, Jacob,' Matthew commanded, triumph in his voice. He took a few paces back to give Jamie enough room to manoeuvre his sword.

'Please,' Jamie said, 'it wasn't like that. It was an accident.'

'Jacob, follow your orders,' Matthew said.

But Jamie ignored him. He had to tell the girl what really happened. That he wasn't a cold-blooded murderer. 'I was hungry, homeless,' he said to her. 'There was a hole in the fence, so I crept into the pool house and fell asleep. Your sister found me. I was scared. I panicked. She screamed and I tried to calm her down. I tried.' He sobbed, tears running down his face. 'I told her I wouldn't hurt her. Tried to stop her running off. But she wouldn't listen and it all went wrong. She fell back through the door. There was glass everywhere. I'm so sorry for what I did. I never meant to hurt her.'

'Liar,' Matthew cried.

'No, I'm not lying. That's what happened, and the girl's sister has a right to know the truth before she dies.'

'Fine,' Matthew retorted. 'Good. She knows. Now, execute her.'

Staring at the girl, Jamie took a step back and held his sword out to the side, ready to slice down onto the white of her neck. Her face showed fear now, but there was nothing he could do about that. Jamie steadied his legs, making his stance wide and solid as he prepared to deal the blow.

'Thank you,' she said, her voice barely audible above his brothers' chanting. 'For telling me. I always wondered what really happened... I forgive you.'

'What?' Jamie said.

'I said, I forgive you.'

'Kill her,' Mathew said through gritted teeth. 'Or will I have to do it myself?'

Jamie took a breath and swung the sharp blade down to her throat. He stopped short by a hair's breadth. Swung it back the other way and made a clean slice through skin and bone and sinew.

Matthew's head was cleaved from his shoulders and landed in the snow with a crimson thud. His robed body toppled to join it. His face stared up from the ground; even in death it wore an expression of demented arrogance.

The chanting stopped and the night was silent except for Jamie's own heavy breaths. No one moved.

Jamie turned his eyes away from the bloody pile and looked instead at the girl. She was drained of colour, breathing hard. He couldn't believe he had the girl's forgiveness. It was more powerful than any of the boy's hollow words. Matthew was supposed to have been a man of God, yet this stranger, this sister to a murdered girl, had a truer heart than Grey, Matthew, or any of their men. Jamie saw things clearly for the first time.

'I'm sorry,' Jamie said again. 'I didn't know she was your sister... It was an accident. I honestly never meant to hurt her.' Those words felt so good. He wondered why it had taken him so long to say them. If only he had stayed after the accident. He could've said sorry back then. Saved all the nightmares and remorse.

Skye. The girl's name had been Skye. It had suited her.

Had this war simply been about punishing a girl? About revenge? Jamie felt used. He realised Matthew hadn't really cared about rescuing James Grey. He hadn't cared about his warriors, who had trained for him and bled for him. Bled for their beliefs. For a way of life. In the end, it had all been about ego. About a boy's self-importance.

Jamie hadn't wanted to believe it. Had wanted to believe in a good way to live. In a higher purpose. But Grey's church was a sham. A lie. The dream shattered around him like so much broken glass.

Jamie's head began to pound. He let his dripping sword fall into the snow. Pulled out his pistol and held it to his temple. The cold metal barrel soothed the dull pounding in his head.

'No!' Skye's sister cried.

She held his gaze as he squeezed the trigger.

CHAPTER FIFTY-FOUR

RILEY

Six Months Later

A heat haze shimmered off the ground, and dust swirled as the copter blades began to spin. In the cockpit, a notepad rested on my lap and I chewed on a pencil, ready to list out all the fence locations that still needed attention. The rebuild was taking months, but it would be fantastic once it was done. Scrub that, it was already beyond everyone's wildest dreams.

I couldn't believe it was almost a year since Skye's death. It felt like an eternity and also like no time at all. All those months I had spent dreaming of tracking down her killer and pulling the trigger. In the end, Jamie had done it himself. But I hadn't been glad or relieved. I'd only felt sadness. I still saw his face sometimes. The haunted expression in his eyes. At least I knew Skye hadn't been murdered in cold blood. That the whole thing had simply been a terrible accident.

On Christmas Eve, after witnessing the deaths of FJ and Jamie out in the snowy wilderness, Grey's disciples had seemed lost. I had stood there, shocked and freezing as their chanting ceased and they lowered their hoods. I had spoken to them.

Reasoned with them and told them a ceasefire would be in all our interests. Told them I could broker a deal that would make everyone happy. They had been as stunned as I was by the turn of events and seemed almost relieved to have a solution handed to them. They took me up on my offer. Removed my chains and returned me to the Perimeter.

When we arrived, it was like everyone was waking after a dream. Grey's soldiers had been driven out by the combined forces of mine and Reece's people, a unifying moment that had not ceased since that day. The shanties helped us clear up, tend to the wounded and account for the dead. And we were forever in their debt. True to my word, we provided Lou, Reece and the shanties with more than enough provisions for the winter and beyond. After all, without them we would have lost everything.

One happy ending was that we discovered Fred and Jessie tied up in one of the trucks. They were suffering from hypothermia and we weren't sure if Jessie would make it. But being reunited with Liss and Annabelle gave them all the incentive they needed to get better.

In the weeks that followed, Grey's church dissolved and his warriors scattered. They had no leader. We'd cut the head off the snake, literally. As word spread, more and more children were reunited with their parents. But there were also hundreds of orphans to be cared for, and Reece was still searching for his missing sisters. Many people had been lost. Friends, families, allies. No one was untouched.

Here, now, in the sparkling sunlight, the whole thing seemed like a distant dream. A hazy nightmare of winter and destruction. I smiled at Luc and he grinned back at me as we took the copter up into the soft blue sky. Being reunited with my parents, Luc and the others was the best feeling I'd ever had in my life. Luc and I did everything together these days. Told each other our deepest thoughts. No more miscommunication and lies. He forgave me for leaving him in the underground stores. Understood why I'd done it. But, at the same time, I had to promise to never do anything like that again. I had to trust him. And I realised I did. I trusted him with my life.

We banked north, away from Talbot Woods. We would start by listing out the places which needed the least work and move outwards. Nothing like this had ever been attempted before, but Pa said it was time, and most people agreed. The Perimeters and Compounds were the places which had the most to lose, but Pa argued that we couldn't go on like before. If we did, things would only get worse. The country would never heal. Would always stay fractured.

I peered down at the green lawns and the grey roads of my home. Construction was already well under way and the wide new road now ran from the old entrance straight out into the heathland towards Charminster. Our northern and western fences had been partly dismantled already, and we were making good progress re-building our new southern boundary, which would run for twenty miles from Bournemouth, here in the east, to Puddletown in the west. From there, the boundary would stretch northwards for forty miles, along the old A354 up to encompass Salisbury. The eastern boundary would complete the triangle, from Salisbury back down along the Wessex Way to Bournemouth. Many of Grey's people had fled Salisbury, but the ones who'd stayed were offered the chance to be part of our new way of life. They accepted without hesitation.

My heart gave a leap of excitement as I looked down from the air to see new villages and houses without fences around them. To see rectangular fields of crops and animals, where once was only dangerous scrubby heathland.

This new region was to be called Wessex and would have its own government and its own police force, made up of representatives from each of the old settlements. No more Perimeters, Compounds or guards. No more lawless stretches of wasteland.

We were going to aim for a new kind of civilisation with a new set of laws. A vast island of safety.

A few people from the Perimeter said it was too ambitious. Too perilous. That all we needed to do was rebuild a stronger fence to hide behind. But, thankfully, enough of us were ready to try a new way.

Maybe, if this worked, we could extend our boundaries further, and keep on extending until we reached the very edges of our nation. Then we would have no need of fences and no one would be left outside. We would reach a day when the whole country was free. When we could walk alone and unarmed, without fear of being attacked.

Wouldn't that be something?

A LETTER FROM SHALINI

Dear reader,

Thank you so much for reading *The Perimeter*. I do hope you enjoyed the Outside series; it was a real labour of love to write. If you'd like to read similar action, romance and adventure, you might like my Vampires of Marchwood series.

To keep up to date with my latest releases, just sign up here and I'll let you know when I have a new novel coming out.

www.secondskybooks.com/shalini-boland

I love getting feedback on my books, so if you have a few moments, I'd be really grateful if you'd be kind enough to post a review online or tell your friends about it. A good review absolutely makes my day.

When I'm not writing, reading, walking on the beach or spending time with my family, you can reach me via my Facebook page, through Twitter, Goodreads or my website.

Shalini Boland x

KEEP IN TOUCH WITH SHALINI

www.shaliniboland.co.uk

facebook.com/ShaliniBolandAuthor

twitter.com/ShaliniBoland

goodreads.com/shaliniboland

ACKNOWLEDGEMENTS

Huge thanks to my wonderful publisher, Natasha Harding, for taking this series and making it shine. I'll be forever grateful.

Endless thanks to the dedicated team at Second Sky: Jenny Geras, Ruth Tross, Jack Renninson, Noelle Holten, Sarah Hardy, Kim Nash, Melanie Price, Mark Alder, Alex Crow, Natalie Butlin, Jess Readett, Alexandra Holmes, Mandy Kullar, Emily Boyce, Saidah Graham, Lizzie Brien, Occy Carr and everyone else who helped relaunch this series.

Thanks also to Madeline Newquist for your fantastic proof-reading skills. Thank you to designer Eileen Carey for another incredible cover.

Huge thanks to Billie for proofreading and deleting the cringy lines that no sixteen-year-old would ever say.

Big thanks to Jordan Spellman at Tantor Audio and Henri-etta Meire for creating fabulous audiobooks for the series.

Massive thanks and love to my husband, Pete, who has lived and breathed this series with me since 2006 when I first had the idea. Thank you for looking after the children while I 'just finish this chapter'. Thank you for making dinner and getting me chocolate and making cups of tea and reading the scenes I wasn't sure about. Thank you for your help with all the battle scenes and the complicated technical bits. But most of all, thank you for being my best friend and for making me laugh when it all got a bit much.

Thanks to my gorgeous mum, Amara, who was always so enthusiastic and encouraging, telling me everything was brilliant. Even though she was my mum and kind of had to say that, it was still just what I needed to hear back then. I still hear your encouragement now.

Thanks to my beta readers, Julie Carey, Amara Gillo and Peter Boland. I'm so grateful for your eagle eyes. You never let me down!

In those early days of writing, I was lucky enough to have an incredible author support network. People who were – and still are – always there to help with writerly issues and dilemmas: B. Lloyd, Suzy Turner, Sarah Dalton, Reggie Jones, Robert Craven, Johanna Frappier and so many more. I love you, guys!

While researching information for my novels, I sometimes hit a brick wall. Thank you to the following people for your solid advice: Weapons guru K.P., you're a legend. And Poppet, you got me out of a hole. My snipers and I thank you!

Thanks also to you fabulous book bloggers and reviewers who spread the word. You guys are the absolute best. To my readers: I adore you. I love it when you stop by online to say hi. I love it when you leave reviews. And I'm forever grateful that you choose to read my books. Thank you.